DEMOCRACY UNDER SEIGE!

"Who do we need?"
"Sam Jack Dodd!"
"When do we need him?"
"Now!"

To a man and woman, all of the marchers carried mounted posters of Samuel Jackson Dodd, the charismatic billionaire who had captured the nation's fancy in the wake of a disastrous first eighteen months for the new president. The gridlock that was supposed to end only tightened, and a slew of broken promises later, his approval ratings had sunk into the high twenties. After a brief respite, the economy faltered again with no measures the administration enacted able to halt the slide. With nowhere else to turn, much of the nation was turning away.

Toward Samuel Jackson Dodd.

"Give me a crackling fireplace on a cold night, a damned good cognac, and Jon Land's DAY OF THE DELPHI .. then leave me the hell alone so I can enjoy myself."
— David Hagberg,
author of *COUNTDOWN* and *CRITICAL MASS*

"Tom Clancy and Stephen Coonts step aside. Jon Land is the new master of the political thriller, with plot twists for the '90's. Characters that jump off the page and breathless pace make him the new one to beat."
—Ralph Arnote, author of *FALLEN IDOLS*

Other books by Jon Land

DAY OF THE DELPHI

JON LAND

TOR®

A TOM DOHERTY ASSOCIATES BOOK
NEW YORK

DAY OF THE DELPHI

Cover art by Paul Stinson

A Tor Book
Published by Tom Doherty Associates, Inc.
175 Fifth Avenue
New York, N.Y. 10010

Tor® is a registered trademark of Tom Doherty Associates, Inc.

ISBN: 0-812-53434-4

First Tor edition: November 1993

Printed in the United States of America

0 9 8 7 6 5 4 3 2 1

For the men and women of the U.S. Special Forces

DE OPPRESSO LIBER

From oppression we will liberate

ACKNOWLEDGMENTS

Day of the Delphi marks a new beginning for me with the Tor publishing family, the wonder of which starts at the top with Tom Doherty, as great a man as he is a publisher. Tom is even greater for assigning me to a brilliant editor, Natalia Aponte, who took *my* final draft and helped turn it into something much better.

Of course none of this would have ever happened without my agent Toni Mendez's dogged persistence and faith. Toni, you just keep getting better, as does Ann Maurer, who lived every line of this book with me from the first draft.

Walt Mattison (the real Blaine McCracken) and Emery Pineo continue to keep me on the straight and narrow when it comes to armaments and technologies. Genuises both, especially Emery, who makes answers to all my questions just a phone call away. And now that Dr. Mort Korn has retired, South Florida's loss has become my gain, since he has more time to peruse my early drafts.

For a great weekend in Washington where much of this book took shape, my thanks to Skip Trahan, the ultimate tour guide, although I think next time we'll skip Dupont Circle.

Thanks to Andy Stearns, Michael Weinberg, and Colin Burgess for help with the Coconut Grove geo. And to Jane Bosman for South Africa, Dick Shartenberg for New Mexico, Nancy Bercovitz for promotional input, and political scientist Gary Eddins for his help deciphering the inner workings of the government. Acknowledgment must also go to a superb study of trilateralism edited by Holly Sklar.*

And finally a special thanks to the gang at Steeple Street, who suffered through my weekly progress reports, and especially Joni Kopels, who made it through a whole manuscript!

*Trilateralism: The Trilateral Commission and Elite Planning for World Management, South End Press, Boston 1980.

PROLOGUE

"Testing one, two, three . . ."

The miniature tape recorder spit his voice back at him and David Kurcell hit the STOP button. Satisfied with the test, he rewound the tape and raised the Sony back to his lips.

"Two o'clock A.M.," he said softly, gazing down from the hillside. "Picked up convoy on Route 16 near Hoocher's Gap ninety minutes ago. Followed it onto unmarked road after a half hour of driving. Trucks show no markings, no license plates. Troop concentration inside base heavy."

David placed the Sony on the ground by his side and brought the binoculars back to his eyes. A new figure had appeared on the base below, the first one David had detected not in a standard army uniform. The man wore black slacks and a black turtleneck. He was so broad that his shirt looked to be stuffed with padding. He towered a full head over the troops he passed as he moved by the trucks. Even in the dark, David could tell there was something strange about his straw-colored hair, something wrong. It stopped short of the big man's ears and rimmed his scalp, as if only those strands protected by a bowl had survived his last trim. The thought made David reach up to his long brown locks and run a hand through them.

He heard a distant rumble and turned his binoculars away from the base toward the unmarked road that ran before it. Holding them with one hand, he picked the Sony up and pressed RECORD. "Three more trucks approaching. Also no markings, no license plates. Identical in all respects to the ones I tailed here."

Again the trucks were of the heavy transport variety, modern and sleek. Space-age eighteen-wheelers built of shiny hard green steel. Probably armored. David followed them as they edged toward Miravo Air Force Base, a former Strategic Air Command site that had been shut down two years before.

His heart continued to pound with excitement. He wasn't going to mess things up; not this time, not again. He had learned his lesson a few months before as a feature writer for his college newspaper when a dorm mate who worked in the school's infirmary insisted that three students had contracted the AIDS virus after brief stays there. After the story ran, though, the source had disavowed his statements, leaving David with only a few scribbled notes for corroboration. He had been dismissed from the paper's writing staff as a result, his dream of becoming an investigative journalist marred forever. Embarrassed and alienated, he barely managed to finish the rest of the semester before dropping out and heading west in his Jeep Wrangler.

By mid-April he had met up with some friends who were camping in the Colorado Rockies. David was halfway through a six-pack late that first night when a quartet of heavy transports had rolled down the road just barely in view.

"Man," one of his friends mused, "this is getting to be a habit."

"Huh?" uttered David, already trying to chase the beer from his system.

"Three nights, three convoys. What the fuck?"

His curiosity piqued, the next day David accompanied his friends only as far as the next town to pay a visit to the local electronics store. From there he returned to the hills and began his vigil with the tape recorder and a camcorder ready at all times. This time he wasn't going to fuck up. This time he was going to get hard evidence. His dream had been returned to him and he wasn't about to squander the chance.

Still, he had been ready to give up the wait after three eventless nights when tonight, in the dead quiet of the Colorado dark, he heard the trucks coming from a half mile away.

David was already behind the wheel of his Jeep Wrangler when the convoy passed. Knowing it wouldn't be hard to follow, he pulled out well back and drove slowly by moonlight, keeping the low rumble of the convoy within earshot. Without headlights, the slight bends in the road became treacherous curves that had the Jeep Wrangler clinging for dear life.

The longest hour of his life passed before the headlights of the convoy illuminated the shape of the mothballed SAC base. David had hidden the Jeep Wrangler and found this vantage point in the hills overlooking the base five minutes later. That was a half hour earlier, and now this second convoy had arrived. He followed the big trucks all the way to the entrance through his binoculars. They wheezed to a halt and waited for the gate to be opened.

Hurriedly David lifted the camcorder from his pack and brought it to his eye in place of the binoculars. He wasn't sure if the night would yield much, especially from this distance, but it would be enough to show these latest trucks entering the base. He had no idea what he was onto here. Whatever it was, though, without documentation it might as well be nothing.

He was trying for better focus on the camcorder when the sound of a jet engine burst from the air above him. A plane swooped out of the sky on slow descent for the base. David followed its approach and watched a line of lights snap on beyond the row of buildings lining the base's center. Runway lights. He returned the camcorder to his eye.

The camera caught the sinking plane as it dropped beneath the buildings. Instantly the big trucks revved their engines and headed in convoy fashion for the lights of the runway.

"Damn," David muttered, lowering the camcorder. "Damn!"

The base's buildings would shield from him whatever happened next. Either the contents of the six trucks were going to be loaded onto this plane, or vice versa. And from this vantage point there was no way to determine what those contents were. He had only one choice, one chance: get onto the base and film the troops in the midst of the loading process. David's mouth had turned desert dry, but the canteen stayed in his pack. He stowed the camcorder next to it and pulled his arms through the straps. Then he sprinted down the hillside for the steel fence enclosing the base.

He reached it barely four minutes later after easily avoiding the cursory vigil being performed by the patrolling troops. Scaling its ten-foot height nonetheless remained formidable, and David crept toward a darkened corner totally out of view from the guards, a corner, he noted with satisfaction, where the barbed wire was missing.

David took a running start and hit the fence just three feet from the top. The rest was easy. He scrambled over the top and hit the ground. He took a quick look around him and then started off, keeping to the dark reaches of the base on a circuitous route to a building very near the runway. After a few deep breaths, he pressed himself against its side and moved toward the upward spill of the runway lights.

Several floods perched on nearby buildings added more illumination to the scene before him. The plane, a powerful transport, sat squarely on the runway two hundred yards away. The big man with the straw-colored hair that didn't seem to match his head stood next to it, hands coiled by his sides. As David watched, he signaled the first of the trucks parked in a neat row to approach. Instantly the lead rig backed up toward the plane's open cargo bay. David's heart rose in anticipation, then quickly sank in disappointment when he saw the truck actually slide enough up the ramp to hide the loading process from him. The man in black disappeared into the bay after it. There would be no shots now of whatever was being carted onto or off the trucks, no way David could get close enough to make use of the camcorder.

Still surveying the scene, he had a sudden inspiration. A hundred yards away, one of the latest trucks to arrive had just slid to a halt apart from the others on the tarmac, its rear angled diagonally toward him. No guards were in the area; all of those he could see were concentrated around the waiting plane.

David made his decision between heartbeats. The night continued to cloak him for a brief stretch into his dash, but then he was in the open, breath tucked deep in his gut. In the end he figured the idling engine had kept the truck's occupants from hearing the thumps of his steps across the asphalt. He reached the truck's rear and placed his back against it. His shoulders sagged inward and he realized its cargo door had already been raised, a canvas flap dangling in its place. David reached up and pulled the flap away in order to peer inside the hold.

The sight within confused him at first until he looked closer. His breath turned to icicles. His blood seemed to thicken and slow.

"My God . . ."

David wasn't sure whether he uttered the words or merely thought them. Trembling, he dropped into a crouch and pulled the pack from his shoulders. He eased the camcorder out and brought it to his eye. Pan for a few seconds, zoom in, and then get the fuck out of here. His hand shook as he struggled to hold the camcorder steady. He completed a quick sweep of the truck's contents and rotated the lens for a close-up.

"Hey!"

The shout jolted him. He twisted around and caught a glimpse of two soldiers bolting toward him from the runway before he swung and charged off for the front of the base.

"*Stop!*"

Gunshots split the night when he refused to oblige. Brief flurries of rapid thuds followed him between a pair of buildings that dissolved back into the sea of darkness.

What was going on here? What in God's name was happening?

He had to get out, had to get the *tape* out, and stuck the camcorder in his jacket when the fence came into view.

He threw himself up onto it without breaking stride. He grabbed steel link just a foot from the top this time. But here the barbed wire was still intact, and his right hand exploded in pain as he pulled himself up and over.

He felt the wire dig deeper into his flesh when he dropped off the fence onto the other side. He landed with a thud, fell, and clawed his way back to his feet. The air burned in his throat. He couldn't catch his breath, yet he didn't dare slow up. He crossed the road and raced into the hills toward the Jeep Wrangler. He reached it, heaving for air. A quick glance at his right hand showed a deep, bloody gouge stretching across the length of the palm. David held it against his chest while his left hand worked the keys from his pocket and then yanked open the door. Fighting back nausea, he climbed into the jeep's cab and stowed the camcorder on the passenger seat. His left hand wedged the key home and twisted.

The Jeep Wrangler jumped to life.

David left the headlights off as he roared down onto the unmarked road, the jeep's pedal dangerously close to the floor. He balanced the wheel with the heel of his ruined right hand while his left tore a sweat-soaked strip of his shirt away. Using his teeth, he managed to turn the strip into a makeshift bandage and then wrapped it about his right palm as tight as he could. He knew some back roads that would help him elude pursuit, but he would have to take them at top speed with only a single hand for control.

He sped by the first of the back roads and screeched into reverse. A fearful glance in the rearview mirror revealed no signs of pursuit and he pulled down the turnoff, switching on his headlights.

"Come on! Come on!"

David fought the jeep for more speed. He tried to close his right hand over the steering wheel, but a bolt of pain shot through it. He yanked the hand off and felt a fresh surge of blood soak through the makeshift bandage. The jeep took a bump hard, jostling the camcorder from its perch on the passenger seat. David stretched his mangled hand over to secure it. Blood oozed over the camcorder's steel housing, but the tape inside remained safe, untouched.

His eyes darted nervously once more to the jeep's rearview mirror. Still no headlights shined back at him.

David's insides rattled as another jarring bump gave the jeep's shocks all they could take. He was checking the rearview mirror again when a wave of nausea hit him. He managed to get the Wrangler stopped just before the vomit flooded his throat.

"Oh, God," he muttered after the last heave out the open door left him breathless. "Oh, God."

David drove on.

His plan had been to drive toward the sun, toward the light and the first hint of safety. A police station, a highway patrol barracks—anything. But it was clear now he couldn't make it that far. The pain in his dripping hand had made him woozy. He kept biting into his lower lip in an effort to cling to consciousness.

Suddenly his headlights caught a roadside sign in their spill. David slowed the jeep and tried to focus. The sign flapped in the breeze, evading the light. David flipped on his high beams to capture its words: GRAND MESA.

The years had spared enough of the sign's wood to make that much out, along with an arrow pointing to the right.

A town! It had to be a town!

David swung right at the next turn-off and pushed the jeep on.

At the outskirts of Grand Mesa, a motel flashed a vacancy sign that was missing half its bulbs. There were a dozen or so units laid out in an L and only a trio of cars in the parking lot.

David maintained the sense of mind to drive by the motel

and park the Wrangler three blocks past it in the lot behind
a combination gas station/repair shop. Walking back toward
the flashing vacancy sign, he kept his bad hand pressed
against the pocket he had tucked the camcorder in to reassure himself it was there.

He would check into the motel and call his sister. It was
five A.M. back in Washington. An hour from now she would
be rising for another long day as chief of staff for Senator
Jordan of Florida. David had always made fun of her for being a flunky. Now her position might be the only thing that
could save his life.

The door to the motel office was locked, and David hit
the buzzer a half-dozen times before a light snapped on. His
eyes swept the street continually for any sign of Humvees
from the base.

"Morning," a man in a red bathrobe greeted sleepily.

"I need a room," David said as calmly as he could manage, his numb, dripping hand hidden from sight.

"I figured that much. Come on in."

As he staggered into the office, David managed to work
a pair of twenties into his good hand and told the clerk to
keep the change. He'd cleanse and wrap the bad one as best
he could in the room. Maybe even ring up the clerk for
some alcohol and bandages in exchange for another twenty.
But first the phone. Reach his sister Kristen, then do something about the pain.

David locked and chained the door to Room 7 behind him.
The room had a bed, a desk, a chair, a television, and a bureau. That was all, besides a bathroom. God, how he needed
a shower. The stench of fear and blood formed a thick coat
over his flesh. What remained of his shirt was soaked through
with sweat. His long hair was wet and matted.

But the shower could wait. The telephone was on the
desk, and he turned on the small lamp over it before dialing
Kristen's number. Eyes perched on the drawn blinds in
search of stray headlights, he willed it to ring, his sister to

answer. He let his torn hand dangle and blood from it dripped freely onto the carpet.

One ring. Two.

"Come on," he urged. "Come on."

Three rings. Then a click.

Thank God!

"Kristen," David started.

"Hi, this is Kristen Kurcell. I'm not home right now, but at the tone leave—"

"Damn!"

Five o'clock in the fucking morning and she wasn't home. Or maybe she was home and just had the machine on so the phone wouldn't wake her. The message ended. The beep sounded.

"Kristen, are you there? Kristen, it's David. If you're there, please pick up. Pick up!"

He was almost shouting in the end, realizing either she wasn't home or couldn't hear him.

"Okay," he continued, settling himself. "I'm in trouble, Kris, big trouble. You're not gonna believe this, but about an hour ago I saw— "

The door to the motel room smashed inward. The chain rattled. Splinters and shards of wood flew everywhere.

"No," David muttered, then screamed, "*No!*"

The big man in black with the ill-fitting straw-colored hair from the base emerged through the remnants of the door. David's mouth had dropped for a scream when the gun the man was holding coughed twice. The bullets felt like kicks to his chest, pushing his shoulders back against the wall. The telephone slid out of his grasp. His feet weren't his anymore. He felt himself sliding downward, eyes locking at the last on the receiver floating above the patch of blood that had oozed from his hand.

Then the big man loomed over him, something shiny sweeping down toward David's head, about to dig in when the darkness swallowed everything.

PART ONE

COCOWALK

CIA HEADQUARTERS:
THURSDAY, APRIL 14, 1994; 10:00 P.M.

CHAPTER 1

Clifton Jardine, director of the Central Intelligence Agency, looked up from the final page of the report before him.

"How many copies of this are there, Mr. Daniels?"

"You're reading the only one," Tom Daniels replied, his voice high and slightly strained. "I typed it myself."

"On disk?"

"By Olivetti. Sorry for the typos."

Daniels was forty and had joined the Company straight out of college. Since then he had served effectively in a number of foreign bureaus before returning home to assume the mundane role of assistant deputy director of intelligence. It was a token promotion and one that would allow the Company to bury him in the bureaucracy he seemed best suited for. Nothing about him bode well for future advancement, especially his appearance. Tall and lanky, his plain suits were invariably ill-fitting. He wore his hair slicked down against its natural wave; his glasses were the photosensitive variety, but they never seemed to lighten sufficiently indoors, cloaking any expression his eyes might have shown. His voice was high and squeaky. Clifton Jardine could never recall meeting a man of less charisma. Daniels inspired no degree of confidence whatsoever, but the report the director was shuffling through again now spoke for itself.

"You'll note that the appendix details the specific travel itineraries of the subjects, sir."

Jardine looked up from the pages. "Subjects or suspects, Mr. Daniels?"

"The latter, by my interpretation."

Jardine found the proper page in the appendix and spoke as he studied it. "For men like this, extensive travel is hardly unusual."

"Again, sir, you should note that each of them visited the *same* eight countries over a six-month period. And the people they met with there . . ."

"By your own admission, you're not certain of that. No hard data."

"I wouldn't expect there would be. The point is, we can place them together *in this country* five times over the past six months." Daniels paused. "My report includes their backgrounds, their dossiers, what they had been a part of."

"Emphasis on *had*, Mr. Daniels. Tense becomes crucial here."

"It never stopped, sir. It redefined itself and kept pursuing its agenda underground."

"And suddenly it resurfaces. Why now, Mr. Daniels?"

"Dodd, sir. He was the missing variable and the most important one."

"An assertion totally lacking in hard evidence."

"No, only indications. But they're strong, irrefutable." Daniels took a deep breath. "Dodd's the one who will finally allow them to bring this off."

"Bring *what* off exactly?" the director charged without giving him a chance to answer. "Your report seems to skirt that issue."

Tom Daniels took a deep breath. "The overthrow of the United States government."

The room became heavy with silence. Clifton Jardine's eyes blazed across his desk, all at once uncertain.

"Then those foreign meetings—"

"The same agenda, by all indications, is being pursued across the globe. Maybe the United States isn't enough for them anymore. Maybe watching events unfold dramatically in other countries is what finally brought them back." Daniels paused and removed his glasses to let his eyes meet the director's. "Maybe, in fact, they caused those events."

"And you're confident the timetable you suggest is accurate?"

"Yes, sir, I am."

Jardine digested this information, then rose, a clear signal for Daniels to take his leave. "You were right to bring this to me, Mr. Daniels. When the response team is in place, I'll make sure you liase."

Daniels stood up, but made no move for the door. "Sir, if I may . . . "

"Please."

"The fact is that the individuals mentioned in my report have been around longer than we have, longer than anyone in government has. We have no idea of how far or deep their sphere of influence extends."

Jardine's features flared. The notion that an underling with a token title could intimate such a thing was unthinkable. "Mr. Daniels, are you suggesting that my own people are not to be trusted?"

"I'm suggesting only that an operation of this scale involves too many people to be certain of them all, and under the circumstances, I'm sure you agree we must be certain."

"You have something to propose as an alternative, I assume," Jardine responded grudgingly.

"The smaller we keep the scale of our response, the better our chances of finding out how the subjects of my report intend to accomplish their goal."

"How small, Mr. Daniels?"

"One man."

Jardine fanned the report's pages. "I see no inclusion of names of possible candidates in this."

"Because there's only one who is suitable, and I didn't want to be logged pulling his file from the flagged pile."

"Who are we talking about, Mr. Daniels?"

"Blaine McCracken, sir."

Jardine's response was to sit back in his chair and

squeeze its arms. "A strange choice, considering your past history with him."

"Not when you consider McCracken is expendable, denounceable, and highly mobile."

"Mobile?"

"You know his background. Nobody's fought for, this country harder than McCracken. No one's proven himself more often in situations comparable to the one we're facing now."

"Your analysis, Mr. Daniels, would seem to indicate there is *nothing* comparable."

"Granted, sir. McCracken has faced his share of madmen and psychopaths, but never anything like this. We could be talking about the end of government as we have come to know it in the United States. And it's already begun. The indications are there."

"You really believe they can pull this off, don't you?"

"*They* think they can."

"That's not what I asked you."

"But that's the answer that matters. Because by all rights, what they're planning to do is impossible. The mechanisms, the levels, the built-in protections of our government—they know about them as clearly as we do, clearer even. That can only mean they've found a way to transcend all of that."

"An awful lot to transcend."

"They're planning something that makes it all possible, sir, something that we aren't considering because we can't. And unless we find out what it is, how they intend to pull this off, we won't be able to stop them."

"But McCracken will . . ."

"It's what he does, sir."

" . . . because he's highly mobile."

"If he uncovers the how, that might be enough."

Jardine tapped his fingers atop the lone copy of Daniels's report. "Given your past dealings with him, what makes you think he'll listen to you?"

"He won't be able to pass up the meeting, sir, for that very reason."

"You'll want to run him yourself, then."

"No one runs Blaine McCracken, sir. But if you mean liase, yes. As I said, the fewer people involved in this, the better."

"He won't trust you, Mr. Daniels."

"That's what I'm counting on, sir. I don't want him to trust me or anyone else totally. It'll be enough if he believes."

Jardine lifted the report from his desk uneasily, as if portions of it were hot. "I'll want to be kept informed of every step," he said finally.

"Of course, sir."

"When you reach McCracken, I'll want to know."

"Yes, sir."

"When the meet is set, I'll want to know."

"I understand, sir."

"And one more thing, Tom. Knock off the sir business. It's Cliff from now on." Jardine tried for a smile and failed. "With the secret the two of us are sharing, we should at least be on a first-name basis."

CHAPTER 2

"Throw him the fuck out the window!" Vincente Ventanna ordered.

The ferret-faced man in the baggy floral shirt sank to his knees pleadingly. "Please, Mr. Ventanna, it won't happen again. I promise!"

Ventanna snorted a line of coke right off his fingertip. "You're right, Hector. It won't happen again because you're gonna go splat eight stories down." His glassy eyes climbed to the muscle-bound shapes looming over the drug dealer who had tried to cheat him. "Luis, Jesús."

"Please," Hector moaned, stinking of sweat and yesterday's cologne. "Please!"

By then, though, Jesús and Luis had already dragged him out onto the balcony overlooking the ocean. Worst thing about tonight, Ventanna figured, was that he'd never be able to return to this, his favorite residence. Located off the Rickenbacker Causeway in the heart of Key Biscayne, Key Colony was one of Miami's most fashionable condominium developments. Ventanna had owned this penthouse in the Tidemark building for a couple years now. Threw lots of good parties and did lots of good shit. Place brought him luck. But everything comes to an end, and shit, the Key hadn't been the same since Hurricane Andrew gobbled up all the trees.

He reached the balcony just as Jesús finished prying Hector's right hand off the railing. "Have a safe flight, *amigo*."

Ventanna blew the remnants of the white powder off his fingertip. It caught in the wind and swirled about.

Jesús and Luis hurled Hector out into the night air.

"Ahhhhhhhhhhhhhhhhhhhhhhhhh!"

Hector's scream tailed off as he dropped. Ventanna reached the railing after he had landed with a thud on the cement between the building and the pool.

Ventanna began laughing hysterically. "Throw 'im the fuck out the window," he wheezed between guffaws, an arm slapped around the shoulder of each of his henchmen. "Throw 'im the fuck out the window!"

His eyes had teared up from the laughing fit and he dabbed them with his sleeve as he stumbled back into the living room. "Okay, Marco, who we got next?"

A man in a peach-colored suit moved away from a door leading into one of the condo's bedrooms. "Dude that's been asking about you around South Beach. We picked him up at Strumpet's."

The smile vanished from Ventanna's face. "A fag joint?"

Marco shrugged.

"You're telling me this dude was looking for *Vincente Ventanna* at a fag joint?"

Marco nodded.

Ventanna started laughing again. "I'm gonna throw him the fuck out the window, too."

Hysterical, Ventanna dropped back into his chair and waved for the man to be brought out into the living room. He emerged between a pair of hulks who might have been twins of Jesús and Luis, Uzi submachine guns slung from their shoulders. Dude was a big man himself, upper body layered in a muscular V. He had a scruffy close-trimmed beard, curly hair, and the darkest eyes Ventanna had ever seen. His arms were tied in front of him, the sleeves pulled up to reveal a pair of thick, sinewy forearms. Dude had a hard face that didn't waste an expression, angular with thin furrows cut out of his brow and lots of shadows to hide his secrets. Ventanna had the man dead to rights, but look at him and it seemed like he was in charge.

Ventanna settled himself down and took a sip from his hefty glass of iced vodka on the rocks. "Hey, *amigo*, what you doing looking for me in a fag joint?"

Those black eyes didn't blink. "Seemed the best place to find the biggest asshole in Miami."

Ventanna spit out a mouthful of vodka. "Hey, you got a sense of humor. You a funny dude." He pulled himself to his feet and noticed a jagged scar that ran through the big man's left eyebrow. "I like that. So you know what I'm gonna do?"

"Can't wait to hear."

"I'm gonna throw you the fuck out the window."

Ventanna had barely got the sentence finished before collapsing in another fit of laughter. He looked up to see that, surprisingly, the bearded man had joined in.

"You think that's funny, *amigo*?"

"No, I think you are."

Jesús and Luis touched the Glock nine-millimeter pistols

wedged uncomfortably in their belts. Ventanna shook them off.

"You got balls, eh? You a reaaaaaaal tough guy."

"A couple questions, then I leave." The man's dark eyes drifted to the balcony, empty like glass. Maybe the muscles in his forearms flexed a little. The shadows on his face seemed to spread outward, threatening to swallow it. "I'll even forget about unscheduled Flight Hector."

Ventanna climbed back to his feet. "Hey, thanks ever so much, maahn. I guess I owe you big time."

"Your choice, Ventanna. Easy or hard."

Ventanna tapped his finger against the air. "You know I mighta let you go if you hadn't looked for me in a fag joint. I could overlook everything else except that. Now you know what I gotta do?"

"Throw me the fuck out the window?"

"You catch on fast, *amigo*." His drug-glazed stare struggled to stay fixed on the black eyes of the big man. "Jesús, Luis!"

The two monsters came forward and grabbed the captive at either arm. The two who had been holding him backed off submissively.

"Throw him the fuck out the window!"

Jesús smashed the big man in the stomach, doubling him over. Luis followed with an elbow to the back of his head, which sent him to the marble floor.

"Hard, maahn," Ventanna taunted. "I choose hard."

They dragged the big man onto the balcony. Ventanna reached the sliding glass door just as they hoisted him back to his feet. His head had slumped over the rail.

"Bye-bye."

Ventanna flapped his hand childishly, laughing as his monsters started pulling the big man forward.

Then something happened.

Because of the mind-dulling drugs he'd been downing all night, Ventanna saw it unfold in slow, surreal motion. First the big man's arms, suddenly not bound at all, came up behind the monsters' heads. Then his whole frame was behind them, yanking the hulks brutally backwards by the collars and then shoving with equal force forward.

The monsters flew over the balcony screaming. The Glocks that had been wedged through their belts were now in the big man's hands. They came up as Ventanna stood there, his feet melting into the marble.

The two other hulks back in the living room fought to get their Uzis unslung, and Blaine McCracken shot them both before either had touched his trigger. The man in the peach-colored suit had managed to free his pistol and aim it. But McCracken ducked behind the cover provided by the rigid Ventanna. When the man hesitated, McCracken put two nine-millimeter bullets in his chest. His peach suit turned red.

Blaine grabbed the still-stunned Ventanna and slammed him against the balcony. "You should have chosen easy."

"Wh-wh-who are you?"

"The man who's gonna throw you the fuck out the window."

"No, maahn! Please! Just tell me what you want."

"Might be too late for that," Blaine said and shoved Ventanna's head farther over the top rail.

"Please, *amigo!*"

Blaine pulled him back. "One chance, Ventanna."

"Yes! Anything! *Anything!*"

"That's good."

Cassas stood on the corner of Florida Avenue and Mayfair Boulevard in Miami's Coconut Grove, hating what he saw around him and loving what was about to become of it. Any night of the week will find Miami's Coconut Grove cluttered with people into the early hours of the morning. Sidewalk and bar space is staked out and held fast to. Moving anywhere without jostling or being jostled becomes impossible. Salsa and rock music from jam-packed bars pour into the streets, lyrics warring to form little more than babble. Teenagers cluster by the doors eyeing the mostly college-age patrons enviously, waiting for the proper moment to duck through. It all makes for an experiment in chaos.

No one in the Grove paid any attention to Cassas. He had spent a good part of his life blending in, and it was especially easy to blend in here among those who cared nothing for those they did not recognize. For all intents and purposes, he was invisible.

The cellular phone made a slight bulge in his inside jacket pocket, and Cassas kept his eyes directed toward the Cocowalk mall diagonally across the street. Pounding chords of rock music drifted from within it, courtesy of a live concert that had begun at midnight. A new song had begun; "Sympathy for the Devil" by the Rolling Stones, Cassas noted. How fitting.

In the sky above him, a helicopter swooped lower to better direct its spotlight upon this cluttered mass of decadent humanity. To Cassas it seemed like one of those old war movies where the searchlight cuts back and forth across the prison camp through the long night in search of potential escapees. Well, this, too, was a prison, except no one was going to escape.

Cassas turned his gaze upward again. The chopper continued its sweep, cutting neat patterns out of the sky.

Not long now, he thought as he nearly collided with a big, bearded man in a white suit. Not long at all.

McCracken had first thought the man was drunk, then realized he was just staring up at the helicopter that was carving up the darkness with its spotlight. Blaine turned off Florida Avenue onto Mayfair Boulevard toward the centerpiece of Coconut Grove: Cocowalk, a four-story indoor/outdoor mall complex formed of retail stores squeezed amidst sprawling nightclubs. He had left Vincente Ventanna bound and gagged in a garage storeroom of the Tidemark back at Key Colony just two hours before. It was closing on one A.M. now, and the night in the Grove was still heating up. Blistering guitar riffs battled a Mick Jagger wanna-be for control of the air as "Sympathy for the Devil" continued.

"I'm looking for a gunrunner," McCracken had said to Ventanna back on the penthouse balcony, the sound of approaching sirens drifting through the night. "Calls himself Manuel Alvarez. I believe you've made his acquaintance."

"Yes, but he is little more than a strang—"

McCracken shoved Ventanna's upper body over the edge. "You've decided to get into guns, Ventanna, and Alvarez has agreed to become your connection. In fact, he's half of South Florida's connection. Big market in the schools now, I understand. I want him."

Ventanna looked in Blaine's eyes fearfully. "I don't know who you are, *amigo*, but you cannot get close to Alvarez."

"No, Vincente. But you can. In fact you've got a meeting set with him for tonight. You're going to tell me where." McCracken eased back on the pressure and straightened Ventanna's lapels. "And you're going to lend me a suit."

Since Ventanna wore his clothes long and oversized, the fit was acceptable. So, too, was the drug lord's confirmation of the fact that tonight would mark the first time he would ever actually be meeting the mysterious Alvarez. He was to enter the Baja Beach Club in Cocowalk through the nightclub's second-floor entrance wearing a white suit with a rose pinned to the right lapel. Alvarez would have people waiting.

Stepping into the palm-lined courtyard center of Cocowalk, McCracken was instantly aware of how much he stood out. There were few adults, certainly none his age, and his manner of dress was all wrong. No one else in view was wearing a suit, which would make it all the easier for Alvarez's people to spot the man they thought was Ventanna once he entered the Baja Beach Club. Overhead the helicopter's spotlight poured through Cocowalk's roofless structure and caught him briefly. The crowd was cheering and hooting. "Sympathy for the Devil" was finished and the band-leader announced a tune by Led Zeppelin was next.

The concert had been set up on a makeshift stage erected at the base of a second-floor mezzanine. The top of the Cocowalk complex was rimmed with gold inlay, but the dominant shades of the lower levels were chic pastels of mauve and cream. Salesmen who didn't rate a glass-covered storefront like the Gap, The Limited, Victoria's Secret, or B. Dalton hawked their T-shirts or costume jewelry from pushcarts and kiosks set up anywhere they could squeeze them.

McCracken climbed to the second-floor veranda level. He passed by a bar called Fat Tuesday's and approached the entrance to the Baja Beach Club on the right next to a restaurant called Big City Fish. There was a line to get in, but Blaine flashed Ventanna's gray private membership card and went right on through.

His ears were instantly assaulted by a screeching rasp of a voice singing lyrics to the accompaniment of a karaoke machine. The words slid down a screen on the wall of a large inner room as a balding patron fought to match the Bob Dylan classic "Tangled Up in Blue." Few of the Baja Beach Club's young patrons seemed to be familiar with what he was singing. Bikini-clad waitresses loped across the floor toting trays of multicolored drinks.

"Body shots!" one advertised above the din. "Body shots!"

"Mr. Ventanna?"

Blaine turned to his right and found a young man dressed in a baggy olive suit.

"Mr. Alvarez is waiting upstairs. If you'll just follow me . . ."

They moved toward a doorway with an arrow pointing up over it. The door led back outside and onto a narrow set of brick steps. On the Baja Beach Club's second floor, Cocowalk's third, the clutter of people was the tightest yet. McCracken followed the young man through a crowd loud enough to all but drown out the Led Zeppelin song being pounded out down on the first level. Blaine saw a covered outdoor balcony just up ahead, strangely deserted considering the excellent view it offered of the festivities. A trio of figures leaned over the far railing. A pair standing vigil at the doorway halted McCracken's progress after his escort had slid through. The escort moved to the railing and spoke briefly to the shortest figure peering over it. The figure turned and started McCracken's way.

It was a kid; sixteen, seventeen maybe, wearing baggy cuffed jeans and a silk floral shirt. Dark curly hair wet with mousse or gel. Deep tanned, with the sharpest blue eyes Blaine had ever seen.

"I'm Carlos Alvarez," the kid said when he neared McCracken.

He didn't stick out his hand. Neither did Blaine.

"I was supposed to meet with Manuel."

"Yeah, well, my father don't meet with just anybody." The kid paused. "You carrying?"

"Your instructions were not to, *amigo*," McCracken followed, trying hard not to register his shock at the fact that South Florida's biggest gunrunning operation was being run by a father-and-son team.

"I'm not your *amigo*," the kid told him in perfect English. "You want to do business, let's do it."

A canopied table was set out on the balcony, and two of the kid's goons led Blaine toward it. The view from this vantage point took in all of Cocowalk. For the first time McCracken had clear sight of the cineplex occupying the fourth floor and the Oriental gazebo-like structures sitting atop the open U-shaped roof that sloped around the courtyard.

"You sure you're not carrying?" Alvarez said, taking the seat across from him. The kid had both a beer and some foamy pink concoction within easy reach. But he seemed more interested in working a wad of gum noisily about his mouth. "I mean, I don't want us to get off on the wrong foot or anything."

"What's this about?" Blaine snapped, pulling open his jacket to invite a frisk.

"Just want to give you a chance to own up to a fuck-up if you made it."

"Vincente Ventanna gave his word," Blaine said with just enough toughness while one of the kid's henchmen patted him down.

The kid leaned forward slightly. A smile full of white teeth spread across his face.

"Trouble is, *amigo*, you're not Ventanna."

CHAPTER 3

Down on Florida Avenue, Cassas checked his watch. Around him the street continued to swell with additional throngs of people. He figured South Beach must be dead, so its patrons had hit the Grove for what remained of the night. Red lights meant little to drivers in search of a parking space or familiar face. No one was going anywhere, or if they were, they weren't going fast.

Perfect.

Cassas drew the cellular phone from his pocket. The sight was not unfamiliar in the Grove, giving him no reason to disguise it. He pressed out the numbers and waited.

"Here," a voice greeted.

"It's time," Cassas signaled.

Five guns had been thrust McCracken's way before he could move. Slivers of the chopper's spotlight caught the Alvarez kid's face as he continued. "You think I'm stupid, man? You think I don't check out who wants to meet with me?" His white teeth twisted into a half snarl. "This is Miami. I *own* this city."

"Then you should be taking better care of it. Stay home and finish your homework instead of moving guns."

"Funny, man."

"Maybe study for midterms."

"You're a regular fucking riot."

"I hope you're not a dropout."

"A average, shit for brains," the kid boasted. "At Ransom."

"Must be the local juvenile detention center."

"Keep it up, asshole, and maybe I'll have you killed slow."

"You're out of your league, kid."

Alvarez leaned back, cupped his hands behind his head, and shifted his eyes among the five gunmen spread over the balcony. "This is fun. I'm glad I let you up here."

"This your operation or your father's?"

"Both."

"Keeping it all in the family."

"Hey, man, the American Dream!" Alvarez shook his head disparagingly. "And you come here hoping to spoil it."

"Kids are killing each other with your guns."

"I got national distribution now. Branching out."

"That's why I came."

The kid chuckled. "You gonna stop me, that it?"

Blaine shook his head. "People like you always end up stopping themselves. I just might help the process along."

The kid's eyes bulged incredulously. "Look around you, man. *I* got the guns. I snap my fingers and you're dead right here."

"Your father wouldn't like that."

"Somewhere else, then. Don't matter to me."

"*Doesn't* matter," Blaine corrected. "I told you, you should be studying."

The kid snarled again. "You gonna be sorry you tried this, man You gonna be soooooooo sorry."

A second helicopter dropped down from overhead, descending right above them. Two of the Alvarez kid's guards stole glances at it from their posts near the balcony railing.

"Hey," Alvarez shot Blaine's way when he noticed

McCracken's eyes drifting toward it as well, "I'm talking to you."

Blaine watched the second chopper lower in a direct line with the Baja Beach Club's balcony and dropped to the floor.

Rat-tat-tat . . . rat-tat-tat . . .

The machine-gun fire tore through the men at the railing first. Blaine was going for Alvarez to take him down when the kid swung the chopper's way and was greeted with a volley of bullets. Impact threw him over the table, blood jetting from his silk shirt. Bullets dropped another of his guards to the floor. Two more were cut down in the back as they tried to flee.

McCracken crawled to the nearest one and yanked the nine-millimeter Beretta pistol out of his holster, then a trio of clips from his jacket pocket. He lunged to his feet and slammed his shoulders against the lone outdoor wall. At the same time, the chopper's pilot did his best version of a quick drop in a hot landing zone and deposited a half-dozen black-clad gunmen atop the second-story roof of Big City Fish. The helicopter banked immediately back into a rise as the gunmen broke into a spread formation and leveled their M16s toward the crowd on the first floor.

McCracken opened fire. A pair of his bullets punched one of their number backwards. The way he went down could only mean body armor, ruling out body shots to effect a kill.

The other five gunmen swung the balcony's way and Blaine managed to direct a bullet dead center into one of their foreheads. He dove back to the floor just ahead of the barrage of 7.62mm fire and crawled for the doorway leading back into the Baja Beach Club.

Throughout Cocowalk, meanwhile, confusion had given way to chaos. The band giving the concert had stopped in the middle of another Stones number and its members were scurrying for cover. The initial hail of bullets that in the original plan would have been fired into the crowd had alerted it instead. The complex's front provided the most convenient means of exit by far, and the thousands gathered rushed that way in a stampede-like charge until the attacking helicopter dropped low to cut off their escape. Automatic fire rained down from within it, effectively pinning the occupants of Cocowalk in their tracks. Bullets thumped into bodies and dropped them where they stood.

McCracken emerged through the chaos of the Baja Beach Club onto Cocowalk's second floor just as the enemy chopper started into another rise. The carnage it had left sickened him. Screams rose over the last of the gunfire pouring from within it.

"Jesus Christ," he muttered, "Jesus fucking Christ!"

McCracken held his Beretta overhead and fought to angle through the crowd for a shot at another of the gunmen. All five had dropped off the roof and would be moving through Cocowalk, no doubt distracted by the presence of a man who had drastically altered their plans.

Meanwhile, the dozen police officers who were on duty in Cocowalk struggled to maintain a semblance of order, at the very least to track the movements of the gunmen spreading through the mall. The walkie-talkies the officers carried meant backup would already be en route in the form of every bit of firepower the Miami police could muster. But Blaine had to assume that it was too far away to do much good at all and would be hard-pressed to penetrate the crowds in any case.

The throng McCracken was caught in suddenly stopped its surge for the stairs. One of the gunmen had appeared on the opposite side of the mall. The policeman who had been posted near the second floor entrance to the Baja Beach Club frantically shoved patrons aside to clear a path for his bullets. The gunman didn't wait. He simply fired into the crowd. The policeman went down. The survivors around him hit the floor, exposing the gunman who had begun to move on.

"Down!" Blaine screamed to those nearest him and got off a trio of bullets.

The first thumped into the gunman's bulletproof vest and drove him backwards. The second caught him just under the collarbone, while the third found his skull. The man keeled over.

McCracken pulled himself on, briefly alone now as he neared the mezzanine that overlooked the makeshift stage and panic-seized Cocowalk entrance. Gunfire traced him from the third floor and he had no choice but to thrust himself over the railing down to the first.

He hit the concert stage with knees tucked to his chest, landed in a sea of wires and cables. One of the big amplifiers tipped over at the same time the spotlight from the civilian chopper inadvertently found him in its spill.

"Shit!" McCracken rasped and threw himself into a roll that saved him from a barrage originating on the second floor in front of B. Dalton.

Blaine came up firing the Beretta in that direction. No way to hope for a killshot this time. Four hits into the gunman's legs, though, pulled his feet out from under him. His machine gun was still erupting when he went down, and the bullets shattered the plate-glass window fronts of B. Dalton and the stores on either side of it.

Sirens were wailing in the distance. But from the traffic Blaine had witnessed in the Grove streets, certain to be worsened tenfold by now, their arrival was hardly imminent. In addition to cars, the streets had filled with those people lucky enough not to have been within Cocowalk and others even more lucky to have escaped it. The asphalt seemed to buckle under the weight of so many charging onto it at once, the panic spreading fast.

McCracken realized the enemy chopper had temporarily abandoned its murderous vigil over the main entrance to swoop toward him. He threw himself behind the cover of a marble planter and felt bullets tear chips of it away on impact. When he heard additional gunfire but felt no more pounding, he knew the chopper had returned its attention to the young people, who, suddenly unimpeded, had launched a massive rush for Cocowalk's front once more.

Blaine rose from his cover and opened fire on the helicopter. He emptied the rest of the clip into its frame and succeeded in drawing the chopper toward him again. The remaining three gunmen he could let go for now. The chopper was his main concern. It had to be neutralized. But not with a simple nine-millimeter, or even a machine gun. Movie scenes of bullets downing helicopters were hardly realistic. There were other ways, though.

Blaine's eyes drifted up from the mass of rock music equipment on the small stage, following the thick lines of coaxial cable all the way to what must have been a fourth-floor power source. He had his answer.

McCracken snapped a fresh clip home into the Beretta and bolted for the stairs. Bullets from two of the remaining gunmen who had been laying in wait for him burned his way and he returned the fire, forcing them to take cover. One reemerged as soon as Blaine reached the second floor, but McCracken's lightning reflexes served him well. He fired three bullets dead on, while the best the gunman could manage was a harmless spray. The first shots took the man in the right shoulder and arm. The third obliterated his throat and showered the panicked bystanders nearest him with blood.

Blaine then slid across the linoleum to avoid a burst fired down from the third-floor perch of one of the two remaining gunmen. Still in motion, McCracken drained the rest of his second clip, and the gunman dropped over the railing, dead.

The helicopter swooped for another attack. Blaine dove for cover beneath a collection of empty pushcarts stored near a wall on the second floor. He covered his head against the exploding splinters of wood and waited once more until the chopper whirled for a return to the Cocowalk entrance before reemerging.

Only one of the gunmen remained between him and the point on the fourth floor where the other ends of the concert

cables were plugged. McCracken took the stairs quickly to
the third floor and was halfway to the fourth when a bullet
grazed his side. As hot pain seared through him, he spun to
see not the last gunman, but the one he had shot in the legs
lying forty feet away. A trail of blood lay in his wake where
he had dragged himself. The gunman tried for the trigger
again, but McCracken had already measured off a head shot
with the first bullet in the last clip salvaged from Alvarez's
dead guard.

Having neutralized all but one of his adversaries,
McCracken sprinted to the fourth floor to follow the tangle
of the coaxial cables to their source. This vantage point af-
forded him a clear view into the street. A quartet of police
cars had managed to work their way through the snarl and
were moving forward.

The helicopter, which had started back for him, again
turned its attention on them. It pummeled the closest squad
car with a fusillade that sent it careening down Mayfair
Boulevard. Spinning wildly out of control, the car smashed
through the front of Johnny Rocket's, an old-fashioned fif-
ties soda fountain that until tonight had boasted the best bur-
gers in Miami. A grenade fired from a launcher inside the
chopper turned a second police car into a spinning hulk of
burning metal, while a third cruiser crashed into a row of
parked cars trying to avoid it.

McCracken felt it all like kicks to his stomach. He
reached a large junction box the coaxial cables had been
plugged into and yanked one out. He took up what remained
of the slack and then, with all his strength, jerked the other
end of the cable up from the first floor. On the makeshift
stage, an amp tipped over and in true domino effect took a
row of equipment with it. Out of the jumble the cable began
to rise.

Directly across from him, on the other side of Cocowalk,
the enemy helicopter was cutting a horizontal path through
the air, strafing the many buildings. Glass shattered and
showered over those patrons still stuck within the complex.

More sirens wailed. McCracken could see a police helicopter speeding through the air in the Grove's direction.

Clang!

A bullet slammed into the steel railing on his right, and McCracken hit the floor with the cable pinned beneath him. The final gunman charged toward the stairs, M16 firing nonstop. Blaine pumped a quartet of shells into his armored midsection, and the force was sufficient to separate the gunman from his rifle and pitch him down the stairs he had just mounted. He slammed into the floor and crawled behind the nearest cover.

McCracken regained his feet and reeled the rest of the cable up from forty feet below. When the process of curling it like a garden hose was complete, he turned his attention to the enemy chopper.

Before Blaine could consider the matter any further, though, the police helicopter soared in directly over Cocowalk's rear, not fifty feet above his head. Gunfire spit from within it in the enemy chopper's direction. The enemy chopper flitted in the air briefly before swinging toward its adversary and surging forward. The police chopper rose slightly and the enemy followed suit, return fire pouring from the open side door.

The two helicopters converged on each other, swooping and swerving, like great birds of prey. Blaine watched as the civilian chopper rose over both of them and settled in the air, spotlight sweeping the sky beneath it. Confused at first, he quickly realized that the civilian chopper's pilot was trying to blind his counterpart in the enemy helicopter with the beam. The ploy forced the pilot who had ferried the gunmen in to bank downward and slide back in McCracken's direction.

Just what he needed!

As Blaine readied his looped-together cable, another grenade jetted out from within the enemy chopper. The grenade struck the police helicopter broadside and sent it spinning out of control, black smoke belched in its wake. The pilot managed to steady it into an uneasy descent that would hopefully hold long enough to find a parking lot or rooftop to try for a landing.

During the course of the battle Blaine had glimpsed the remaining captives of Cocowalk seize the opportunity to flee. Now, though, with nothing left to impede it, he knew the enemy chopper could simply move its attack to the streets where the endless sea of bodies would make equally inviting targets.

McCracken pulled his coiled mass of cable back behind him to gather momentum. The helicopter had begun to turn his way again when he tossed the cable outward. McCracken watched it unspool as it neared its target and then dove to the floor beneath the spill of the bullets pouring at him from within the chopper. From the corner of his eye he saw a section of the snakelike cable land upon the main rotor blade. In the next instant, the rest of the spool had been reeled into the rotor and swallowed in a blur. Control compromised, the chopper began wobbling and then fell into a severe list to the left. The pilot overcompensated and the helicopter turned nearly all the way onto its right side. It began spinning wildly, lifting into the air only to drop again as the coaxial cable wrapped itself ever tighter around the rotor blade.

The pilot fought desperately to regain control. He tried to bring the chopper into a rise, but the move spilled it all the way onto its side. The rotor sputtered, choked by the spool of cable. McCracken watched the chopper plunge toward an indoor parking garage behind Cocowalk and covered his head a moment before impact.

The chopper crashed into the top of the garage, caught fire but didn't explode. Blaine's eyes lingered on it briefly before turning back toward the shattered insides of the mall. Not a single shop or storefront was left whole. The glass and debris were everywhere, much of it layered atop the bodies the killers had left in their wake. Miami SWAT teams flooded the complex in a black wave. McCracken started to raise his arms to signal them toward him.

The last gunman he had shot lunged into his line of vision, diving for the M16 McCracken's barrage had torn from him. The figure's black ski mask was gone, allowing a mass of blond hair to slide down to its shoulders. A woman!

"Don't!" Blaine yelled down, Beretta in hand once more and poised her way.

The woman's hand grasped the M16 but didn't right it. Alerted to the commotion, Miami police rushed to the fourth floor in combat fashion.

"Stop!" a voice screamed.

"Hands in the air!" followed another.

"Give it up," Blaine called to the woman. "It's over."

"No!" she ranted, eyes darting between the gun and McCracken. "It's just beginning. A revolution in the streets, starting tonight. We're going to take this country back!"

"Who is? Who are you?"

"You can't stop us! No one can stop us! You'll see, everyone will see!"

"*Drop the gun!*" a Miami policeman yelled at McCracken. "Don't move!"

A trio of police closed on the woman from separate angles.

Blaine dropped his pistol and showed his hands. "Don't shoot her!" he screamed to the officers. "We need her al—"

The woman's eyes blazed. She started to bring the M16 up.

"*No!*" Blaine screamed.

The policemen's fire tore into her, spinning the woman's frame around and slamming it to the floor. Her legs kicked once and were still.

McCracken leaned over the railing. "Shit," he muttered.

"Don't move!" another policeman bellowed his way.

The spotlight from the civilian chopper caught McCracken in the midst of a dozen rifles thrust his way. A pair of officers thumped up the stairs toward him.

"On the floor!" one of them ordered. *"Now!"*

Blaine took one more look at the young woman's corpse and then sank to his knees before spreading himself out over the floor. A foot jammed hard against the base of his neck. His hands were jerked behind him and a pair of cuffs snapped home.

"In case you didn't notice," he said out of the corner of his mouth that had been spared the tile, "I'm on your side."

"You're under arrest," a cop's voice told him.

CHAPTER 4

"Thanks for seeing me, Paul," was Kristen Kurcell's greeting as Paul Gathers emerged from his office in the J. Edgar Hoover Building.

"Don't worry. I'm sure you can return the favor next time my department comes up for funding before your senator's appropriations committee."

He took her outstretched hand in both of his, and she nervously returned his grasp.

"You're trembling," he said and touched her shoulder.

Kristen shrugged. At five-foot-eight, Gathers was only an inch taller than she. They had met for the first time after he had called her following a *Washington Magazine* pictorial entitled "Women on the Hill." Kristen had been one of those featured, thought by many who didn't read the captions to be a professional model. It was no wonder. Tall and lean, she had maintained both her youthful vitality and her athletic lines. A full, easy smile highlighted a rosy complexion that made her look perpetually tanned. Her hair was an auburn composition of curls and waves that tumbled neatly beneath her shoulders, sometimes stubbornly slipping across her face until she pushed it away. One of the shots in the pictorial caught her doing just that, the one that Gathers had checked the caption under. Kristen's beauty was more innocent than sultry. She needed little makeup and wore even less. Enough eye shadow only to help her big brown eyes not stand out on her face.

Gathers had called her at Senator Jordan's office six months before on the pretext of needing some appropriations input. He confessed clumsily while they were still shaking hands at the restaurant. Despite that first meeting coming up just short of a disaster and her continued deflections of his persistent overtures, Kristen and Paul had become friends, sharing an occasional dinner or drink. In any case, he was the only FBI agent she knew well enough to contact directly. Gathers was a special agent with the counterterrorism division. He traveled frequently, but fortunately he was in on this Friday morning.

Gathers looked more stocky than the last time they had met, a man at best doomed to carefully watch his weight and at worst destined to see it stage a significant rise. He kept his kinky dark hair closely trimmed.

"You bring the tape?" Gathers asked, letting his hand slide off her shoulder.

Kristen tapped her worn, soft leather briefcase.

Paul Gathers led her into his office. "No calls," he said to his secretary before closing the door behind him.

"My brother's the only family I've got left, Paul. There's nobody else. If anything's happened to him . . ."

"One step at a time, Kris. Sit down."

Kristen rested her briefcase on one of the chairs set before Gathers's desk. She withdrew the cassette tape and held it briefly before handing it to the agent.

Kristen had first heard the message herself ninety minutes earlier, having called home from the office at about ten A.M. to retrieve her messages. She had already spent three hectic hours checking memos and returning phone calls on what was turning out to be an especially busy Friday. The only conceivably pressing calls would have come from the senator, and since that was where she had been overnight, she might have gone the whole day without getting her messages.

The only one on the machine had been from her brother.

The phone in her office nearly dropped from her hand as the message wound to a close. She felt faint, cold briefly, and then hot all over. She stood up shaking, grabbed the edge of her desk to steady herself. Dazedly she walked into the outer office and stopped at the receptionist's desk. The senator was at an important meeting and could not be disturbed. They had planned to meet immediately afterwards. That would have to wait now.

"Sally."

The receptionist swung her way, startled. Kristen didn't realize she had spoken so loudly.

"Could you tell the senator I had to go out for a while? Personal business. Something of an emergency."

"Of course," Sally said with honest concern. "Is everyone all right?"

"Yes. At least, I think so. It's just that . . ."

The final sentence was still uncompleted when Kristen reached the door.

At her apartment just two blocks from the Russell Senate Building, she listened to her brother's message three more times before calling Paul Gathers. Paul would help. Paul was a friend. Looking at him now as he lowered the tape toward the cassette player resting on his desk blotter made her feel more at ease. Maybe everything really was all right. Maybe she was overreacting.

Gathers popped open the top of the cassette player and slid the tape home. Then he hit PLAY. Kristen didn't take a seat. Neither did Gathers. An instant later her brother's voice filled the room.

"Kristen, are you there? Kristen, it's David. If you're there, please pick up. Pick up!"

His voice had risen to almost a shout by that point. A sound she thought was a deep breath followed as he settled himself.

"Okay, I'm in trouble, Kris, big trouble. You're not gonna believe this, but about an hour ago I saw—"

The sound of something breaking or crashing cut off his words.

"No."

A mutter.

"No!"

A shout.

Then nothing, save for two soft raps that sounded like someone tapping a knuckle against a window. Several seconds passed before the phone on the other end was hung up. The machine clicked off.

"5:13 A.M.," droned the synthesized voice that chirped in at the end of every message.

Kristen turned her gaze from the tape player back to Paul Gathers. "I think those last sounds were gunshots," she said after he had pressed STOP. "That's what they were, weren't they?"

"Sit down, Kris."

"Tell me I'm wrong, Paul. Please tell me I'm wrong."

He settled into his chair and Kristen sat down stiffly on the edge of the one before his desk. More of her frame was actually off the chair than on it.

Gathers leaned forward. "We have equipment that can enhance all the sounds, computers that can identify them. I'll take this down to our lab boys. Let them have a go at it."

"You don't need them to find out where the call was placed from. You've got the exact time, the exchange it came into."

"One step at a time."

Kristen bounced back to her feet, ran a hand across her chin. "Don't do this to me, Paul, not you."

Gathers stood up and came round to the front of his desk. He grasped her near the shoulders and felt her trembling anew.

"You were out when this call came in."

"What's the difference?"

"You think it would have made a difference if you'd been home?"

She looked away. "At least I would have known where he was. Maybe he would've had enough time to tell me what he saw. I could have done something."

"You *are* doing something. You came to me. Yes?" When Kristen didn't answer, he squeezed her arm tighter. "Yes?"

She nodded passively. Then her eyes turned back briefly toward the tape player. "You heard his voice, Paul. He sounded so scared. I never heard David sound like that before."

"This is your brother we're talking about, right?"

"What do—"

"Answer me."

"Yes."

"The one who dropped out of college, the free spirit when measured against his eminently regimented sister. Two months ago, you told me he was driving cross-country in a jeep. Bugged the hell out of you."

"So?"

"So maybe he's still bugging. Maybe you're forgetting about all the jokes you said he's been playing on you since you were kids."

"You think this is *a joke*? God, Paul, his *voice*." She thrust a finger toward the tape player. "Listen to his voice!"

"I will, Kris, and so will the experts. But answer me this: does your answering machine keep any track of the number of callers who hang up before the beep sounds?"

"No, only those who leave a message."

"Then it's possible David called back again, perhaps even several times, and just didn't want to leave another message."

"No, he wouldn't do that to me."

He grimaced. "This *is* David we're talking about, isn't it?"

"Okay. Granted."

"I remember you telling me he fancies himself a journalist."

"I told him I could get him an internship up here when he said he was leaving school again."

"Too much the crusader to take it, though."

"That's how he saw himself, yes."

"Maybe he pissed the wrong people off, then. It happens. He'll turn up, if he hasn't already." Gathers hesitated before going on, as if to choose his words carefully. "Would he have known where to reach you last night?"

"No," Kristen said softly.

"Right."

"Which is all the more reason why you've got to tell me where he called from. I've got to find out where he is."

Gathers nodded, holding Kristen's arm supportively. "You'll be in your office this afternoon?"

"Yes."

The agent's eyes blanked a bit. "I'll need a number where I can reach you after work."

"I'll be home."

"Maybe you want to give me another number just in case. I've heard, well, what they've said about you and the senator."

"You believe everything you hear, Paul?"

"Should I, Kris?"

"I'll be home. Let's leave it at that."

"I'll call you as soon as I have something." He eased an arm over her shoulder. "Come on, I'll walk you down."

"As soon as you know *anything*."

"We'll find David, Kris. I promise."

The cab taking her back to the Russell Senate Building got snarled in yet another protest march. Kristen had stopped keeping score of them all months ago, but as of late they had begun harping on a common theme. She rolled her window down to better hear the participants' cadenced chant:

"Who do we need?"
"Sam Jack Dodd!"
"When do we need him?"
"Now!"

To a man and woman, all of the marchers carried
mounted posters of Samuel Jackson Dodd, the charismatic
billionaire who had captured the nation's fancy in the wake
of a disastrous first eighteen months for the new president.
The gridlock that was supposed to end only tightened, and
a slew of broken promises later his approval ratings had
sunk into the high twenties. After a brief respite, the economy faltered again with no measures the administration enacted able to halt the slide. Internationally the President had
stumbled and stammered his way through recent hard intelligence reports that Iran was now in possession of strategic
nuclear weapons obtained from former Soviet republics who
had collectively refused to sign the START II agreements.

But these storms his administration could have weathered
and survived. Not so the pair of events in the space of a single week three months before that had brought about its un-
ravelling. He had committed a large contingent of American
ground troops to the peacekeeping force in Bosnia against a
groundswell of public opinion that turned into a flood when
a troop of three hundred U.S. soldiers walked into a massacre outside the city of Vitez. Just days later, national guards-
men called in to maintain order at a huge rally in Houston
against American involvement panicked and fired into a
crowd that suddenly surged their way. Eleven were killed,
including three college and two high school students.

A second massacre, this time at home.

Never mind that Vitez only happened because the American convoy took a wrong turn. Never mind that pistols
were found on the bodies of two of the dead in Houston.
The country needed someone to blame and the President's
acceptance of responsibility and his stumbling apology
made him the target of unprecedented anger and wrath. One
political cartoon labeled him "Half-term Harry" and pic-

tured him ducking through the back door of the White
House (or the "Red" House, as it had come to be known)
with bags packed, moving out. Another, perhaps more pro-
phetic cartoon showed a figure in a Superman suit charging
up the White House steps with a cheering throng behind
him.

The figure was Samuel Jackson Dodd.

The smiling countenance caught on the posters brimmed
with confidence. The face rolled and soft, like a movie
star's. The neatly coiffed brown hair too thick for a man in
his midforties, flecked with patrician gray. It was the picture
of strength, of hope.

"Who do we need?"
"Sam Jack Dodd!"
"When do we need him?"
"Now!"

The chanting continued as the marchers surged on up
Constitution Avenue. Kristen noticed that some of their
posters had the election year printed beneath the picture.
Only in this case it was not 1996; it was 1994.

Simmering discontent had turned into a boiling caldron of
militant protest. Everyone with an ax to grind was making
his or her feelings known, and everyone, it seemed, had an
ax to grind. Needing a rallying point, they turned to Sam
Jack Dodd, who did nothing to diffuse or discourage their
efforts. He publicly derided those politicians who had allowed the nation to sink to its present depths. He spoke of
a machine that plainly didn't work well anymore and
needed to be drastically overhauled before it broke down altogether. The country embraced his message, willing to accept the drastic changes he painted in broad strokes, *any*
changes.

"Who do we need?"
"Sam Jack Dodd!"
"When do we need—"

Kristen rolled up the window, insulating herself from the
chant, and gazed out at the faces of those hoisting Dodd

posters as they snailed past the cab. After more than a decade in Washington including her years at Georgetown, Kristen had found herself able to identify a group's cause swiftly by its mere composition. No more. This group defied analysis in its lack of homogeneity. It included all types, as if this were some pollster's random sampling of the country. It wasn't fair—or maybe it was. For generations, Washington had been changing the rules on the people. Now maybe the people were ready to change the rules on Washington.

Traffic started moving again in maddening stops and starts. Her brother's phone call had exaggerated all the worries that had been plaguing her recently. Now more than ever nothing made any sense, and it wouldn't again, she knew, until her brother was located.

Their parents had been killed in a car accident two summers before, just before the start of David's freshman year in college. Kristen had blamed the tragedy for the off-the-cuff style her brother's life had taken on since. He left school for a semester, then transferred, and now was taking another semester off. To get his head straight, he had told her. She was infuriated when he wouldn't listen to reason. David was smart, brilliant even. Senator Jordan had offered to smooth the way for him into Georgetown; then, at least, he would have been close to her. But David hadn't wanted that. They had always been diametrically different personalities, and the death of their parents had further polarized them. David, always the free spirit, ran wild. Kristen, forever structured, sought security in regimentation.

Working for Senator Jordan had become her one salvation. She had performed an assistant's job with enough vim and vigor to end up in just three years as the senator's chief of staff, a position she had held since the election in '92. The sixteen-hour days, the never-ending chain of phone calls, juggling the senator's itinerary to fit everything in— Kristen loved it all. It never occurred to her that maybe she was running just like David was, only in another way.

The rest of the afternoon passed in a blur. There were two conference calls and a trio of press briefings on different issues for different segments of the media. Kristen got through it in a fog, her eyes never far from the phone.

"A Mr. Gathers on 410," the receptionist's voice hailed over the intercom finally, just before four o'clock.

Kristen lunged for the receiver. "Paul?"

"Right here, Kris."

"What's all that noise? You sound far away."

"I'm not in the office. Listen, can you get out of there, say in about an hour?"

"Of course." Her heart was pounding against her rib cage. Her throat felt heavy and the words had trouble sliding out. "What is it? What have you found out?"

"I've got a few more things to follow up. David's call was placed from Colorado. A town called Grand Mesa."

"Colorado?"

"You had no idea he was there?"

"He hasn't been sending postcards from every stop. What else, Paul?"

"I'll tell you when we meet, when I'm sure. An hour, like I said. You know L'Escargot?"

"Restaurant on Connecticut Street."

"I'll be there at five. No, better make that five-thirty. I might be at my next stop for a while."

"What's going on, Paul?"

He had already hung up.

Kristen arrived at L'Escargot fifteen minutes early, desperately afraid of being late. Not surprisingly, Gathers had not arrived yet, so she chose a small table on the right of the entrance and tried to pass the time reading a copy of the morning *Post* grabbed off the bar. The articles slid by just as the rest of the day had, misty and vacant. She found herself staring at the headlines, unable to concentrate on the stories beneath them. Kept flipping pages and sipping ginger ale just to be doing something.

Grand Mesa, Colorado . . .

Somehow Gathers's discovery soothed her. Grand Mesa hardly seemed a place that could be a hotbed of controversial activity. A big city, any city, would have frightened Kristen much more. She checked her watch.

5:31.

Her eyes had been moving to the entrance every time the door opened. Now she fixed her stare upon it. A few times her heart rose at the sight of a man she thought was Gathers. But she was disappointed on each occasion. It had started to rain outside, and most of L'Escargot's patrons came straight from work wrapped in overcoats and shaking umbrellas in the vestibule. Kristen realized she had brought neither.

5:47.

She tried not to feel nervous. Gathers said he had to check out a few things, that his next stop might take some time. It must have simply taken longer than he had expected.

Why hadn't he called her from his office?

Kristen began to fixate on the tone of his voice. Had it been rushed, panicked? She replayed the background noises in her head. Where had he been calling from?

Stop! *Stop!*

She was driving herself mad with this. But it was closing on six o'clock and there was still no sign of Paul Gathers. He would have called if he was going to be this late. Unless he couldn't call.

The door blew open again and Kristen's heart rose. Another man entered dripping, the brim of his hat soaked clear through.

It wasn't Gathers.

Kristen moved to the pay phone. A man was using it. He took one glance at her and turned away, covering his free ear with a finger. Kristen was furious. It seemed that he was staying on the line just to antagonize her. She was desperate enough to consider grabbing the receiver from him when he at last hung up. The receiver had barely touched the switch hook again when Kristen snapped it to her ear and dialed Gathers's office number, bypassing the Bureau's switchboard.

"Mr. Gathers's office," a female voice greeted.

"Yes. Could you tell me if Mr. Gathers has called in?"

"Excuse me?"

"We had an appointment and he seems to be late."

"Who is this, please?"

"Kristen Kurcell. I was in to see him this morning. We made arrangements to meet later and I was worried he may have forgotten."

The woman on the other end paused briefly. "I'm afraid Mr. Gathers is in transit. He was called away suddenly on assignment."

"You don't know how to reach him?"

"He'll be calling in for his messages, I'm sure. Would you like to leave one?"

The phone was trembling in Kristen's hand. "No, I don't think so. Er, when was he called away?"

"Early this afternoon, I believe. He left in a hurry." Another pause. "Are you sure I can't—"

Kristen returned the receiver numbly to the hook. As far as his secretary knew, Paul Gathers had been called away on assignment *before* he had called Kristen's office from somewhere outside the Hoover Building at four!

"I've got a few more things to follow up. . . . I'll tell you when we meet, when I'm sure."

And now he was gone. Not in transit, not on assignment. Just gone.

Like her brother.

But Gathers had left her something: the place where David had called from the night before.

Grand Mesa.

Colorado.

CHAPTER 5

"I want to know the death toll," McCracken insisted.

His side ached where the bullet had grazed it, the pressure of the bandage making the throb worse. A pair of painkillers he had no intention of downing had been waiting in his pocket for almost twelve hours now.

"I want to know how many people were injured."

Captain Roy Martinez stood against the glass front wall of his office as he spoke. "I thought we had extended you enough courtesy, Mr. McCracken, by not putting you in a cell."

"How many, Captain?"

"Why is it so important that you know?"

"Because I was there."

"And maybe you feel guilty. Maybe you were responsible for at least a few of them."

"Do you really believe that, Captain?"

"Do you?"

McCracken's response was a knowing stare. Though much of what had unfolded in the Coconut Grove in the early hours of Friday morning remained muddled, enough was clear to point to the fact McCracken's presence had put a severe crimp in whatever the actual plan had been. By turning the gunmen's attention on himself and away from the patrons of Cocowalk, he had saved countless lives. But that hadn't been enough.

The police had placed Blaine under arrest and taken him under heavy guard to Mount Sinai Hospital. An intern had barely finished taping the bandage over his wound when his escorts whisked him away to police headquarters and a holding cell. He refused to speak to anyone other than the commanding officer who at that point was on scene in the Coconut Grove.

"Thirty-seven dead," Captain Martinez said finally. They had spoken twice during the morning, but this was the first time Martinez had provided any information. "Over three hundred wounded. Both numbers expected to rise."

"They always do."

"You've seen this kind of thing before, then."

"What does my file say?"

"Since you had to give clearance before we could access it in Washington, I'm sure you know."

McCracken rose and joined Martinez near the glass wall. "Most of the good parts were left out. Trust me."

"If half of what that file says is true, I want to know what the hell you were doing in Miami."

"We come back to that again."

"And we'll keep coming back to it."

"Guns brought me down here, Captain. Thirty percent of the illegal traffic in this country originates in South Florida, and I had a line on one of the biggest distributors."

"Alvarez—"

"As in father and son, I learned last night."

"The son is—I mean—was Carlos. His father's name is Manuel." Martinez took two steps away from the glass wall. "You see, we're not totally ignorant down here, Mr. McCracken. We just have this little thing called due process to keep in mind, something I get the feeling you stopped bothering yourself about quite a while ago."

"Captain, due process for me went out the window even before those blank spaces in my file started appearing."

"Did you come down here to kill Alvarez, Mr. McCracken?"

"Father or son?"

"Does it matter?"

"Well, the father sells to adults, the son specialized in

other kids. No, I guess it doesn't matter. And no, I didn't come down here to kill either one of them. Huge shipments of heavy firepower have been moved through Miami and the Alvarezes over the past few months. I came down here to find out where it all ended up, who has it."

Martinez nodded as if his own point had been made for him. "So maybe, just maybe, the men in that helicopter came to stop you from finding them."

"It wasn't me."

"How can you be so sure?"

"Because if it was, they couldn't have had time to set up such a complicated strike. They must have been watching the Alvarezes for quite a while. The kid was the one they were after."

"And, on the chance you're wrong, maybe you're responsible for those thirty-seven deaths."

"And if I'm not, number thirty-eight might well be Manuel Alvarez, unless you find him first."

"You think he was the actual target?"

"Since he and his son worked so closely with one another, both would have been on the list."

"Whose list?"

"One of the parties they were selling to. A party that must want to hide what they're up to awfully bad to pull off what they did last night."

"I don't suppose you can prove that," Martinez persisted.

"I think I can, Captain. Have you been able to identify any of the gunmen yet?"

"No, but we will."

"Then you've fingerprinted them."

"Waiting for something to come back from Washington as we speak."

"Nothing will, Captain. Their fingerprints won't be on any file you can access."

"You're quite the expert on this, aren't you?"

"You wouldn't be able to identify me under similar circumstances, either."

"Meaning . . ."

"Meaning the group that hit Cocowalk last night is part of something much bigger. The Alvarezes had to be removed before that group's real business can start."

"Manuel's still alive."

"For now."

Some of the female killer's final words fluttered through Blaine's head.

"You can't stop us! No one can stop us! You'll see, everyone will see!"

"Give me copies of the fingerprints," Blaine offered. "I'll fax them to someone who'll be able to access the right files."

"And then you'll share the information with me, is that it?"

"There won't be anything you can do with the information, Captain. But yes, I'll share it with you, if you like."

Martinez's face grew taut with exasperation. He was about to speak when the phone on his desk buzzed. He moved to it and snapped the receiver up angrily.

"I thought I told you not to— Oh. . . . Yes, I'll take it." Martinez pressed the button of one of the incoming lines. "This is Captain Martinez. . . . Yes, I understand. . . . Of course. . . . No, it's no problem at all. . . . He's right here."

McCracken moved to the front of the desk and accepted the receiver from Martinez.

"Yes?"

"It's Tom Daniels, McCracken," a high voice greeted.

"Sorry, I think you've got the wrong number."

"Back off. I just got you sprung."

"So you can recommend my file be flagged in red yet again, no doubt."

"Hear me out."

"I'm all ears, Daniels."

"Not now. In Washington. In person. I've got you booked on a two P.M. flight into National. Reservation's under the name of Lord. There'll be a room waiting for you at the Four Seasons under the name Troy."

A detective came to Martinez's office and knocked gently on the glass. The captain crossed the room and opened the door.

"This just came in, Captain," Blaine heard the detective report as he handed a piece of paper to Martinez.

"Why all the subterfuge?" McCracken asked into the phone.

"I don't want anyone to know you're in Washington," Daniels replied, "and I especially don't want anyone to know you're meeting with me."

"I hadn't realized I'd agreed yet."

Daniels paused long enough for Blaine to figure he'd given up. Then his voice returned, calm and deliberate.

"The attack last night was just the beginning. You know that."

Blaine tried to keep the interest from his voice. "And you know who was behind it?"

"I think so, yes." He stopped. "And I know they've got to be stopped."

"Go on, Daniels."

"Sorry, McCracken. In person. In Washington. Captain Martinez will have someone take you to the airport. Check into the Four Seasons and wait for my call."

The phone clicked off in McCracken's ear. He hung it up himself.

"Your file didn't mention you were CIA," said Martinez, sounding suddenly reserved and accepting.

"Because I'm not. Sometimes the trails we follow just happen to cross."

Martinez showed Blaine the sheet of memo paper the detective had given him. "Well, the trail down here just went ice cold. Coast Guard just reported finding what's left of a yacht belonging to Manuel Alvarez. It blew up at sea." He swallowed hard. "I'll get you copies of those fingerprints."

* * *

Daniels had chosen Rock Creek Park for their meeting, and McCracken arrived at ten P.M. sharp as agreed upon. They were to meet in the wooded picnic groves not far from the Carter Barron Amphitheater near the banks of the creek itself. McCracken approached from the south and walked across a bridge constructed over the creek, ducks paddling atop its still waters. The specific grove where he was meeting Daniels was fifty feet to the left. A small yellow cooler would be waiting on one of the picnic benches. Its absence was the signal that the meeting was off.

The cooler was there. Daniels wasn't.

Daniels wasn't the only person Blaine had spoken to before leaving Miami. He had put in a call to Sal Belamo from Miami police headquarters.

"Sal's Sweet Shop," a gravelly voice answered. "You got the cherry, I got the cream."

"Your cream's seen better days, Sal."

"McCrackenballs! I was beginning to think all my friends forgot my private number."

"Spending your days at home now?"

"Hey, those morning talk shows and afternoon soaps beat the fuck-all out of real life. You ask me, guys like you and me could learn something from this shit."

Sal Belamo had saved McCracken's life the first time they had met eight years before, and they'd been working together off and on ever since. Until recently Belamo, a pug-nosed ex-boxer whose greatest claim to fame was losing twice to Carlos Monzon, was Blaine's prime contact inside the intelligence community. But helping McCracken destroy the Tau had earned him an indefinite suspension and permanent ostracism. Belamo still had plenty of friends on the inside, though, and he was always there to help.

"Need a favor, Sal."

"Name it. Just give me time to turn off yesterday's episode of 'The Young and the Fuckless' on the VCR. . . . Okay. Gaw 'head."

"I'm gonna fax you six sets of fingerprints that the locals here in Miami couldn't get anywhere with."

"Soakin' up some sun, MacBalls?"

"Never even saw it shine, Sal. See what you can find out."

"Hey, you need backup, I'm here. 'The Bold and the Bosom' can wait."

"Not yet, Sal, but stay close."

"By the phone, boss."

And now, ten hours later, McCracken found himself hanging back amidst the trees waiting for Tom Daniels to appear. Several occasions in the past had brought them together, none of them pleasant. A number had culminated in Daniels petitioning Company directors for Blaine's "removal," the bureaucrat ultimately being rebuffed in each instance, which only added to his hostility. As a result, Blaine had no reason to really trust Daniels, but he had recognized the fear in Daniels's voice that morning and later again when the meeting was set up. Fear was something that transcended hostility, made allies out of even deadly adversaries.

Blaine unzipped his jacket to more easily reach the SIG-Sauer nine-millimeter pistol holstered inside it. He held his ground, nervous. Daniels was the kind of man who was nothing if not punctual.

The bushes ruffled behind him. McCracken swung, pistol drawn.

Nothing.

"Daniels," he called softly. "Daniels."

He turned one way, then the other. His back against a thick nest of shoulder-high shrubbery, Blaine regretted not taking Sal Belamo up on his offer to serve as backup.

What might have been footsteps or just a trick of the wind sounded from somewhere in the distance. McCracken's shoulders bent the bushes inward now, waiting.

A rustling noise and a low moan came from behind the

shrubs he was nestled against. McCracken spun away, gun leading.

"Help ... me." And Tom Daniels fell against him with what remained of his life spilling out on the ground.

"Jesus," Daniels moaned, collapsing forward.

Blaine let him down easy and crouched to join him. Daniels's midsection had been shredded. In-close work, a knife probably. His eyes burned with pain. Blood was already sliding out his mouth.

"Left me for dead," Daniels managed.

McCracken kept his SIG palmed, eyes searching.

"Who did this to you, Daniels?"

Daniels's fading stare tried to find McCracken's. "You've got to stop them. They're close...." He took a muffled, gurgling breath. "It's theirs."

"*What's* theirs?"

"The country ... They're ... taking over."

"How, Daniels? *Who?*"

"Indications, signals," Daniels said, his mind drifting. "Needed you to flush them out. That was the plan."

"Flush them out with what?"

"Operation Yellow Rose," Daniels wheezed. "That's where it began. Everything comes back to it."

"Comes back to *what*?"

With death very near, Daniels's pain receded slightly. He began to shiver.

"They're writing the future." His eyes faded again. His mouth dripped blood. "Not here. Never here.... Prometheus! They can't do it without Prometheus!"

"What's Prometheus?"

"Ten days! You've only got ten days!"

McCracken grasped Daniels more tightly and lifted him from the ground. "Talk to me, Daniels! Talk to me!"

The blood was bubbling in a pool from Daniels's mouth now. His eyes had locked open. Blaine eased him back to the grass.

The hackles on his neck rose. The sound of fresh foot-steps gliding across the park's grass had reached him. Daniels's killers were approaching from different angles. He couldn't be sure how many. But it was enough.

And he was trapped.

The gunmen entered the clearing in unison from five different vantage points. Three wielded Ingram submachine guns and two held M16s, scopes that would have helped them lock in on whomever Daniels had come to meet still attached. Except for Daniels's body lying facedown, the clearing was deserted.

"Shit," the leader muttered.

He approached the still, bloodied form alert for movement, but focusing as well on the surrounding bushes and trees. The Telefunken long-range listening probe now dangling from his neck had not only allowed him to find Daniels but had also filled his ears with another voice that could only be that of the man Daniels had come here to meet. Where was he now? The leader reached Daniels, wary eyes still casting about him. He started to kneel down.

A gun snapped up and exploded in front of his eyes.

McCracken had donned Daniels's blood-soaked suit jacket after dragging the dead man into the bushes. He barely had time to throw himself back onto the grass before the hit team stepped into the clearing.

The killers had responded just as he had expected. Blaine had kept his eyes facing the ground until the approach of the leader halted and the air shifted to indicate he had knelt down. Then McCracken sprang, pistol firing.

The first three had gone easily, the element of surprise too much for them to overcome. The fourth managed to find his trigger before Blaine shot him in the face, and the fifth actually fired a wild burst before a pair of the SIG's bullets hammered into his chest.

McCracken lunged back to his feet and sprinted toward

the nearest exit, not knowing whether more killers lurked in the park, perhaps attracted by the gunshots. The full moon could give him away to a professional as easily as daylight.

Once outside, he walked for a few blocks to make sure he wasn't being followed before hot-wiring an inconspicuous car parked along the side of the road. His immediate goal was simply to flee the area. Beyond that, though, a plot that Daniels had died for uncovering had been dumped in his lap.

"They're taking over."

Operation Yellow Rose . . .

Prometheus . . .

Places to start.

"Ten days! You've only got ten days!"

McCracken gunned the stolen car's engine and drove off.

Clifton Jardine, director of the CIA, replaced the phone on its cradle and massaged his eyelids. The news that Tom Daniels's body had been found in Rock Creek Park had shaken him badly, because the murder seemed to confirm Daniels's incredible conclusions. But the plot he had uncovered could still be stopped if the right people could be convinced of its existence.

The phone on the desk of his downstairs study rang and he fumbled the receiver to his ear.

"Yes? . . . No, I don't want you to *wake* the President. I just want to see him first thing in the morning, before breakfast, if possible. . . . Yes, I know how late it is. . . . Yes, I know his schedule is set. It's imperative that he change it. . . . That's right, just him and me. . . . No, I can't tell you. . . . I can't tell you that, either. . . . Right. I'll be there."

Jardine hung up the phone and heard the soft click of the French doors leading into the house from the patio being opened. He swung round in his leather chair to be greeted by a burst of cool spring air.

"Oh, it's you. It's about time."

The doors clicked closed. The breeze retreated behind them. The man who had entered came forward.

Jardine gestured at the phone. "That was the White House duty officer. Tomorrow morning, seven o'clock, God help us all. I didn't believe him, you know. Right up until—"

The man had stopped. Jardine saw the gun in his hand. "Jesus God . . ."

The man gave him time to say no more. Two soft spits spilled Clifton Jardine to the floor.

The French doors opened once again and the man disappeared into the night.

PART TWO

OPERATION YELLOW ROSE

The Maine Woods:
Saturday, April 16, 1994; 7:00 a.m.

CHAPTER 6

"He has killed again. That is why I had to come to you, *Wanblee-Isnala*."

Chief Silver Cloud raised the cup of tea to his lips in a trembling hand. Across from him, in the cabin he had fashioned with his own hands and tools, Johnny Wareagle sat listening and watching intently.

"The spirits showed me the killing in a dream," the chief continued, his voice cracking.

The trip to Maine from the Oklahoma reservation where he presided as elder had obviously taken its toll. Silver Cloud was approaching eighty now, and to Wareagle finally looked his age. His leathery skin was sagging, its bronze tone faded to a dull olive. His eyes seemed old for the first time.

"You must stop Traggeo, *Wanblee-Isnala*. You must hunt him down before he can do further damage to our people. He is not one of us, and yet each killing brings more shame upon our people."

Wareagle slid one of his huge hands forward and helped Chief Silver Cloud ease the heavy mug back to the table between them. The mug was homemade too, and as with everything Johnny fashioned, it had been made with his seven-foot, 275-pound proportions in mind. His hair was tied back in a ponytail, its coal black shade marred by an occasional strand of gray. His massive chest was covered by a leather vest he had sewn himself. He leaned his hands on his knees and his shoulders stretched to a girth that made even the old chief's eyes widen.

"You know him from before, do you not, *Wanblee-Isnala*?"

"Only as one knows another stranger in the Hellfire."

"Where it started," the chief recalled.

Traggeo was a hulking monster of a man who arrived in Vietnam calling himself half Indian even though neither of his parents boasted a direct bloodline. He went on patrol with braided black hair and war paint smeared over his cheeks. He was thrown into a stockade after killing and scalping three Vietnamese villagers suspected of being Cong collaborators. But the war did not end for him there, thanks to a Special Operations colonel named Tyson Gash.

Gash was a renegade himself, his methods and manners unacceptable even to the accountless lot who ran the only part of the war America actually won. He ended up leaving Special Ops to form his own splinter group for missions even Johnny and Blaine McCracken's Phoenix Project group couldn't handle. Gash pulled men like Traggeo from military stockades and piles of Section Eight discharges. He selected them from a rogues' gallery of the most immoral, brutal, and ruthless. He convinced the hierarchy who approved the scheme that he could control them, that their expendable nature made them perfect for missions deemed unsurvivable.

And to some extent he was right. Gash's "Salvage Company," as it became known, did prove quite effective on several occasions. The problem was it got started too close to the war's end. By the time it was fully up and running, the cease-fire agreement was signed and Nixon was claiming peace with honor. The members of Salvage Company, though, knew little about peace and even less about honor. The ones who survived encounters in Laos and Cambodia were given amnesty and let loose back in the real world.

Traggeo was one of them. The war paint and braids became his trademark. The tale that a great Indian warrior had been reborn within his soul left the war with him, even though he lacked any true Indian heritage. After Vietnam he had bounced around several mercenary groups before returning to the States. Five years ago he had beaten four men to death in a fight and had scalped them all, then escaped from jail before his trial. There'd been a number of other killings over the years, all with the same pattern.

Three nurses on a single night in Chicago.

An entire family in Idaho.

Two unfortunate off-duty policemen outside of Los Angeles.

The list went on. All the victims had been scalped. And each time that trademark act linked Traggeo to a killing, his fabricated Indian heritage came back to haunt the people he claimed to be a part of. It had become a question of honor for the Sioux tribe Chief Silver Cloud presided over. Traggeo had to be found, had to be stopped. But just over a year before, the old man explained, he had disappeared.

"Another of our tribe thought he had finally located him. Will Shortfeather." Chief Silver Cloud produced a dog-eared color snapshot of a tall man with stringy, straw-colored hair that neatly rimmed his scalp. "He disappeared. We never heard from him again. That was two weeks ago."

Wareagle nodded. "And this other killing?"

"The night before last. I came out here by bus on the morning after the dream came. I knew it had started again. But worse now. Somehow worse."

Silver Cloud's eyes pleaded with Johnny, and Wareagle felt a pang of affection for the man who had been one of his spirit guides. The thought of this old warrior spending more than twenty-four hours on a bus ride east to ask for his help was humbling. And if Johnny refused his overtures, Silver Cloud would be on the next bus without question or rebuke, thinking no less of him.

But Johnny wasn't going to say no. And neither was he going to let the old man return west on anything but an airplane.

"Will you help us, *Wanblee-Isnala*?"

Wareagle held the picture of the Indian with the straw-colored hair at arm's distance. "Where was Shortfeather when you heard from him last?"

The lines on Silver Cloud's ancient face seemed to ease. His shoulders straightened from their slump as if a great weight had been lifted from them.

"Gainesville," he replied. "Gainseville, Texas."

CHAPTER 7

The President swam his laps in the White House pool while his chief aide, Charlie Byrne, walked back and forth alongside.

"I don't want to talk about the polls, Charlie. The polls give me gas."

"You can take a pill for gas, Mr. President." Even though they'd been friends since high school, Byrne insisted on addressing him formally at all times. "There's no pill I know of that can take care of our problem in the polls."

The President switched to the breast stroke. "The good news is I've still got two and a half years to set things right."

Byrne continued to walk along the pool's rim. "And the bad news is it's taken only one and a half for things to get this bad."

The President dunked his head and came back up, squinting the chlorine from his eyes and starting toward the ladder. "Is there anything you would have done different, Charlie? I mean if we had everything to do all over again from scratch, what would you change?" When Byrne made no effort to reply, the President continued, "It's not me, it's not us. It's the damn system. We've been penalized for trying to effect real change, for facing up to problems that have been ignored for so long that no one wants to look at them anymore. Maybe we'd have been better off doing nothing."

"Or moving slower."

The President started to pull himself slowly up the ladder. "We couldn't afford to move slower."

"Your approval ratings—"

"Is that what this is about? Is that what everything comes down to?" The President reached the rim and stood there, dripping. "Make no move unless it gives us a positive read? Attain popularity with rhetoric? More of the politics of nothingness."

"Sir—"

"Or maybe we need a war. Bomb Iran or North Korea unless they surrender their nuclear capability. Do wonders for my approval ratings, wouldn't it? At the very least it might make people forget about Half-term Harry for awhile. Hell, they might even start calling this place the *White* House again."

"That's not what I was suggesting."

"But there's really no other direction to move in. Eighteen months and I'm already a lame duck. And you know the worst thing, Charlie? I'm not sure I care. Maybe I'll just spend the next two and a half years shoving the truth down this country's throat and then pack my bags willingly."

Arms wrapped around himself, the President stepped away from the pool and accepted a towel from Charlie Byrne. The few laps he'd managed to swim had fatigued instead of refreshed him, and he sank into a chair by the wall to dry himself. He held the towel over his face for a time, as if hoping that when he pulled it away his features would be as they were when he assumed office. He considered himself robust then, in excellent health. Now it sometimes took his breath away just to climb the stairs. His hair had thinned and whitened. The lines already on his face had deepened into crevices, with fresh cracks spreading out from them. The muscle he had worked so hard at keeping had turned to flab. The office was to blame or, more accurately, the frustrations of it. The terrible plight he had inherited had left him with a set of expectations that were impossible to meet. When things got worse instead of better, coupled with a succession of broken campaign promises, the country turned on him in a heartbeat. The people had become like drowning swimmers, willing to accept a lifeline from anyone who tossed it their way.

"I believe you were talking about the polls, Charlie."

"You've got company in them this morning, sir."

"Sam Dodd again?"

"You're down fifty-five percent to seventeen to him with twenty percent undecided and none of the other party's likely candidates beating the margin for error."

"Well, at least I'm still in second place," the President said, trying to sound jovial. He tightened the towel around his shoulders. "Think I'll stay there?"

"Dodd's no Ross Perot. He won't self-destruct, and as an independent he won't be subjected to normal scrutiny either. Besides, he's already opened his closet to reveal his skeletons and nobody cares. The man can afford to make sense. People like him. Jesus, *I* like him."

"Maybe I should offer him the vice-presidency."

"He could just as easily be thinking the same thing about you."

The President leaned forward. "Well, then maybe I should let him try my job for a while and see if he can do better. Let him have a whack at convincing Congress to stop torpedoing all the programs *he* tries to get passed. Then take a look at *his* numbers six months down the road while I'm on vacation."

Byrne's eyes looked as empty and still as the surface of the pool.

"Jesus, Charlie, I'm sorry."

"No, you're discouraged. I can't blame you for that." Byrne paused. "I'd blame you only if you quit."

"Do you think I have already?"

"I'm not sure."

"Thanks for your honesty."

The life returned to Charlie Byrne's eyes. "We can still get it done, sir."

"Sure," the President sighed, "by watering down all the proposals we know this country needs. By kowtowing to the demands of those who couldn't care less where it's going. By choosing pragmatism and polls over principle."

"You can't change things overnight."

"We've had eighteen months, and you know what? I don't feel I've done a damn thing. I go to bed at night trying to figure out what I accomplished during the day, and usually I can't find anything."

"Your expectations were too high."

"And now they're too low. I want to make a difference, Charlie," the President sighed. "It's just getting tougher to figure out what the difference can be."

The door leading to the pool opened and FBI director Ben Samuelson entered escorted by the Secret Service duty officer who instantly took his leave.

"I didn't know we had a meeting scheduled for this morning, Ben," the President said, pushing himself up from the chair.

"We don't. I apologize for the intrusion, but I know you'd want to hear this face-to-face."

The President saw the glum reserve in Samuelson's normally bright hazel eyes. The FBI director was a thin, almost gaunt man who had recently exchanged his glasses for contact lenses, part of a makeover that included the Bureau as well. Samuelson has been one of the President's most successful appointments, the FBI flourishing in both morale and performance under his charge.

He took a deep breath. "Clifton Jardine was found murdered in his study less than one hour ago."

The President sat back down. "My God, how?"

"He was shot. Sometime between midnight and three A.M. by all accounts."

The President let the news sink in. Jardine had been another of the few feathers he'd been able to stick in his cap.

Charged with the monumental task of redefining the CIA in the post–Cold War world, he had been doing a brilliant job.

"Ben, we're talking about the second-best-protected man in this government. His own people round the clock, and you're telling me he was shot in his *study*?"

For a few seconds Samuelson was silent. "We're interrogating the guards on that watch, sir."

"I'm sure you already have something preliminary."

"All of them claim they saw nothing."

"Meaning . . ."

"Either the killer was an elite assassin . . ."

"Or?"

This time Samuelson said nothing at all.

"Jardine made an appointment to see me first thing this morning," the President continued tensely. "It was penciled into my daily schedule some time late last night. That means something must have come up very suddenly, and then not much later he's dead." The President looked to Byrne. "Charlie, find out exactly what time the call was logged." He turned back toward Samuelson as Byrne took his leave. "Unavoidable connection, isn't it, Ben?"

"There may be another connection, sir. One of Jardine's men was killed in Rock Creek Park last night. The word was passed to me by local authorities just before I left to come here. An apparent mugging."

The President wrapped the towel around his shoulders. Suddenly he felt chilled. His robe was hanging on a hook by the door, but the walk over to get it didn't interest him.

"Apparent," he repeated. "This agent who was killed—"

"Career Company named Daniels. Nothing very much outstanding in his background. He was a gatherer and sorter, nothing more. A career bureaucrat with a competent but hardly distinguished career."

"In other words, not the kind of man Cliff Jardine would take into his confidence."

"Correct, sir. But the coincidence remains difficult to accept."

Charlie Byrne came back through the door. It closed behind him with a slight rattle.

"Jardine's call was logged in by the duty officer at just after two A.M.," he said after he passed the start of the pool. "The duty officer returned that call at precisely eleven minutes after two. I just spoke to the officer at home and he said Jardine sounded harried, even panicked. He insisted on an early morning meeting but stopped short of having you woken up. He wouldn't say what the meeting pertained to, or why no one else could be in attendance besides him and you."

The President looked back at Samuelson. "What time was Daniels killed in Rock Creek Park?"

"Between nine P.M. and midnight is our best guess, pending an autopsy, sir."

"Next questions: Was Daniels working on anything he would for some reason have reported to Jardine directly on? Had there been any contact between them in recent days?"

"The answers are forthcoming. This afternoon at the latest."

"And maybe they'll help us uncover what we need to know most of all." The President paused. The chlorine had cast his light eyes in a red haze. "Finding out what Cliff Jardine wanted to see me about this morning."

As was their custom, the two men met on the Metro under the heart of Washington itself. It made them feel they were living in the underworld, a stairway's distance from claiming what lay above. They found the symbolism appealing.

The codes and procedures were complicated but remarkably unencumbering. Two hours after contact was initiated, inevitably, a meeting would take place. No disguise or subterfuge. Just two men taking a routine ride in the capital's subway.

The larger of the two was astonishingly big, from his protruding forehead and almost grotesque jowls to the girth of his midsection and tree-trunk legs. The second was tall and lithe, with a disheveled crop of hair and round horn-rimmed glasses that made him look like an academic. The bullish-looking man had called the meeting and was waiting when the academic boarded the car. He sat down in the next seat and opened his newspaper.

"I gather from this meeting that things did not go completely as planned," the academic started.

The bigger man's expression remained flat. "The entire team dispatched last night was killed."

The academic's eyes flickered as much in anger as surprise. "By a *bureaucrat?*"

"No, not Daniels. Someone else."

"The man he was to meet with?"

"By all indications, yes. The team erred in leaving Daniels for dead. He slipped away from them and managed to reach his rendezvous point."

"With whom?" the academic wondered. "I imagine you know by now."

The big man nodded without enthusiasm. "The bullets used were encased in full platinum jackets. While these are not uncommon in professional circles, one man is especially distinguished for their use: Blaine McCracken."

The academic could not hide the uncertainty that stretched a grimace across his usually emotionless features. The train slid to a half in the next station, and he waited for the familiar chimes signaling new movement before speaking again, glad for the opportunity to compose his thoughts.

"Containment?"

"We managed to remove the bodies and sanitize the scene, so the authorities would not be able to make an accurate appraisal of the situation," the bullish man reported. "None of this would have been necessary if we had carried things out as I suggested," he added.

"Then our complicity in this failure is mutual. Yes?"

"Granted."

"And we should move forward while the situation remains contained."

"Agreed."

"Good," the academic said in a conciliatory tone. "Do we have reason to believe that Daniels passed on to McCracken what he knew?"

"Which amounted to little, virtually nothing."

"To Daniels perhaps, but not McCracken. A few words, phrases, even inferences—that's all he needs. Please answer."

The bullish man nodded reluctantly. "We must assume at this point that Daniels had time to relay information to McCracken prior—"

"—to your team being executed," the academic completed.

"They were not expecting him."

"He wasn't expected in Miami either, was he?"

Now it was the bullish man who hedged. "Could he have already been aware—"

"Not then. Now, well, what we're facing here is a coincidence with potentially dire consequences once McCracken makes the connection."

"Unless we can find him before he does."

A look of taut concentration had returned to the academic's features. "Or use the inevitability of his succeeding action against him."

"How?" the bullish man wondered.

The academic told him.

For Vasily Conchenko, Russian ambassador to the United States, lunch at the Mayflower Hotel was a daily ritual, even on Saturday. The hotel was only a few blocks from the Russian embassy and Conchenko always enjoyed the walk, especially in spring. In fact, he enjoyed everything about America, more so than ever now that the old divisions were a thing of the past. He could walk the streets freely without concern of being followed or watched. His moves were no longer scrutinized because there was no reason to scrutinize them. He felt exuberantly free.

He ordered the Mayflower turkey club without bothering to gaze at the menu, then began to read Saturday morning's edition of *The New York Times*, which he preferred infinitely to *The Washington Post*. He had barely gotten through the first article when a shape hovered at his side. Thinking it was the waiter with his sparkling mineral water he gazed up politely.

"Good afternoon, Comrade Conchenko," greeted Sergei Amorov.

Amorov had been the final KGB station chief ever to serve in Washington. The Soviet Union's tumble had left him nothing to return to. As a result he had remained here in the capital city of the United States he, too, had come to love very much. If his wardrobe was any indication, Amorov must have amassed quite a fortune in his years as KGB station chief. Today he wore an olive green full-cut Armani suit that fit him exquisitely. Conchenko had never seen him wear the same suit twice.

"We have nothing to say to each other, Sergei Ivanovitch," the ambassador snapped at him, scanning the restaurant carefully in case anyone had noted their meeting. Fortunately, since it was Saturday, the restaurant was all but deserted.

"Ah, but we do. I've ordered a cocktail. It's being sent over."

"Have it sent somewhere else."

Amorov frowned. "How, then, would I be able to do you the great favor I am prepared to, comrade?"

"Don't call me that."

"Habit. Forgive me."

Conchenko tensed as Amorov sat down after unbuttoning the jacket of his double-breasted suit. Again his eyes swam about across the other tables. He shifted his chair away from the former KGB station chief with noticeable distaste.

"This is not the way to treat a man who is going to make you a hero, comrade—excuse me—Vasily Feodorov."

"Or make me a pariah."

"You must learn not to judge so harshly."

With that, Amorov pulled a small shipping envelope from his pocket and placed it within Conchenko's reach. The ambassador made no move to touch it.

"What is this?" he demanded.

"More old habits, I'm afraid. Just to pass the time, you understand."

"No, I don't."

"The greatest coup of my career. Even when the Union dissolved, I could not abandon it."

"Abandon *what*?"

Amorov slid his chair closer and this time Conchenko made no effort to pull away. "I was able to have a bug planted within the office of the director of the Central Intelligence Agency."

"*What*? How?" Conchenko had to remind himself to stifle his enthusiasm. Old habits die hard and this was something that would have been cause for great excitement only a few years before.

"The CIA seal hangs behind his desk. When it was sent out to be refinished some years ago, we managed to plant a bug within it. The paint we used acted as a screen against detection."

Conchenko fidgeted nervously. "Get to the point!"

"After my . . . reassignment, I, er, neglected to have it removed. I still listen to the recordings, out of habit mostly, I suppose, and boredom. They make for great entertainment sometimes." Amorov tapped the mailing envelope. "Thursday night's was a prime example."

"This is a *tape*?"

"Yes, comrade, it is."

Confusion crossed the ambassador's features, then suspicion. "You've heard, of course, that the CIA director was murdered early this morning."

Amorov slid the envelope closer. "I think you should listen to the tape, Vasily Feodorov, and maybe you will understand why."

CHAPTER 8

"I don't see any file folders in the vicinity, Hank," McCracken said to the figure seated on the steps of the Lincoln Memorial.

"And you won't, either," Belgrade returned, shielding his eyes from the sun. "Sit down, McNuts. I'm giving you three minutes. After that, it might not be safe anymore."

"Sounds ominous."

"Two minutes fifty-five seconds. I don't know what you got yourself into last night, but Washington's gone crazy this morning. Langley, to be more accurate."

Blaine had called Sal Belamo from a room in the Jefferson Hotel after fleeing Rock Creek Park the night before. He had abandoned that room as soon as the phone call was complete and checked into a second hotel in Alexandria's Crystal City.

"Wow," Belamo commented after McCracken had filled him in. "Looks like I might be missing tomorrow's episode of 'As the Shit Churns.' "

"Find out what Operation Yellow Rose and Prometheus are and I'll spring for a big-screen TV. Get Johnny Wareagle down here," Blaine added, referring to the big Indian he called upon in situations like this, "and I'll throw in a stereo."

In hardly typical fashion, by this morning Belamo's efforts on all fronts had proven futile. He could find no mention of Operation Yellow Rose or Prometheus on any data bank, accessible or otherwise. And Johnny Wareagle was nowhere to be found.

"That's not all," Sal had finished grimly. "Cops found no

trace of the five guys you waxed. Can only mean somebody came in and got them, boss, and they must have been damn quick about it."

The best Sal could do was set up a meeting for Blaine with someone who might have the answers that he lacked: Hank Belgrade. Belgrade was a big, beefy man who like a select few in Washington drew a salary without any official title. Technically both the Departments of State and Defense showed his name on their roster, but in actuality he worked for neither. Instead, he liaised between the two and handled the dirty linen of both. He had access to files few in Washington had any idea existed.

"Clifton Jardine was murdered," Belgrade resumed after a long pause.

McCracken sat next to him on the far left-hand steps of the Memorial. The news didn't surprise him. A man like Daniels wouldn't requisition a paper clip without proper clearance. It figured the director would have been involved and aware. If Daniels was killed for what he knew, the same fate would very likely have awaited Clifton Jardine.

"My clock still ticking, Hank?"

"Depends on whether the reason for this meeting's linked to Jardine's death."

"You really want to know that?"

"I bring it up or what, McNuts?"

"Fine. Your choice. Jardine wasn't the only Langley man killed last night. You get back to the office, see if anything's come in on Tom Daniels."

"You in the area at the time?"

"After the fact, mostly."

"Mostly?"

"Daniels had time to talk, Hank. Someone's moving on the country. Someone's trying to take over."

Belgrade fixed his stare on Blaine. "We talking about an overthrow of the government here?"

"Daniels told me I had ten days to stop it, then died before elaborating further."

"Ten days . . ."

"Maybe nine now. I killed the five men who killed Daniels. But don't bother checking that part out on the wire, because the tracks have been covered."

Belgrade's hand swept nervously across his double chin. "Christ, that explains it."

"Explains what?"

"It was Daniels who mentioned Operation Yellow Rose to you, right?"

"That and Prometheus."

"Well, I drew a total blank on Prometheus and near total blank on Yellow Rose."

"Near?"

"File's been deleted, McNuts."

"Even from your eyes?"

"You should've called me yesterday."

"What are you saying?"

"That the deletion was logged on at two-thirty A.M. *this morning*. Sound familiar?"

"Jardine's and Daniels's murders . . ."

Belgrade nodded. "Somebody musta figured you or someone else would be looking."

Blaine looked right at him. "And you wouldn't be here if they didn't leave something behind."

"I did some cross-checking. Had to log on myself to do it, which means my access code was recorded. That means whoever made the file disappear will know I was looking for it. Under the circumstances, that doesn't make me a very happy man."

"Tell me what you found before my time runs out."

"Two obscure references, MacNuts, the first being the term 'Delphi.' Mean anything to you?"

"Nope."

"Likewise here. Data banks came up with *nada* when I ran a search."

"And the second reference?"

"A name: H. William Carlisle."

"Never heard of him."

Belgrade slid a little closer. "Ever hear of the Trilateral Commission?"

"A conspiracy theorist's dream, wasn't it?"

"And remains so today," Belgrade told him. "The commission's founding dates back to the early seventies, its stated purpose being to foster an enduring partnership between the ruling classes of the United States, Western Europe, and Japan—hence the term 'trilateral.' "

"Make the world safe for Western business interests, right?"

"In a big way."

Belgrade went on to provide a capsule summary of the Trilat's history, beginning with its formation in 1973 by David Rockefeller and Zbigniew Brzezinski. A series of international and national shocks in the late sixties and early seventies, culminating in the Arab oil embargo and Nixon's New Economic Policy, led the Western business community to fear for its very survival, or at the very least hegemony. The Trilateral Commission became the means by which the international elite fought back. Together the multinational corporations represented by its members believed *they* could control or at least affect world policy through the pursuit of a carefully charted dogma. These members saw themselves as custodians more than manipulators, but the difference, in theory as well as action, was little more than semantics.

For men like George Ball, Henry Kissinger, and Jimmy Carter the ideal response was to pursue collective management of world economic affairs. So vague had the line between politics and economics become that their goals could be brought within reach by achieving a broad-based global corporate capitalism. Foremost among these goals was guarding against future international events that might adversely effect the collective. Unilaterally none of the international legs of the Trilat could wield sufficient power to bring about that end. But joined together they had unlimited potential.

"Never did pull it off, though, did they?" Blaine broke in.

"Hey," retorted Belgrade, "they're still trying. The commission's listed in the Manhattan phone book if you want to give them a call and see how things are going."

"Organizations bent on world domination usually have unpublished numbers."

"Only if they're trying to disguise their methods."

"Which brings us back to Operation Yellow Rose."

"And H. William Carlisle. . . ."

"A Trilateral commissioner, no doubt."

Belgrade half nodded. "And before that the boy wonder of Wall Street, alias Billy the Kid, who had branched out into politics and had become a kingmaker before his thirtieth birthday. Prime force behind Eisenhower's two terms and counted as his only failure Nixon's near miss in 1960. He'd made up for that, though, in the '68 election, but pulled away from the Dickster after Nixon tried to reinvent the economy in '71. Ended up as one of the Trilat's founding members. Then in 1978 he disappeared. Walked out of his mansion one morning and never came back. Suicide was strongly suspected, or even foul play."

"And Operation Yellow Rose?"

"Like I said, MacNuts, all I've got is cross-references to Carlisle and the Delphi, whatever that means. No dates, no prospectus, nothing else."

"Doesn't sound like I'm gonna be able to learn much from him under the circumstances," McCracken said drolly.

Belgrade leaned a little closer and lowered his voice. "Carlisle's still alive, MacNuts. He never even left D.C.; just changed his address. To the streets."

"He became a bum?"

"He dropped out. I got limited surveillance files on him dating back to '78, but ending in '90. They must've figured why waste the money and gave up on the effort. But if he's alive today, you can bet he's still out there. Trick becomes finding him."

McCracken was already standing up. "I think I've got a good idea where to start."

Lafayette Park fronts the White House on the Pennsylvania Avenue side and is therefore often cluttered with protesters. Today the park was crammed with a relatively quiet lot who were content to hoist their hastily scrawled picket signs the White House's way. DODD, most of the signs read, a number adding FOR PRESIDENT, and several of these NOW. The message was there for the President to see every time he gazed out his window.

McCracken slid behind the protesters, who were almost eerie in the reserved, singular devotion they brought to their cause. Their seeming lack of emotion underscored their commitment. A few bystanders watched, snapping pictures from up close or taking it all in from a seat on the rim of the park fountain. Several of Washington's homeless, meanwhile, loitered the day away in a cherished patch of shade atop spread-out blankets, their life's possessions stored in bags never beyond reach of an outstretched hand.

The numerous benches were deserted for the most part. One set in the sun instead of shade featured a single man sitting comfortably with his arms outstretched on either side of him and legs crossed. The man wore a black overcoat marred by a number of bad stitching jobs and faded at the shoulders and ankles. His white hair and beard were thick and unkempt. A pair of torn canvas luggage totes lay beneath the bench, guarded closely by his legs. As Blaine looked on, the man began twirling the long strands of his beard. McCracken pulled out the picture Hank Belgrade had supplied of H. William Carlisle and tried to match the face to this one. Any resemblance was slight, but after this many years, how could it not be?

Blaine approached from the side so as not to draw any attention. The man didn't so much as look his way, even when McCracken sat down on the end of the bench. But

Blaine noticed him tuck his legs a little tighter around his two packs of belongings.

"Nice view, Mr. Carlisle," McCracken said, taking a chance. "Of the White House, I mean."

"My bench," came the raspy reply, years of wear telling on the voice.

"You come here every day?"

"And no one ever bothers me." He still hadn't turned Blaine's way. "You hear that, sonny? Get on home now. Shoo, shoo, shoo."

McCracken slid a little closer. A crust of dirt and grime covered the man. The smell was revolting. Blaine cocked his gaze toward the White House.

"You're already close to home, aren't you?"

"Belongs to the people, doesn't it?"

"It's supposed to. Sometimes a few see it as more theirs than others."

"Right or wrong?" the man snapped.

"Depends, I guess. Or maybe it doesn't."

A pair of red-stained, beaten eyes regarded Blaine for the first time. "You're damn right it doesn't. 1600 belongs only to those smart enough to own it."

"Tell that to them," said McCracken, gazing toward the stoic supporters of Samuel Jackson Dodd.

The eyes looked at him more closely. "Who the fuck are you?"

"Name's McCracken."

"You got a reason to think you know me?"

Blaine didn't hesitate. "Operation Yellow Rose."

McCracken stared at the raggedy pile of a man seated next to him, and only then was he sure that it was indeed H. William Carlisle, Billy the Kid himself. The man's chapped and broken lips pulsed. His eyes narrowed into slits of suspicion.

"Go to hell," Carlisle said without much resolve.

"You've been there for almost twenty years, Mr. Carlisle."

Carlisle smirked. "I left hell, Mr. What's-your-name."

"Why don't you tell me about it?"

"What makes you want to listen?"

Blaine's eyes gestured across Pennsylvania Avenue to the White House. "Take a good look, Mr. Carlisle, because the tenants just might be changing ahead of schedule."

"What are you saying?"

"Someone dug up Operation Yellow Rose. Unless I miss my guess, it's somehow connected to a plot to overthrow the government."

Fear blanketed Carlisle's grime-encrusted face. He lurched toward Blaine in a sudden motion and reached to grab him at the lapels. Blaine let him, closing his nostrils as best he could against the stench.

"Who are you? *What* are you?"

"Tell me about Yellow Rose."

Carlisle let go of Blaine's jacket and slid away. He spoke distantly with his eyes cast straight before him. "It was all so grand at the outset. What we Trilateralists set out to do to the world, for the world."

"And yourselves, of course."

Carlisle swung back toward McCracken "It's the same thing, damnit! We offered stability, consistency. At a price."

"What price?"

The slightest of smiles crossed over the old man's face. His gaze tilted toward the White House. "A wonderful thing, democracy. But it's an illusion for the most part, bullshit like everything else. The only governable democracy is limited democracy. Give the people enough to make them think they've got what they want. But not everyone back in the seventies was ready to buy into that. We were challenged."

"We?"

"Trilaterals, elitists, the upper class—call us what you want. Militant protests pounded us from all sides, threatening our attempts to produce stability, threatening the very foundation we were endeavoring to build. Women, Indians, the poor, environmentalists, the militants—especially the militants. Rivals! Everywhere we turned." Carlisle's eyes sought out Blaine's. "Something had to be done. We needed to get the nation's house in order. I was chosen to lead a subcommittee of the Trilat."

"To eliminate these rivals, no doubt."

"To save the country from itself, from anarchy, you ass! Our enemies, the country's enemies, were singled out. Operation Yellow Rose would have rid the nation of their menace." Carlisle's lips quivered. "Jesus Christ . . . *Jesus Christ!*" He slid close to Blaine again but stopped short of grasping him. "What you said before, about the overthrow of the government, we knew! We knew, goddamnit, but we didn't do enough about it! The enemy went underground to wait his turn, to grow strong enough to make his move. We could have stopped what's going to happen, but the others were too weak."

"What others?"

"The bulk of the Trilateralists who didn't have the stomach to carry out real governing. Buried themselves in theories, postulates, and position papers, but weren't willing to pay the price for carrying out the recommendations the papers contained. Hell, Carter was a Trilateralist, Bush too. Even they wouldn't listen. They goddamn fucking wouldn't listen. And now, *now!*"

Carlisle's yellowed eyes swung in the direction of the picketers. "Take a look. The enemy's still there. I come here every day and I watch them. I don't even know who I'm watching most days. But it's getting worse, escalating. People are angry, capable of accepting anything that qualifies as change." Eyes back on Blaine now, as much sad as furious. "And we could have prevented it. We had them all selected. The seeds of discontent plucked away so this could never happen."

"That's why you quit, withdrew."

"I walked out, on the Trilateralists and the world."

"And what about the Delphi?"

Carlisle's eyes blazed at Blaine's abrupt mention of the word, then seemed to sink back in his head. His lips trembled.

"Who are they, Mr. Carlisle?"

The old man reached over suddenly and grasped McCracken's lapels again. But this time the fury was gone from the move, desperation in its place.

"Stop them," he urged pleadingly. "You've got to stop them."

"I've got only ten days. Not enough time maybe to do it on my own." Blaine lowered his voice. "I need your help, Mr. Carlisle."

Carlisle let his grasp on McCracken slip away and slid a trembling hand into the vest pocket of what remained of his three-piece suit. It emerged with a key he pressed into Blaine's hand.

"Greyhound/Trailways Bus Station," Carlisle said softly, eyes on the key.

McCracken could feel the grit of rust layered over what had once been smooth steel. "A locker?"

"A grave."

McCracken didn't open the locker right away. He loitered about the bus station providing intercity service for an hour before even approaching it. Anyone in the waiting area whose seat faced the bank of lockers was subject to his scrutiny. He was looking for a man or woman who lingered while paying little attention to the boarding announcements. After the hour had passed, he felt confident that no one had the station staked out. Whatever secrets locker 33 had to offer had remained just that.

Still wary, McCracken guided the key into the lock. It resisted and he was careful not to bend it in the process. At last it turned to the right and Blaine pulled the locker door open.

The first thing he saw inside were rumpled clumps of cash, some wrapped in bands, others simply rolled or folded. Big bills for the most part, many of them new, part of a stash William Carlisle must not have made much use of anymore.

Partially concealed by the scattered bills was an old soft leather briefcase. The conditions of the locker had dried and cracked it. The case had a zipper that was open enough to let some of the bulging contents slip out:

Tabs, the tabs of manila folders.

Blaine brought the briefcase from the locker as nonchalantly as he could manage. One of its handles was torn from its stitching, so he placed the case under his arm. He closed and relocked the locker behind him. Then he glided back out into the warm afternoon air.

McCracken had found a spot inside a nearby parking garage for the car Sal Belamo had arranged for him. There, in the darkness broken only by the domelight, Blaine unzipped the briefcase all the way and removed a hefty chunk of its contents.

The first five manila folders Blaine opened contained detailed personal files with photographs included. Three of the names meant something to him. Two didn't. All five had only one thing in common:

Affixed to the top of the first page in each was a sticker of a yellow rose.

One of the subjects was a college professor. Another was a union organizer. Two more were leaders of the antiwar movement who had organized the march on the 1968 Democratic convention in Chicago. The fifth was an Indian leader who had led the '72 protest at Wounded Knee.

All champions of leftist protest movements and all designated enemies of the Trilateral Commission.

In that context the files made a great deal of sense. The Trilateral Commission's grand scheme allowed no quarter for civil disobedience. The Vietnam war protests had clearly illustrated how public policy could be swayed by left-wing militancy. Carlisle and the other Trilateralists would have learned their lesson from that, opting for a strategy of pre-emption in the form of Operation Yellow Rose: remove the perpetrators and leaders from the scene before they had a chance to set back the commission's plans.

Blaine massaged his eyelids and resumed his scan of the stack of personal files. Somewhere in here was what Daniels must have been seeking. Somewhere in here might well be the identities of those behind the coming attempt to topple the government.

Something in the file before him now froze McCracken's eyes. "Well, I'll be damned," he said out loud. "I'll be goddamned."

CHAPTER 9

"Excuse me," Kristen Kurcell said to the old man sweeping up in front of the building marked GRAND MESA MUNICIPAL OFFICES. "Excuse me, I'm looking for the chief of police's office."

The old man kept sweeping and didn't look up. "Don't have one."

"What?"

"Now if you were looking for the sheriff, I might be able to help you."

"The sheriff, then."

The old man looked up. Though his white hair was thin, it covered all his scalp. He had a scraggly beard of the same color. His face was tanned and creased. He wore a thin plaid jacket over a red flannel shirt and khaki trousers.

"You got an appointment?"

"Do I need one?"

"Asked if you had one."

"No."

The old man leaned forward against his broom. "Come with me. I'll see what I can do."

Kristen followed him through the door of Grand Mesa's municipal building. She had driven here early Saturday morning after spending Friday night in Denver. She had considered driving out as soon as her plane got in from Washington, but it was after midnight by then and there wouldn't be anything she could accomplish. Besides, she was exhausted and needed at least a few hours of sleep to settle herself down. Every time she closed her eyes in the airport hotel, though, she saw images of her brother and Paul Gathers of the FBI.

Both were gone. Both had disappeared.

Kristen hadn't told anyone where she was going. She left a note for the senator that it was personal and she would call in as soon as she could. Until she had some grasp of what was going on, she could not involve anyone else. Paul Gathers had uncovered something and vanished as a result of it. Whatever that something was, it must have been connected to the source of her brother's frantic, unfinished phone call.

The trail began in Grand Mesa. Grand Mesa might hold the answers.

She had not called ahead in the hope that surprise might be her best ally. Now the scope of the town before her made her question the need for that strategy. Grand Mesa's town center consisted of one main street, a few cross streets, and a small complement of shops and stores for its two thousand residents. A single gas station doubled as the only choice for automotive repairs. There were two restaurants and a small L-shaped motel. What had been three additional motels lay not far from the center of town. But they were mere shells now, boarded-up relics that hadn't seen guests in well over a decade by the look of things.

"Here we are," the old man said and closed the door behind them.

The municipal offices were laid out in neat, precise fashion. There was a door marked COURT. Separate walled-off counters with desks behind them were labeled respectively

TAX PAYMENTS, ASSESSOR'S OFFICE, and AUTOMOTIVE REGISTRY. Two were not labeled at all. Not that it mattered: not a single person was on duty behind any of them. There was no label for sheriff, but Kristen did notice a nameplate that read SHERIFF DUNCAN FARLOWE atop a desk in the room's front left corner.

The old man moved down the center's aisle toward an open doorway, taking his broom with him. "I'll get the sheriff for you," he called back to Kristen.

She had barely begun to assess the municipal office's furnishings when he reemerged. The broom was gone. A dull silver badge was pinned to the lapel of his jacket.

"Sheriff Duncan Farlowe, miss," he said, extending a hand. "What can I do for you?"

He twisted rubber bands about his fingers as she spoke, hardly looking at her. He took notes, although Kristen couldn't tell whether he was really listening as she told her story.

"You don't have this tape," Farlowe said at the end, still toying with the rubber bands.

"No."

"Too bad. We coulda used it." Farlowe's eyes darted up from his fingers. One of the rubber bands flew across the room. "You sure your FBI friend said Grand Mesa?"

"Yes. Why?"

"Because there's maybe a hundred towns in Colorado called *something* Mesa. Maybe you got the wrong something."

"No, I'm sure he said Grand Mesa."

"Your brother, he sounded pretty spooked on this tape?"

"Very."

Farlowe nodded at that. Another of the rubber bands jumped off his fingers. "Not much here been known to spook folks. He probably came from somewhere else, just passing through."

"I've thought of that, yes."

"But he wouldn't have been driving long. Way you tell it, he woulda wanted to call ya from the first phone he saw."

Kristen nodded.

"That time of night, only thing open woulda been the motel, if Harley didn't leave the TV on when he dropped off to sleep and couldn't hear the buzzer." The sheriff opened the bottom drawer of his desk and reached a hand inside. "What d'ya say you and me go over and have a talk with him?"

Duncan Farlowe rose with an old-fashioned leather holster in his hand and wrapped it around his waist. He drew a long-barreled black pistol that looked even older and spun the cylinder.

"Colt Peacemaker," Farlowe said proudly. "Been in the family for generations."

"You really think you'll need it?"

Farlowe shrugged. "Reminds folks they got a sheriff."

"Yeah, I remember him," said Harley Epps, owner of the Grand Mesa Motel, as he looked up from the most recent picture Kristen had of David. "Checked in either two or three nights back. I'm almost certain it was two."

"That'd be Thursday," Farlowe prodded.

"Yeah," Epps nodded. "Thursday. Paid in advance and was gone come morning."

"Make any phone calls?"

Epps checked the log for that day. "Not that I got record of, but he could've used a credit card or called collect. I wouldn't know about it then."

Farlowe looked Kristen's way.

"I'm not sure," she told him. "The FBI agent didn't tell me how my brother placed the call."

"What room he stay in?" Farlowe asked the clerk.

"Seven."

"Any other guests here that night?"

"I was just packin' 'em in, as usual."

"Yes or no, Harley?"

"Yeah, two, as I recall. Business has been slow lately, like about the last dozen years."

Duncan Farlowe turned slightly toward Kristen. "Right about the time the silver veins went dry." He looked back at Epps. "Might want to talk to those other two, Harley."

"They checked in late, too. I didn't ask for their addresses."

"Tough to send 'em Christmas cards that way."

"Cash in hand does fine by me."

Farlowe extended his hand across the counter. "Give me the key, Harley."

Room seven was dark for daytime. Farlowe flipped on the light switch by the door and then opened the blinds and drapes. Kristen followed him in tentatively, perhaps afraid of what the room might yield. All it gave up, though, was a musty, stale scent of disuse and a distant odor of disinfectant.

With Kristen hovering in back of him, Farlowe checked all the drawers. He made a quick inspection of the bathroom and then felt about the bed. His last stop was the small desk where the telephone was perched. He leaned over and sniffed the receiver.

"Been cleaned recently?" Kristen raised.

"No, little lady—replaced. This phone's brand spanking new."

"New?"

"According to the way you described that tape, it sounds to me like your brother was attacked in this room. Maybe he tried to use the old phone as a weapon. Maybe it just broke when he dropped it. Either way it would need replacing."

"That means someone had to come back to replace it after they got David out."

Sheriff Farlowe crouched down. The long barrel of his Peacemaker dropped beneath his leg and scraped against the carpet. "That's not all they came back for. Check out this rug. See how the nap's all going in one direction."

"No. Wait a minute, yes, I think so."

"Well, Harley Epps ain't vacuumed since you were still in diapers, and even if he did, it wouldn't straighten the nap this much. Nope, I'd say somebody washed this carpet, real recent, too."

Kristen felt the hollowness building in her gut. "My brother *was* here."

"Seems that way."

"But there's nothing to tell us where they took him, where he is now."

"No, little lady, but I got me a notion on how he got to Grand Mesa in the first place."

"He drive a jeep, one of those little Jap jobs?"

"How did you know?"

"Figured as much."

Farlowe hadn't elaborated further. They climbed back into his 4 × 4 and drove three blocks down to the town garage and filling station. Inside a cluttered repair bay, a mountain of a man with red hair and a matching beard wearing blue denim overalls had his head beneath the hood of an old Ford.

"Jimbo," Farlowe said to him.

"I'm a little busy, Sheriff."

Farlowe turned off the work light dangling from the open hood. "So am I."

The man mountain straightened up, towering over Farlowe, who stood back with this thumbs cocked in his pants pockets. Kristen noticed the butt of the Peacemaker was poised outside his jacket.

"Need to talk to ya about that jeep you found."

"It was parked on my property. Nobody claims it, it's mine."

"Strange how it had no papers inside."

"I figure it was stolen," said the man mountain. "Abandoned here."

"Could be. Mind if I take a look?"

"Long as you leave it just where it is when you're finished."

"In the back bay?"

"Where it's stayin', Sheriff."

Farlowe tipped his wide-brimmed hat and led Kristen through the obstacle course of grease and oil that darkened the floor in splotches. The rear bay was accessible through a missing door, and the jeep was there waiting for them.

"This your brother's, little lady?"

Kristen circled about it. "I don't know. I never saw it. But it's the same model, I think. I just can't be sure." She looked down. "The license plates are gone."

"Big Jimbo probably dumped 'em in the river by now. Eliminate anyone else's claim on it, that way."

"I assume the glove compartment will be empty as well."

"For sure." Farlowe tapped the Wrangler's hood. "Your brother was a smart boy, little lady. He musta parked his jeep out of sight so whoever was after him wouldn't know he was in town. I mighta been the one callin' you if Big Jimbo hadn't've come upon this first. Don't matter much really, I suppose."

"Why?"

"Because what matters is figurin' out where it was at 'fore your brother drove here. I mean, whatever got him hurt happened a ways out of town. We find out where and maybe we find out what."

Kristen whisked her hand across the shiny-clean fender. "Looks like your friend Jimbo wiped off whatever evidence of that there might have been."

"Not all of it, little lady," countered Farlowe, kneeling by one of the front tires. "Looks like he hasn't gotten to these yet."

Farlowe drew a pen from his pocket and stuck it in the tread. A layer of clay-colored dirt coated the tip when he pulled it back toward him. He brought the pen to his nose and sniffed.

"Looks like your brother was up in silver country."

"What?"

"This part of Colorado used to be known for its silver mines. People came on through to stake their claim," Farlowe explained. "Plenty got rich. Plenty didn't. Town did fine either way."

"You think my brother was looking for *silver*?"

"Be damn stupid if he was, little lady. See, there hasn't been any silver in these parts for a good dozen years now, like I said before. That's why Grand Mesa's little more than a ghost town these days. Anyway, all I'm saying is his jeep was up in the hills off Old Canyon Road where the mines used to be. Pretty dangerous territory. Man could fall in one of the abandoned shafts if he took his eyes off the ground for a second."

"What else is out there?"

"Not much. Miravo Air Force Base, but that was shut down a couple years back. With SAC gone, they mothballed it. Killed whatever was left of Grand Mesa's economy. Nobody even uses that old road anymore. We'll drive out that way. See if anything strikes our fancy."

They moved from the rear bay back into the front section of the garage where Big Jimbo was coolly working under the hood of the Ford.

"You find what you were looking for, Sheriff?" he asked, without poking his head out.

"Funny thing, Jimbo," Farlowe told him. "Glove compartment got itself emptied."

Farlowe stopped just to Big Jimbo's right. As Kristen looked on, the old man reached up and brought the hood down hard on Jimbo's head and shoulders. The man mountain screeched in pain. Farlowe let the hood bounce back up and grabbed a fistful of red hair. Before Big Jimbo could respond, the sheriff's Colt Peacemaker was cocked dead center against his forehead.

"That jeep back there belongs to this here lady's brother, Jimbo," he said quite calmly. "Now there's two things you're gonna do. First, you're gonna give me everything you took out of the glove compartment, since something important mighta been in there. And second, you're gonna park the jeep right outside my office sometime in the next ten minutes. Have I made myself understood?"

Big Jimbo nodded.

"I think I wanna hear you say it."

"Yes, Sheriff."

Farlowe let the Peacemaker's hammer release and pulled the gun back from the red-haired man's forehead. "Much obliged."

They waited near the garage's entrance for Big Jimbo to retrieve the contents of David's glove compartment. After Big Jimbo had handed them over, Farlowe led Kristen outside, keeping his eyes on the man mountain until they were halfway to his truck.

"Now, little lady," he started, only then returning his trusty Peacemaker to its holster, "let's see if we can figure out what your brother was trying to tell you he found."

Farlowe gave Kristen the contents of the glove compartment and watched her quickly thumb through them. She got halfway into the pile and stopped. The wind ruffled the papers in her hand. She looked up from them at Farlowe.

"I think I've got something, Sheriff."

CHAPTER 10

"This is a receipt for a camcorder my brother bought three days before he disappeared," Kristen explained, handing it to Farlowe.

"You thinking maybe he taped whatever it was he was trying to tell you he saw?"

She nodded. "And maybe he hid the tape somewhere. Maybe Big Jimbo still has it."

Farlowe smiled slightly. "Nope. I don't think he'd be thinking 'bout adding it to his video collection, under the circumstances."

"Would you have shot him back there?" Kristen wondered.

"Big Jimbo talks a tough game, little lady, but he never woulda made me."

"But would you have shot him?"

"My great-uncle on my mama's side would have, I can tell you. Man by the name of Wyatt Earp."

Kristen looked at Farlowe in surprise. "Wyatt Earp was your great-uncle?"

"Not what you'd call a close relation, but my mama always told me I had the same blood he did in my veins. She gave me that Peacemaker when I was all of sixteen and told me Wyatt had fired it himself on occasion. Thinking back, I guess that's what made me want to become a lawman. I grew up down in the Panhandle in the last of the boon times. Spent my formative years as a Texas Ranger. Man, I could tell ya some stories . . . Later, maybe. Right now we'd best head out to where I'm pretty sure your brother may have used that camera he bought."

Kristen used the drive to scrutinize the contents of her brother's glove compartment more carefully. Other than the receipt, though, they seemed utterly routine: the registration; an insurance card; a number of gas company credit card charge slips that might aid her in piecing together the route he had taken across the country. Perhaps whatever had led to his desperate phone call Thursday night had not occurred near Grand Mesa at all. Perhaps it had happened several hundred miles away, and only as he neared Grand Mesa had David realized he was in danger. If that was the case, the charge slips might come in very handy indeed.

"Uh-oh," she heard Farlowe mutter and looked up from the receipts to see thick clouds of chalky brown dirt swirling in the air before them, stealing visibility in blizzard-like fashion.

"In these parts, we call this a brown-out," the sheriff explained. "It's like them whiteout snowstorms they have in other parts. All kinds of theories as to what causes them and why they come mostly in the spring. Me, I can smell 'em just before they hit. Come and go fast, though."

Farlowe slowed the truck to a crawl. The reduced engine sounds allowed the pounding wind to make its presence heard as well as felt. The truck shook from the pressure. For Kristen, the effect was akin to a New England northeaster, with dirt in place of snow or rain. A little over five minutes later it was over. The sky returned as quickly as it had disappeared. Farlowe gave the engine gas, but the 4 × 4 hesitated a bit, as if needing to shed the layers of dirt that had battered it too. He pulled over a short time later and reached behind him for a can of window cleaner and a rag.

They started down Old Canyon Road again after the windows were clear. Farlowe drove for ten or twelve miles, keeping the pace slow enough for him to survey everything that they passed by. Suddenly he pulled over and climbed out of the 4 × 4, leaving the engine on. Kristen joined him on the road and watched the sheriff kneel down gingerly. Stray blowing dirt created a film over his glasses and speckled his beard and hair. After a few seconds he rose, his knees creaking, and proceeded further down the road, only to kneel down again.

Kristen joined him in a crouch the third time he stopped. "What is it?"

"Tire marks. Trucks, big ones. Looks like a whole convoy came to a sudden halt right in this area not too long back."

Kristen gazed about. "But there's nothing around here."

"Could be something made the lead truck come to a quick stop. Maybe an animal dashed out in front of it. Caused a chain reaction. Whatever the case, there were trucks, all right, several of 'em. Since Old Canyon Road leads nowhere fast, I can't tell you where they were headed."

She followed Farlowe back to the 4 × 4. He pulled back out onto the road and continued on at an even slower pace, looking for more signs of the convoy. The minutes and miles passed in silence. He slowed again after passing the abandoned air force base he had mentioned, then stopped altogether and climbed out.

"That's funny. Those trucks didn't get this far," he announced after careful inspection of the road. "Trail they left ends at the base."

Kristen fixed her gaze on the chained entrance to Miravo. "But it's deserted. What could they have been doing there?"

"Why don't we go inside and have ourselves a look?"

"Can you do this?" Kristen asked from behind Farlowe as he aimed his Peacemaker at the lock holding the chain in place over the gate.

"I'm the law, little lady. I can do anything my little heart desires. Cover your ears now."

She did as she was told but the reverberation still stung them. The lock shattered. Farlowe pulled the chain off and swung open the gate.

Before them, Miravo Air Force Base boasted all the eeriness of a ghost town. Windows of many of the buildings had been boarded up. Beyond the buildings and hangars, the runways and tarmacs were collecting dirt. Where once upwards of a thousand people had occupied this SAC base, there was no one. Wind whistled by the steel hangars and Quonset huts. The sunlight struggled to glimmer off their rusting hulks.

Duncan Farlowe checked the soft ground just inside the base entrance, kicking dirt and then smoothing it with his feet. He moved about stiffly; crouching had obviously become too much of a chore for him.

"The trucks came in here, all right," he told Kristen. "And lots more than just that one convoy we found evidence of back on the road." He managed to half bend over. "They pulled through the gate and eventually headed . . ." He paused to check the ground more closely and brought his hand up. " . . . that way."

Farlowe was pointing toward the airfield that occupied the area beyond the last row of buildings. He led Kristen toward it and inspected the runways when they got there, apparently with little satisfaction.

"Concrete this firm doesn't leave signs like that good ol' roadbed that got us here," he said, ruffling his foot through the layer of dirt that had accumulated. "Could be some planes been landing. Could be they haven't." The sheriff turned suddenly toward Kristen. "You say that phone call came at night?"

"Morning, actually. Around three A.M. your time."

"Now that's interesting." He moved to the edge of the main runway and followed the line of lights, stooping to check each one. "Bulbs are still present. Seems strange folks would abandon a base and leave the bulbs behind. . . ."

"They could have forgot."

"Didn't let me finish, little lady. See, the thing is these bulbs don't show much dirt and their filaments are barely worn. I'd say they been inserted sometime in the past month."

"Trucks and planes," Kristen muttered. "Then something could have been flown out of here!"

"Or flown in. To be loaded onto those trucks, or unloaded from them. Either way, as I figure it, could be your brother got close enough to get a real good look at the proceedings."

Farlowe swung and fixed his gaze on the hillsides almost hidden from view by the tight clutter of buildings enclosing the airfield.

"Except he couldn't have seen anything from up there in those hills. The trucks, yeah, but not the planes. Means he musta come down and entered the base. Maybe got to use his brand-new camera to record what they was holding."

"But we don't know he was here at all," Kristen re-minded, afraid of what it meant if David had been inside. "Without the tape, we can't prove anything."

"Might not need the tape to prove it, little lady."

"Your brother was 'bout the age I was when I started out with the Rangers," Farlowe picked up, as they walked across Old Canyon Road toward the nearby foothills that had once been rich in silver. "Back then, if it was me, I'd want to park my jeep out of sight, but within fast reach. Like to know I could get out in a hurry if I had to. 'Cept now I don't do nothin' in a hurry, save for drawing Uncle Earp's Peacemaker. That's something that don't leave you so fast."

They trudged along the hillsides, covering paths wide enough to handle the Jeep Wrangler. Every time Farlowe found a spot to his liking, he stopped and kicked the dirt about. A few times he leaned over and ran his hand through it. Mostly he just walked with thumbs cocked in his pockets.

"Here," he said all of a sudden, thrusting a finger downward even before making a careful check of the spot. "Your brother's jeep, or another damn like it, was parked right here." He eased himself into a crouch to point out what he had picked up to Kristen. "Sunken tire marks. And here, in these ruts, this is where your brother hauled ass out." His finger came up and pointed down Old Canyon Road. "That way."

"Toward Grand Mesa."

Farlowe nodded and held up a handful of dirt. "See this? Matches the dirt I found stuck in the treads of his jeep's tires."

"He got as far as the motel in town and called me."

"Seems to be the case," Farlowe affirmed somberly.

"He was trying to tell me what he saw happening on the base."

"Yup," Farlowe said, already in motion up a swirling path that cut between adjacent hillsides.

At the top the gap widened to create a gully that provided a clear view into the front of Miravo Air Force Base. As Farlowe had suggested, though, the row of buildings kept the outlying runways hidden from sight. Kristen watched the old sheriff check the dirt with his eyes and then his hands.

"Nothing up here to suggest this is where your brother perched himself," he said, "but it's the perfect hiding place. I'm betting he was here. Only thing we don't know now is—"

Kristen saw the expression on Farlowe's crusty face change, as if a shadow was suddenly cast over it. In a blur of motion difficult for even a young man, he had torn the Peacemaker from its holster and fired two shots that whizzed by Kristen's side toward the hillside behind her. There was a gasp and she turned to see a man holding a rifle crumpling, his hands reaching for his midsection. In the next instant Farlowe threw himself toward her. The impact took both of them to the ground.

Crack!

A bullet sliced a chasm cut out of the hillside directly where Kristen's chest had been. A series of muted echoes followed, and more dirt and shale showered over them.

"Yup," muttered Farlowe, Peacemaker still in hand, "this is the place, all right."

More gunshots rang out from both south and west, then east again as another man replaced the one the sheriff had shot.

"I'd say they got us surrounded, little lady," Farlowe said after Kristen assumed a sitting position next to him in the cover of the small gully.

He held the Peacemaker near his chest.

"And I only got three bullets left. Rest are in the truck, 'long with the radio."

Kristen found herself not only terrified but also deeply

saddened. The fact that they had been ambushed by men with the obvious intention of killing them did not bode well for the fate of her brother. Up till now she had been clinging to the hope he had simply stuck his nose where it didn't belong and was being held prisoner or might still be on the run. Now she realized whoever was behind what David had uncovered, what he had witnessed inside the base, would stop at nothing to prevent their secret from being revealed. If they were trying to kill her and Farlowe, then . . .

The sheriff saved her the trouble of completing the thought. "They'll be closing in on us now," he said as soon as the gunshots had abated. "Know they got us boxed in. No reason for them to rush."

"What can we do?"

"I could make a run for the truck, or . . ."

Farlowe seemed to change his mind in midsentence. He sniffed at the air, a narrow smile stretching across his lips.

" . . . we wait."

"Wait? Wait for wh—"

And that's when she felt it, just as a slight wisp of wind at first, but then a gush against her face a few breaths later.

Another brown-out! Duncan Farlowe had sniffed the air and known it was coming!

"Cover your eyes and mouth as best you can," he instructed as swirls of dust began to whip about in dozens of mini-tornadoes. The air darkened with them. The sun was already gone. "Take my hand and follow me when I pull you."

Kristen had her sleeve over her eyes. "Follow you?"

"Yup. I know these hills as well as I know my own face. I'm figuring our gunslingin' friends don't have quite that advantage."

The blowing dirt filled his mouth and turned his last few words to little more than garble. He spat it out and then tied the red bandanna that had circled his neck over the lower part of his face.

"Come on!" Farlowe rasped from behind his bandanna, tilting his wide-brimmed hat low to better shield his eyes.

He took the steps of the hillside blindly but surely. Kristen thought she had lost her bearings when they started off, then realized they weren't retracing their route down the path toward the truck; they were heading south further out into the hills toward the abandoned silver mines.

Kristen heard gunshots crackling in the brown air, fired wildly. There were distant sounds of men shouting. Then came a yell from what seemed not more than fifteen feet away. She felt Farlowe tense and stopped a step behind him. She managed to open her eyes enough to make out a shape feeling its way sightlessly almost right before them. Farlowe's Peacemaker roared once. The shape was gone, its wail lost to the howling wind that swept the dirt into a heavy brown blanket tossed over the day.

The sheriff had only two bullets left now. He pulled Kristen on again a bit faster, aware that the distinctive roar of the Peacemaker would draw the remainder of the enemy force to the area. She could tell from his pace that this didn't seem to bother him. In fact, she could almost sense it was exactly what he wanted. The brown out was theirs to use for as long as it lasted. The one they had encountered on the drive here had lingered five, maybe six minutes, Kristen recalled. That meant there were six or so left.

Farlowe steered Kristen around a narrow hole in the ground leading into one of the hundreds of abandoned silver mines that were like pockmarks on the land. He angled to the right and brought her to a halt directly over the rim of a larger entryway.

"We're going down!" he tried to scream over the wind.

"What?"

"Follow me!"

He pulled her down with him and eased her to the rear of the shaft's head just before it sloped forward into the vein. At first she thought they were going to hide in here or perhaps even use the vein as an escape route. But Farlowe moved away from her and perched himself right beneath the shaft's rim at ground level, listening for whatever sounds of approach the brown-out would let through.

Something made Farlowe tense. He cocked the Peacemaker's hammer and waited, propped up on his toes. A few seconds later, he bounced upward.

The cracking in his knees was audible above even the swirling sounds of the brown-out. So again was the Peacemaker as it barked twice.

Farlowe turned back Kristen's way and pulled the bandanna down from his mouth.

"That's another down. Let's go."

Kristen could see how hard he was breathing, the strain draining the color from his eyes. She approached Farlowe, and once again he grasped her jacket. The Peacemaker was holstered, empty.

"This is where it gets tough, little lady. Just watch my feet and follow them. Keep your eyes *down*!"

And then the bandanna was back over his mouth and they climbed out from the mine's entrance.

Farlowe headed off toward the southwest this time, the world a brown curtain before them. Kristen could taste the dirt in her mouth. She felt as though the insides of her throat had been coated with ground-up chalk. She couldn't swallow. It was as if she had taken a bite out of a desert.

Farlowe's tightening grasp alerted her to employ extra caution just before she made out a rolling collection of foothills that were dotted with mine entrances. Only narrow slopes of turf separated one shaft from another. This area had been bled dry of life and silver. The land had died. The holes, deep and ominous, were lesions on its corpse.

Farlowe led Kristen behind a slight rise. He pressed down on her shoulders as a signal to crouch behind the cover it provided.

"Stay here," he ordered, holding his bandanna away from his mouth to make sure she heard him.

She tried to ask him what he was going to do, but the

caked-up air stole her words. Farlowe disappeared into the brown cloud, and Kristen peered around the rise to follow him with her eyes as best as she could.

She locked her gaze onto the sheriff's shape and refused to blink. He was retracing their steps, heading straight back toward the enemy. The brown-out had begun to abate slightly, enough for slivers of clear air to appear. Kristen noticed the approaching shapes when they crossed these slivers: three, she thought, though it could have been four. She looked back toward Farlowe. He was gone.

Then his shape reappeared in her line of vision fifty feet away. He was running, a dark blur amidst the storm. Kristen heard shouts, then gunfire crackled. The approaching shapes that had been coming her way turned round and charged toward Farlowe.

A scream sounded as one of them seemed to drop off the world, simply disappearing.

Into one of the mine shafts.

Farlowe darted through the brown-out again and a second rapid burst of gunfire sounded. Another enemy gave chase, and he too fell with a scream as a different shaft welcomed him. It was like being caught in a treacherous mine field, Kristen realized, and Farlowe was using himself as bait to lure the enemy into its reach. Kristen pulled back behind the rise to wipe her eyes and then slid round it again to find out what was happening.

One of the enemy was coming straight for her. As she watched, though, the man suddenly turned away and steadied his rifle into the storm.

For Farlowe, no doubt!

Kristen lunged to her feet and charged into the dirt-clogged air. She struck the man as he pulled the trigger, and an errant barrage stitched across the sky. He wobbled on his feet but didn't go down. Kristen clung tight and he turned the butt of his rifle on her and smashed her in the shoulder.

Stars exploded before Kristen's eyes. She knew the pain was there, but refused to feel it. She wrapped herself tighter around the gunman and tried to find his rifle's trigger to keep him from pulling it. He hammered her under the chin with another blow and then rammed her in the sternum. Kristen lost her grasp. She sank to her knees and fell over on her side gasping for air, which allowed the storm to flood into her lungs and choke her on dirt.

The man struggled to tilt his gun down to take aim at her. He had managed to angle the barrel Kristen's way when the shape of Duncan Farlowe lunged at him through the swirl of the storm. Kristen saw that Farlowe was holding the Peacemaker by the barrel. The handle swooped sideways and down, smacking into the back of the gunman's skull. His head snapped forward. He staggered and tried to turn Farlowe's way.

The sheriff cracked him with the handle again, this time right over the bridge of his nose. Kristen heard the bones mash and watched the gunman keel over backwards like a felled tree, his face reduced to pulp. Not taking any chances, Farlowe tore the gun from his grasp and held it before him as he approached Kristen.

"Nice work, little lady," he said through his bandanna as he lifted her to her feet.

Kristen realized her chin was swollen, the pain rising from a dull ache to a throbbing agony that made her feel faint. She couldn't move her mouth, even if the brown-out would have let her speak.

They stopped over the body of the man Farlowe had dropped with the butt of his pistol. The man's eyes had locked sightlessly opened. The sheriff reached down and checked his pockets for identification, but found none. His gaze slid about the pockmarked land through the clearing air. The two men she had seen fall into shafts remained unaccounted for, and he kept the rifle steady in case they reappeared.

"I think we seen enough here," Farlowe told Kristen and led her away.

* * *

Back in town she insisted they stop back at the motel.
Only when another search of David's room failed to turn up
the missing camcorder did she accompany Farlowe back to
his office so he could tend to her wounds.

"I was a medic in World War II," he explained. "Then
again in Korea. Some things you don't forget." He swabbed
her gashed cheek with alcohol. "I'll call you a doctor if you
want, but nothing's broke and I don't think this gotta be
stitched."

"No," she managed painfully. "The less people that know
I'm here, the better."

"My thoughts exactly, little lady."

"I'm more worried about something else, Sheriff: they
could have identified you."

"If any of them survived, that is."

"You know what I'm talking about."

Farlowe winked at her. "I can take care of myself just
fine. Got just enough Earp blood in my veins. And where
the blood leaves off," he continued, tapping the handle of
the Colt Peacemaker he had reloaded as soon as they'd
reached his car back outside Miravo, "there's always this."

He placed a gauze pad gingerly over the wound and taped
it down. Then he adjusted the way Kristen was holding the
ice bag atop her head.

She looked at him with grim resolve. "We've got to find
out what happened to my brother after he called me from
the motel. We know now where he was before." She swallowed hard. "Those men in the hills could have been the
same ones who . . ."

Farlowe leaned over and grasped her shoulders. "Nothin'
you can do on that account. Leave it to me."

"I've come this far."

"You want to help."

"More than that."

"Then start lookin' at this thing a different way. Could be
the trail your brother's left has taken us as far as it can.
Leaves us only with finding out who's behind whatever he

saw happening at Miravo." He paused briefly. "Now I got to figure you got friends who can help on that account."

"How?"

"Way you handle yourself, for one thing. The fact that I saw your plane ticket from Washington stickin' out your bag for another. Everyone there has friends."

Kristen shrugged. "Granted," she said, thinking of Senator Jordan.

"Use your friends, little lady. You got any old favors, call 'em in. Never gonna be a better time to do it."

The phone rang and Farlowe moved back to his desk to answer it. Kristen didn't bother listening, too busy rechecking her wounds. It still hurt to talk and her head pounded with each breath. Similarly, every inhale sent a bolt of pain surging through her bruised sternum. In sum, she was a wreck. The last thing she was looking forward to was the long plane ride home, especially since she'd be leaving Grand Mesa with matters even more unsettled than when she had arrived.

She looked up again suddenly to find Duncan Farlowe standing right before her. He had put his wide-brimmed hat back on and a grim expression was stretched over his features.

"We gotta take a ride, little lady."

Kristen came slowly out of her chair. "What? What is it?"

"Nobody's sure yet, but it ain't good."

"Maybe you oughta let me do this," Sheriff Farlowe offered when they reached the river. "If it's David, I'll know it from that picture you showed me."

Two kids had spotted the body while walking along the riverbank. The highway patrol had already pulled it from the river by the time Farlowe parked his truck as close to the bank as he could. Kristen was out of the truck before him and on her way down to the bank. Farlowe hustled to get ahead of her and held her back.

"I've got to see for myself."

Farlowe nodded reluctantly and tucked an arm over Kristen's shoulder to lead her on. An ambulance had backed up to the river's edge. Its rear door was open and two attendants were dragging a dolly across the rocky shoreline to where a black body bag lay. Two pairs of highway patrolmen looked on, overseeing the process emotionlessly.

"Afternoon, Duncan," one of them greeted when they saw Farlowe approach.

Farlowe tipped his cap. The ambulance attendants were lifting the body bag up onto the dolly.

"Mind if I have a look at that first?"

One of the patrolmen nodded. The other looked at Kristen.

"This might be a relative," Farlowe explained.

Kristen slid by Farlowe as one of the attendants unzipped the body bag a third of the way. She gasped, then sank to her knees on the wet rocks. Farlowe supported her from behind. She was wheezing. Her chest hammered as she heaved for breath.

"David," she cried. "Oh, God, David!"

Farlowe nodded at the closer pair of highway patrolmen, who backed off a bit. One of the attendants had started to zip the bag up again when Kristen shot out a hand to his arm and stopped him.

"No!" she screamed, pulling herself back to her feet. She grimaced as she moved closer to the corpse. She took a longer look this time and began trembling horribly. David's face was blank and milk white. His eyes were bulging. His mouth hung grotesquely open and seemed twisted to the side.

But worst of all was the top of his head. His scalp was dark and raw, missing all but a few stray patches of hair.

"Look at him!" she heard herself scream. *"Look at him!"*

That was the last thing she remembered clearly until she was back inside Grand Mesa's municipal offices. A blanket Farlowe had draped across her shoulders did nothing to ease her shaking. Neither did the hot soup or coffee he made her drink. She had never felt this cold, thought her teeth might break from chattering so hard against each other.

"You saw the body," she said halfway through her second cup of coffee.

"Let it go for a while, little lady."

But she couldn't. "You saw the body."

He nodded.

"H-h-how, how was he killed?"

"I'm no expert."

"How?"

Farlowe sighed and leaned his chair closer to hers. "Looks to me like he was shot."

"What happened to . . . his head?"

Farlowe turned away slightly. "Could've been after they dropped him in the river. Fish could've got to him."

"No."

He looked her way again. "Little lady, I—"

"Don't hold back. Don't hold anything back. I've got to know. Do you hear me? *I've got to know!*"

Farlowe sighed deeply. "I think he was scalped."

Kristen felt faint. "Oh, my God . . ."

The cup dropped from her hand and burst on the floor. Coffee splashed upward. Farlowe stopped her from falling, enveloped her in his embrace.

"Easy now, easy."

But the pain had taken hold and wouldn't let go, everything hitting her at once. Her brother was dead. She would never see him again. He had been murdered; no, more than murdered—violated. How could anyone have done this to him? *How?*

"I shouldn't have said anything," Farlowe said softly. "I was wrong."

Kristen pulled back from his grasp, rage and resolve battling sorrow over her features. "No, you were right."

Farlowe's eyes filled with concern. "Leave it be, little lady. Let the professionals sort everything out."

"I am a professional, Sheriff," Kristen told him, "by

Washington standards, anyway. My brother saw something at Miravo that got him killed. Miravo is Washington's business." She paused and held his stare. "And I'm making David's murder mine."

CHAPTER 11

The limousine deposited Samuel Jackson Dodd in front of the Grand Hyatt on H Street for his hastily called press conference Saturday afternoon. The press was getting used to these precision fits of fancy; every time there was something on Dodd's mind, he'd summon them together. Originally only a few reporters had shown up, with no representatives from television among them. Now an hour's notice was enough to pack a room, with all major networks represented.

Dodd had thrown the limousine's door open before it had come to a complete halt. He lunged out and approached the Hyatt entrance, leaving his private security detail to catch up. He glided through the door, a tall, elegant figure in a medium gray suit. He moved like a wide receiver in the open field, slipping by gawking onlookers with a handshake fast enough to make them wonder if they'd felt it. His face was an amazingly close likeness to the one pictured on brochure covers and picket signs all over the country. The ever-present smile exuded warmth and confidence. This man could do *anything*, in point of fact *had* done pretty much everything already.

His security detail caught up in time to usher him down the first of three escalators, past a bubbling indoor fountain pool where a piano player worked the keys on an islet built into the center. Dodd hurried down the final two escalators to the Hyatt's lowest level, where the press had squeezed itself inside the Franklin Square Room. Some of the participants from television were still setting up and turned their pace frantic when Dodd entered. Camera lights blazed. Video cameras whirled. Samuel Jackson Dodd strode to the front of the room, where a large-screen television and VCR were waiting.

"There's something I want you all to see," he announced by way of introduction.

Without further explanation, Dodd switched the VCR and television on and signaled for the room's lights to be dimmed. Instantly a picture of screaming protesters filled the screen. They thrust picket signs high into the air, as they surged forward toward a closed gate fortified with riot police on the other side. The camera focused on one of the signs. It read simply LIFE!

Dodd froze the VCR there and spoke again, his figure silhouetted eerily by the glow off the screen. "You know where this is, ladies and gentlemen? San Quentin Prison, where Billy Ray Polk is scheduled to be put to death at dawn tomorrow. The crowd you see here doesn't want Billy Ray Polk to die. They say death by lethal injection is cruel and unusual punishment."

Dodd's tall figure moved a bit away from the screen's glare.

"Cruel and unusual punishment? Did you notice that no one was there to protest what he had done to those two boys? How he tortured them before he killed them, how they begged for their lives and then begged for him to kill them? And there are those in America who don't want to see him killed. There are those in America who don't care if no one speaks for those two boys and their rights."

Dodd drummed a fist before him in cadence with his words. "Well, *I* speak for them, and I speak for all the other victims of crimes that go unpunished because our judicial system can't handle the backlog and police are too hamstrung to even guarantee the case will get that far. The system's out of control. The system stinks."

A soft murmur moved through the crowd of reporters.

"We've got the highest per capita crime rate in the world.

Know why? Because somehow, somewhere along the way
things got all twisted around in this country. We ended up
caring more for the rights of the criminals than the rights of
the victims. We're losing the fight because we're playing on
the wrong side. Things have to change. We've got to make
crime punishable. We've got to make it safe for people to
go out of their houses again. The police can't do it alone.
We need a national militia to work alongside them, a feder-
ally charged and authorized force to break down the crack
houses and break up the gangs."

"Mr. Dodd?" came a call from the near darkness of the
press gallery.

"Yes. Over there."

"It would seem, sir, that what you're advocating runs
counter to several amendments to the Constitution."

"Is that a question, son?"

"Only if you choose to respond."

"I do," Dodd said, coming forward toward the questioner.
"I know all about what the Constitution says and guaran-
tees. I know all about the freedoms on which this country
was founded. Like the freedom to be able to walk the street
at night without being afraid. The freedom to send a child
to school without a pusher on every other corner with his
wares carried in a knapsack. Over ninety percent of the laws
we live by are over a hundred years old. Laws for a different time, a different age. We need laws for this time, for this
age, for today."

"Could you give us an example?" a female reporter asked
him.

Dodd moved her way. "We've got schools in this country
where more guns are carried than lunches. I say a kid who
gets caught with a gun should be sent away to a juvenile detention center for a year. No warnings. No second chances."

"What about the individual child's rights?"

"What about the rights of the other kids in the school?"
Dodd shot back at his questioner.

"Do you think this country has sufficient facilities to incarcerate the number of resulting offenders?"

"My feeling, son, is that if these kids knew about the punishment in advance, they wouldn't *become* offenders."

"All the same," the reporter continued, "many of your platforms seem to advocate wholesale change."

"I'm advocating change where it's needed. I'm advocating change before it's too late."

"Too late for what?" chimed in a new voice.

"Too late for us who don't want our society being dominated by the Billy Ray Polks. When are we gonna learn? When are we gonna stop fooling ourselves? This nation's approaching free-fall and none of the people here in Washington seem to give enough of a damn to do anything about it."

"Why are you here?" from a young female reporter.

"Ma'am?"

"In Washington, I mean, Mr. Dodd. What brings you to the capital?"

"I'm still trying to find somebody on either end of Pennsylvania Avenue to listen to what I've got to say."

The female reporter was still standing. "Are you preparing to run for president?"

"The next election's over two years away. I'm not sure the country can wait that long."

"What's the alternative?" raised a network Washington correspondent.

"Why don't you tell me?" Dodd shot back, striding about the front of the room with fist pumping. "Better yet, let's work it out together." He stopped back at the television screen frozen with the picket sign reading LIFE. "We've got everything all screwed up and turned around in this country. For every person who'd hold this sign, there's another hundred thousand who'd pull the switch on Billy Ray Polk. But where are they? Why do we never hear from them? Lots of them have even given up voting because they don't believe it makes a difference anymore. People are frustrated. People are angry."

"What makes the picketers in front of San Quentin different from the ones who marched on the Capitol yesterday in support of you?" chimed in the voice of a male reporter.

Dodd turned his way and stopped. The room became dead quiet, except for the whir of camera motor drives.

"Plenty. The people who support me want to see this country built back up. These," he said, thrusting an angry hand toward the frozen screen, "want to see it broken down even more than it is. And there's lots of them out there, more than we can possibly realize. I'm talking about people who've just been looking for an excuse to bring this country down, son. I've seen them and I've felt them. A seamy underbelly that hates everything America is and stands for. They're just waiting for their chance to do what they've always wanted to. And unless we shape up fast, we're gonna give it to them."

A collective murmur slid through the crowd, the reporters wondering if the impenetrable Sam Jack Dodd had at last been caught committing a Perotism.

"Are you talking about a *revolution*, sir?"

"No, I'm talking about random violence," said Dodd, recovering nicely. "I'm talking about the Los Angeles riots of '92 on a national scale. Do you think the country is equipped to respond to that? Of course not. So what choice do we have other than to take steps to avoid it?"

"By steps, you mean—"

"I mean setting things right and setting them right now. We need a system that works. We need a country that works. No more gridlock. No more compromising principles in favor of politics."

"Spoken like a candidate for president, Mr. Dodd."

At that, Sam Jack Dodd flashed the famous boyish grin that had become his trademark. "Too bad this isn't an election year, son, isn't it?"

CHAPTER 12

"Yeah, I remember him," the Gainesville, Texas deputy told Johnny Wareagle late Saturday afternoon.

Johnny took the picture of Will Shortfeather back from his outstretched hand.

"He was here about two weeks ago, stirring up a nest of unpleasant memories," the deputy continued, the tone of his voice indicating he was in no mood to rehash them either. "Was another deputy who talked to him."

"He came to ask about a man named Traggeo."

The deputy nodded.

"What happened in your town? What did Traggeo do here?"

"Was a little over a year ago. Got into a fight with four men in our local bar," the deputy explained. "It didn't last long. One of them's dead. Two are still in the hospital. One of 'em be lucky if he keeps one of his eyes. The other can't talk anymore on account of something happened to his throat. And the thing is they were tough guys, toughest this town had to offer anyway. It was almost like your friend knew that, like he went looking for them."

"He's not my friend."

"But you know him."

"I . . . know him."

"And what he did don't surprise you."

"No."

The deputy looked angry. "Your friend picked the fight. Four on one and he started it. Witnesses claim he was drunk."

"That was probably the only thing that kept him from killing all of them."

The deputy eyed Johnny briefly before resuming. "Somebody cracked him over the head with a bottle. Me and two other deputies get there and he's still doing damage. Bar was closed for over a week to handle the repairs. We walk in and he's got his hands on the head of the guy he almost blinded and is tearing at his hair, like he's trying to rip off his scalp. Whooping it up the whole time. I think he was smiling." The deputy's gaze became one of suspicion. "He's one of you, isn't he, an Indian?"

"No, he's not."

"Looked it."

"What happened next?"

"We drew our guns, told him to get his hands up. When he didn't, I shot him in the shoulder. Slowed him down enough for us to get the cuffs on him. Son of a bitch plea-bargained the charges down to manslaughter two or something, self-defense. Accepted the five years. He smiled through that, too."

"You mean he's in jail?"

"Huntsville State Penitentiary, far as I know, with four more years left on his sentence."

McCracken shifted uneasily in his seat. Just over a day had passed since he had left Miami, and now, thanks to the files found in Bill Carlisle's locker and information uncovered by Sal Belamo, he was on his way back.

"Any luck finding Johnny?" Blaine had asked Sal at the outset of that conversation.

"Nothing, boss. Seems to have made himself scarce, and that's no easy trick for the big fella. You ask me, boss, what you're after down there, be a good idea I come along in his place."

"Love to have you, Sal, but I need you to track down H. William Carlisle again, and my feeling is that he won't be as easy to find this time."

"Why's it so important we find him?"

"Because some of the files marked with yellow roses stretch up to 1980, even though Carlisle supposedly dropped out in 1978. Makes me think he may have decided to stick around for a while, after all, at least on the periphery. That means Carlisle might know a hell of a lot more than he told me about who's going after the government."

"Got something here that might help in that regard," Belamo followed. "I just got a make on two sets of those prints you faxed me from Miami of the shooters at Cocowalk. Belonged to a couple of big old bad dudes who were part of a group called the Midnight Riders way back in the sixties. Ever hear of them?"

"I wasn't around much in the sixties, Sal."

"You didn't miss much, let me tell you. Anyway, the Midnight Riders were made up of nuts even the Weather Underground and Students for a Democratic Society couldn't control, what became known as the lunatic fringe. The Riders advocated a full-scale revolution. Enough people listened to keep gas in their engines. Their leader was one very mean bastard named Arlo Cleese."

"Cleese . . . His file was one of those inside the locker, Sal, yellow rose and all."

"Just the kind of dude Carlisle's committee and the Trilat would have loved to see out of the way."

"Only they couldn't pull Yellow Rose off, and now maybe Cleese is back with a vengeance. Fits right into what Daniels hinted at and Bill Carlisle alluded to."

"Say Cleese has been buying his gear from the Alvarezes, boss," Belamo picked up. "Sounds like you showed up at the Coconut Grove when he was trying to cover his trail."

"But he left me with a trail to follow in the process, didn't he? Tap into Alvarez's line and maybe I can trace the arms shipments that went Cleese's way. Follow them all the way to the top."

To accomplish that Blaine was returning to Miami to re-trace the steps that had led him first to Vincente Ventanna

and then to Carlos Alvarez at Cocowalk in the minutes prior
to the battle that had virtually destroyed the mall.

"Can I get you something to drink, sir?"

"Club soda," McCracken said to the stewardess in the
A-300 Airbus's first-class section. "With a twist."

She smiled and moved back toward the galley.

Blaine hadn't had even a sip of alcohol since Vietnam
over twenty years before. There were times over there when
booze was the only thing that helped him get through, so
much so that he swore off it entirely as soon as his service
was finished. Maybe he was afraid drinking would bring the
feeling of the war back to him. Maybe he was afraid of ex-
panding the down-time dependence he had developed.

At last the big plane began to back away from the gate
and start its taxi toward the runway. The flight had been delayed for nearly an hour, first by an anomalous on-board
count apparently caused by a passenger who'd checked in
and failed to get on the plane. Then a new cart of meals arrived to replace one that contained the wrong entrées.
McCracken tried to relax through it all, but his thoughts
wouldn't let him.

He gazed down and saw his club soda resting in the
proper slot on the center armrest. He didn't even remember
the stewardess bringing it. The seat next to him was empty,
as were most in the first-class section. The captain came
over the PA to report that they were rapidly climbing toward
their cruising altitude of 35,000 feet. A flight attendant's
voice replaced the captain's to announce that the meal
would be served shortly.

An uneasy chill slid up McCracken's spine. A passenger
had checked in but not boarded. The new meal cart had
been loaded *after* this anomaly had shown up.

The chill deepened.

Blaine's thoughts tumbled through his brain. It was possible, even probable, that by now those he was pursuing had
placed him with Tom Daniels in Rock Creek Park last night.
And if they presumably knew that Daniels had uncovered

Operation Yellow Rose, and by association Arlo Cleese, the Miami connection would be obvious. But if Blaine was simply being watched, his tail should have been on board right now. Unless the tail's failure to board indicated a different strategy had been opted for, the meals replaced in order for the opposition to place something else on the plane.

Blaine got up from his seat and moved through the curtain into the coach section of the plane. A pair of meal carts were being wheeled down either aisle, just behind the drink wagons. Flight attendants were politely asking the passengers for their choice of entrée and beverage. McCracken angled toward the meal cart in the left-hand aisle. He pretended to be patiently waiting to slide past it, uncertain at this point what his inspection could realistically entail, under the circumstances.

He might have remained uncertain if he hadn't heard the voice of the flight attendant from the other aisle: "There's one wedged in there. If you'll just be patient, I'll . . ."

McCracken slid sideways across a center row of four seats. He shoved the lowered tray tables upward, spilling two plastic cups of soda and jostling against the knees of the dismayed passengers.

In the neighboring aisle, the flight attendant was still struggling to free the jammed food tray. She seemed to have located the problem and was about to yank when Blaine snapped a hand down to hold her forearm in place.

"Sir?"

"Take your hand off the tray and remove it slowly."

"What seems to be the problem here?" another flight attendant was asking.

McCracken ignored her. His eyes remained fixed on the blue-clad young woman whose hand was still resting on the stuck tray.

"Do as I told you." And he squeezed her forearm just enough to force her to comply. The stewardess removed her arm slowly. A slightly older flight attendant who seemed to be in charge approached from the rear of the coach cabin.

"I'm going to have to ask you to return to your seat, sir."

McCracken closed to within a foot of her and leaned forward. "I think there's a bomb in the cart," he said softly.

Fear and uncertainty mingled in the head flight attendant's eyes. She looked back and forth from Blaine to the meal cart.

"You're really going to have to return to your seat," she repeated. "Please, sir."

"Fine, as long as this cart comes with me."

McCracken started to wheel the cart forward. The head flight attendant thought about trying to stop him, then simply helped steer the cart to avoid a commotion.

The captain was waiting back in the first-class cabin when Blaine slid the cart through the curtain. "I'm going to have to insist that you take your seat, sir. The alterna—"

"He says he thinks there's a bomb in the meal cart," the head flight attendant whispered.

"What?"

"Not thinks," Blaine corrected, his hand feeling for the tray the younger stewardess thought was stuck. "It's here, all right." His face squinted as he struggled to reach in deeper. "And I ... think ... I've ... found it."

Several of the first-class passengers had turned toward him. The captain took a step closer to the meal cart to block their view of what McCracken was doing.

"Who *are* you?" the captain demanded.

"The man this bomb was placed here to kill. Also the man who might be able to disarm it."

"*Disarm* it? If you're right, I'm declaring an emergency and turning this plane around."

"Probably not a good idea."

"Get your hand out of there!"

McCracken removed it slowly, his cursory inspection completed. "Listen, Captain, unless I miss my guess this bomb was activated at a certain altitude and is rigged to explode when our descent eventually takes us to that same altitude again."

The captain's expression wavered. "How can we be sure?"

"I remove it for closer inspection."

McCracken set up shop in the cramped confines of the first-class galley. A set of tools pulled from an emergency chest were at his disposal, along with steak knives and other utensils from the galley. With the help of the head flight attendant, whose name was Judy, and Captain Hollis, he removed all the trays in the cart except the ones in the immediate vicinity of the bomb. Then he angled himself backwards and with the help of a flashlight peered in at what remained.

The bomb was there, all right: sophisticated, a kind he had seen several times before. The wiring was all internal, connecting the microcircuits to four inlaid layers of C-4 plastic explosives. A pair of computer chips acted as the bomb's brain and controlled its intricate sensor system. It was wedged against the back wall of the cart, built to the specifications of a food tray and attached to the ones immediately above and beneath it. The bomb was not rigged to timer detonation. It could be triggered either by the removal of one of the attached trays or, on the chance neither tray was withdrawn, by the change in pressure that accompanies descent to a certain altitude.

"Well?" the captain inquired when McCracken eased himself out.

"Hand me a steak knife and a screwdriver," Blaine said to Judy before responding. Then he turned to Hollis. "Five minutes, Captain."

Actually it was closer to ten. The sophisticated guts of the bomb were enclosed in a black steel casing, custom-drilled to allow the proper number of wires to be snaked out from it. It was affixed to the back of the cart with simple adhesive which Blaine was easily able to slice through. In fact, he felt the explosive slide free before he was ready.

"Captain," he called.

"Right here."

"I want you to reach into the cart and slide the two remaining trays outward when I tell you. I can't take a chance on severing the wires connecting them to the bomb's housing until I've had a closer look."

Sweat dropped into McCracken's eyes and he paused to blink it away.

"Okay, Captain. Reach inside and tell me when you've got the trays."

Blaine felt the captain's arms graze up against him en route to the trays.

"I've got them."

"Both?"

"Yes."

"Start sliding them toward you now. I'm holding the bomb in my hand and it's still wired to the trays. We've got to move exactly together . . . That's it . . . Easy . . . Easy . . . ."

McCracken brought the bomb forward from its perch in rhythm with the captain's pace. As soon as the trays began to clear the cart, Judy took the top one in hand, leaving the captain with only the bottom.

The bomb emerged in Blaine's hands last, behind a trail of wires attaching it to the trays. It was a foot long by ten inches wide and three inches in depth. Its black casing revealed no exterior controls.

McCracken straightened himself up so he was between Judy and Captain Hollis. Together they approached the area of the galley that had been cleared of all clutter. The contents of the trays clanged a bit when placed down on the counter. Blaine laid the bomb between them.

He leaned over and inspected the steel housing with the flashlight. He probed some of the screw holes with the end of a steak knife and then a screwdriver. Apparently satisfied, he pulled a pair of scissors to him and cut the wires connecting the bomb to the trays.

Captain Hollis sighed audibly. "Is that it?"

"Not by a long shot. I've only deactivated the sensor mechanism. It'll still blow up sometime in the midst of our descent when the proper pressure sets off the internal detonator."

"Can you disarm it?"

Blaine looked up and shook his head. "The casing is booby-trapped. Remove it and the bomb detonates."

"You're saying you can't disarm it, and if I take us down, it will explode," Captain Hollis concluded.

"Yes."

"In other words, we're stuck up here until our fuel runs out."

"Not necessarily."

"No?"

"There's one alternative." Blaine's eyes held the captain's. "We can get the bomb off the plane."

CHAPTER 13

It took Captain Hollis a long moment to realize that McCracken wasn't kidding.

"In case you haven't noticed, that bomb is too big to fit through a window, and opening a door at 25,000 feet isn't a very good idea."

Blaine thought briefly. "Is there access into the baggage compartment from this level?"

"You're standing on it," said Judy, the head flight attendant.

"There's a panel we can remove," Hollis elaborated. "But if you're thinking about opening one of the cargo doors—"

"I'm not."

"Then—"

"I'll need a rope, or the closest thing you've got to one," McCracken continued, moving his eyes from Hollis to Judy. "And all the vodka you've got on board."

"I hope Absolut will do," she returned.

"So long as it's hundred proof, it'll do fine."

Blaine explained his plan while a eight-foot length of strung-together nylon seat belts soaked in three liters of vodka in one of the galley sinks. He had already sliced the mask extremity off a small emergency oxygen tank, so that activating it would send the oxygen rushing out the tube like an open nozzle.

"Wait a minute," Hollis said before McCracken had finished his explanation, "even if this works you're still gonna get yourself sucked out of the aircraft and crash us in the process."

"I won't get sucked out if I tie myself down to the frame somehow. And if I can get the compartment sealed again before total depressurization, you'll be able to maintain control."

"Sealed? How do you think you can go about sealing a two-foot square hole in the bottom of the plane?"

Blaine's mind worked quickly. "Lots of luggage be jostling around, of course."

"For sure."

"All being sucked toward the hole."

"Plenty right on through."

"But not all."

The captain's face brightened for the first time. "Yes! Yes, goddamnit, it just might work!" Then he sobered again. "Doesn't do much to help you down there, though."

"There's a tie line strung across the width of the baggage hold," Judy pointed out. "I've seen handlers use it to tie down bags. It's connected up with the frame. If you strap yourself onto it, you won't be sucked out."

McCracken nodded.

"Just give me time to get this thing turned around and headed back for Washington," Hollis instructed. "Best-case scenario, we're still gonna need an emergency landing."

"I could live with that, Captain."

* * *

"It'll take me a few minutes to get everything rigged," McCracken said after they had returned to the Washington area.

On the ground at National, emergency preparations were under way. On the plane the thin carpeting had been pulled up on the galley floor and a panel removed to reveal the entrance to the cargo hold.

"Time for me to prepare the passengers," nodded Hollis.

Blaine started to lower himself through the hatch. "Happy landings."

"See you on the ground."

The bomb was tucked carefully in a pack strung to his shoulders, padded with towels to prevent it from being jostled. Also contained in the pack was the vodka-soaked eight-foot length of seat belts as well as the customized oxygen tank. A larger portable oxygen tank dangled across his chest. The mask attached to it was wrapped about his neck. Around his waist he had looped a twenty-foot length of tight nylon rope pulled from an emergency kit. He would use the rope to fasten himself to the cargo hold's tie line to keep from being sucked out of the plane.

The dark cold embraced McCracken as he descended into the hold. Thin ceiling lights streamed down, casting a dull glow over the neatly arranged luggage. The flight was crowded, and as a result the baggage compartment was packed. Blaine reached the floor as the hatch above him was sealed.

He followed the tie line toward the front of the plane and cleared a spot on the floor of luggage. The hole he needed to create in the plane's aluminum skin had to be large enough to drop the bomb through but not so large that it would be impossible to plug with the flying luggage. With that in mind, he removed the alcohol-laden seat belts from his pack and arranged them carefully into a two-foot square on the floor of the hold where only an inch of aluminum lay between him and the open air. He then rose and began using the rope looped around his waist to adhere himself to the tie line.

This was the most sensitive task of all, for he needed to be fastened tight enough to keep him from being sucked out but loose enough to allow for the easy and swift completion of the task before him. Blaine achieved the best compromise he could manage and pulled an emergency flare from his pocket. He yanked the fuse free and the bright orange flame flickered and flared. McCracken let it drop on the squared seat belts and the alcohol caught instantly. Flames rose along the rectangular outline, blackening the floor.

Alone, these flames would hardly be sufficient to burn through the Airbus's outer skin. But feed the fire with a flood of oxygen from the portable tank he'd brought with him, and the heat of the flames would rise exponentially, eating through the aluminum like paper. It would happen fast and Blaine had to be ready to drop the bomb through as soon as it did in the last moment before depressurization. For this reason he drew the bomb from his pack and held it against his chest with his left hand while his right tightened its grip on the emergency oxygen tank. It felt like a large can of hair spray to him, and with the mask sliced off to expose the tubing, it functioned pretty much the same way as one as well.

His shoulders, waist, and legs strapped to the tie line, Blaine leaned over to bring the oxygen as close as possible to the alcohol-fueled fire. First he made sure the mask attached to the larger tank strung to his chest was fitted around his mouth. Then he tightened his grasp on the bomb and pressed the smaller, hand-held tank's nozzle.

An audible *poof!* followed as the flames first swelled upward and then burned white-hot. They cut through the plane's outer skin in no time, a two-foot-square hole burned open right before his eyes. The first gush of outside air shoved the last of the flames back up at him as he dropped the bomb toward the opening. McCracken feared that the sudden rush had stripped him of the stability required to ac-

curately release the steel casing. But the bomb slid straight
through the hole he had created, certain to detonate harmlessly at whatever altitude it had been set for.

In the next moment it seemed that all the air was sucked
out of the hold. Even with the oxygen pumping home
through his mask, Blaine felt as if something had reached in
and stripped the air from him as well. His ears bubbled and
his head pounded. He could feel the plane wobbling, shaking in the air as it plunged through the sky nose-first. His
insides seemed to join it. He felt himself being whipped
about, the pressure testing his bonds to the tie line to the
fullest.

The feeling conjured thoughts of a wild free-fall while
parachuting, albeit one through an obstacle course as
McCracken was jolted from all directions by flying luggage.
A suitcase smashed him from the rear. He got his hands up
in time to ward off a leather tote and then ducked under a
duffel bag heading straight for his face. He caught glimpses
of larger pieces of luggage being sucked through the hole in
the bomb's wake. He knew even now the fissure he had created would be widening, soon to spread the length of the entire hull unless the flying debris was able to plug up the
hole and relieve the pressure.

Luggage continued to fly about. Pieces of all shapes and
sizes wedged briefly in the fissure before being sucked
through. The loss of pressurization continued to toss
McCracken about at will, even as he searched for a means
to aid the plugging process before it was too late. Directly
beneath him pieces of luggage swirled and shifted about as
if hurrying for their turn to be expelled, swirling through in
a whirlpool-like stream. It was like watching water going
down a drain, no hope of the hole being plugged up in the
process.

Blaine felt the nose of the Airbus dip even more, time
running out faster than he had expected. That realization led
him to tear his legs and arms free of the holds he had tied
them into. Fastened in only at the waist now, McCracken

began reaching out to shove luggage forward and pile it atop the fissure to keep the chasm closed for more than an instant. He heaved for oxygen with each hoist. He felt light-headed and willed himself not to pass out. The layer of suitcases thinned as soon as he built it up, and he just kept heaving piece upon piece into the center of the maelstrom. Staying even was as good as getting ahead, so long as he could keep up the pace.

He felt the plane level off briefly before settling into an uneasy emergency descent toward National Airport. Blaine continued to work the chasm desperately until he heard the whir that signaled the lowering of the Airbus's landing gear. He barely had time to refasten himself haphazardly to the tie line before the plane swooped in for what he expected would be a jarring jolt of a landing. He could barely believe it when he felt Hollis bring the Airbus down gently and ease into a slow glide down the runway. In the passenger compartment above him, Blaine could hear the cheers and applause.

The Airbus was still taxiing when he began the process of clearing the luggage he had piled from the fissure. A jagged tear stretched out five feet in both directions from the hole that was now twice as large as the one he had fashioned. Blaine dropped out through the fissure a moment before the emergency chutes activated and helped the first passengers down the nearest chute get to their feet.

Captain Hollis was the last one to slide off.

"I'd fly with you anytime, Captain," Blaine said, helping him up.

Hollis grabbed Blaine at the shoulders. "You've earned your wings, Mr. McCracken."

More emergency vehicles continued to arrive, sirens and flashing lights preceding them. The rescue workers had little to do other than gather the passengers up and begin the chore of loading them onto the waiting buses.

"Then do me a favor, Captain," Blaine said, "and don't mention to anyone that I was on board."

Hollis gazed back at the hole Blaine had dropped the bomb through to save his plane. "Not an easy trick, under the circumstances."

"Stall them, then."

Hollis took a long look at the bruises across Blaine's face, courtesy of the flying luggage. "I get the feeling this kind of thing is nothing new for you."

"You might say that."

"I'll do what I can."

"Captain!" a new voice rang out.

Hollis turned briefly to acknowledge the rescue boss. "Thing is," he began as he turned back Blaine's way. He let the sentence dangle.

McCracken was gone.

CHAPTER 14

Ben Samuelson's call reached the President while he was dressing for a state dinner with representatives of both the Israeli and Arab negotiating teams. The Mideast peace process had become yet another quagmire that had bedeviled his eighteen-month tenure. Tonight's dinner marked a concerted attempt on his part to get the process going again. As soon as he got off the phone with Samuelson, though, the President buzzed his appointments secretary and instructed him to bump the dinner back an hour at the risk of offending his guests.

The FBI chief was ushered into his private office twenty minutes later. A handleless briefcase was tucked tightly under his arm. He had asked to see the President alone, without even Charlie Byrne in attendance.

"Only you can make the decision of who should share the information I'm bringing with me, sir," Samuelson had explained.

"You were rather coy on the phone, Ben," the President started, the door to his private office closed again.

The head of the FBI stood before him stiffly. "Let me go in order, sir. First off, Langley has confirmed from the logs that Tom Daniels met with the director on three separate occasions over the past ten days. The last meeting took place this past Thursday, the evening prior to the murders."

"Is that unusual?"

"In and of itself, yes, because by all accounts Daniels skipped channels and went straight to Jardine. I could accept that happening once. But three times could mean only that Daniels had Jardine's blessing to pursue whatever he was on to."

"I don't suppose those logs included a summary of what they discussed."

"No, sir, they didn't. At that point I was at a dead end, with no more to go on other than the feeling that the two murders were connected."

"I gather you have more to go on than that now."

"If I may, sir . . ."

"Please."

Samuelson moved to the Queen Anne writing desk over on the right. He placed his briefcase atop it, careful to skirt the unkempt piles of the President's personal correspondence.

"Two hours ago I received a call from the Russian ambassador insisting he had to see me immediately on a matter vital to national security."

"Ours, I assume."

"Quite," Samuelson acknowledged and withdrew the cassette tape former KGB station chief Sergei Amorov had given to Vasily Conchenko. "Apparently, one of the last accomplishments of the KGB was to plant a bug inside Jardine's office."

"And it went *undetected*?"

"By all indications, yes. For years."

"Years? Then . . ."

"Yes, Mr. President, the bug remained active after the KGB was withdrawn. Ambassador Conchenko assures me no foul play was intended. Either way, the placement of the bug proved most fortunate." Samuelson's eyes shifted to the cassette. "Thanks to it, and thanks to our friend Ambassador Conchenko, we now have a copy of this tape which was made Thursday night."

"My God," the President realized. "Jardine's final meeting with Daniels."

Samuelson removed a thin tape player from his briefcase and popped the cassette in. He pushed PLAY and the voice of Clifton Jardine filled the room.

"How many copies of this are there, Mr. Daniels?"

McCracken used the chaos enveloping all of National Airport as cover to flee. A cab brought him to Dulles, where he just made the evening's last plane to Miami. A half hour after the thankfully uneventful flight had landed, Blaine was back at Strumpet's, a mostly private club located in the basement of another building in South Beach. The lack of windows, if anything, added to the ambience. Strumpet's was dark enough for people to hide out in the open. The single bar room was decorated in shades of peach and mauve, lit by electrified reproductions of Victorian gaslights. Its large bar was slightly curved and paneled in dark wood that matched the room's walls.

The man who had put Blaine on to Ventanna was drinking in the same corner booth he had been in Thursday night. He was dressed all in black. Oil slicked his hair back and had taken the wave from it. The gold chains dangling from his neck glinted faintly in the dim light. He pretended not to see Blaine approaching.

"Hello, Rafael," McCracken said from over him.

Rafael didn't look up. "You fucked me good, you asshole."

"Did I?"

"You set up Alvarez. They find out I helped you, I'm dead."

"I had nothing to do with the Coconut Grove hit. And I came back to Miami to go after the real perps, Raffy."

Rafael drained the rest of what looked like vodka on the rocks. "I buy you a drink?"

"I'd settle for more info."

"Sorry. Fresh out."

Blaine continued to stand. "Alvarez was selling to Arlo Cleese. Name ring a bell?"

"Can't say that it does."

"Sixties revolutionary who apparently hasn't given up the cause. It's possible he wants to finish the revolution he helped start a generation ago, with the help of firepower supplied by Alvarez."

"He and his kid both got whacked for their efforts. That's what you're saying?"

McCracken nodded. "Because Cleese must have all that he needs. That means whatever he's planning to do is going to happen soon."

"He's who you're after . . ."

"And I can find him by following the trail of the guns Alvarez shipped out of Miami."

A waitress arrived and set a fresh vodka on the rocks down on a napkin in front of Rafael.

"I could make some calls," he offered when she was gone.

"Tell them I'm after whoever it was killed their boss and his kid. Tell them I don't usually fail."

McCracken accompanied Rafael to a private dock on Biscayne Bay two hours later.

"Must be them now," Rafael said as a sleek 32-foot Gulfstar cabin cruiser approached, running with a single light.

The cabin cruiser slid up against the dock. A big man in shiny clothes jumped off and held it against a pylon while

Blaine climbed on board. Instantly flanked by an armed man on either side of him, McCracken looked back toward Rafael.

Rafael held his ground and waved. "Have a good life, *amigo*."

McCracken couldn't have said for sure at that point what the intentions of the men on the crowded cruiser were. He counted five in all: the two flanking him, the one who had held the boat in place, a driver, and a final man atop an open air bridge who was holding a Mac-10 submachine gun.

"Your gun, please," the one closest to him said.

Blaine surrendered his SIG-Sauer and the man wedged it into his belt. The Gulfstar set off.

His escorts gave no indication where they were heading and McCracken didn't ask. He simply stood at the rail in the warm night air and tried to relax.

The cruiser made good speed through the calm night waters. An hour into the voyage, Blaine made out the shape of a large yacht silhouetted against the moonlit horizon. When it came clearly into view, he recognized it as an 82-foot Hatteras motor yacht, complete with twin Detroit 875-horsepower engines. Strictly top of the line, at a cost of maybe two million dollars. The captain drove it from a high-perched, enclosed bridge. Even from this distance, Blaine noted a figure standing high on the large top deck following the approach of the Gulfstar.

As McCracken tried to get a better view of the figure through the night, a pair of speedboats roared from around both sides of the Hatteras and sliced toward the Gulfstar. They took up positions along the cruiser's port and starboard and guided it the last stretch of the way.

A steel ladder was secured from the stern of the 82-foot Hatteras, and a pair of men on the cruiser's foredeck reached up to steady it for McCracken. Taking the signal, Blaine began to climb.

"This way," one of them greeted after McCracken had pulled himself onto the deck.

The man, conspicuous by the fact that he was unarmed, led him up to the top deck where the figure Blaine had glimpsed before stood with eyes gazing over the yacht's port. The figure turned round slowly and the moon illuminated his face.

"Manuel Alvarez," McCracken greeted, recognizing a man who was supposed to be dead from pictures Captain Martinez had shown him the day before.

"I see you are a difficult man to surprise, Mr. McCracken."

"Not always. I'm surprised you had me brought here."

"But not that I'm still alive."

"I read your file," Blaine told him. "You let them blow up the *smaller* of your two yachts."

Alvarez smiled thinly. "Vanity, I'm afraid." The smile disappeared. "You came down here expecting to find me."

"Hoping, anyway. I knew the bait would interest you."

"I was interested even before you left it. I might have contacted you myself earlier if I had known how. I looked at it as a godsend when word reached me you had returned to Miami."

Blaine started forward. "Why?"

"I have well-placed contacts inside the Miami police. They informed me of who you were, what you managed to do in the Grove. It seems you saved many lives."

"Not your son's, Mr. Alvarez."

"You would have. I know that."

"If I'd had the chance, yes."

Blaine met Alvarez at the halfway point of the upper deck. Alvarez leaned his elbows on the railing and turned his gaze back to the sea, anguish squeezing his features into a taut grimace. His naturally dark skin looked sallow. The wind ruffled his neatly coiffed hair and his thin mustache seemed to droop.

"That's why I've been hoping I'd have this chance, Mr. McCracken." He turned toward Blaine again. "I need you to avenge my son."

"That means finding Arlo Cleese, Mr. Alvarez."

Alvarez's hands tightened around the railing. "It was Cleese's people in the Grove, wasn't it?"

"If you asked the question, you don't need me to answer it."

"I warned my son to lay low. I *warned* him! He thought himself beyond danger." Alvarez sighed. "The folly of the young."

"Then you must have suspected something. That's why you faked your own death, let Cleese blow up that other yacht."

"The indications were subtle, yet present. Contact had been broken off. My man who served as conduit with Cleese disappeared last week."

"Leaving you and your son as the only sure links to him."

"I told him what he should do. I warned him of the danger. I thought he would listen."

"He was too greedy, Mr. Alvarez, a lesson learned at your knee, perhaps."

Alvarez nodded painfully, conceding the point. "You can't hurt me any more than I already have been. I know the responsibility for my son's death"—a heavy sigh—"is mine."

"You might soon be responsible for far more deaths than that."

"Because of Cleese . . ."

"You never questioned what he intended to do with your merchandise."

"He was like any other customer, Mr. McCracken. He placed his orders and I filled them." Alvarez swallowed hard. "The guns that were used in the Grove, I had them checked. I . . . I had to know." His eyes glistened. "They were part of one of the shipments I made to Cleese." A look of detached resignation crossed his features. "My own guns had been used in the killing of my only son. For that, I must make amends and you must help me."

"Stopping Cleese from killing anyone else would make a nice start."

"Whatever it takes. I can give you the location of the storage facility where our shipments to him ended up." More pain stretched over Alvarez's face. "I could have had the cache of weapons I supplied him destroyed, I suppose, but that hardly qualifies as justice. It's Cleese who must pay for this, but he has to be found first."

"And for that you need me."

Alvarez turned his gaze vacantly in the sea's direction once more. "After you find him, Mr. McCracken, I will supply any and all help that you need to do what must be done." His eyes came back to Blaine. "For my son."

"For the country, *amigo*."

CHAPTER 15

Kristen Kurcell had called Senator Jordan from Duncan Farlowe's office before leaving Grand Mesa.

"You should have told me what was going on before you left," Jordan said softly. "I've been so worried. Jesus, I would have helped you."

"I'm sorry. I just panicked. I . . . didn't know it was going to be this bad."

"I'm the one who's sorry, Kris. But I'll be waiting at the airport when you land. We're going to take this on together. Hell hath no fury like an angry senator with a crucial committee seat."

Jordan's driver was standing next to the Lincoln's rear passenger door when Kristen stepped out of the terminal Saturday night. The man saw her and pulled the door open. Kristen hurried over and placed her single small overnight bag in his outstretched hand. Then she plunged into the backseat.

Inside the senator was waiting. They embraced and Kristen felt Jordan's lips sliding toward hers and turned away at the last.

"It's okay," Jordan said soothingly, kissing her on the cheek instead. "You're home now."

Samantha Jordan held Kristen tightly against her as her driver restarted the Lincoln's engine.

Samantha Jordan had not made any advances toward Kristen until the night they had celebrated her promotion to chief of staff eighteen months before. A wonderful dinner had been followed by a bottle of champagne at the senator's townhouse. They sat together on the couch sipping glass after glass, Kristen becoming uneasily aware that Jordan was moving ever closer to her. One of the senator's hands began to stroke her knee and then slid slowly up the inside of her thigh.

Kristen pulled away. Their eyes met and in that instant of silent embarrassment she knew. It was in Samantha Jordan's stare even if it hadn't been in her words. Kristen had left the townhouse and walked home in a stupor.

Perhaps she should have resigned the next day. She could never recall a time in her twenty-seven years when she'd felt more uncomfortable and ill at ease. But that would have meant throwing away a friendship with the person who had been there for Kristen during the most difficult time of her life in the summer preceding the election in '92. Samantha Jordan had canceled two days of campaigning to be by her side for her parents' funeral. She had helped with the arrangements, helped with everything. Kristen didn't know what she would have done without her, glad to be able to return the favor when an unpleasant divorce ended with Jordan losing custody of her two children just two months later.

Kristen had spent the night the final decree had come down with the senator just talking, and she did not see the inside of Samantha Jordan's townhouse again until the night they celebrated her promotion in November. She knew Jordan was lonely and, since the divorce, given to frequent bouts of depression. She accepted the attempted seduction as an upshot of that tumultuous emotional combination.

But more attempts followed in the succeeding eighteen months, inevitably mirroring Jordan's lowest times. They always ended in the same innocent fashion with Kristen helping the senator up to her bedroom and then sleeping downstairs to be there in case Jordan awoke with the bout of depression still in progress.

Washington loves rumors, and those linking the two women amorously were among the hottest for a time. They continued to simmer in large part because Kristen did not bother to refute them, afraid that drawing more attention to the situation might bring Samantha Jordan's emotional instability to light and destroy the brilliant career that alone was holding the senator together. Beyond that, there was no man in her life Kristen could point to in order to repudiate the story, and there hadn't been for some time. The death of her parents had torn away any desire she had for a relationship and had severely constrained her urge for physical pleasure. Whenever she started to feel good, guilt inevitably entered in. She thrust herself into her career, because working was the only thing that took her mind off everything else.

Kristen would languish through the long nights alone downstairs in the senator's townhouse, glad at least to be able to share the hole her emotions had fallen into. The only man she could see herself taking up with again would be one who could provide the kind of strength she tried to provide Samantha Jordan during her worst spats with depression. A friend first, who asked for nothing more than what she was capable of giving, who wouldn't let her down.

Following Kristen's desperate call from Colorado, Samantha Jordan hadn't let her down. With Kristen on the verge of slipping into a vortex of hopelessness after the

gruesome death of her brother, she had reached down and
pulled her up.

"We've got an appointment tomorrow morning at the
Pentagon with the head ordnance officer for all stateside
military bases," the senator said as her driver pulled the Lincoln away from the curb.

"On a Sunday?"

"The Pentagon knows who to open their offices up to,
babe."

"Have you found out anything about Paul Gathers?"
Kristen asked her.

"From what I've been able to piece together, his assignment was strictly routine."

"But did you speak to him?"

"It's not time to force the issue yet, Kris. But when the
time comes, there's no one better at doing the forcing."

At the Pentagon Sunday morning, it was all Kristen could
do to keep up with the senator's pace down the corridors.
The woman was a dynamo. Nothing and no one got in her
way. She had bulldozed her way through subcommittee after
subcommittee until the spot on the appropriations committee
opened up. The party hierarchy was afraid of what she
might do if they didn't choose her. Samantha got the seat.

Jordan double-checked the number on the office they had
stopped at and then stepped in without knocking or an-
nouncing herself to the receptionist.

"Senator Samantha Jordan, Colonel," she announced to a
uniformed figure seated behind the desk after closing the
door. "And this is my chief of staff Kristen Kurcell."

Colonel Haynes came out of his chair, checking his
watch. "I'm sorry, Senator, but I thought our appointment
was for—"

"I'm a little early. Now let's cut the bullshit and get right
down to it, if that's all right with you, Colonel Haynes."

"Of course," Haynes said, tripping over his words. "Of
course, Senator." He didn't sit down.

"I want to talk to you about Miravo Air Force Base in Colorado."

"Miravo?"

The senator turned to Kristen and nodded.

"My brother saw something happen there last Thursday night," Kristen began and then proceeded to tell the story, steeling herself from more tears when she came to the part about identifying David's body.

Colonel Haynes listened intently, an increasingly perplexed look drawn over his features. When Kristen had finished, he moved from behind his desk deliberately and closed the door to his office.

"Senator Jordan," he said, standing rigid, "what's your security clearance?"

"I serve on two subcommittees of the Senate Armed Services Committee, Colonel. My clearance is G-5, and they don't come any higher than that."

"Then I'm going to assume for the moment that Ms. Kurcell's is the same. I think the two of you should sit down."

"I think we'll stand."

"As you wish. Senator, your assistant—"

"Chief of staff."

"—chief of staff claims Miravo is abandoned, mothballed."

"Yes," Kristen chimed in. "As of yesterday anyway."

"That's impossible. You see, it's been up and functional again for six months."

"Not according to the logs furnished my subcommittee, Colonel," said Jordan with a hard edge to her voice.

Haynes hedged. "I think perhaps my superiors should brief you on this."

"You report directly to the Joint Chiefs, Colonel, and both of us know it. I believe you can handle the chore equally well."

Haynes nodded slowly. "Miravo's reopening was authorized under a blank standard your appropriations committee authorized, Senator."

"Wait a minute, did you say *re*opening?"

"Yes. Miravo along with several other mothballed bases in strategic locations across the country."

"Why? What exactly is it that was supposedly authorized by my committee?"

"The dismantling and destruction of nuclear warheads in accordance with the latest disarmament treaties. Miravo and the other similarly isolated bases were retasked and reoutfitted accordingly."

"I'm telling you it was deserted," Kristen insisted.

"Then you weren't at Miravo."

"I'm sure it was Miravo. Christ, I was almost killed in the hills surrounding it!"

"I toured the base myself just last month, ma'am."

"My brother was killed because of something he saw going on there. I was almost killed because I followed his trail to the base."

"I'm sorry about your brother, but he couldn't have been at Miravo."

"You're saying the base was active *Thursday* night," Kristen badgered.

"Yes."

"As well as yesterday?"

"Yes, ma'am." Haynes relaxed just a little. "Senator, I'm going to order a full investigation. I'm going to—"

"No," interrupted Samantha Jordan. "No investigations. I'm flying out there today to see for myself, and I'd appreciate it if base personnel were not forewarned of my coming."

"That's highly irregular, Senator."

"So is Miss Kurcell's story."

"Which, apparently, you believe."

"Yes," Jordan said, eyes on Kristen. "Yes, I do."

* * *

En route to Huntsville State Penitentiary in Texas from Gainesville, Johnny Wareagle tried to tell himself that Chief Silver Cloud had been mistaken. If Traggeo was in prison, he could not have been responsible for Will Shortfeather's disappearance, nor could the old chief's vision of another, more recent murder be correct. Johnny wanted to believe that the killer was behind bars, as the sheriff's deputy in Gainesville had assured him; that the years had finally blurred the great Silver Cloud's eyes. But the resolve that had burned in the old chief's stare ruled out any error on his part, a fact confirmed by the warden of Huntsville Sunday morning.

"Traggeo was granted early parole five months ago, after serving seven months of a five-year sentence," he reported, a manila file open on his desk. A pudgy, balding man, the warden peered up at Johnny through Coke-bottle glasses.

"Who granted it?"

"The governor, it says here. Got a paper inside with his signature."

"I didn't think Texas was in the habit of granting early parole to brutal killers."

"I don't make the rules, Mr. Wareagle."

"Is there a forwarding address?"

"Of course. Let me just— Wait a minute . . . That's odd." The warden looked back at Wareagle through his thick glasses. "I'm afraid many of the blanks on this form have been left empty."

"Is there anyone here who can help me fill them in?"

"If you mean furnish information not present in this file, the answer's no. Unless . . ." The warden sifted through the file once more. "Apparently Traggeo's cellmate is still with us. Elwin Coombs, doing twenty years to life for murder. I doubt he'll be cooperative, though."

"Where can I find him?"

"You didn't let me finish. Coombs has been cited numerous times for threatening guards. He broke a chaplain's nose and hospitalized a psychiatrist during an annual examination. He doesn't like answering questions."

"Where can I find him?" Johnny repeated.

The warden relented with a shrug. "He'll be in the yard now helping to get the afternoon show of the annual rodeo ready."

"Rodeo?"

The warden explained that every year the prisoners of Huntsville Penitentiary put on a rodeo for the public. Admission was charged for bleacher seats erected in the huge yard and all the money went into a fund to be dispensed as an inmate board saw fit. The rodeo had opened on Friday and would close after this afternoon.

"He's over there," said the guard who had escorted Johnny into the yard, gesturing toward a corral. "Good luck."

Wareagle glided toward it.

The huge, barrel-chested Coombs was pouring feed into the trough before the pen of one of the bucking broncos that were the rodeo's central attraction. When he leaned over to drain the rest of a bag, Johnny shoved him through the rails into the pen.

"Hey!" he screamed as the bronco inside bucked and kicked at him. "Hey!"

Coombs climbed to his feet and circled away from the snorting monster. Its legs kicked out toward him and Coombs slammed against the pen's rear.

"Hey!"

No sooner had he yelled than Coombs saw the huge figure of an Indian grab hold of the bronco's reins and, impossibly, hold him steady.

"What the fuck, man?"

"We're going to talk about Traggeo," Johnny told him.

Wareagle gave the bronco just enough slack to lash out at Coombs again. Its hooves whistled by his face and grazed his shoulder.

Coombs waved his hands frantically. "Okay, okay! I'll talk! Just let me outta here!"

"Talk first," Johnny said and reined the bronco back in.

"Sickest fuck I ever met on the inside or the out, and let me tell ya, I met my share. I don't know why they put us in together while he was here. It wasn't like he was a bro or anything." Coombs gave Wareagle a long look. "Least not of mine."

"Mine, either. What made him sick?"

"Way he talked about people he had offed. Said it gave him a charge. Said he lived for it."

Wareagle swallowed hard. His grasp tightened on the bronco's reins.

"I remember him telling me he'd figured things all out. That's when he shaved his head."

"What had he figured out?"

"Didn't make much sense to me. Something about absorbing people's strength after he offed them." Coombs looked at him shuddering. "Said he was gonna start *wearing* the scalps of his victims."

It took all of Johnny's resolve not to show any response. He thought of Will Shortfeather's straw-colored hair atop Traggeo's shaven head.

"Then one morning 'bout, I don't know, maybe six months back, they culled him to the warden's office and he was history. Sprung from here just like that." Coombs was trying to swallow. "He musta had some major pull. That's all I know."

"Who came for him?"

"I dunno. Shit, that's the truth. Why don't you ask the goddamn warden?"

"He doesn't know, either. Tell me what you think."

"I don't think nothin' . . . but I heard stuff. 'Bout the cars that came and took him away."

"Go on."

"They had government license plates."

CHAPTER 16

The private jet landed in Denver five hours after taking off from Dulles Airport. Kristen Kurcell and Senator Samantha Jordan were the only occupants of the cabin. At the senator's insistence, their presence and plans had been made known to no one else. A rental car would take the two of them to Miravo Air Force Base.

For Kristen, the turnaround seemed impossibly quick. The truth of her brother's death had not even settled in, numbing shock still blurring the reality of it. And yet, not even twenty-four hours after identifying his body, she was returning to the place where he had witnessed something that had led to his murder.

"It's just up ahead," Kristen told Senator Jordan, who had enjoyed the rare experience of driving so much that she insisted upon doing all of it herself.

The ride had stretched into early evening Sunday, only the two hours gained in the time difference allowing them to arrive before sunset. The base appeared after the next bend in Old Canyon Road. Kristen braced herself to reexperience the same emotions she had felt when she and Farlowe had approached it little more than twenty-four hours ago.

But all she felt when Miravo came into view was shock.

Miravo Air Force Base bustled with activity. Trucks moved about and were parked where none had been present just yesterday. And troops loomed everywhere, starting with those manning a pair of Humvee vehicles that straddled the main gate as a first line of defense.

"I'm going to have to see your pass, ma'am," one of the armed soldiers said to Senator Jordan.

"Will this do?" she asked, flashing her senate ID.

The guard looked twice to make sure the picture matched her face. He stiffened briefly, saluted, and then said he would summon the base commander.

"I'm Colonel Riddick," another man greeted the two women not five minutes later. Riddick was a stocky, big-boned man with a belly that hung over his waist. "What can I do for you, Senator, er . . . ?"

She had stepped out of the car to greet him. "Jordan, Colonel."

"I'm sorry to keep you waiting, Senator."

"That's quite all right."

"I'm afraid your presence here caught me by surprise."

"As it was supposed to, Colonel."

Kristen had joined Senator Jordan outside the car now, hanging back on the passenger side.

"That's the problem, ma'am," Riddick explained. "My understanding was that Miravo and other bases like it were financed off open appropriations. You shouldn't know this place exists. No one on your committee should. That's the way everyone from the President on down wanted it."

"I'll bet the towns in the area don't even know, right, Colonel? Your civilian neighbors find out what's going on here, they're gonna come to Washington screaming." Senator Jordan hesitated to let her point sink in. "Look, you can forget all about open appropriations. Before I authorize a billion dollars in spending, you can be damn sure I'm gonna get briefed on where the money's going. In this case I happen to believe in what you're doing. Others won't once the truth gets out, as it always does. When the outcry starts, I want to have an argument ready. That's why I'm here, Colonel."

Riddick stood there taking it in. He nodded slowly in apparent satisfaction.

"Then allow me to give you the tour myself. We have on-site control teams, a half-dozen checks on each stage of the dismantling process. All our systems have redundant back-ups. You can rest assured we play things safe."

"You said dismantling," Jordan noted. "What about destruction?"

"That's not our role, Senator. Miravo was retasked to act as a clearinghouse for ordnance stockpiled stateside. The weapons brought here were never shipped overseas, never became battalion specific."

"Battalion specific?"

"Specific codes that can be authorized only by the President are required to unlock the firing mechanism of the warhead, and each overseas battalion is issued its own, specific to its ordnance."

"You're not saying the warheads are brought here *unlocked.*"

"Not at all, ma'am. They come locked, and requisite personnel are furnished with the proper code to unlock them just prior to removal of the warhead itself from the shell casing. We disassemble each unit into its component parts and then ship those component parts to bases specifically tasked to deal with them." Riddick paused. "This will all become clear once you've seen the inside of the base, Senator."

"Then what are we waiting for?"

Riddick led the way, with Kristen and Samantha Jordan walking beside him. He returned the gate guards' salutes and led them into Miravo.

"How long have you been operating here?" the senator asked just inside the gate.

"Six months now," Riddick replied, confirming Colonel Haynes's assertion back at the Pentagon.

"Straight?"

"Well, we do have occasional layovers between incoming shipments."

"Just how long do these layovers last?"

"The longest was just under a week."

"Do any personnel remain on the base?"

"Just a skeletal staff."

Ask about earlier in the week, Kristen pleaded with her eyes. *Ask if anyone was here Thursday night when David was killed.*

But the senator ignored her.

"Guards?" she asked instead.

"Round the clock, of course. You're about to witness our security precautions first-hand." Riddick started walking again. "How much do you know about the nuclear disposal process, Senator?"

"Only that we have undertaken a serious commitment to accomplish it."

"What about procedure, priority?"

"Extraordinarily little."

"Then let me give you a little background, ma'am. First a question: what do you think the first nukes off line to be brought to places like this are?"

"The big ones?"

"Strategics?"

"Yes."

"No, Senator," Riddick corrected. "The big high-yield long-range missiles that could take out Rhode Island in a heartbeat don't pose the biggest threat to the new order or world peace. It's the smaller tactical units we're responsible for dismantling here, because they're virtually maintenance free and are easily transportable."

"How are they brought here?" Kristen chimed in suddenly.

Riddick looked her way, his tone conveying a hint of annoyance. "Mostly they're flown in."

"Mostly," she echoed. "What about trucks? Are shipments ever delivered by truck?" she asked, thinking about the tracks Sheriff Duncan Farlowe had discovered leading onto the base off Old Canyon Road.

"Occasionally, ma'am."

"Under tight security?"

"Of course."

"Usually at night, right?"

Riddick had started an abrupt response when Samantha Jordan cut him off, her eyes signaling Kristen to back off.

"I think what Miss Kurcell is trying to do is get an idea of how the process works."

Riddick seemed to accept the explanation. "That's what I'm about to show both of you."

They approached an airplane hangar that from the outside looked relatively mundane, except for the armed guards that surrounded it, each stationed every ten feet. Kristen also noticed, as she peripherally had yesterday, that all the windows had been covered over by shiny steel sheeting.

Drawing closer to the entrance, she was surprised to find only a single ordinary door with guards poised on either side of it. Riddick exchanged salutes with them and then extracted an ordinary key from his pocket. He opened the door and beckoned the senator and Kristen to follow him inside.

They stepped into a cramped vestibule with off-white walls. A steel door lay directly before them. Again armed guards stood on either side of it. At waist level behind them, a pair of matching slots protruded slightly from the wall. In this case another pair of guards toting automatic weapons stood ominously by in the corners of the room.

"Good afternoon, Colonel," the guard on the right-hand side of the door greeted.

"Who has the watch, Sergeant?"

"I do, sir." The man gazed at Kristen and Senator Jordan but didn't question their presence.

"Let's do it, then."

"Today's code first, sir."

Riddick moved to a keypad behind the guard's shoulder and pressed in the proper combination of numbers. A green light came on. At that point both he and the sergeant pulled thin chains from around their necks. Dangling from the ends were matching flat rectangular metallic keys. Kristen watched as the sergeant moved to the slot on the door's left, while the colonel started his key toward the one on the right. He inserted it slightly ahead of the sergeant.

"On my mark," Riddick ordered. "One, two, *three*."

They turned their keys to the right simultaneously. A chime followed and then the door slid slowly open. Kristen had started to walk through when Colonel Riddick reached out and grabbed her.

"Bad idea, ma'am."

And she looked up to see a dozen automatic rifles poised at her from inside a much larger vestibule. Riddick turned to Senator Jordan.

"Standard three-zone security, Senator," he explained. "At our bases in Europe it's done with barbed wire. At Miravo we elected to make use of what the spacious hangars provided."

"They shoot anyone who enters without access," Jordan concluded. "Is that it?"

"It's much more complicated than that, ma'am. The idea is to create a number of zones that must be penetrated before final access is achieved. The team inside here is charged with assessing the situation and then determining if self-destruct is mandated."

"And if it is, Colonel?"

"Let me show you."

Inside a chamber that occupied the remainder of the hangar were dozens of green fiberglass rectangular storage containers. The security detail inside, though, was surprisingly light when compared with that of the previous zone.

"Nine men," Riddick explained, watching Kristen counting. "If penetration gets this far, the self-destruct order would have already been given. Three of the nine constantly on duty have the proper code to activate the procedure into a transistorized control. The duty rotates on a daily basis.

No one on the shift knows who has it. All they know are their own orders."

"I'm impressed, Colonel," complimented Senator Jordan.

"This final fail-safe measure is actually superfluous, ma'am, because even if someone managed to get the tacticals contained in those green storage containers out, they'd still need the proper codes to activate the warheads."

"Which even here continue to be changed on a daily basis as well, I assume."

"Yes, ma'am. But there's something else to consider: since these particular warheads were never shipped overseas, they lack the fuses needed to complete the arming process. So even *with* the right code, they couldn't be made to fire."

Kristen wrapped her arms about herself, suddenly feeling chilly.

"The temperature in this chamber is kept at a constant sixty-eight humidity-free degrees, ma'am," Colonel Riddick explained. "To keep what's inside each of these green boxes stable. You see, this building was specially reconstructed and retrofitted prior to work at Miravo commencing. Reinforced to be able to handle a tornado and outfitted with blast doors and shutters in the unlikely event of an attack on the base."

"But there's no chance that these warheads could be detonated, even if that transpired," Senator Jordan mused.

"None at all, Senator."

"How difficult would it be to make them active?" Kristen asked him.

Riddick looked perturbed, but answered her anyway. "Assuming you had the fuses, you'd need the unlocking code of each charge both to install them and to activate the warhead."

"That's all."

"That's quite a lot, ma'am. As I said before, the fuses aren't even present on this base."

"Just how powerful is one of these, Colonel?" the senator

wondered, her hand stopping just short of the nearest green container.

"Each charge is two or three times as powerful yield-wise as the bombs used on Hiroshima and Nagasaki, Senator. So far as damage rendered, that would depend on too many variables for me to give you an accurate analysis. For instance . . ."

Kristen continued listening as Riddick's words grew increasingly technical. Everything he had said made perfect sense, except there was no way he could account for this base being utterly deserted only yesterday. And the only explanation for that was his involvement in what was going on.

Involvement in whatever was responsible for her brother's death.

CHAPTER 17

"Riddick's lying," Kristen said from the driver's seat after the colonel had escorted them back to their car. "There was nobody here yesterday, Sam."

"Meaning . . ."

"They put all this back together when they found out you were coming."

"They?"

"Yes."

"Who?"

"*I don't know!*"

The senator touched Kristen's arm tenderly. "Yesterday could have been one of those down periods Riddick mentioned."

"Riddick also mentioned a skeletal force and full-time security. They weren't around when I was here."

"Because you didn't see them."

"Yes."

"But you didn't go near any of the hangars, did you?"

"No."

"And besides what's inside them, this base looks totally ordinary. Right?"

"Yes."

The senator took a deep breath. "Then maybe security *was* here, Kris."

Kristen looked at her quizzically across the bench seat.

"You said you and that sheriff were accosted."

"We were shot at, almost killed."

"After you broke into the base."

"Well . . ."

"Yes or no?"

"Yes."

"Is it possible, then, is it at all possible, Kris, that the men who shot at you were guards?"

Instead of vehemently denouncing this assertion as she intended, Kristen paused to think. The senator was proposing something she hadn't stopped to consider herself.

"They fired on us without warning, Sam."

"You said the wind had started to whip up. Maybe you didn't hear them. Maybe those first shots were warning shots. Listen, Kris, I just want to be sure."

"They weren't wearing uniforms and they weren't patrolling the base when we checked it."

"I'm not saying you're at all to blame for what happened. I'm just trying to determine the degree of fault. There *was* a security breach, a major big-time fuck-up. And maybe, just maybe, you ended up right in the middle of it. Now somebody's trying to cover their ass. Could be Riddick. Could be those lots bigger than Riddick."

Kristen swallowed hard. Her throat felt heavy. She felt herself starting to give in until she remembered David's fate. "No, Sam, it's more than that. It's more than that, and my brother saw it. He *filmed* it."

"If only we had the tape . . ."

"They must have taken it when they killed him. And

when Duncan Farlowe and I came snooping around yesterday, they tried to kill us too."

"Kris—"

"No, Senator, let me finish. Something's wrong here.
Riddick was convincing, I'll grant you that, but there's too
much he can't account for. There's a base operating that nobody, including the committee that approved the money for
its reactivation, knows about. They may have the procedures
and priorities down pat, but something went wrong. Jesus,
can you imagine some of those warheads falling into the
wrong hands?"

"You think that's what happened?"

Kristen's face twisted in anguish. "I don't know, but my
brother did. And that's why he's dead."

Riddick placed the call from the private, secure line as
soon as he returned to his office. He let it ring twice, replaced the receiver, and waited. Less than one minute later
his phone rang.

"Delphi," a voice announced simply.

And Riddick gave his report.

The man on the other end of the line hung up when Colonel Riddick finished speaking. He then unlocked the bottom right-hand drawer of his desk and slid it open to reveal
a built-in phone. The man lifted the receiver and pressed out
a long series of numbers. A beep sounded and he pressed
out more. Then two beeps, followed by one last series.

The seconds passed, stretched out to nearly a minute before a click sounded.

"System activated," droned a computer-synthesized voice.

"Delphi," the man said.

"Designation?"

"One-four-zero-two-niner. Mother's baby boy."

A brief pause.

"Voice recognition successful. Access allowed. Ple

wait for the beeps to begin message. Press the pound key to terminate message and send."

The man waited. The beeps sounded, three of them. He spoke again.

"Voice meeting tonight, ten P.M. Washington time. Necessary all members in attendance. Subject matter top priority."

The man hit the pound key.

"Message sent," said the mechanical voice.

"You're not listening to me, Sam!" Kristen repeated ten minutes into the drive.

"Pull over," the senator instructed. "Over there in that gravel lot."

Kristen pulled over and turned off the engine.

"It's you who's not listening, Kris. But you've got to start now. I'll get to the bottom of what's going on at Miravo, but you've got to give me time."

"No one gave my brother time, Sam."

"That's not fair!"

"No, it's not. It's not fair that he's dead because he saw something he wasn't supposed to on that base."

"We don't know what he saw, and we're not sure that what happened to him had anything to do with Miravo."

"He was there!"

"I'll grant you that. Only we don't know if he was there immediately before he was killed. It could have been something else altogether. Probably was."

"No!"

"Kris, be reasonable. Please." Samantha Jordan sighed impatiently. "I dropped everything else and came out here with you. I riled the whole Pentagon and compromised my position in the Senate. I went out on a limb and I'm willing to stay on it until we know the truth. But you've got to back off and let me work." Jordan stopped and lowered her voice. "Listen, Kris, I know how you feel."

"No, you don't!" Her mouth quivered. "David was all I had, Sam, all I had left."

The senator reached over and stroked Kristen's hair affectionately. "You have me," she said softly.

Kristen stiffened and grabbed the older woman's hand, forcing it from her head. "I was talking about my brother, my family."

"You're the best thing that's ever happened to me, Kris. What I've done for you—you don't understand what I've done for you."

Something in Jordan's tone disturbed Kristen, and she pulled away toward the window.

"Tell me you can put it to rest, Kris. Tell me you can let it go."

"You know I can't do that, Sam. You know I can't."

The senator's pleading eyes filled with sadness and resignation. "I wish you had come to me first. Before Gathers, before coming out here. There would have been hope, then. There would have been a chance."

"What are you talking about, Sam?"

"I told them to let me do it my way. I told them you were too important to me."

"Told *who*? Sam, what's going on?"

"I'm so sorry, Kris. God, I'm so sorry."

"Sorry for what, Sam?" Kristen snapped.

"For this," Jordan said with quivering lips.

Kristen looked down and saw a small blue-steel semiautomatic pistol in her hand.

The pistol trembled slightly.

"It didn't have to be this way, Kris."

"Sam, what are you doing? *Sam!*"

"But you're just not willing to be convinced. I was hoping after today that—that—"

Kristen felt her shock recede in favor of an all-encompassing rage. "You're a part of this! You're a part of what *killed* my brother!"

"You're a part too, Kris, because you *believe*. I know y

do. Give me a chance to explain. I can still bring you on board. I can convince them to let me."

"Convince *who*?"

The pistol was steady in Samantha Jordan's hand now. "Listen to me, Kris. I'm sorry about your brother. I'm truly sorry. It was just a terrible coincidence, a tragedy, that he was there, that he saw."

"What did he see, Sam? Tell me what he saw!"

"Join us and I'll tell you. I'll make it right, I promise. We can be together. We can always be together."

Kristen squared her shoulders toward Jordan. "You killed my brother."

"I would have stopped it. If I had known, I would have stopped it. For you, Kris. I'd do anything for you. But don't make me do this!" Samantha Jordan begged. "Don't make me kill you! I *love* you. *Please,* just listen. Hear me out."

Kristen looked her square in the eyes. "Shoot me, Sam, or I'm getting out of this car and walking away."

Senator Samantha Jordan held the gun out further, steadied in both hands now.

"Kris . . . Oh, Kris . . ."

In that moment of Jordan's lament and indecision, Kristen lunged. She went for the gun and managed to shove it up over both their heads.

The boom of a gunshot stunned them both as it echoed through the car's interior. Kristen threw herself on the older woman and fought to keep the barrel away from her. Gritty resolve filled Samantha Jordan's features. Gone was the saddened gaze present just seconds before. Eyes that had tried to show love now showed only intense anger.

Kristen gripped the senator's trigger hand to keep her from moving the barrel downward. She worked her other hand under Jordan's chin and shoved with all her strength to slam the senator's skull against the passenger side window. The glass spiderwebbed and Jordan gasped, eyes clouding slightly.

Kristen tried to tear the gun free in that moment, but

screaming, Samantha Jordan raked her face with her nails. Kristen yelped with pain and felt her hold on the senator's gun hand loosen. Jordan yanked the pistol downward and Kristen lunged atop her, struggling anew to twist the barrel from her.

The gun went off. Kristen shrieked at the sound and the hard kick to her stomach that meant the bullet must have ripped home.

"Sam," she moaned. "Sam . . ."

Her eyes gazed down into Jordan's. They were still and bulging. Kristen pushed herself up and saw the crimson stain spreading across the senator's blouse from the bullet that had found her instead.

Kristen couldn't make her mind work. Everything was fuzzy and dull. The gun was forgotten. The inside of the car smelled like spent firecrackers.

And her own blouse was wet with Samantha Jordan's blood.

Trembling, Kristen managed to move back behind the wheel. Still in a fog, she drove off, kicking dirt and rocks behind her. The senator's head thumped against the window as Kristen pulled back onto the road.

"You're a part too, Kris, because you believe. *I know you do. . . ."*

Believe in *what*?

"Give me a chance to explain. I can still bring you on board. I can convince them to let me."

Samantha Jordan clearly was just an underling, part of something vast and horrifying that was somehow connected to what David had witnessed at Miravo Air Force Base.

Night was falling. Kristen flipped on her headlights and drove on. She would drive to Grand Mesa, to Sheriff Duncan Farlowe. Farlowe would help her. There was no one else.

Kristen was glad it was getting dark because she hated looking at Samantha Jordan's corpse in the passenger seat. She regretted there was no way to avoid hearing it bounce against the door with every bump in the road, or to block out the smell of blood. Still, she had no intention of stopping until she reached Grand Mesa.

A roadblock appeared suddenly just over the crest of a hill on Old Canyon Road. Kristen hadn't realized how fast she'd been going and barely managed to get the sedan stopped in time before the inevitable collision, skidding onto the shoulder. Cold fear struck her with the reality of what was occurring and she threw the sedan into reverse in hopes of finding the road again to turn around.

Two more sets of headlights veered in from that direction as well. A bullet shattered the top of the windshield, forcing Kristen to duck. She heard two more volleys blow out the sedan's front tires. She rose to see armed men approaching through the glare of the headlights aimed her way, led by a monster of a man whose face was terrifyingly ugly and who looked—

His hair! Oh my God, his hair! ...

A picture of David's mutilated corpse flashed through Kristen's mind. Duncan Farlowe had said her brother had been scalped.

And this man monster was wearing his hair. ...

She shrank back in her seat transfixed by the sight of him, flailing desperately for the pistol she had discarded after it had killed Samantha Jordan. But her mind went numb before she could find it, and Kristen could do nothing but watch with open-mouthed horror as the man monster wearing David's hair reached her door.

CHAPTER 18

The President fixed his gaze on the tape recorder placed atop the desk in his private office. Listening to the tape obtained by FBI director Ben Samuelson had become an addiction for him. A mostly sleepless Saturday night had been spent playing it over and over again, a process that had dragged long into Sunday as well. This time, the President fast-forwarded to a precise spot on the counter before pressing the play button.

"*It never stopped, sir. It redefined itself and kept pursuing its agenda underground.*"

"*And suddenly it resurfaces. Why now, Mr. Daniels?*"

"*Dodd, sir. He was the missing variable and the most important one. . . . Dodd's the one who will finally allow them to bring this off.*"

"*Bring what off exactly? Your report seems to skirt that issue.*"

"*The overthrow of the United States government.*"

The President reached out and pressed STOP. The words chilled him just as they had the previous times he had listened. It was unthinkable. Not here, not in the United States. The safeguards of democracy aside, power was too decentralized. No cadre or cell was in a position to transcend the levels and tiers. The Constitution and the Bill of Rights existed to assure orderly transitions of power and a fair say for all opponents.

The President ran his hands over his face and held them there. The opposition had gotten around all that, an opposition led by a man whose popularity was equaled only by the extent of his power: Samuel Jackson Dodd. Until now, Tom Daniels and Clifton Jardine had been the only men outside his sinister cadre who had glimpsed what was coming, and both had died for possessing that knowledge.

The President fast-forwarded again, keeping a close eye on the counter until the time came to hit STOP and then PLAY. Daniels's voice filled his ears once more.

"*The smaller we keep the scale of our response, the better our chances of finding out how the subjects of my report intend to accomplish their goal.*"

"*How small, Mr. Daniels?*"

"*One man.*"

The President stopped the tape there and gazed at the

photograph the FBI director had brought last night along with the tape. The shot was a poorly cropped one in blurred black and white. But the face it pictured was clear in its intensity and intimidation. The President felt the eyes reach out from the picture and grasp his own. He had to shake off the feeling that Blaine McCracken was studying him just as intently as he was studying the photo. According to the card clipped to the photo's top, those eyes were black. A scruffy, close-cropped beard hid the balance of what appeared to be a ruddy complexion. A nasty scar cut through McCracken's left eyebrow. His hair was thick and wavy, dark as the eyes. The profile card listed Blaine McCracken as six-foot-one and 200 pounds. Based on his neck and the part of his shoulders that were visible, the President figured all of it was muscle. Something about this man made him want to turn away. Something else made him want to reach through the glossy paper and bring Blaine McCracken into the room.

"Just who is this McCracken, Ben?" he had asked.

"Ex–Special Forces, ex–Phoenix Project, ex-Company—ex–just about everything. Works rogue now, outside the system, and nobody gets in his way."

"And just why is that?"

"Because they've seen what happens to those that do. McCracken once blew out the groin area of Churchill's statue in Parliament Square because he thought that was what the British were missing after they failed to heed his warnings and a plane load of hostages got blown up as a result. That's how he got his nickname."

"Nickname?"

"McCrackenballs."

"Daniels thought he was the right man for this job."

"He might well be."

"You're missing my point, Ben. Daniels discusses setting up a meeting with McCracken and then shows up in Rock Creek Park the next night, where he's murdered. I read the autopsy report you sent over. He didn't die right away, did he?"

"No, sir, he didn't."

"Then maybe he was there to meet with McCracken. Maybe he stayed alive long enough to share information not included on this tape. That would mean McCracken might have the answers we don't. And he hasn't come forward because he doesn't know who to trust."

"Just like we don't."

"Find Blaine McCracken, Ben. Find him fast."

Samuelson had been about to take his leave when the President spoke again.

"One more thing, Ben."

"Sir?"

"What do you think of the job I've done in the office? Straight answer, please."

"I wouldn't want your chair, Mr. President."

"That's not what I asked you."

Samuelson swallowed hard. "I'm disappointed."

The President smiled. "Thank you, Ben. So am I. Now tell me why."

"I think you've chosen to fight the wrong battles at inopportune times."

"I've won some, lost more."

Samuelson shrugged an acknowledgment.

"But now we've got ourselves a battle we have to win, don't we? Samuel Jackson Dodd isn't going to wait until the '96 election to take that chair you want no part of." A resolve unseen since the campaign and his early days in office filled the President's eyes. "Well, I'm not going to let him. If it's a fight he wants, we'll give it to him. Bring this government down and the country falls with it. Not on my watch, Ben. Whatever it takes, we're going to stop him."

And now, a day later, the President held the photograph of Blaine McCracken away from him at arm's length and pressed PLAY again. When the words he was waiting for began, he turned up the volume and leaned closer to the machine.

"They're planning something that makes it all possible,

sir, something that we aren't considering because we can't. And unless we find out what it is, how they intend to pull this off, we won't be able to stop them."

"But McCracken will . . ."

"It's what he does, sir."

"For God's sake, I hope so," the President said out loud.

CHAPTER 19

The big truck wobbled slightly as McCracken drove it through the entrance of the stockyard late Sunday afternoon. The choice of this locale by Arlo Cleese as his weapons storehouse seemed oddly appropriate.

Commandeering the meatpacking truck from a stop fifty miles back had provided Blaine's means of access to the stockyard. Its real driver would be able to work his binds free by nightfall, and by then Blaine would be long gone from the area.

Manuel Alvarez had traced the stockpiled weapons he had supplied to Arlo Cleese to this location in central Oklahoma, and McCracken had come here hoping to find a clue to where Cleese himself could be found. His Midnight Riders had been the most militant of all the radical cells of the sixties. They avoided the mundane kidnappings, bank robberies, and small bombings in favor of large-scale destruction. A courthouse, an office building rising out of what had once been a block of tenements, and a church frequented by top members of the Washington establishment were all counted among their successful targets. A dozen people had died in those three bombings alone. Another ten had perished in several shootouts with FBI agents when Midnight Rider lairs were compromised, during which Cleese had been left with a bullet in his thigh and a permanent limp.

Cleese had surfaced occasionally until 1970, when he

vanished into the underground, along with a substantial portion of the lunatic fringe, without a trace. He managed to elude capture, despite spending three consecutive years in the early seventies on the FBI's most wanted list and remaining thereafter a much-sought-after fugitive. McCracken knew that Cleese and others like him operated in an entire sublayer of American society. The underground was a world unto itself and would have provided the ideal breeding ground for Cleese to expand the revolutionary furor he had helped foster in the sixties.

There were three other trucks ahead of McCracken's being loaded with sides of beef fresh from the slaughterhouse building. Blaine parked his truck in the appropriate slot and climbed down, engine left on to keep the refrigerator going in the hold. The stockyard workers were dressed in long white coats. All wore gloves. A few donned masks outside the building, while inside the slaughterhouse all undoubtedly wore them to block out the stench. Get himself into an outfit like that and Blaine would be able to check out the grounds at will, as well as walk to the main office in search of some indication of Arlo Cleese's present whereabouts.

Blaine ambled away from his truck and walked around the back of the death-filled building. There was a door marked EMPLOYEES ONLY. It was locked from the inside, but half a minute later he had it open and had slipped into a dark hallway. A number of rooms lay along it. In the fourth one several pairs of white coveralls hung from pegs on the walls.

McCracken needed less than a minute to don one of the standard stockyard uniforms. He located a mask that covered most of his face and strapped it into place. The pair of gloves came last, after he had tucked his SIG-Sauer inside the white overalls.

The corridor continued directly into the slaughterhouse itself. The mask did little to quell the scent and nothing to stanch the sound. Blaine hated everything about it, revolted by the process required to put food on plates all across the country. He stayed to the outer perimeter of the line, well away from the frightened clutter of animals and from clear view of any of the other workers. He took the first door marked EXIT and found himself on a platform overlooking the stockyard complex.

Large pens of animals filled the horizon. Beyond them rose a number of buildings and what looked like small houses that gave the outskirts of the stockyard the look of an old-fashioned commune. This appearance was further supported by the fields of crops stretching out as far as he could see.

In the nearby corrals workers dressed in similar garb were busy spreading out feed in long bins. The doomed cattle fought each other for what might be their final meal, occasionally perking up their ears at the sounds coming from the building all would enter eventually.

Blaine's eyes were drawn to the corral nearest the slaughterhouse, where a man wearing a hip-length denim jacket over his white uniform was shoveling out feed. The man had combed his brown hair back into a ponytail that could not hide the streaks of gray. His skin had the dark, creased look of someone who had spent a good portion of his life outdoors. His shoulders were narrow, but firm layers of muscle were evident even beneath his jacket. He moved backward to grab another bag of feed and Blaine noticed his limp. Judging from his apparent age and long-injured leg, McCracken realized that, incredibly, he was looking at Arlo Cleese himself!

His shock was tempered somewhat by the realities posed by this unexpected stroke of fortune. Now that he had found Cleese, what should his next move be? Blaine had never considered himself a simple assassin, and executing Cleese would leave him without a viable escape route in any event. Additionally there was the problem of how far all this extended *beyond* Cleese. If what was coming could go on without him, than killing the leader of the Midnight Riders was pointless. A thorough interrogation was called for, after which Blaine could turn Cleese over to Manuel Alvarez for his just rewards.

McCracken descended from the platform and headed toward the corral, crossing into the view of a pair of rifle-wielding guards en route. He kept moving forward as if he were doing exactly what he was supposed to. He'd noticed no one out here was wearing a mask, so he had brought his to neck level before leaving the platform.

The harsh stench of the animals grew stronger as he neared the corral. The ground within it was wet and oozing with mud and cow dung. Blaine noticed that the muck covered Arlo Cleese's high rubber boots up to the ankles. A number of additional pairs of boots had been placed on a sill outside the corral. Still wary of the guards, Blaine leaned against the fence to steady himself and pulled the rubber boots over his shoes. His feet felt awkward, but at least now he would be able to walk freely about through the ooze.

Blaine pulled open the gate, scattering the cattle nearest it as he entered. He moved through the maze of snorting beasts straight for Cleese, who continued to seem oblivious to him, shoveling more feed into the trough without missing a beat. A door had opened at the far side of the corral and several of the animals were disappearing through it to their deaths. McCracken grabbed a stray shovel to further disguise the last stretch of his approach. He was barely two yards away when Cleese finally started to turn.

"Take the south end. I'll finish up he—." Cleese interrupted himself when his eyes finally rested on McCracken. "Don't think I know you."

"You don't."

Cleese's eyes lowered for the gun Blaine held concealed from view by his hip. "You come here to kill me, I'd be dead already."

"We're going to take a walk."

"My guards wouldn't like that."

McCracken followed Cleese's gaze toward the pair of

armed guards perched fifty yards away. "No reason for them to be any the wiser."

"Been expecting somebody like you."

"Really?"

"Surprised it took so long," Cleese continued, pulling another feed bag toward him and tearing open its top. "I guess it means you fuckers are getting close." He stood up straight and rigid. "You wanna dance, we do it here and now. I ain't going anywhere with you."

The SIG felt suddenly heavy by Blaine's side. Something was all wrong here. Six feet before him a militant leader he thought was on the verge of launching a revolution was standing knee-deep in muck, sounding more like a victim.

The indecision must have shown up on Blaine's expression.

"Wait a minute," Cleese muttered, "wait a minute . . . I'll be fucked! You ain't one of them at all!" Looking suspicious now, wary instead of resigned. "Then what the fuck are you doing here?"

"I thought I was trying to save the country from an old asshole who can't let go."

Cleese tossed the first shovel full of feed from the fresh bag into the trough. The animals that had bunched together further up the line spread out to reach it.

"You're way off base, man."

"Not way off in figuring Manual Alvarez was your weapons pipeline. Not way off in figuring you're finally well enough stocked to finish what you started twenty-five years ago with the Midnight Riders and the rest of the lunatic fringe."

Cleese smiled. "You figure I offed the two Alvarezes?"

"Makes sense."

"Yeah, for somebody else trying to make it look like I was responsible, for that and plenty more. Hey, I got the men and the materials to move, but what the fuck for? Me and all the other old assholes kinda settled down now. The lunatic fringe is still fringe, oh yeah, but we're not very lunatic no more."

"Two of you were. In Miami. The Coconut Grove."

"If I'd sent them, I'd've made sure they had links to no one. Like you would." Cleese stared hard at McCracken, shovel held like a spear before him. "And, don't tell me, guns that were used in the Grove were part of one of my shipments."

Blaine didn't bother to confirm Cleese's assumption.

"You got a name?" Cleese asked him.

"McCracken."

Cleese stuck his shovel in the feed but didn't hoist it. "We got ourselves a bunch of nice little communities like this all over the country. I keep myself on the move between them. I'd ask you if you wanted to hitch on, but I get the feeling you're not the type."

"Part of your stockpile from Alvarez stored in each?"

"Damn right."

"For the revolution that's not coming anymore?"

"Just to stay alive now."

"Daddy!"

A child's gleeful cry stopped Cleese before he could go on. From McCracken's rear, a boy of about six was charging through the muck, adult boots reaching nearly up to his waist. He slid past Blaine and jumped into Arlo Cleese's arms.

"You said you'd be done in ten minutes, Daddy. You said you'd be home."

Cleese set the boy down. "I got a guest."

The boy looked at Blaine. "Is he staying?"

"Nope."

"Lot's of people stay, you know," the boy said to McCracken.

"Run along. Wait for me on the porch," Cleese told his son, and quick as that the boy was gone.

"His mother left here three years ago," he continued to

Blaine. "I got a few other kids, too, but he's the only one with me now."

"Seems like you're settling down."

"Ain't got it so bad, far as things go. I had a lifetime's worth of complications already. Be a good idea to avoid them for a while."

"Then why the need for all the firepower?"

"We got to be ready, that's why. You're here 'cause somebody filled your mind with some thick shit, Mac. People who want you and everyone else to think I'm behind what's gonna go down. That's who I thought sent you. All part of the plan."

"What plan?"

"You standing there, you must know it."

" 'Long as I'm here, why don't you give me your version?"

Cleese pulled the shovel from the feed bag and leaned against it. Around him animals began to cluster impatiently.

"Got a feeling you weren't around much for the sixties, Mac. Two tours maybe?"

"Close."

"No record you was ever there?"

"Close again."

Cleese stuck his shovel back in the feed. "You and me, Mac, we both went to war and we're both survivors. 'Cept back in the sixties, surviving didn't seem to matter much. War's all that mattered, and I'm not talking about where you shipped out to. I'm talking about the homeland. While you were fighting for freedom, I was watching it being threatened in the good old U.S. of A. Subtle but concerted effort to make sure everybody toed the mark. Got scary for a time and we did what we could to fight it, till they turned up the heat and we went away. Fringe wasn't lunatic enough to stick around for the finish. But the real bad guys were. They never stopped. They never *will* stop till they get what they want."

"Which is?"

"Nothing'll satisfy 'em short of the country itself. That's what they been planning for. That's what they wanted us out of the way for way back in the beginning."

McCracken's thoughts were swimming. Conceivably Tom Daniels's dying mention of Operation Yellow Rose might not have been meant to point him to the Midnight Riders at all, but at the force *behind* Yellow Rose: William Carlisle's shadowy Trilateral Commission subcommittee. Carlisle had intimated that the current crisis was due to the failure of that subcommittee to wipe out men like Cleese when they had the chance. But what if that failure had led to another stage of development, a more complex plan to gain the control they sought? In that event, the former residents of the lunatic fringe were being set up, the blame cast upon them for the plot Daniels had uncovered by its true perpetrators.

"Operation Yellow Rose," Blaine muttered.

Cleese's eyebrows went up at that. "Like I said, you standing there, you know."

"Keep talking."

"Trilateral shits didn't have the guts to go through with Yellow Rose. So things get quiet for a while until somebody new takes over. Somebody real good. Got himself a real agenda that makes the old one look like a shopping list. Knows just how to get what he wants without anybody knowing they gave it to him."

"For example . . ."

"Check out House Resolution 4079. Cut through the bullshit and check out what it really says, what it paved the way for."

"Care to give me a hint?"

"You be better off seeing this for yourself."

"The word 'Prometheus' mean anything to you?" McCracken asked Cleese suddenly, recalling another of the shadowy clues passed on by Tom Daniels.

"Should it?"

"If Operation Yellow Rose does, maybe. They're connected."

"How?"

"I don't know. Not yet." Blaine thought briefly. "What about the Delphi?"

Cleese shook his head. "Means nothing to me, man. Best thing you can do is stick to what you know, what I told you. You wanna see who's driving the train, start with what they're hiding in the caboose."

"That House resolution . . ."

Cleese's next shovelful of feed landed beyond the trough. The cattle scattered quickly to retrieve it.

"It'll prove what I'm telling is the truth, 'cause what 4079 does is—"

Cleese's words ended in an agonized scream. He fell to the ground, clutching his shoulder. McCracken dropped just as quickly and readied his SIG as he heard another burst of silenced spits. Blaine's eyes probed for the two guards who'd been watching them the whole time. One had vanished from view. The other still lay in the mud.

"Fuck!" Cleese screeched, rolling in the ooze, shielded by cattle.

"Don't get up."

"If they yours, motherfucker, you'll die remembering!"

"Not mine, Cleese."

More gunshots sounded. The rhythm, the spacing, the cadence made Blaine realize something. All these guards, both seen and unseen, and still Cleese's security had been penetrated without so much as an alarm.

"Yours," Blaine finished.

The fuck you say—

"A few, enough. They let the attackers enter the property."

McCracken had slid slightly away from him, searching for the gunmen. Illusion and reality, at least, had clearly parted, his true enemy having revealed itself.

Bill Carlisle had it all wrong. This wasn't happening because his subcommittee had failed in its mandate; it was happening because that still-thriving offshoot of the Trilateral Commission was pursuing a *different* mandate.

Blaine guessed they could have killed Cleese at any time, but they'd waited until now. After the bomb on the Miami-bound plane had failed to do the job, they had set a trap where they knew McCracken's trail would ultimately lead.

"Can you get out of here yourself?" Blaine asked Cleese.

"I ain't stayed free all these years to die like this," the leader of the Midnight Riders grimaced. "Still got some tricks up my sleeve."

"Use them. Get out."

"I ain't running," Cleese said stubbornly, breath misting before his face.

"Think of your son." Blaine knew he had him with that. "Roll away. Keep to the mud, between the cattle."

Cleese nodded. "Gonna give you a number to memorize. Safe line. 'Case you need to reach me someday. Thing is, I owe you now."

Cleese recited the number. Blaine memorized it.

"Now get yourself outta here," McCracken ordered.

CHAPTER 20

Blaine watched Cleese disappear into the cattle crowding toward the corral's rear and began pulling himself through the muck. Mud spit into the air in his wake as he moved. The converging gunmen were fast drawing a bead on him. The trajectory of their bullets gave him a vague indication of their position. In the narrowing distance he was able to grab glimpses of them when the spaces between the cattle allowed. Blaine still held his SIG-Sauer but hadn't yet fired it. Just as he brought it forward and started to sight down the barrel, a steer's leg slammed against his arm.

The pistol went flying, a wild shot blasting skyward. McCracken felt through the muck for the gun. Cattle blocked his search in all directions, their hooves coming dangerously close to crushing his fingers. He was wasting time. Not only was he weaponless now, but the errant shot had signaled the attackers to his position. Only one avenue of cover, perhaps even escape, remained for him: the slaughterhouse itself.

The huge complex was a hundred feet away, accessible via the corral if he could negotiate his way past the frightened, bellowing cattle. The doors leading into the slaughterhouse from the back of the corral had opened and the animals squeezed toward them.

Blaine sank lower and tasted the rancid mud. The animals that weren't clustered about the fresh feed Cleese had shoveled out were still pressing toward the entrance to the slaughterhouse. The mass of brown hide made for an indistinguishable blanket, awkward in its slow motion forward.

Beyond the corral he could hear screams, shouts, and the heavy thumps of footsteps. A pair of shotgun blasts rang out. More of the soft spits answered them. Some of Cleese's still-loyal guards must have arrived to offer resistance, at the very least buying Blaine some time. He continued to haul himself through the muck on his elbows. Above him, the hooves of the snorting beasts promised disaster with each step.

The double doors started to swing closed. McCracken frantically picked up his pace, squeezing and slithering between the animals. He lunged through the doorway just as the doors thumped shut behind him. Blaine rose into a crouch, still shielded by the cover of the milling cattle. Revolted by the stench, he pulled his now-muddied mask up to cover his face again. It would steal some measure of sight from him, but the cost was worth it for the moment. The herd was inching its way forward through the massive building, funneled into three separate lines leading onto conveyor belts which would take their carcasses through the stations of the assembly line process.

The ceiling was high and the building's light quite dim.

The machine noises had hidden the sound of gunshots from those within, accounting for their ignorance of the gun battle raging outside. Blaine caught glimpses of soiled white uniforms as he dodged amidst the cattle.

The cattle pressed onward, herded on by workers who hadn't yet spotted McCracken. His plan was to launch into a rush once he reached the head of one of the lines the cattle spiraled off into. The conveyor belt would eventually lead him to the doors the beef would be carted through to be loaded onto trucks like his.

Blaine chose the middle of the three lines. When he was still fifteen yards from the entrance, a sudden wash of light cut neat slivers in the chilly darkness. The enemy had trailed him here and had thrown open the main doors to continue their pursuit. Blaine could hear nothing of their approach above the animals' snorting and see nothing of it over their hulking shapes. All he could do for now was let himself continue to be swept forward by the impetus of the surging animals.

Blaine was close enough to the elevated central opening to see a worker on a slightly raised platform controlling the flow of animals to their deaths. When the light from the open doors reached the man, he turned his masked face rearward and stiffened. Unarmed, he tried to reach for something on his belt when he was jerked against the wall. Huge scarlet chasms opened where only dried blood had been before. The man slumped down. The face of another man on his right vanished in a burst of blood and bone.

The enemy was closing. McCracken could not possibly enter the killing zone without being seen. He was trapped.

Unless . . .

Blaine stopped. Around him the animals bunched briefly together, then slid by. He lowered his shoulders and peered backward at ground level through the endless hooves.

There! Thirty feet back and just to the right, a pair of boots advanced through the pack. Blaine shuffled to the left. His progress came in agonizing fits and starts as he pushed himself between the bunched and nervous animals. He angled in toward the approaching killer after covering six yards. He calculated that, at the pace the herd allowed him, he would intercept the man just before the final ramp leading up onto the conveyor belt.

Blaine launched his attack through a narrow gap between a pair of animals stalled in their tracks. He came in low, slamming the stalker in the knees and taking him down. The animals gave ground and the two men tumbled to the slimy floor.

The killer was holding a Kalashnikov assault rifle, ineffective in close. Nonetheless, Blaine made sure to pin it against his body before he launched his free hand forward. He had wedged as much mud and feces in his grasp as he could hold and jammed the oozing contents against the killer's nose and mouth. The man gagged, eyes bulging. In that instant Blaine brought his second hand up to join the first and pounded his face. The third blow landed with a crunching impact. His hands came away bloody. The man moaned and was still. Blaine struggled to free his Kalashnikov.

The sudden nervous shifting of the animals above him provided warning of the rapid approach of another adversary. McCracken gave up on the rifle and lunged to his feet. He caught the second surging attacker by surprise across the jaw with an elbow. The man staggered briefly, then lashed outward with the butt of his rifle. The blow caught Blaine in the chin. His head whiplashed to the side, neck muscles seizing. His torso slammed into the rock-hard bulk of one of the herd and he bounced back the man's way.

The man's finger had closed on the trigger just as Blaine grabbed the barrel and shoved it away. The bullets from his Kalashnikov sped errantly into a nearby clutter of cattle. Around them, the already terrified herd erupted into panic. Animals began slamming into each other, discarding the orderly flow and heading in any direction that would have them.

The man kicked out at him, but Blaine refused to release

the gun barrel. Ignoring McCracken's hold on it, he drove forward with the butt as he had before. At impact, the momentum carried the two of them up the ramp leading into the middle of the three killing zones.

They landed at the start of the conveyor belt that ferried cattle along the slaughterhouse's assembly-line process. Blaine slammed into it hard and felt the tread churning beneath him as his assailant shoved a rifle butt into the soft flesh of his throat, choking off his breath. The man continued to jam the stock downward. A look of triumph started to spread over his filth-laced face.

McCracken held fast to the rifle but couldn't budge it. He had only seconds left to act before unconsciousness claimed him, but *how* to act?

Blaine stole a glance behind him and glimpsed the mechanical ramrod that was the only automated feature of the line. A laser guided the ramrod dead-on with each animal's head and sent it into a swift punching motion forward once the sensor line had been crossed. The result was instantaneous death, the animal then hoisted by its chained forelegs into the air and spirited toward the now-abandoned stations. Being automated, though, the ramrod should still be functional.

Blood hammering inside his head, McCracken abruptly released his hold on the rifle and reached for the hair of the figure above him. He grabbed hold and jerked the man forward enough to break the plane of the ramrod's sensor. A brief mechanical whine was followed by a swift blur jettisoning forward just within Blaine's line of vision. It punched against the man's forehead and drove him violently backward, a strangely bloodless chasm dug out of his skull.

McCracken lunged to his feet and started down the center of the three slimy, blood-soaked catwalks to the slaughterhouse's rear. The surface was formed of heavy slats positioned with gaps to allow for drainage. The flooring was solid only at each of the major stations along the way where workers alternately sliced, skinned, and quartered the carcasses. Above it the conveyor belt rose to carry the suspended corpses conveniently through the process.

Blaine dashed along the planking beneath the shackles left empty by the sudden breakdown in the system. He stopped long enough to retrieve a pair of bloodied, machete-like slicers dropped when the workers ran for their lives. He heard a man shouting to another behind him and swung. He flung the knives before his aim was sure. One flew hopelessly errant. But the other grazed one of the gunman's arms and spun him into the path of the ramrod. The steel end caught him in the throat and punctured it, the man struggling wildly as the ramrod impaled him and snapped him backward with its recoil.

Others pushed by his flailing frame and began firing McCracken's way. Blaine charged away from them, catching up with the last of the cattle to be hoisted upon the line. With the bullets bearing down, he jumped up and grabbed hold of a pair of shackles harnessing a steer's forelegs so that the carcass behind it would serve as his cover. He tucked his legs up so they wouldn't dangle below the animal's length and just managed to avoid incurring a nasty gash from a huge scissor-like contraption suspended from the ceiling at the quartering station.

Suddenly the belt stopped. Blaine dropped back down to the planking and nearly slipped in an oozing pile of entrails and stray limbs.

"There he is!"

The shout barely preceded the fresh hail of gunfire. Blaine crouched and ran along the last of the planking toward an opening where ordinarily the conveyor belt deposited its finished products for storage. Quite expectedly here too Cleese's workers had deserted their posts, leaving the six freezers unattended. To confuse the closing opposition, McCracken cracked two of the freezers open and then charged into a third one. He slammed the door behind him and his body was instantly engulfed by the intense cold. Quartered and halved steer carcasses were stacked or hung everywhere. The air was rich with ice crystals. Clearly he could not last long in here. But escape was on his mind, not refuge.

Blaine had glimpsed enough of the loading process outside to know these freezers were equipped with rear hatch-type doors. He dashed to the back and yanked the hatch door open to reveal a steeply angled slide the carcasses were dropped onto for easy packing on the trucks. Twenty yards beyond this chute, his truck waited, its engine still idling.

Blaine heard the door to the freezer burst open behind him and threw himself onto the slide head first. A slimy coat of oil and blood quickened his ride down. He started pulling himself upward when the slide bottomed out. His feet touched hard-packed gravel already running, and he leaped behind the wheel of his truck

Ignoring the bullets already slamming into its side and rear, he jammed the truck into drive and tore off through the parking lot. The truck bucked and rattled, and Blaine shut down the refrigerator in the rear to gather more power. Almost like a boost from a turbo, the truck surged gratefully toward the refuge promised by the open road.

The refuge, of course, was temporary; McCracken abandoned the refrigerated truck in the woods ten miles from Arlo Cleese's stockyard. He then set off on foot until he came to a small farmhouse that had a clothesline strung between two trees in its rear. The one-piece stockyard uniform he'd stripped off had prevented most of the dirt and blood from reaching his own garments. The stink, though, seemed in them forever. Fortunately, hanging with the other clothes on the line were a pair of jeans and a shirt that looked to be about his size. After a silent apology to the owner, he yanked them off and pulled them on in place of his own ruined garments.

Blaine's next goal was to obtain a vehicle to replace his abandoned truck. A long hike down the road brought him to a combination filling station and general store. From the small parking lot alongside it he chose the car with the coldest engine, indicating it belonged to someone who worked inside and likely wouldn't miss it for a few more hours. The owner had carelessly left the key in the ignition, an unexpected bonus for McCracken, who was intent on saving as much time as possible. He pulled into a motel just past nightfall, the plates on the stolen car changed once en route.

The first thing he did was phone Sal Belamo to tell him to dig up everything he could on House of Representatives Law 4079, the law Arlo Cleese had alluded to just prior to the attack at the stockyard. It took two hours for the pug-nosed ex-boxer to call him back.

"This is crazy shit, boss," Belamo began. "Crazy."

"You talking about HR 4079?"

"I ain't much good with the technical lingo, so let me give you HR 4079 as I understand it. To begin with, it centers on penalties for drug offenders, specifically dealers. It authorizes, get this, the construction of special prisons to deal strictly with their incarceration. What you make of that?"

"Sounds like concentration camps to me."

"My thoughts exactly. They're called detention centers in the bill."

"That's what they were called in Nazi Germany, too."

"Anyway, going by this wording I'm not even sure Congress knew what it was passing. But whoever was behind 4079 got it through. I made a call to someone at the Office of Management and Budget who owes me a favor. Sure enough, he tells me that funding was line-itemed for the construction of six of these centers under—big surprise—'miscellaneous.' One of them's already been completed. In New Mexico, boss. White Sands. Guy I talked to said it's dead-filed as Sandcastle One."

CHAPTER 21

Johnny Wareagle wasn't totally surprised that the government had been implicated in Traggeo's early release from prison. There would always be need, demand, for the killer's brutal skills in some circles, and Johnny had a pretty good idea which of these circles might be involved.

Colonel Tyson Gash, Traggeo's commander in Vietnam, had not let being drummed out of the service five years before deter him from his life's work. The former head of Salvage Company had used the opportunity to found his own private and secret army, a survivalist group of former Rangers and Special Forces types who trained at an isolated camp in Arizona in the shadow of the New River Mountains. If anyone had a reason to spring Traggeo, it was Tyson Gash.

Wareagle was detained at the compound's front gate late Sunday afternoon while Gash was informed of his presence. The three guards still had their M16s aimed at him when Gash pulled up in a jeep, looking no different from the last time they had met over twenty years before, right down to the unlit cigar wedged into the side of his mouth. Colonel Tyson Gash was a rawboned man who wore his muscle lean and hard. He was tall and maybe the least bit chunkier now, sporting a bushy black mustache and the same crew cut Johnny remembered from 'Nam. A .45-caliber pistol was holstered around his waist. Although the temperature still hovered in the mid-eighties, he was outfitted in full combat dress.

"At ease, soldiers," Gash ordered his men.

The three weapons were lowered simultaneously.

Gash spoke again to his men while he looked upward to meet the gaze of the seven-foot-tall Wareagle. "You boys don't know it, but you just received a lesson better than any I could teach ya. You had three guns aimed at a man who's only packing a knife, and he could've taken you all at any time he pleased." He eyed them sternly and the soldiers snapped to attention. He yanked the cigar from his mouth and pointed it at them as his voice picked up its cadence. "Boys, you're in the presence of greatness. Next time you meet a man of this stature, if there is a next time, you'd better recognize him for what he is or find yourself another outfit. Now get back to work."

The soldiers saluted before backing off. Gash stepped up to Johnny to shake his hand.

"Pleasure to see you, Lieutenant."

Wareagle swallowed Gash's hand in his grasp. "I am not worthy of the words you spoke of me, Colonel."

"You mean you couldn't have taken those three cherries with one eye closed and the other squinting?"

"I mean they were not in the presence of greatness. Neither are you."

Gash nodded, still smiling. "I always knew you'd show up here someday to take me up on my offer. I figured all you needed was time."

They started for the jeep, Gash still looking up at Wareagle.

"That is not what I have come about, Colonel."

"But you'll take a look at the place, check it out. Maybe stay for dinner."

"As you wish."

"I wish you'd decide to join up. We need you, Lieutenant. And the time's coming fast when this country's gonna need us."

"I am looking for one of your men," Johnny said when they reached the jeep.

"They're all here. No such thing as leave in my command."

"Not one of your current men, Colonel, one from the past."

"How past?"

"Salvage Company."

Unlit cigar back in his mouth, Gash gunned the engine without responding and threw the jeep in reverse.

"Got a few of those with me," Gash acknowledged as the jeep eased through the wooded outskirts of his private compound. "Who is it you want?"

"Traggeo," Johnny told him.

"Hell, I thought he was dead."

"No. But a number of those who have crossed his path are."

"I haven't been keeping tabs."

"He was supposed to spend five years in prison. Someone arranged his release before even the first was up. Someone official."

"And you thought it was me."

"The logic was there."

"You musta missed the sign outside the front gate, Lieutenant," Gash told him. " 'No lunatics allowed.' "

"Then both of us may well have been denied entry, Colonel."

Gash laughed. "Granted. But Traggeo's a whole 'nother level. I can't work with anyone I can't control."

"You did in the hellfire."

Gash stopped the jeep. He yanked the cigar from his mouth and threw it to the ground. "They weren't supposed to survive! That was the point. Hell, I called Salvage Company 'Suicide Company' in internal memoranda. They ended the damn war too early. If they had given me another ten thousand like Traggeo early enough, I could have won the damn thing. He may have been a crazy son-of-a-bitch, but he was as loyal a soldier as ever served under me. Never failed to perform, no matter the circumstances, and I don't have to tell you how difficult plenty of them were."

Wareagle looked away so Gash wouldn't see the scorn in his eyes.

"This personal, Lieutenant?" Gash asked.

"Traggeo claims to be one of my people, Colonel. The claim is a lie. He darkens his skin to pretend. He learns our tongues and our ways to fool others. But he carries none of our blood. And he must be stopped before more darkness is shed on the spirit of my people."

"He's still"—Gash made a slicing motion over his head—"his victims?"

"Worse now," Johnny said and related what Elwin Coombs had said about Traggeo's wearing the scalps of his victims.

"Lord Jesus . . ." Gash thought for a moment. "Sounds to me like you got a bigger problem now. If it wasn't me who sprung Traggeo, then who was it?"

"You said others from Salvage Company were here."

"A couple."

"Recent arrivals?"

"Within the last year."

"May I speak with them?"

"They don't talk much, Lieutenant."

"I don't require long answers."

Seconds later the jeep reached the massive open area containing training fields, target ranges, and a fully equipped base right down to the buildings, barracks, and vehicles. It was in many respects a replica of the Delta Force training center at Fort Bragg where the colonel had finished his career in less-than-distinguished fashion.

"This was built entirely with private donations, Lieutenant," Gash explained. "Donations from individuals who believe as I do that someday a force will be needed to defend this country at home. We've gotten soft, Johnny; not you, not me, but the country as a whole. It's all busted up and weak from the inside out, and sooner or later something's gonna give. That's why we're here. When it does, we'll be ready."

Gash waited for a response. When none came, he continued. "I got fifteen hundred men here with me now and I can move them anywhere in the country I want inside of six hours. Even got our own transport planes. And you should see our equipment. Strictly top of the line. Desert Storm checked plenty of it out for us and it passed with flying colors." Gash stopped again, not for a response this time. "They can call us survivalists, they can call us fascists, they can call us whatever they want. But all we are is people who love this country and can read the writing on the wall and don't like what it says. You know what they're calling us now?"

Johnny did, but didn't respond.

"The 911 Brigade." Gash laughed heartily. "It's the goddamn truth, so I let the name stick. When the real emergency comes, we'll be there, Johnny, and my guess is that'll be sooner, not later. Stay and sign up, or you just might miss it."

"I prefer trying to stop it."

"Right," the colonel said knowingly. "You and McCrackenballs. Been following your work. When McCracken's ready, tell him I got a bed waiting for him, too."

"I will."

"You won't, but thanks for humoring me. If only I could make you see that this place, what I'm trying to do here, is made for the two of you. Take a good look around you, Lieutenant. This is the Alamo. We're surrounded on all sides by weakness and mediocrity. We're the last stand. Anyone with a gun could take this country, and all I'm hoping is we get the call in time to stop them."

They were creeping along the main drag of the base to a chorus of commands calling the troops to attention as the colonel passed by. The salutes were endless. Discipline never wavered when Tyson Gash was involved.

"Let me see what I can do," Gash said suddenly.

"Thank you, Colonel."

Gash slid the jeep to a whining halt in front of the base headquarters and stuck a fresh cigar in his mouth. "Don't thank me for helping you meet up with a man like Traggeo, Lieutenant. I should've killed him myself, let him come out of the grave and suck Charlie's blood when we were gone. He was convinced he was immortal, claimed he had the power of his ancestors in his veins."

"He has blood in his veins, Colonel, and when I meet up with him, it will spill."

The man called Badger, like Traggeo an alumnus of Salvage Company, was ushered into Gash's office and snapped instantly to attention.

"At ease, soldier," said the colonel.

Badger seemed incapable of managing anything close. His attempt at relaxing brought only a slight lowering of his shoulders. He was tall and lean, the crew cut worn into his head. His mouth twitched madly. His eyes were furtive and darting, forever in motion, as if unable to focus.

"This is Lieutenant Wareagle, soldier," Gash started. "You will answer any and all of his questions truthfully to the best of your ability. Understood?"

"Yes, sir!" Badger snapped back to attention. The twitching dulled but the eyes kept darting.

"Proceed, Lieutenant."

"You served with a man named Traggeo many years ago in another place. Have you heard from him any time in the past year?"

Badger's eyes locked finally on Wareagle. "Only once, sir. Months ago, before I came here. I don't know, I can't remember exactly."

"Whatever you do remember will be enough. Go on."

"A single phone call, sir, asking me if I wanted to join him." Those eyes grew uncertain again. "I don't know how he found me."

"Join him in what?"

"He didn't say, sir. Or if he did, I don't remember. It was . . . a difficult time."

"I understand. Do you remember anything?"

"Only the place he said he was calling from. I remember it because I think I've been there: Carrizozo."

"New Mexico," Johnny returned.

"Yes, sir. Located right before you reach White Sands."

CHAPTER 22

The limousine dodged through the Washington streets, its rider impatient to be rid of them as night tightened its hold on the city.

"Clear, sir," the driver's voice informed the limo's lone passenger.

"You know the route, then."

"Of course, sir," the driver responded, just a vague outline against the blacked-out partition.

The last twenty minutes had been spent making sure the limousine was not being tailed. The driver was a professional who had run many sophisticated surveillance operations. He knew all the tricks, and therefore how to subvert them.

As the big car headed toward the Beltway, its lone passenger opened a leather case that had been resting between his legs. Inside was an advanced communications system the size of a small television. It took both of his hands to lift it out and place it upon the limousine's built-in pedestal. He ran a connecting cable to a similarly built-in computer and slid it home. Then he switched the computer on and turned his attention back to the pedestal.

The communications system resting atop it had a simple square front that looked as though it might have been part of a sophisticated telephone. There was no receiver, just the oval-shaped dot holes of a speaker. The touchtone board located beneath it had twice as many numbers as the mundane variety, along with a half-dozen additional keys marked with symbols. To the board's left, and comprising the rest of the square front, was a series of seven electronic lines equipped with LED readouts. The man leaned slightly forward and touched a small button that activated the system.

Instantly, four of the LED readouts began flashing, an indication that three others were on-line and ready for the meeting to start. The red letters were all capitals, detailing the respective cities now in attendance: England, France, Germany.

The fourth—his—read WASHINGTON.

Japan and Johannesburg were lagging, while the seventh, the only speaker who would remain unidentified, would come on-line only when all others indicated their readiness.

The man in the limousine could do nothing but wait.

Since sophisticated scramblers made voice recognition impossible, the top six LED readouts existed to indicate to all participants which representative was speaking. The seventh and lowest simply flashed when the unidentified chairman was speaking.

Japan came on. A few seconds later JOHANNESBURG lit up red, leaving only the bottom slot unfilled. Lights bobbed forward like a bar grid across it when the chair's voice opened the meeting.

"Communications check," began the voice altered into a computer-synthesized monotone that was identical to the six others. "England."

"Here."

"Germany."

"Present."

"Japan."

"Yes."

"France."

"Present."

"Johannesburg."

"Here."

"And Washington."

"Present," the man in the limo's rear responded.

Traditionally whoever called an unscheduled meeting was mentioned last. Today was no exception.

"Proceed, Washington," ordered the unidentified voice.

"Complications have arisen."

"Severity?" The bar grid danced in place of a name.

"Difficult to gauge at this time."

"Have the Delphi been compromised, Washington?"

"Not yet," the man answered, emphasizing the second word of his response. "But the approved strategy I enacted to deal with McCracken has failed."

"You are saying that he survived his expected meeting with Cleese," concluded England.

"And indications are that Cleese did as well."

GERMANY flashed on as the next voice spoke. "Following your failure to finish McCracken with the explosive on that plane, I believe you said we had the opportunity to kill two birds with one stone. Now you tell us both have flown away."

"The responsibility is mine."

JAPAN replaced WASHINGTON. "Do we know where McCracken is?"

"No."

FRANCE. "Do we have any idea where he will surface next?"

"At this point, also no."

ENGLAND. "Then how are we to accept any further assurances that the Delphi have not been compromised?"

"Along with assurances that our present operation remains sterile," Germany added.

"Have I missed something?" Johannesburg wondered. "Are we not speaking of a *single* man?"

It was the unlabeled line that replied. "Let's not be naïve. All of you have been made aware of McCracken's proclivity for dealing with this sort of situation."

GERMANY. "I would have thought he might be more inclined to join us, under the circumstances."

"Then study his file again."

FRANCE. "The question of what is to be done with him remains."

"I am satisfied that up till now McCracken has obtained no information that could possibly make him aware of either our existence or the scope of our operation. The issue now becomes one of containment in these final days before activation. And with that in mind, Washington, I believe you should now detail the other complication that led to your calling this meeting."

"Miravo has been compromised," the man in the limo's rear said. "And, as a direct result of the way matters were handled prior to my involvement, Senator Samantha Jordan was killed earlier today."

"Another failure on your part?"

"No, England, a failure on hers. She chose to attempt to enlist a subordinate instead of following the specified course of action. We have that subordinate in custody now and must determine if there are others to whom she passed on the information she possessed."

"Beyond that," the chairman stated, "I have suggested moving the last of our stockpile out of Miravo."

"Why not simply ship the materials ahead of schedule?" raised Japan.

"We can do nothing of the kind until we are satisfied the senator's subordinate did not involve anyone else in her quest. I assure you that it will not affect the timetable of the operation."

"It is difficult to accept such an assurance when you have yet to inform us of that timetable's specifics."

"Then allow me to now," returned the unnamed chairman. "One week from this coming Tuesday, on April 26, the President is scheduled to address a joint session of Congress on his new plan for the economy. At that time, and in full view of the entire country, he will be assassinated along with the vast bulk of those charged with governing the country."

The chairman paused to wait for a response. When none came, he continued. "The military will be forced to take over to maintain some semblance of order. Our representatives within it will then act to suspend the Constitution so that a special election for the office of president can be called. Only one candidate will be deemed worthy, gentlemen, only one."

Silence replaced the chairman's voice once more, but it was the silence of acceptance, of awe.

And inevitability.

When the electronic meeting had ended, Sam Jack Dodd remained at his desk staring at the communication system that had been designed to his own specifications.

The charismatic billionaire, the man with the Midas touch who controlled the world's largest communications conglomerate, had joined the Trilateral Commission a decade ago and quickly become one of its most outspoken supporters. Even more quickly he had become one of its most frustrated. Dodd's early impressions had proven as exhilarating as his later ones had been frustrating. Here was a collection of the nation's greatest minds gathering to map out and sway world policy toward a worthy and unified goal. Yet the scope of their tangible accomplishments was immeasurably small. The Trilateral Commission was unable to respond fast enough to the ever-changing dynamic. They were reactive instead of proactive. Meetings went nowhere, well-attended conferences impressive only for the categorical brilliance of the men and women they attracted.

Dodd stopped going.

But then another group made contact with him, a group thought to be a dead offspring of the Trilat whose views mirrored his own. They called themselves the Delphi after the Greek oracle whose council determined action and thus history. That was, after all, the way the members of what had evolved from a subcommittee into a separate entity saw themselves. And they were a step away from achieving their grand vision.

Sam Jack Dodd became that last step. Over the next few

years he helped steer the Delphi in that direction, taking the helm. Every stratagem, every move, was undertaken with a single day in mind. A day in which the country—and the world—would change forever.

The day of the Delphi.

Expansion had been gradual, a power base formed and built upon. The Delphi seized upon the international goals proposed in the commission's charter but carried out by the Trilat only in modest. The original Trilateralists had shared a similar vision but were unwilling to take the steps necessary to achieve it. Their brilliance bred caution and conceit. They believed their logic to be so sound that eventually, irrepressibly, it would take hold. The Delphi knew that same hold was something that had to be forced, generated out of necessity. From the seeds the commission had planted had sprouted men and women the world over who felt the same way. A cabal had formed, an impatient cadre waiting only for a man like Samuel Jackson Dodd to bring it all together.

But in the end desperation had dictated the final timing. The country and the world had run out of chances. It had floundered and fallen, sinking ever deeper into economic chaos. Nothing anyone tried had been able to reverse the trend. Dodd wasn't surprised. No stopgap maneuver was going to work. A total overhaul was the only hope. But the people had to want it. The people had to want *him*.

The idea—to seize the moment by going public with his platforms and wage a popularity campaign for himself designed to bring him to the brink of the presidency—proved as effective as it was brilliant. Dodd had watched the failed campaign of Ross Perot with great interest, invigorated by its vast and ultimately squandered potential. In the process Perot had proven that it could be done, that the country was ready to elect a political outsider.

The *right* outsider.

Dodd had studied Perot's mistakes with an eye on not repeating them. The man lacked charisma, spoke in broad generalities, and became a pariah to the media. Dodd made sure the media embraced him, vowed never to dodge a question or speak in veiled terms. And charisma had never been a problem for him. He was starting out ahead; both his approval and recognition ratings were considerably higher than Perot's at the outset.

But unlike Perot he had no plans to wait for a presidential election to prove his mettle. Even if he won, an ordinary president, bound to the current limitations and restrictions of office, could never bring about the drastic changes required to save America and the world. These measures were needed to stem what analysis now indicated was not only a geometric deterioration of the nation's economy but also an equally rapid crumbling of her spirit. Each month that passed meant more irreparable harm.

In a sense that reality had become a godsend, strengthening his resolve and further casting him as the savior the people *had* to believe he was. With the next election so far off, an election that would never take place, he was spared the necessity of specific platforms and policies. And yet the nation became enamored of his dogma and embraced his message of hope and change. When the day of the Delphi came they would flock to him.

Dodd was not reluctant in the task. The scope of what he was attempting did not awe him. It was merely the next logical step in the progression of his life. There was nowhere else to go, nothing else to do. The duty had grown into an obsession. Sam Jack Dodd could no longer settle for anything else. Everything he loved about this country, everything that had allowed him to be, was dying. A terrible price would be extracted to keep it alive, but this was about the nation's survival, and no price could be put on that. So few would ever touch the truth, yet in the end all would have no choice other than to accept it.

As they would accept him when the day of the Delphi dawned in barely nine days time.

PART THREE

WHITE SANDS

THE WHITE HOUSE:
MONDAY, APRIL 18, 1994; 1:00 P.M.

CHAPTER 23

The participants in the Monday-afternoon meeting at the White House arrived at well-spaced intervals and used different entrances so as not to attract attention. Two more had joined the inner circle composed of the President, his chief of staff Charlie Byrne, and FBI director Ben Samuelson.

Chairman of the Joint Chiefs of Staff Trevor Cantrell had been another of the Presidents' key appointees after an exhaustive and difficult search. The President had not known him personally, but his reputation for toughness combined with being a team player had raised him above the other candidates. Cantrell was below average in height but built like a bulldog. He still had no neck to speak of, although the days that required his marine corps uniforms to be custom-tailored to fit his bulk were gone now. He remained in great shape and only some gentle persuasion on the President's part had convinced him to finally let his crew cut grow out a little.

The second was Angela Taft, the National Security Advisor who had been passed off as a token appointment by the President's many enemies; after all, she was black *and* a woman. But in truth she was immensely qualified for the post. A tenured professor of political science at Harvard, Taft had joined the President's team during the campaign and had been primarily responsible for the drafting of his foreign policy platform. She was a pragmatist who was beholden neither to partisan politics nor to the media.

The night before the President had traded a few hours of sleep for a careful scrutiny of some videotapes his staff had

assembled for him on Samuel Jackson Dodd. He tried to
view Dodd not through the eyes of a politician and the
seated president, but as an ordinary, frustrated American
would. Undeniably Dodd was making a primitive kind of
sense, the kind that would appeal to the many citizens who
had joined the ranks of the disenchanted or disenfranchised.
That made him an even more frightening figure to anyone
who understood the true ramifications of his proposals, what
the country would be giving up if they accepted his quick
fix. Hitler, Stalin, and Mussolini had all made similar points
prior to their respective reigns. So long as things went well,
no one would be complaining. And when things stopped going well and the complaining did begin, the normal historic
channels for recourse would no longer be in place.

"All right," the President started. To Charlie Byrne and
the others, he looked like a different man. Recharged and
rededicated, no longer beaten. Even reborn. Recommitted in
the face of a crisis that made all else that had confronted his
administration pale by comparison. Four days ago, he had
just about given up. Nothing could be further from his mind
now. "You've all been briefed on the contents of the tape
that came into Director Samuelson's possession. Ben, why
don't we start with you? That means starting with the man
behind what appears to be an attempt to unseat this government."

Samuelson's expression was grave. "Sir, I've had thirty
agents collecting every bit of data on Sam Jack Dodd in existence, and there's nothing, not a single shred of evidence
linking him to some monstrous conspiratorial group."

"You're talking about hard evidence, of course," surmised
Charlie Byrne.

"Actually, any evidence at all."

"We've got the tape," Byrne reminded. "That's enough
for me."

"Enough to what?" asked the President.

"To arrest the son of a bitch!"

"On what charge?" challenged Ben Samuelson.

"Sedition or treason. Take your pick."

"Without proof, Charlie, it's impossible," the President told him. "We'd never be able to make it stick. Lest we forget, you're talking about the most popular man in the country. How do you think your suggestion would play in Congress? I haven't got many friends left there, and arresting Dodd will give my enemies the impetus they need to move with the impeachment proceedings plenty on the Hill have started to mention in private. Beyond that, we've got to remember that he's not in this alone." The President looked toward Samuelson. "Ben, your report on Cliff Jardine's murder concluded that it could never have happened in the manner it was carried out given on-site security unless—"

"Unless that security had been compromised."

"Meaning . . ."

"My conclusion pertained to a handful of agents."

"But how much more in this country has already been compromised beyond the Company? In the military, at Defense and State, on the Hill. How many people has Dodd got in his pocket?"

"My feeling, sir," Samuelson added, "is that it might be the other way around. Daniele's taped assertions would seem to indicate that Dodd was only the final piece in a huge puzzle, the 'missing variable,' I believe was the term used."

"And why not?" from the President. "He's the man the people love. The man who's got his hand on the nation's pulse, with his goddamn ninety percent approval rating."

"Then why is he bothering to attempt a forceful overthrow when he can win the next election?" raised Angela Taft.

"Because an election won't give him the power he wants, craves. This isn't about winning and losing; this is about redefining the way this country functions. Dodd and whoever's behind him are convinced that what we're trying to do just isn't working anymore, no matter what. He's after the kind of change even the Constitution wouldn't allow."

"A rather large obstacle," Angela Taft noted.

"Then part of his plan creates a rationale for its suspension, a rationale that has Dodd riding in on the white horse he's been keeping in the barn just to save the day."

"All the same, Mr. President," Angela Taft argued, "this isn't some Third World country where a coup succeeds if four tanks make it to the palace gates."

"General?"

Cantrell took his cue. "We may not be Third World, Dr. Taft, but with a centralized seat of power we face many of the same limitations and liabilities. That becomes especially true if the opposition still had the element of surprise on their side. Our response time would indeed be the problem under that scenario. The right men and weapons on the part of the opposition could get the job done before we could mount an adequate counter." Cantrell paused. "With that in mind, Mr. President, I do have some suggestions."

"Proceed, Trev."

"Speculation on unknown variables here seems fruitless. Our focus should remain on those issues where we have a degree of reasonable certainty."

"I wasn't sure there were any."

"There's at least one, sir: the government cannot be toppled so long as the current administration and Congress is seated. I believe our opposition's plan began with that awareness and took shape when the means to overcome it was discovered."

"What are you suggesting, General?"

"In the military, we'd call it Evac. I'm suggesting we strongly consider moving the seated government to designated safe areas."

Cantrell proceeded to summarize briefly the three primary facilities that were the subject of constant upkeep, but to this point had never once been employed. Mount Weather, located fifty miles northwest of Washington, was built to house the President, justices of the Supreme Court, cabinet members, and other selected officials in the event of a nuclear war. Each man or woman had already been assigned a pickup point within the capital where they would be flown by helicopter to what amounted to an impregnable, invisible fortress.

The equally secret Site R, just six miles from Camp David near the border of Maryland and Pennsylvania, was the largest of the three facilities. All 265,000 of its square feet were contained underground in the area of Raven Rock Mountain. Site R was designed to house the Alternate Joint Communications Center and the Alternate Military Command Center. Effectively it was envisioned as a wartime replacement for the Pentagon.

The final installation had no catchy code name and was known simply as Greenbrier. It was not protected by huge mountains or vast tonnages of rock as its counterparts were. Instead, Greenbrier was simply a massive cavern near the luxurious Greenbrier Hotel in White Sulpher Springs, West Virginia, a cavern dug out of the ground and well fortified to withstand assault. It had been constructed to house the whole of the Senate and the House of Representatives within its concrete walls. Not only did this require the requisite number of living spaces, but it also called for auditoriums and halls spacious enough to allow for full sessions of both bodies. One of these, known as the Exhibit Hall, was capable of housing a joint session of Congress.

Of course, with the dissolution of the Soviet Union, no one in Washington believed any of the three facilities would ever see use. General Cantrell's suggestion that their utilization might finally come to pass thanks to a force *within* the country seemed the ultimate irony. Perhaps at last one of the greatest wastes of taxpayer money in the nation's history would actually prove its merit.

"The most fundamental problem," Angela Taft responded at the end of Cantrell's discourse, "is one of timing, General. Since we at present have no idea of the enemy's timetable, how do we know when to press the panic button?"

"And even if we did," picked up Charlie Byrne, "pressing

it would be tantamount to submission. We'd be running with our tails between our legs."

"Better than having them blown off, Mr. Byrne," Cantrell was quick to point out.

"You believe that's what all this will come down to?" the President quizzed him.

"Sir, what I believe is that our opposition needs to create a state of utter chaos, out of which only they are in a position to restore order. It follows, then, that one of the prime requirements of their plan is to neutralize the chain of command, along with the chain of succession."

"Short of this Evac, General, is there any defense you can suggest—preemptive or preventive military measures, perhaps?"

"None with anywhere near as high a degree of confidence for success, sir, and they would require an open acknowledgment of what we thought we were facing." Cantrell leaned forward over the table. "The Seventh Light Infantry has been trained for this kind of eventuality. We could arrange to have units moved into Washington. Back them up with an armored division or two."

"Washington turned into an armed encampment . . ."

"I prefer to call it a defensive ring."

"I don't think the public would take kindly to setting up a defense against a force we can't even prove exists. Beyond that, how long will we have to keep the ring in place while facing charges of paranoia and downright incompetence? With enough momentum, such things could bring us down as effectively as bullets."

"Okay," Charlie Byrne postulated, "then let me try something else out on all of you: we go public with our suspicions *without* naming names and without calling out the cavalry."

General Cantrell shook his head demonstratively. "Mr Byrne—"

"Hold on, hear me out on this. Dodd and whoever's behind him could never accept being exposed. That's why both Jardine and Daniels had to die. That's why we never found the only copy of Daniels's report and why even the typewriter ribbon on his old Olivetti was changed. As far as the opposition knew, it ended there, and it would have, if not for our friend in the Russian embassy."

"What's your point, Charlie?" the President asked.

"My point, sir, is that fear of exposure might be enough to make these sons of bitches pull back. It's the one thing their plan could never have accounted for."

"You're suggesting we should release the tape."

"It's all we have," Byrne acknowledged.

"But it's not enough," the President said with grim certainty. "Not to avoid embarrassment and disgrace anyway. Oh, we might be able to delay their plan for a while, leaving ourselves so laughably weak that they might not even have to storm the capital to take over not long down the road."

"I still think it beats pulling out of the city or sending in tanks to patrol the streets."

"Don't get me wrong, Charlie," the President consoled, "I think you're on the right track. But to ride it all the way out we need more information, more proof. And that's why we need McCracken." He looked at Samuelson. "No luck finding him, I presume, Ben."

"We've confirmed it was indeed McCracken who managed to get the bomb off that American Airlines Airbus en route to Miami on Saturday night."

"Planted by our enemies to get rid of him, of course."

"They're his enemies also, sir. But he left no trail for us to follow once he reached Miami. We've left messages at all his drop points and tried unsuccessfully to contact a former intelligence operative who often fronts for him. We even sent a team into the Maine woods to search for an Indian he served with in Vietnam and apparently has continued to work with, also without any results."

"He's getting close to them," the President proclaimed, an edge of hope sliding into his voice.

"We can't be sure of that."

"I'm sure. And anyone who's read as much about McCracken as I have in the past few days would be just as sure. We find him and we find what we need to save this nation from Dodd and company."

Charlie Byrne shifted uneasily. "Unless they find him first, Mr. President."

CHAPTER 24

"Thanks for letting me tag along, boss."

"Got a feeling I'm gonna need you on this one, Sal."

McCracken had barely beaten Sal Belamo to Albuquerque Airport Monday afternoon. He had stopped once to buy a change of clothes to replace the ones lifted from the farmer's clothesline back in Oklahoma. Belamo wore a crinkled linen suit over a plaid shirt. The supplies he had brought with him for both of them would already be making their way to the baggage carousel.

Belamo wasn't much more than five-and-a-half feet tall and had carried more flab than muscle ever since Carlos Monzon ended his career in their second fight. The contrast with McCracken's V-shaped, muscle-laden frame and Johnny Wareagle's massive bulk belied the fact that Belamo was as good as either of them in a pinch, albeit in his own style.

"You ready to tell me what's goin' on here, boss, I'm ready to listen."

McCracken explained it all as best as he could on their drive south on Route 25 toward the White Sands desert and Sandcastle One. It wasn't Arlo Cleese and the Midnight Riders at all who were out to topple the government. That was only what the country was going to be led to believe by the true perpetrators, who formed the remnants of Bill Carlisle's shadowy Trilateral Commission subcommittee.

Belamo accepted the tale with a combination of shrugs

and nods. By the time Blaine reached the end, though, his face was twisted into a frown of taut displeasure and disgust.

"Then these detention centers—"

"Are good places to stash those who don't agree with their plans," McCracken completed.

"Gonna be lots who fit that bill, boss. It's a big country."

Kristen's cell was small and windowless, a single recessed ceiling light all that stood between her and total darkness. She lay atop a stiff cot set directly opposite the solid door. With her watch gone, she found that distinctions between night and day had become blurred. Her mind wandered. She tried to hold it steady, to reconstruct what had happened in the fuzzy period since her capture.

Her last clear stretch of memory was of being dragged by the man monster who was wearing her brother's hair from the car where Samantha Jordan lay dead. She was still screaming when another man jabbed a needle into her arm.

Then darkness.

Consciousness returned intermittently after what might have been an hour or a day. She recalled being jostled in the binds of a safety harness. Her ears were aching. A grinding, whirling noise filled them.

A helicopter! She was being taken somewhere on a helicopter!

"She's come around," a voice said.

Then darkness descended once more.

Kristen's next clear memory was awakening inside a tiny room to the monotone voice of a man asking questions.

"Had you spoken to your brother immediately prior to the night he left the message?"

"No."

Why was she answering? Her questioner's round, flabby face loomed above her, caught in the light from the small room's single bulb. The slightest movement he made took his face from the bulb and allowed only slight flickers to dance across it. As her vision cleared, Kristen realized there was a second figure in the room, back by the door, shrouded in darkness.

"Did he at any time tell you what he had uncovered in Colorado?"

"No." She couldn't help answering.

"Did he tell you what he saw at Miravo Air Force Base?"

"No."

"Did you even know he was in Colorado?"

"Not until I found out that was where the phone call had come from."

"Through the FBI agent. Paul Gathers."

"Yes."

"Did you share the information with anyone else prior to coming to Colorado yourself?"

"No."

"And once you reached Colorado?"

"Farlowe. The sheriff of Grand Mesa."

"You told him everything?"

"Everything."

"To your knowledge, did he share the information with anyone else?"

"No."

"Who did you share the information with after your return to Washington?"

"Senator Jordan."

"No one else?"

"Colonel Haynes at the Pentagon."

"Other than Colonel Haynes."

"No. No one else. Only the senator."

When Kristen said that, a picture of Samantha Jordan's dead eyes staring at her in the car flashed through her mind. She shuddered.

"She can't take much more." Her inquisitor had turned round to face the shape hidden in darkness by the door.

"She'll take as much as we need her to. I have my orders."

And then the inquisitor's flabby face turned back Kristen's way. *"Did you speak to anyone after coming to Colorado with the senator?"*

"No."

Kristen felt herself nodding off, unable to concentrate.

"The situation is contained," she heard her inquisitor report to the shape by the door in apparent conclusion. "I'll order a light sedative to be administered. That's all she'll need. She'll be taken to one of the cell blocks to await the next session."

"Fine. Let's go."

The door to the small room opened. Light from the corridor flooded in, catching the man previously lost in the darkness.

A big man, huge. Towering in the doorway, he seemed to fill out its width. He stepped out ahead of her inquisitor and the light caught his face, his hair.

Oh my God . . .

Kristen knew the face, recognized it from back on the road when they had taken her prisoner. It was square and angular, flat as the rock-face side of a mountain, framed still by her brother's hair.

Kristen wanted to scream.

The door closed. Something rattled. Footsteps echoed.

Kristen willed her eyes to stay open, willed herself to stay alert, aware. But her lids were dead weights and closed over her eyes despite all her resolve.

Since then Kristen had come awake sporadically, each re-entry into consciousness lasting longer and leaving her more in command of her senses. She'd been able to avoid closing her eyes for what felt like an hour now, fighting to keep her mind active.

Put it together! Reason it out!

Kristen vividly recalled the imposing sight of the green storage containers, each with a nuclear warhead inside, lined up in the reconstructed hangar at Miravo Air Force Base. Hundreds had undoubtedly come before them and hundreds more would undoubtedly follow.

A fresh chill seized Kristen. Colonel Riddick had been all too happy to display the contents of that hangar. But she had seen no evidence on the base to suggest they were actually being dismantled. Anyone in possession of such an arsenal would become party to incredible power. What if David had witnessed some of those containers being spirited off the base by truck or plane? His death would have been judged necessary to protect the terrible secret he had become privy to.

Could it be that nuclear arms were being pilfered and sold to whomever could meet the asking price? The fuses and unlocking codes needed to activate the warhead could conceivably be provided by Colonel Riddick. She knew Riddick was lying about the base's status on the Saturday she and Duncan Farlowe had nearly lost their lives in the hills beyond it. And that meant he could be lying about everything else.

But there was far more involved here than simply a black-market operation Riddick was part of, something even bleaker than the terrifying thought of brokered nuclear arms. Samantha Jordan's participation proved that.

"Give me a chance to explain. I can still bring you on board. I can convince them to let me."

The words were among the last the senator had spoken. Explain *what*? Convince *whom*? Whatever Jordan was a part of must have intended to make use of the stolen warheads themselves for a purpose other than profit. The balance sheet being kept here was not about dollars. It was about power.

Kristen wrapped her arms tighter about herself and pushed her body up so that she was half sitting, her back pressed against the concrete wall. Her mind remained sluggish and she had to hold fast to her thoughts before they slipped away.

A conspiracy was going on that stretched to the highest corridors of power, extending even into the FBI. Paul Gathers must have made the connection between Grand Mesa and Miravo Air Force Base. When he began to make inquiries, he was silenced. Then she and Duncan Farlowe—

Duncan Farlowe! She had implicated him in all this during the course of her interrogation. That meant the old sheriff was in grave danger. Not being able to warn Farlowe, being responsible for what was about to befall him, made Kristen feel even more helpless.

She let her thoughts veer away and focused on what she knew. She was a prisoner in some sort of ultra-modern high-security prison. She had been kept alive strictly to learn what she had discovered and who else she might have been in contact with. Once her story was confirmed and perhaps another interrogation conducted, her usefulness would be exhausted.

And the man wearing her brother's hair would kill her.

Johnny Wareagle sat in front of the steaming coffee that turned his insides sour on its way down. He never drank coffee, drank nothing like it other than the teas he concocted and bagged himself. But he wanted to seem as normal as possible to those inside Carrizozo, New Mexico's lone diner. He wanted the waitress to accept him so the questioning process would go smoothly.

"I get you anything else, honey?" she asked, holding a fresh pot of the black acid in hand.

"No, thank you."

"Man your size really should eat more. How 'bout it? Bacon and eggs? Maybe a side of flapjacks? Come on, I'll even go back and make them myself."

"Sorry, no."

The diner and Carrizozo were located at the virtual beginning of White Sands, the rolling endless expanse of land in plain view outside any window. He'd come here straight from Tyson Gash and the 911 in the hope that someone inside would know what in White Sands had led to Traggeo being brought to the area. Johnny wasn't getting his hopes up.

"You heading to the reservation?" The waitress appeared eager to talk.

"Excuse me?"

"We got lots of 'em couple hundred miles west of here. Lots like you, Indians I mean, stop here on their way." She chuckled. "Guess they don't have much of a choice. This is the last stop there is."

"Who else stops here?"

"You mean regularly?"

"If there is anyone."

"Not many 'sides tourists and the usual truckers hauling loads to and from Mexico. Used to be better. Not too long ago, either. We actually went back to operating twenty-four hours a day when the construction teams were around."

"Construction teams," Johnny repeated, a sensation like static pricking at his skin.

"Sure. Must have been hundred-man crews, and near as I could tell they were running shifts 'round the clock."

"Building what?"

The waitress leaned forward and lowered her voice to a whisper, the coffeepot a memory in her hand. "I heard it said it was a new army base, but the real truth is that the government needed another place to put all the space aliens that they been collecting for decades."

"Have you ever seen this base?"

She shook her head. "Never seen it myself and never met anyone who has, 'sides the workers. I'm never going to, either, since they never got it finished. Ran out of money or something, or the aliens died most likely."

"I know these parts," Johnny lied, "and I've never noticed such a place."

"That's the point," the waitress scoffed at him. "Don't you get it? A place the government plans to stash aliens they don't exactly want to advertise. They built it on the way to Alamogordo, of all places, on roads unmarked and hidden. They built it so even if you happened to get yourself lost and pass by, you might not even notice on account of it's the same color as the sand. I heard it said it damn near disappears at night."

"Can you show me where it is?" Johnny asked her.

"You got a map?"

McCracken and Sal Belamo first saw the headlights coming toward them fifteen miles down a lonely road deep in the heart of White Sands. Belamo's directions for Sandcastle One had them heading south on Route 54 out of Carrizozo and then west into White Sands at Tularosa.

White Sands was not a desert per se, nor was it even a wasteland. Instead flora bloomed near breathtaking rock formations. The land sloped, curved, and climbed, rebutting the common belief that White Sands was no more than a barren plain. Sagebrush and tumbleweed shifted about, hitching a ride with the wind.

"Company," Sal told Blaine as the headlights gleamed their way.

McCracken slowed their car to a halt after spotting a jeep turned sideways across the narrow road. In typical guard-style procedure, one of its occupants approached in the spill of a blinding floodlight while the other hung back by the vehicle. Both were dressed in army uniforms.

"Just two," Belamo confirmed, a .44 magnum that looked as big as one of his stubby arms eased into his lap.

McCracken had the SIG-Sauer Belamo had replaced for him in hand as well. The approaching soldier reached his open window and Blaine gave him the best innocent look he could manage.

"We're lost," he said.

The soldier held his M16 forward but not leveled. "You have entered a restricted government compound. I'm going to have to ask you to—"

"Just tell me how to get back on Route 70," Blaine said,

stretching his unfolded map toward the window, virtually filling it.

"—vacate the area immediately upon penalty of seizure and arrest."

To punctuate his order, the soldier poked the barrel of his M16 against the map. The paper collapsed as Blaine grabbed the barrel and yanked the soldier forward. Before the man could respond, Blaine's SIG split one of the map's folds and jammed into his ribs.

"Take your finger off the trigger."

The soldier hesitated, even though his barrel had been tilted harmlessly toward the backseat. He stole a quick glance at his partner back at the jeep, thought about firing a burst to warn him.

"Do it and both of you die," McCracken cautioned.

His eyes gestured sideways to make sure the soldier noticed Sal Belamo steadying his .44 magnum against the dashboard in line with the soldier standing back at the jeep.

"Do what I tell you," Blaine continued, "and you both live."

The soldier pulled his hand from the trigger.

"Now tell your friend to come over here. Tell him to hurry."

The waitress in the Carrizozo diner had told Wareagle that the complex in the desert seemed to disappear at night. Accordingly, Johnny had waited until after dark to make his approach, following the directions she had provided through White Sands. He was proceeding on the assumption that Traggeo was part of some outlaw plot whose leaders were taking great pains to keep undetected, a plot the killer had tried to enlist the man called Badger from Tyson Gash's 911 Brigade in as well. Security precautions, then, were certain to be in place around the installation falsely thought to have been abandoned prior to completion.

Well after dusk Johnny had left his rented truck on the side of the road three miles from the spot on his map the waitress had marked for him in White Sands. He left the hood up and tied a white handkerchief to the radio antenna to indicate a simple breakdown to any patrol. He also made sure to leave a clear trail moving in a direction opposite from his true destination, so a patrol would have no reason to believe he was heading for the complex.

This done, he doubled back off the road and headed deeper into White Sands. With the darkness and the sagebrush acting together as a veil, Johnny almost missed the complex altogether. Only the high steel fence surrounding it finally alerted him. Gazing through it from less than four hundred yards away, Wareagle could barely make out the shape of the huge building housed within.

Not only was the complex painted the exact color of the surrounding desert, but its exterior seemed to have the same rough texture as the sand. An unfinished grainy quality ensured that both the light and the darkness would strike the building the same way they struck the land surrounding it.

It looked, well, like a massive sandcastle chiseled out of the desert plain itself.

From this angle, all Johnny could see was a four-story structure that stretched nearly two hundred yards from east to west, built pyramid-style with each level protruding out from the one above it. What little the night gave up indicated that comparable wings extended south from either end. That meant the complex was either U-shaped or a square, a courtyard enclosed by its walls. Without binoculars, Johnny could tell little else for sure. And yet the way the whole compound was laid out made him question whether this was the training center he had expected at all.

Indeed, it looked more like a prison.

Had Traggeo simply left the cells of one for the cells of another? No. No spotlight scanned the spacious grounds. A pair of watchtowers were unmanned. A small complement of armed men patrolled the desert turf within the fence, but that was all. Other than the departure of a patrol jeep through the complex's entrance an hour into his vigil, there was no other activity to indicate this facility was even operational.

Whatever had gone on here seemed to be long over. Conversely, it might be a building still waiting to be used; a building now empty but poised to fill a future role. Either way, the token security force on the premises must have been stationed here to protect whatever secrets the complex held, among which Johnny hoped would be Traggeo's present whereabouts.

Johnny had begun to turn his attention to gaining entry to the complex when a blast erupted from the direction where the jeep had sped several minutes before. He could see an orange glow indicative of a fiery explosion in the flat distance. All at once, the complex came alive. A piercing siren went off and men scrambled in all directions under a sudden wash of light. Two more jeeps tore out of the complex's entrance, backed up by a truck packed with troops. Both jeeps were equipped with .50-caliber machine guns.

The thick spread of light gave Johnny his first clear look at the complex and what he would have to cross to reach it. His eyes catalogued the terrain, potential obstacles, and places of concealment en route to the fence enclosing the perimeter.

Using the fortunate distraction to his own advantage, Johnny started forward into the night and began his approach.

"Right on time," said Sal Belamo, his binoculars lingering on the explosion while Blaine followed the progress of the convoy out of Sandcastle One toward the origin of the blast.

Sal had wired the explosive charge to the jeep to ensure a bright display in the desert dark. Both he and McCracken had learned long ago that nothing aided an unwarranted entry to a secured base better than a distraction which lured security personnel away from it. As it turned out, Sandcastle One was another two miles from the spot where the jeep had confronted them. After stowing the two guards a safe distance from the coming explosion, they drove most of that distance with lights off and then sprinted the last stretch. They took up a position within the cover of a rock formation four hundred yards in front of Sandcastle One just two minutes before the timer charge was set to go off. The night gave up virtually nothing until the explosion brought the expected flurry of men and vehicles out the main gate through the spill of lights. The last of the vehicles had barely passed out of sight of the gate when McCracken abandoned his binoculars and grasped the pack.

"Let's go," he told Belamo.

CHAPTER 25

Inside Sandcastle One, the hair that was not his own bounced raggedly atop Traggeo's head as he hurried along the corridor leading out of Cellblock B. Though muffled by the building's double concrete construction, the explosion from beyond had been easily recognizable to one familiar with the sound.

He was almost to the control center when the siren began to wail.

"Fuck," he muttered. "Fuck!"

He tore the hair of the kid he'd killed in the motel from his head and flung it against a wall. Pieces of glue and the kid's rotted scalp stuck to his flesh and left it a patchwork of dark, grimy splotches. He hadn't had time to chemically treat this scalp properly and was looking forward to the replacement that would be his very soon. Of course, he wouldn't wear the woman's full locks. He would style and fashion them into the braids of his people—a headdress and trophy at the same time.

The first scalp Traggeo had worn had been the straw-colored hair belonging to the Indian who had tracked him to

Miravo. How that Indian had managed the feat Traggeo would never know. Nor did he know exactly the nature of the operation he had been a part of since his release from prison had been arranged. He had managed to recruit several other members of Salvage Company to join him, careful to leave himself the only officer among them. He held the rank of platoon staff sergeant the day he scalped three Vietcong collaborators to set an example. Such news traveled fast through the Delta villages. All he wanted to do was make a point.

The blessing of it all was that Salvage Company had allowed him to explore and come to grips with his true nature. The regular army was all protocol and regulations. Salvage Company just got things done. Brutally. Efficiently. Much to Traggeo's liking.

He knew no Indian blood flowed through his veins; it was a spiritual thing. He could feel the spirit of a great warrior reborn inside him, guiding him on. He saw the warrior in a dream vision and took on his likeness, fashioned his very appearance after what the vision had shown him.

But it wasn't enough. The warrior in his dream vision could not achieve the greatness he longed for so long as another stood in the way:

Johnny Wareagle.

The huge true-blood who had shared the war with Traggeo was more myth than man. A legend Traggeo knew he would have to overcome if he was to achieve what the warrior of his vision prescribed for him. The wearing of his victims' scalps was intended as a means to swallow their energy, absorb their auras into his own, so that he would be up to the task when the day came for him to meet Wareagle.

For now, though, there was a job to do, a task to perform. Traggeo took great pride in being trusted. He wanted to prove to those who had freed him to his destiny that they had chosen well, wanted to show himself to be worthy. Whoever had arranged his release from prison must have known of his work with Salvage Company. While those years had helped hone his physical skill, though, this tour of duty would allow Traggeo to hone his spirit, fashion it in the image he desired.

He reached the control center and entered the proper combination into the keypad. The door slid open. He charged through it and moved straight for the chief of security.

"What's going on?"

The security chief held one earpiece of his headset in place as he spoke. "We've lost contact with the patrol jeep."

"The explosion, you fuck!"

"Our men are almost to the scene now."

Traggeo reached over and grabbed the man by the shirt. A name tag that read CAROSI went flying. "You sent them *out*?"

"I-I-I had to."

"Damn it!"

Carosi's headset had come half off and Traggeo could hear a garbled report coming out through the earpiece. The control center overlooked the front of the place known as Sandcastle One, and he could see the day-bright glow cast over the yard.

"Turn off the lights!" Traggeo ordered.

"But—"

Traggeo lifted Carosi up and slammed him against a wall composed entirely of darkened television monitors. "Don't you see what's going on here? We're being set up. Turn off the fucking lights!"

Johnny Wareagle had reached the fence on the complex's eastern side an instant before the lights snapped back off. His Gerber M-2 knife sliced through the steel links like putty, and he was inside within seconds. Before pressing on, he refastened the ruined portion of the fence as best he could to hide the fact that the base had been penetrated from anyone with the sense to look.

Turning back toward the darkened grounds, Johnny saw

the remains of the security force was beginning a careful sweep of the area. He recognized the black, awkward-looking devices strapped around their faces as AN/PVS-7 night-vision goggles. But the men weren't looking for him.

They were looking for whoever had set off the explosion down the road. Another party, perhaps significant in number, was attempting to gain entry to the complex. Johnny had become so obsessed with catching Traggeo that until now he had totally failed to consider what sort of plot the killer might be involved in. Clearly it involved a force with sufficient resources to either construct or commandeer this facility. And this force's enemies had arrived at the same time Johnny had, something he could make work in his favor.

Wareagle lay flat on the ground and began smoothing handfuls of the desert upon his flesh and clothes. When he once again started to move forward, his frame was indistinguishable from the ground itself. As the complex had melded into the desert, so had Johnny. He pulled himself on with his feet and elbows, lost amidst the sagebrush and tumbleweed, unseen even to those who looked directly at him.

Belamo and McCracken used wire cutters to get through the fence. The lights died again just after they were in, and Blaine reached over to stop Sal from pressing onward.

"Someone knows we're here."

"Huh?"

"That's why they turned the lights back off."

"First bright thing they've done, you ask me."

"Absolutely. An assault team would use the light to pick off the guards one at a time. The dark keeps everything equal."

"Or them ahead, they got that night-vision shit."

"Right."

"So what d'we do?"

"Change the rules."

"Boss?"

"They were expecting an assault team, Sal. They weren't expecting us."

"I've called in our status," Carosi was saying, the headset refastened over his ears. "Reinforcements are en route as a precaution but it's going to take some time. . . . Sir?"

Traggeo didn't even turn the man's way. Instead he continued to strain his eyes out the window in Sandcastle One's control center toward the grounds beyond. The glass had been treated to appear opaque on the other side, making it impossible for anyone below to notice him. The night gave up nothing besides the occasional shape of one of the guards shuffling about in search of intruders.

"It was the patrol jeep, all right," Carosi resumed after accepting the report from the group that had reached the scene of the explosion.

This time Traggeo did turn his way. "Order the men back here."

"We still have two missing, unaccounted for."

"Either they're dead or they might as well be. Order the men back. Fast."

Carosi swallowed a thick gulp of air and again did as he was told.

Traggeo swung back to the window.

"Do your men on the grounds have walkie-talkies?" he asked.

"Of course."

"Ask them to report in. Ask all of them to report in."

"Why?"

Traggeo's eyes blazed cold fire. "Because I can't see them anymore."

McCracken and Sal Belamo had split up to deal with the immediate threat of the patrolling guards. While permitting sight even on the darkest of desert nights, the AN/PVS-7 night-vision goggles the guards wore came with severe limitations. For one thing, their bulk precluded rapid twists and turns. For another they reduced peripheral vision to almost zero. These two limitations were easily taken advantage of by those who understood them.

While trying to find a way to enter Sandcastle One, Blaine had come upon four guards wearing the goggles. All four had been easily and quietly subdued, no weapon required to incapacitate them. McCracken figured it would be different for the ones who crossed Sal Belamo's path. The pug-nosed ex-boxer had learned his trade on the streets and continued to practice it in the same deadly manner. He had no trouble using a silenced semiautomatic in place of savvy, if it meant facilitating matters and saving a few seconds.

Instead Blaine was surprised to come upon a pair of guards hidden in the low brush of the grounds who were unconscious instead of dead. He might have suspected that Sal had finally discovered subtlety if it weren't for the fact that Belamo, according to plan, should have been on the *opposite* side of the complex. McCracken shrugged the anomaly off and continued on as the headlights of the returning convoy burned through the last stretch of road back for Sandcastle One.

"I can't raise any of the perimeter guards," Carosi said dumbly after putting out the call yet again.

"Because they're not there anymore, you fuck!" snapped Traggeo.

A red light began to flash on the main security console, accompanied by a chirping beep. The status monitor flashed two words in rhythm with the beeps:

UNWARRANTED ENTRY

"We have a penetration!"

"Where?"

"First-floor window. Southeast quadrant, sector one-one—"

"Where the fuck is that?"

Before Carosi could respond to Traggeo's question, a second light and fresh chirping commenced. The status monitor's message changed only slightly:

UNWARRANTED ENTRY
UNWARRANTED ENTRY

"Second penetration!" Carosi managed, almost in a gasp. "First-floor door. Northwest quadrant, sector—"

"Just tell me where, goddamnit!" Traggeo demanded.

Before the security chief could oblige, the lights of the convoy streamed toward the main gate.

"I want them deployed inside," Traggeo ordered. "I want them to shoot anything that moves!"

The gate opened electronically and the first jeep had barely cleared it when the explosion sounded. The jeep's carcass was hurled into the air in a burst of flames. It was flung backward and crashed into the second jeep immediately behind it. The personnel truck bringing up the rear swerved to avoid a deadly collision and was caught in a second explosion that twirled it about like a top and then tumbled it over. A third blast caught the fuel tanks of all three vehicles, the result being a massive fireball that lit the whole of Sandcastle One in its glow.

Because he was standing by the window, Traggeo's skin was tinted orange. His expression had remained unchanged through the chaos that had scrambled the other occupants of the control center behind him. He could feel, could taste, every breath. The calm of battle had taken over. His thinking was clear.

Sandcastle One had been penetrated in two places by an undetermined number of men, who had also secured the perimeter. His primary task now was to contain the damage to the overall plan. There was nothing in Sandcastle One's online systems that could give up any hint of what was coming. But there was a prisoner inside who could provide far more than merely a hint.

Traggeo knew what he had to do.

He moved to the control center's door and pressed the proper code into the keypad. Nothing happened.

"It seals automatically when the complex is penetrated," the security chief explained.

"Open it."

Carosi swung back to his terminal. The door slid open with a hiss.

Johnny Wareagle was creeping along a first-floor corridor of the complex when the explosions sounded. Ordinarily he would have thought the other force that had shown up here was launching an all-out attack, but that didn't feel like the case to him. His thoughts were jumbled, confused. He had come here strictly for Traggeo. This other force had obviously come for another reason altogether.

Blainey . . .

Wareagle shook the feeling off as quickly as it slipped into his mind. A distraction was the last thing he needed now, much less one involving the man who had fought next to him so often that he could no longer enter into battle without expecting to see McCracken by his side. But tonight he was alone. No matter what the mystery force's purpose or allegiance was, he was alone, his own purpose singular: Traggeo.

Johnny turned a corner and walked directly into a blanket of darkness, forcing him to feel his way. The earlier corridors he had traversed had been lit by the dull glow of recessed ceiling lights. The walls and doors, the floor tile too, were off-white in color, not quite cream. Though there were no bars or visible locks, the suspicions Johnny'd had outside were confirmed: this place was a prison, its cells presently unoccupied but fully prepared to take on inmates.

Yet something felt wrong here. Wareagle had been involved in enough rescue missions inside Vietcong prison camps to know the feeling of futility they brought with them. He knew the hopelessness, the despair of their very settings. The feeling here was different, though equally ominous and foreboding. There was a powerful enemy at work as well. Johnny could feel that enemy in the walls, could feel it in the awful purpose this place had been constructed to fulfill.

The complex was part of something terrible. The spirits grabbed Johnny's ear and he heeded them. He understood at once why his search for Traggeo had been so important. That was how the spirits had lured him here to take up pursuit of a far greater enemy the madman had joined up with.

Wareagle stopped in his tracks.

Traggeo was here *now*! Traggeo was *coming*!

Johnny stopped in his tracks, as if an invisible thrust had shoved up against him. His senses sharpened. Up ahead he could see light beyond the next bend in the hall.

Wareagle pulled his knife from its sheath.

The rapid series of explosions had drawn Kristen to the door of her cell, ear pressed against it to listen for more hints of whatever was going on. But the hollow sound of approaching footsteps was all that reached her. Kristen lunged backward.

The monster was coming to kill her.

She understood what David had seen. What he had known, she now knew. That information could not die with her.

A weapon! She needed a weapon!

Her eyes fell on the bed frame. Tear one of the steel support rods free, and at least she would be able to mount some sort of defense. Kristen yanked the mattress off and overturned the bed frame. It thumped hard to the floor.

The bed frame was constructed of solid wood.

Beyond, the footsteps had stopped.

Click.

Her door had been electronically unlocked. The knob began to turn.

* * *

"No!"

The word had started as a scream and ended as a rasp. The door came all the way open.

Kristen shrank back against the wall and watched the huge figure enter. Not the man monster, though. Before her stood a giant Indian whose head barely cleared the doorway when he stepped part of the way in.

Kristen was not able to tear her eyes away from the Indian's compelling gaze.

"You have seen him," he said without further explanation, and his eyes darted back toward the corridor. "We must leave. Hurry."

Knowing she had no choice, Kristen stepped through the cell door and joined him in the corridor. They had started forward when a figure turned onto the hallway at its head a hundred feet down.

"That's hi—"

Kristen's identification of the man monster who had killed her brother was cut short when the Indian yanked her in the opposite direction. They charged toward a blanket of darkness as a staccato burst of gunfire echoed along the hall. Chasms were dug out of the walls. Some of the bullets ricocheted in metallic screeches through the air.

Kristen felt the Indian nearly carry her around the corner that led into the waiting blackness.

Traggeo had not hesitated. Even as his eyes recorded the impossible sight straight ahead of him, his aim had been fast and sure.

Johnny Wareagle!

But his ultimate nemesis, the man whose scalp he wished to claim above all others, had moved a bare instant before he had fired. The spirits who had refused to accept Traggeo as a true-blood for so long had given Wareagle all the warning he needed. But those same spirits must have delivered the legendary Indian here for a reason.

Yes!

This was Traggeo's chance, his test. Pass it by slaying Wareagle, and he would finally be accepted by the spirits that had so long scorned him. Wareagle was everything that Traggeo wanted to be. A legend. A hero. An individual more myth than man.

Wareagle melted from the path of his first burst toward the darkness of the next hall. Traggeo charged down the corridor without halting his fire.

Click.

His clip exhausted just as Wareagle and the woman vanished around the corner. The power in this unfinished wing had yet to be turned on. Pursuing Wareagle now meant doing so in the dark, on the legendary true-blood's terms. Traggeo stopped. The spirits were tempting him, but he wouldn't take the bait foolishly. He knew it was Wareagle's game now to string out as he saw fit. Traggeo also knew defeating the legend meant confronting him on his, Traggeo's, own terms, not following Wareagle recklessly into the blackness.

He swung round and started back for the control center.

"Stay here," Johnny ordered in the darkness after gauging that Traggeo had not elected to follow them.

Hearing the thump outside the woman's door had led him to stop before it. The keypad had not been installed yet, but the wiring was in place. He had simply touched the proper ends together and the door had snapped electronically open.

"Where are you going?" she asked him.

"I'll be back."

"You're going after him, aren't you?"

Johnny had his killing knife poised in his hand now. He wondered whether she could somehow see it.

"I'm going with you," the woman insisted. "He killed my brother."

"He has killed many."

"Then what are we waiting for?" the woman asked and Johnny felt her grab hold of his arm again.

* * *

McCracken moved slowly along the empty corridor, his mind struggling to register all that he was seeing. He had entered Sandcastle One at the point where the southern wing intersected with the eastern one. But he guessed that what his eyes recorded would have been much the same anywhere else.

Sandcastle One was a high-tech prison. There were no bars, no cells. Instead there were doors laid out along the hall in dormitory-like fashion. No more than eight feet separated one from the next, which indicated the rooms within were very small. The wall beside each door was equipped with a keypad complete with built-in microphone.

This place had been built to very precise and costly specifications. A civilized element of polish had been added that hardly fitted the class of criminal it had supposedly been constructed to house. Not drug dealers or suppliers by a long shot. The cells of the complex were awaiting a different class of inmate altogether.

Political prisoners, those who were deemed a threat to the new order about to seize the country.

The Trilateral Commission, through a subcommittee chaired by Bill Carlisle, had sought to accomplish that same goal originally through Operation Yellow Rose. Now, nearly twenty years later, militant offspring of the Trilat were on the verge of achieving it.

Blaine checked his watch. Sandcastle One's uninhabited status explained why only a token security force was in place. But he was still hoping that clues might be found somewhere that would bring him closer to the identity of those who were behind the coming takeover.

McCracken continued on, amazed by the expanse of Sandcastle One. Based on this wing, he estimated that the complex contained upwards of 750 cells to house its prisoners. He imagined more structures like this all over the country, five others already under construction and dozens more to follow over time, if necessary, all filled to capacity.

Blaine had swung onto another corridor when the sound of automatic gunfire reached him. A long burst coming from the fourth floor. McCracken steadied his own Uzi submachine gun before him and charged that way.

"We're getting close to where I was interrogated," Kristen whispered to the Indian. "Somewhere on the next hallway, I think."

Before she could finish, the Indian had thrown her behind him.

"Down!" he ordered, and she barely had time to see the man monster whirling into view before Johnny took her with him to the floor.

They crashed to the hard tile together, barely below the spray of bullets. Before she found her breath, the Indian had somehow managed to send the knife he'd been holding whistling through the air.

Fifty feet away the blade embedded in Traggeo's forearm. His hand jerked upward. A fresh burst of bullets carved chunks from the ceiling. He wailed in agony and spun sideways, slamming into the wall against the control center keypad. In the same swift motion he tore the knife from his forearm and passed the gun over to his left hand.

Believing he had the advantage, Johnny had lunged back to his feet and charged down the corridor. But his dash hadn't taken the swiftness of Traggeo's response into account. He had covered barely half the distance to Traggeo before the gun angled for him again. He saw the barrel lowered in his direction in the same instant he realized he was seeing his own death.

Yet the vision of death was a false one, forestalled by a whirling figure that flashed around the corner and threw itself upon Traggeo.

Blaine had recognized the booming voice of Johnny Wareagle an instant before another burst of automatic fire sounded. Rounding the corner, he spotted Johnny first, then hurled himself upon the equally huge and distantly familiar shape that was steadying a machine gun aimed directly at the big Indian. The gunman turned at the last and sliced backward with a bloodied arm, catching Blaine across the bridge of the nose. The blow stunned McCracken enough to keep him from using his Uzi before the huge gunman pressed two numbers on a keypad on the wall beside him.

A door marked MONITOR CONTROL slid open and Traggeo threw himself inside. A hail of gunfire from within greeted Wareagle when he lunged toward it. McCracken managed to fire a spray into the room before the door closed once more. Blaine jumped to his feet and pushed the same two buttons the huge gunman had.

Nothing happened. The door didn't budge. Johnny Wareagle placed his palms against it, as if trying to push his way through.

"Fancy meeting you here, Indian," Blaine said, breathing hard.

He was about to continue when a familiar staccato sound reached him. Though barely discernible through the heavy walls of Sandcastle One, enough of it found both his and Johnny's ears for them to know its origin.

"Choppers, Indian."

"Coming fast."

Their eyes returned to the door marked MONITOR CONTROL at the same time.

"Nothing else we can do here," McCracken told him.

"For now, Blainey."

Blaine noticed the woman for the first time, her eyes glazed with shock and uncertainty.

"Looks like you sprung Sandcastle One's only prisoner, Indian," he said and then turned back to Kristen. "I can't wait to hear what you were in for."

"What brings you to White Sands, Indian?" Blaine asked Wareagle as they rushed for the main entrance on the first floor, the woman they had freed struggling to keep their pace.

"Traggeo, Blainey."

"Thought I recognized that guy from somewhere."

"The hellfire."

"Bringing us together yet again."

"Not for long if we can't escape."

"Don't worry, Indian. I'm sure Sal's got everything under control outside."

CHAPTER 26

"Well, look who we got here," Sal Belamo greeted when the three of them emerged from inside Sandcastle One, his eyes on the lights of the helicopters approaching over the desert. "Join the party, big fella. No wonder I couldn't track you down."

He was waiting with a pair of machine guns in hand next to a Humvee he had appropriated from the underground garage that was accessible from the complex's west side. The same garage he had watched the now-smoldering convoy emerge from.

"Looks like you boys sprung yourselves a prisoner," Sal added, eyeing Kristen as he pulled himself up behind the wheel. "Nothin' beats an old-fashioned jailbreak, you ask me."

McCracken joined Belamo in the front seat. Wareagle and Kristen Kurcell took the back. The lights of the approaching choppers sliced away larger chunks of the night with each passing second.

"How many, Johnny?" Blaine asked.

"Three, Blainey. Bell Jet Rangers."

Sal gunned the Humvee's engine. "Have no fear, boss. These things are built for this kind of shit. We'll be out of sight before the bastards even have a chance to look."

Before McCracken could ask Belamo how he intended to drive without the lights that would immediately draw the choppers to them, Sal pulled a pair of appropriated night-vision goggles from inside his jacket and tightened them in place. In the next instant they were off.

Sal kept the Humvee's initial pace slow so as to guide it more easily past the smoldering debris scattered through the yard of the jeeps and truck that were blown up earlier. The clutter near what had been the front gate was too thick to avoid, leaving Sal no choice but to drive the Humvee over it. It bucked and thumped its way forward, jostling its passengers, and ultimately squeezed nimbly by the twisted carcass of the personnel truck.

Belamo's appraisal of the Humvee couldn't have been more on the mark. Though squat and quirky in appearance, the chosen replacement for the trusty jeep was strong and agile and, as already demonstrated, could chew up even the most hostile terrain. Its efficiency proven in the Gulf War, it would now serve as their means of escape through White Sands. With no more debris in their path, Sal gave the Humvee a little more gas and headed off into the desert.

"Who are you?" the woman asked suddenly as the Humvee thumped over a ridge in the ground. "Who are *all* of you?"

"The Three Musketeers," smirked Sal Belamo, his eyes on the rearview mirror.

"The better question, miss," said Blaine, speaking for all of them, "is, Who are you?"

"I asked you first."

"Sorry. Rules of common decency don't apply here."

Kristen shrugged. "So I've seen."

"We saved your life," McCracken reminded. "That should be worth something."

"It's not worth as much as finding my brother's killers."

"Your brother's *what*?"

Kristen sighed. "Let me put it another way: have any of you ever heard of Miravo Air Force Base?"

"Sal?"

"Mothballed SAC. Its toilets ain't been pissed in for a couple years now."

"Well," countered Kristen, "somebody there got plenty pissed *off* when my brother showed up and spoiled their surprise."

"Surprise?" raised McCracken.

"This may take awhile. Good thing we've got all night."

The story didn't take all night to tell, even though Kristen left nothing out. She started with the tape of her brother's phone call, contacting Paul Gathers, and then her own trip to Colorado after the FBI man disappeared. With a lump in her throat, she told them about meeting Duncan Farlowe and their brush with death in the hills outside of Miravo. The lump got bigger still when she got to the part about the discovery of her brother's body and the condition it was found in.

"That man, that *thing* inside did it."

"Traggeo," Wareagle told McCracken. "Still claiming to be part of my people and turning our collective spirit sallow in the process."

"You tracked him all the way here."

"A lure to bring us together, Blainey, so we might pursue something much worse."

"I'll say," Kristen broke in and resumed her tale with her return to Washington and visit to the Pentagon accompanied by Senator Jordan. Then she told them of going with the senator for a second visit to Miravo, which found the base to be in full working order.

"But not for SAC," she explained. "They reequipped and reoutfitted it for the supposed dismantling of nuclear warheads, the kind used in artillery."

"Supposed?"

Kristen swallowed hard. The lump wouldn't give. She forced the words past it. "I'm sure my brother died because he learned the warheads weren't being dismantled at all. I think he saw them being flown or driven off the base."

McCracken exchanged stares with Sal Belamo. "But when you returned to Colorado with Senator Jordan, the base was operational again. Everything status quo."

"Of course," Kristen acknowledged bitterly. "They had plenty of time to cover their tracks, plenty of advance warning. The senator gave it to them."

"I thought you said that the senator—"

"I killed her on the road after we left Miravo. Not far from where they killed my brother. I *had* to, or she would have killed me."

"She was one of the bad guys, then."

"For all I know, so are you."

"No, you know better than that."

"Do I?"

"You'd be dead if we were," Blaine said and looked more closely at her.

The same hopelessness that kept the tone of her voice maddeningly level did little to diminish her beauty. Even though her long wavy hair was snarled and tousled, the face captured within it remained radiant and vital. Her brown eyes refused to reflect her fear and instead confirmed her determination. Her cheeks were flushed, perhaps radiating a glow of inner strength and resolve. Blaine had pegged her as the type of person who would scrap and claw till the very end, as evidenced by what she had already managed to endure.

"Did the senator tell you anything else? Did she say anything about what she was a part of?"

"Why don't you tell me what she was a part of? I mean, that is what brought you to, what'd you say it was called, Sandcastle One, isn't it?"

"I was told it was a prison."

"But I was the only prisoner."

"Just for the time being," Blaine said.

"*Whose* prison, Mr. McCracken? I think I've said enough

for now. I'd like to hear from you. I think I've run into your kind a few times on the Hill. Out-of-work spooks the end of the Cold War left in a lurch."

"I was left in a lurch a long time before the Cold War finished up, Kris."

Sal Belamo took a rough spot in the desert too fast and the Humvee's tires thudded, bouncing off the ground.

"CIA?" she raised.

"Used to be."

"And now?"

"On my own. There's plenty to keep me busy."

"Like whatever brought you to the complex."

Blaine had to crimp his neck at an odd angle to look her straight in the eye. "Someone's after the government this time. They want to bring it down."

"As in overthrow?"

"By all indications, yes. And there's only a week left before they try."

Kristen's expression softened a little. "That's the first time I've heard your voice waver."

"Because the prospects scare me."

"I can't picture you being scared of anything."

"Pictures can be deceiving. It's what keeps me going."

"And you're scared now?"

"More maybe than ever before."

"Care to tell me why?"

"Because I'm not sure I can prevent it this time."

"*This* time? There've been others?"

"More than I can count, all focused around power and control. Everyone has a vision, and sometimes the people with the resources to realize their vision decide that they know best what's right for everyone else. The scary thing is that they believe in what they're doing and that's what makes them difficult to stop."

"Yet you stop them."

"I believe in what I'm doing more."

"But this time it's different," Kristen Kurcell concluded.

"Plenty. And thanks to you I'm beginning to understand why."

"Me?"

"The nuclear weapons you believe your brother witnessed being taken out of Miravo. If I'm right, they're going to be used, and soon."

"And just how do we find out when?"

McCracken didn't hesitate. "We go back to Washington and find the one man who might know."

PART FOUR

THE DELPHI

GRAND MESA:
TUESDAY, APRIL 19, 1994; 3:00 P.M.

CHAPTER 27

Sheriff Duncan Farlowe stepped back into Grand Mesa's municipal offices Tuesday afternoon bone-weary and aching all over. He had barely slept at all since Kristen Kurcell had departed early Saturday evening, preferring instead to spend the last three nights in an old rocking chair with black coffee in his stomach and a twelve-gauge in his hands. The old chair faced his front door and gave him a clear view out windows on both sides of the house.

He had spent Sunday and Monday further retracing the trail of Kristen's brother David. Farlowe started with the store a hundred miles down the road in Alfona where the kid had bought his camcorder. The clerk remembered he was in a rush, remembered him asking an off-the-cuff question about any nearby military bases. The clerk had mentioned Miravo but made sure to point out it had been shut down two years earlier.

Farlowe figured the kid must have glimpsed some of the trucks going by and then staked out the road waiting for others to follow. The next convoy must have come through on Thursday night and led David to Miravo. After that the only thing Farlowe knew for sure was that the kid ended up in Grand Mesa's last operating motel. He had searched room 7 and the kid's jeep thoroughly again on the chance that David might have hidden the videotape he had made, but the search turned up nothing. He got AT&T on the line Monday to learn that the only call charged to the kid's credit card in the week prior to his death had been the one to his sister. Another dead end.

All Duncan Farlowe had to go on was whatever David Kurcell had seen at Miravo Air Force Base. The sheriff had returned there for another look yesterday afternoon to find the base up and active, cobwebs shed and none the worse for wear.

Farlowe turned his truck around on Old Canyon Road before, he hoped, the guards posted in front of the gate saw him. It followed that whoever was inside now had been party to his and Kristen's near murders on Saturday; six or so men poorer thanks to the old mines and the Peacemaker, and Duncan didn't want to give anybody a chance to even the score.

Back in town, the numbers Kristen Kurcell had given him to reach her went unanswered. Farlowe had spent Monday night in his chair with more black coffee and the Peacemaker stuck in his belt to supplement the twelve-gauge.

He had returned to Miravo again this morning, Tuesday, taking up a post in the same hills David Kurcell had; no camera, though, just his eyes. He couldn't tell what was going on inside, other than to be sure it had nothing to do with SAC. For one thing, the troops inside were army, not air force, or at least they looked like army. He came back to town to collect his thoughts, determined to share his findings with *someone*. FBI maybe, or the state cops for starters. Sit down at his desk, jot down a few notes, and then make some calls.

The explosion that came barely a minute after he had stepped inside engulfed the entire municipal offices building in a massive fireball. The blast's percussion blew out most of the windows along Main Street. The wooden exteriors of the neighboring structures were creased by black, charred patches that bled smoke into the air. The street was littered with fragments coughed free by the explosion, including the sign MUNICIPAL OFFICES, which had somehow survived whole. An old-fashioned town fire alarm wailed to call in the volunteer fighters.

Squeezed between a pair of houses set well back from

what had been his office, Sheriff Duncan Farlowe watched the twenty-year-old red engine speed onto the scene and screech to a stop. He was more angry than scared, a part of him wanting to walk up to the two men he had glimpsed in the rented car parked down Main Street and blast away with his Peacemaker. He had walked into the front of the municipal building and then rushed out the back, hoping his instincts were wrong.

They weren't, of course, and now it was time to head for the hills. Literally. A cabin he owned in the mountains near a ski resort that was closed for the season. He had a shortwave radio and a phone to keep the outside world as close as he needed it. Hole up for a while and figure out what to do, who to call, and try to figure out what the hell was going on.

CHAPTER 28

"You sure this is the place, Sal?" McCracken asked when Belamo stopped at the head of an alley.

"Abso-fucking-lutely, boss," Belamo replied. "Checked it out myself 'fore I rode out west to meet up with you. Followed Bill Carlisle's trail this far and found a dead end. Literally."

The alley was located off Good Hope Street in Washington's rundown Anacostia district just over the 11th Street Bridge. They walked the last stretch of the way through the Washington night, passing a number of dark figures standing about in clusters. Ordinarily outsiders would have been accosted instantly. But the presence of Johnny Wareagle bringing up the small group's rear discouraged anything but stares and a few threatening comments.

McCracken led the way down the alley toward its cluttered rear. Belamo had managed to trace the last known residence of former Trilateral Commission member, and chairman of its shadowy subcommittee, William Carlisle, to a suite of wooden crates at the far end. McCracken reckoned that Carlisle might well be the only man who could fill in the missing components of the plot he had uncovered.

They had come here straight from New Mexico, driving all the way out of concern that the forces behind Sandcastle One would be intent on tracking them down. They took a circuitous route, changing cars often and grabbing food on the run. They reached the Anacostia section of Washington just after ten P.M. Tuesday night and left their car in an auto body shop's lot on Good Hope Street three blocks away from the alley so it wouldn't be noticed.

"He ain't in there," Sal assured Blaine as McCracken poked his head into one of the crates with Kristen Kurcell peering over his shoulder.

"I don't expect him to be," McCracken returned. "In fact, I'm guessing he seldom ever was."

"Come clean, boss."

"Not until I'm sure. Excuse me," Blaine said to Kristen and backed away from the crate.

He glanced briefly toward the head of the alley where Johnny Wareagle was maintaining his vigil. Then he stuck his head and shoulders through the opening of Carlisle's second crate and rummaged about in the crinkled newspapers, feeling for the cement beneath them.

"I might have been wrong," Blaine said, backing out once more.

"You ask me, we're wasting our time here."

"Wait a minute."

McCracken moved to an ancient Porta-John resting against the side of an abandoned building. His hand reached down for a rusted handle.

"Wouldn't go in there 'I was you, boss. . . . Shit," Belamo added when he saw Blaine yank open the door in spite of his protestations.

"Right," McCracken followed when the stench assaulted him.

Blaine pushed against the walls to see if they would give. He was about to summon Johnny from the head of the alley to help him move the rusted hulk aside when he felt the floor section shift slightly beneath his touch.

"Give me a hand, Sal."

"There's limits, boss."

"I promise it won't get dirty. Just hold on to the frame here. . . . That's it."

As Kristen Kurcell looked on intently, McCracken jimmied the Porta-John's floor all the way free and wedged a hand beneath it. One wrench was all it took to lift the floor away. He tossed it behind him.

"Holy shit!" gasped Sal.

"Right again," said Blaine, gazing through the missing floor into a dark hole that led into the sewers of Washington.

Actually, Blaine realized as he touched down at the bottom of the ladder, this was more likely an abandoned section of the Metro, the city's subway system. Kristen Kurcell was slower in her descent, but nonetheless determined to accompany him. Sal Belamo was quite happy to remain topside with Johnny Wareagle to stand guard.

Kristen's feet touched the murky bottom. "Thanks for letting me tag along. I really mean that. I know it would have been a lot easier for the rest of you if you had dropped me off along the way."

"Then I wouldn't have anyone to enjoy this lovely smell with."

"I'm being serious."

"So was I when I asked if you wanted to join me down here."

"I thought you'd take Sal. I was ready to argue."

"This isn't about Sal, so I saved you the trouble. It's your stake, Kris. You bought in when your brother got killed at the outset. You didn't have a choice then. You deserve one now."

Before she could answer, McCracken turned and started walking along the pathway.

The corridor before them bent in angular, almost mazelike fashion. In some spots the water was deep enough to cover their shoes. In others the concrete floor was bone dry and drew an echo from the clicking of their heels. Thin rows of work lights dangled from the ceiling to illuminate their path. Strangely, not a single bulb was burnt out. Once in a while a powerful rumbling shook the nearby walls, evidence of a functional Metro tunnel not too far off.

The farther they walked into the tunnel, the less they could smell the putrid sewer stench, and finally it dissipated altogether. The rumbling also abated, allowing a soft hum of voices to reach both their ears at the same time. Kristen stiffened. McCracken didn't. She looked at him.

"The voices. You recognize them," she said in what had started as a question.

"Listen, and so will you."

McCracken had already moved on ahead of her and Kristen hurried to catch up. Another twenty yards down the unfinished tunnel, the air suddenly turned cool, almost fresh, as if drained of humidity.

"Air conditioning and filtration," Blaine said by way of explanation.

"You were expecting this."

"We're almost there," he told her.

"Almost *where*?"

After another ten yards, the lighting directly in front of them changed dramatically. A bright spot like a beacon in the darkness lay dead ahead: barely a glow at first, but quickly sharpening into an even layer of light coming from what seemed to be the very end of the tunnel.

The tunnel narrowed toward a single doorway. The muted voices they had detected were coming from beyond it. Kristen followed McCracken through the doorway and her jaw dropped at what lay before them.

In a massive cavern that might have been a sewer reser-

voir abandoned when the Metro encroached upon it, a luxurious residence had been erected. It was composed of two
exquisitely furnished levels joined by a spiral staircase. On
the first floor, a pair of matching Chesterfield sofas sat
facing each other atop a lavish Oriental carpet. A
Regency-style chair stood next to an elegant writing desk,
which was perched upon another carpet of similar design.
Behind the desk a fireplace burned with a gas-lit fire that
threw more atmosphere than heat into the conditioned cool
of the cavern. Shelves and shelves of books lined the walls
to camouflage the concrete of the cavern, and Blaine and
Kristen could see doors leading to what they assumed
were other rooms. A priceless George III long-case clock
stood opposite the fireplace, and a collection of Waterford
crystal dominated an open breakfront.

The second floor, more of an open loft actually, was supported by heavy post and beam construction. Part of a large
canopied bed was visible, as well as even more bookshelves
crammed with books, many of them bound in leather. Their
pleasing aroma drifted throughout the cavern. Hanging on
the few vacant stretches of wall were French impressionist
paintings, mixed with statues and art in an Oriental motif.

"This is CNN."

The familiar voice and music that followed drew
Kristen's attention to an alcove just to the left of the Chesterfield sofas. She noticed McCracken too was staring that
way, where the easily identifiable glow of a big-screen
television shone outward.

A quick burst of rushing water on the second level was
swiftly followed by a door closing, and then a man emerged
from the master bedroom. "Ah, guests," noted H. William
Carlisle as he reached the top of the spiral staircase, a newspaper tucked under his arm. "If I had known you were coming, I would have dressed for the occasion."

In place of the tattered rags the former member of the
Trilateral Commission had been wearing in Lafayette Park
on Saturday, Carlisle was dressed in an old-fashioned smok-

ing jacket and pleated trousers. His slippers were fluffy and padded. His face was clean shaven and free of grime.

"You look a hell of a lot better than the last time I saw you," McCracken noted.

"The disguise allows me to move freely in the streets, to mix in. Priceless."

"I get the feeling you haven't been out since you met me."

"If you could find me, so could someone else. Not a good time to be seen, by all accounts."

Blaine moved slowly forward, eyes sweeping the residence before him that seemed like a cross between the Phantom of the Opera's lair and the rooms of Captain Nemo on board the submarine *Nautilus*. "I congratulate you on building yourself such an impressive hideout."

"I prefer to call it a retirement home. Either way, it was no easy task, I assure you."

"How did you manage to furnish it?"

"With the help of a pair of robberies staged at my house, one before my disappearance and one after. Alas, as it is with all home builders, I found my measurements were a bit off. Lots of empty space."

Halfway into his walk down the spiral staircase, Carlisle seemed to notice Kristen for the first time. "I have not had the pleasure of your aquaintance, miss. H. William Carlisle," he said, his head bowing slightly.

"You're Billy the Kid," responded Kristen, instead of introducing herself.

"You've heard of me, I see."

"I *studied* you."

Carlisle reached the bottom of the staircase and stopped. "And that, my dear lady, is what I have been reduced to: a course requirement."

"Not exactly," noted Blaine.

"I furnished you with a piece of history, Mr. McCracken."

"*Current* history, Mr. Carlisle, because your subcommittee never stopped operating."

"I was referring to Operation Yellow Rose."

"So was I. You said your subcommittee was dissolved in 1978, when you dropped out. But the files in the bus station locker ran through 1980."

Carlisle stood before Blaine rigidly, expressionless.

"You knew the subcommittee was still active," McCracken continued. "You knew it was active then, and you knew it remained active to this day. I'm also betting that you knew all along what its members were up to. And even though you weren't a part of it anymore, you pointed me in the wrong direction."

An ironic smile inched across Carlisle's face. "Because a part of me wanted to see if they could pull off such a grand and glorious scheme. A primitive and juvenile part, I admit, but I was there at the beginning, when discussions hatched the very fate I suspect is about to befall the country."

"Then why tell me anything at all?"

"Simple. I thought telling you nothing might have helped you discover the truth faster than setting you on the wrong path did."

"In other words, you wanted me to fail."

"Because that same juvenile part of me honestly believes that what they offer is the only hope this nation has. Our conversation in Lafayette Park brought all the excitement back to me, made me long to be part of the loop again. Until that moment I hadn't realized how close they were. I suspected, of course, but you provided confident confirmation."

"You sound proud," Kristen interjected bitterly.

"Perhaps regretful that I left when I did."

"You must have had your reasons," Blaine picked up. "And they must have been very good ones."

Carlisle turned away from both Blaine and the question and moved stiffly toward the fake fireplace. McCracken stood by his side and the two stared into the gas-fueled, unwavering flames. Carlisle rubbed his hands together before them, as if to ward off a chill.

"I walked away, Mr. McCracken, because I couldn't go along with what our subcommittee became in the wake of Yellow Rose's demise. You see, the Trilateralists themselves deemed the operation an unnecessary distraction. By 1976, after all, they had what they really wanted."

"The presidency," Blaine picked up. "Jimmy Carter was one of their own."

"And he took plenty more into office with him, twenty-five major appointments by conservative estimates. Can you imagine a better, more favorable scenario for the commission? At last the Trilateralists were in a position to turn theory into policy."

"A miserable failure by all accounts."

"Of course, because history conspired against them."

"The hostage crisis?" suggested Kristen.

Carlisle shook his head. "It was already over by then, miss. When faced with the true managing of government, they found themselves overwhelmed. They weren't willing to go far enough; exposed and accountable for their actions, they didn't dare take the risk."

"So the burden shifted to a group considerably less exposed and thus not accountable—your subcommittee," McCracken concluded.

Carlisle turned his eyes from the fire to Blaine. "The goal being to achieve a more active degree of control over government. It was . . . determined that the commission's goals and priorities could never be achieved through traditional means."

"Meaning the political system as is."

"Yes. The Carter fiasco proved that. The prevailing thought was that a different kind of government was required, one that would allow us to more ably achieve our mandate for world order."

"And you disagreed with that."

"Not the ends, oh no. The ends I believed in with the

deepest conviction. Back then I couldn't stomach the means." Carlisle's brilliant eyes seemed flustered. "The discovery of which, I suspect, has brought you back to me. Tell me what you know, Mr. McCracken. Let us examine how far my old comrades have come."

"Farther than you suspect, Mr. Carlisle," Blaine said and proceeded to summarize the salient points as concisely as he could.

Starting with a brief recap of what the dying Daniels had shared with him in Rock Creek Park, he explained making the connection between Arlo Cleese and the Alvarezes in Miami. He moved on to the revelations gained in his near-fatal meeting with Cleese and then described his trip to New Mexico and Sandcastle One. Blaine nodded toward Kristen when he was done. She related her own tale and finished by repeating her surmise about the apparent pilfering of nuclear weapons by party or parties unknown.

Throughout both their stories, Carlisle had grown progressively more agitated and fidgety. He seemed alternately excited and shocked, accepting the tales the way one does when catching up with an old friend. By the time Kristen had finished, his gaze had become distant and withdrawn, full of nostalgia and longing.

"Better than I thought," he commented. "Much better."

"Whose side are you on, Mr. Carlisle?" McCracken demanded.

"Why does this have to be about sides? I chose mine almost twenty years ago, in any case."

"Because you didn't approve of the means. What's changed?"

"Only the very real possibility that they're going to succeed."

"Obviously you couldn't live with that twenty years ago."

"Different."

"Why?"

"The desperation of today."

"No," Blaine argued, "because you were a participant instead of a spectator. And from the inside looking out you knew what the subcommittee sought was all wrong. But now you're on the outside looking in. They don't scare you anymore because they can't affect your own private world here beneath the city they want to own."

"This country needs what we have to offer it, Mr. McCracken."

"Not 'we' anymore, Mr. Carlisle—they. You walked away because you couldn't stomach their methods. You knew the costs would outweight the benefits. The country would be losing more than it would be gaining. That equation hasn't changed. If anything, the costs have grown even greater."

"And if we don't pay them now, we may never have an opportunity to save ourselves again."

"Save ourselves by incarcerating those who disagree, who speak out? Save ourselves by restricting the very freedoms that define who we are?"

"Necessary sacrifices!" Carlisle insisted. "I realize that now. If I had been smart enough to realize it back then—" He stopped suddenly.

Blaine took a step closer to him, understanding in his eyes. "Fifteen years ago it was you who was sacrificed, wasn't it? You didn't walk away. You were forced out."

Carlisle's lips quivered, uncertainty tightening his features. "We could have had it both ways. They wouldn't listen. They were the Delphi, after all. The future belonged to them."

"The Delphi," Blaine repeated, recalling Daniels's mention of the term and Carlisle's denying any knowledge of it last Saturday.

"Named after the oracle in Greek mythology who was consulted by those in power before any action was undertaken," Carlisle elaborated now. "And thus, to a great extent, its council *determined* the future. Our subcommittee took that name because in essence that was how we envisioned ourselves. When the commission disbanded us, we continued to meet in secret. The Trilat members thought controlling the White House would be enough."

"Carter showed them different."

"They were shattered, devastated. They had the power and it slid right out of their grasp."

"And right into yours."

"In terms of opportunity, yes. We knew that the only way to achieve the commission's entire vision was for our man to come to power at a precise moment in time, a moment when the people were so discouraged and disgusted with the state the country was in that they were willing to accept anything to achieve change. I told the others we had to be ready, prepared to move as soon as that moment came."

"But the others didn't want to wait, did they? They wanted to manufacture this moment to create history instead of merely reacting to it."

Carlisle nodded slowly. "It wasn't necessary. If we had waited long enough, the outcry in the nation demanding the kind of change we represented would have happened on its own."

"And that's when you parted company from them."

"I advised caution, reason. That's all. They thought I had turned on them. There was no middle ground, no other choice for me," he said regretfully.

"They kept working toward the creation of their moment."

"The illusion of a revolution would be provided to set the stage," Carlisle acknowledged, his thoughts coming together as he spoke through quivering lips. "Washington would be overrun, the President assassinated along with the bulk of Congress in an all-out attack. The result would be chaos, even anarchy, with the chain of succession rendered useless, leaving the way open for a special election in which the Delphi would have positioned a man to emerge victorious. After my ... dismissal, I kept a close watch on them, never believing they would ever find the one element they needed to bring their plan to fruition."

"A worthy candidate," Blaine concluded.

"But then they found one," Carlisle told him. "One of their own, in fact."

"Samuel Jackson Dodd," Kristen said barely loud enough to be heard.

"A man with a popular consensus and broad-based program already in place," added McCracken. "Elected with a mandate allowing him to do whatever the hell he—and the Delphi—want."

"Charged with rebuilding a country shattered by the strike your Midnight Riders will be blamed for. I suspected as much after you mentioned Yellow Rose to me." Carlisle's eyes lost their surety. "Dodd will be given a blank check to bring about the changes the Delphi has been working toward for decades. But even that won't be enough for them."

"What?" McCracken and Kristen spoke at the same time.

Carlisle looked at McCracken. "Keep in mind that Trilateralism grew out of the belief that left to itself the United States could not accomplish the goals the commission had in mind for it. A concerted, unified effort on an international front had to be achieved to assure long-term hegemony. The commission groomed representatives in countries all over the world, focusing primarily on those nations rich in resources and manageable economies. The Delphi sought to help similar representatives achieve the same degree of control we sought here in the States. They—we—wanted foreign representatives who could themselves be manipulated, representatives who were more than willing to accept the Delphi's aid in destabilizing their own nations and ultimately coming to power as well. The economies would thus come under a single, unified control."

"Thanks to a twisted international cabal," Blaine concluded.

"The members of which shared a large measure of the Delphi's politics along with their ruthlessness," Carlisle continued. "Groups that had already proven their willingness to do whatever it takes to gain control."

"Terrorists?" Kristen raised.

"No," said Blaine, before Carlisle had a chance to. "The Trilateral Commission and the Delphi were conservative by nature from the beginning, and their failures would have turned them even more conservative. So abroad they would have turned to those whose dogma was the nearest mix: the far right."

Carlisle nodded, impressed. "Precisely, Mr. McCracken. The Delphi needed such groups to achieve what they wanted, and only by accepting the Delphi's help could these groups rise to power."

"How?" Kristen wondered.

"You've already explained that yourself, miss."

"I have?"

His blazing eyes pierced her. "Those nuclear weapons from Miravo."

McCracken's spine stiffened. "Supplied to ultra-right wing leaders who undoubtedly intend to make use of them to help them gain power in their respective nations, or at least to destabilize the current governments."

"Each of those shells from Miravo is two or three times more powerful than the ones dropped on Japan at the end of World War II," Kristen noted dazedly.

"And they will be put to good use, I assure you," picked up Carlisle.

"But you didn't know this before today," McCracken concluded. "You couldn't have."

"No, but I did know the kind of people in whose hands the weapons will end up. You see, the notion of developing an international right-wing cadre dates back to my years with the Delphi. One of my final tasks was to act as liaison with the South African representative. A man named Dreyer."

"*Travis* Dreyer? Head of the AWB?"

"No, his father, Boothe. But young Travis sat in on all the meetings. He took over the AWB after his father died."

McCracken considered the prospects. The AWB, which

stood for Afrikaner Weerstand Beweging (Afrikaner Resistance Movement), was a very well-armed, neofascist organization devoted in principle to maintaining apartheid and in theory to the eventual extermination of blacks. Its members were the reactionary offspring of the Afrikaners from Holland who had originally founded the system of apartheid. They would do, and very often had done, anything in the name of racial purity and their own interpretation of nationalism. In calmer moments they would parade around the countryside on horseback proudly displaying their trademark insignias, which bore a curious resemblance to swastikas.

"Are you saying the nuclear weapons my brother saw being smuggled out of Miravo are going to end up in the hands of men like *Dreyer*?" Kristen said disbelievingly.

The former member of the Trilateral Commission looked at her for several moments. "And what we will be witnessing as a result is a protracted World War III. Civil wars and hopeless entanglements will break out all across the globe. Radical right-wing groups, chosen for the very ruthlessness that makes it possible to manipulate them, will throw the balance of government into utter chaos worldwide. Conceivably it could all happen, the world could be unalterably changed, in a single day.

"The day of the Delphi," he finished.

"And in spite of that knowledge, you sat here and did *nothing*?" Kristen scorned.

"Because I could not help but acknowledge that the scope of the Delphi's ambitions could allow them to seize control in a form purer and more direct than anything the Trilateralists ever imagined, and yet true to their original vision. That's why I couldn't help you stop it last week. That's why I had to send you in the wrong direction. Because a part of me still believes in the sanctity of the vision, that Trilateralism holds the only means by which our way of life can survive."

"But another part of you still remembers that you were

thrown out of the Delphi for speaking your mind, for daring to voice a dissenting opinion," Blaine challenged. "That's not leadership. Or if it is, only at the price of wide-scale nuclear proliferation. That wasn't your vision. If it was, you'd still be with them."

Carlisle remained silent. McCracken continued.

"You didn't just walk away from them, you walked away from society. You had to, didn't you? Had to because you knew the others would never have settled for simple expulsion. You posed too much of a risk. Your only chance was to disappear."

"There was nothing else I could do, Mr. McCracken."

"There is now," Blaine said and looked at Carlisle until his stare was met. "They would have killed you, and you know it. They'd kill you now if they knew you were still playing watchdog. But the last card is yours to play."

"How?"

"The Delphi, Mr. Carlisle. You knew they were wrong then and you know they're wrong now. It's been a long time, but most of them will still be there; enough anyway. You can tell me who they are. Help me stop their day from ever coming."

For a moment suspended in space and time, Carlisle stood frozen and expressionless, his mind wandering through the lost years. Then slowly, ever so slowly, he nodded.

Back on Good Hope Street, a man hidden in the shadows between a pair of burnt-out buildings held the walkie-talkie against his ear and mouth.

"We'll be moving out now," a voice told him.

The man gazed again at the head of the alley where the huge Indian had been visible just an instant before. "Bring an army."

Sal Belamo was waiting just where Blaine had left him when he and Kristen reached ground level in the alley.

"Looks like you just saw a ghost, boss."

"Close enough," said Blaine. "Anything?"

"Nada."

"Johnny?"

"I can't see him, but—"

"We must get out of here, Blainey," said Wareagle, emerging from the shadows.

"Indian?"

"Quickly."

McCracken didn't question Wareagle further. Johnny turned and started back toward the head of the alley, the others falling in behind. They reached Good Hope Street and McCracken noticed instantly that the threatening young men they had passed en route here were gone. The night seemed to have grown even darker.

Wareagle stiffened. McCracken slid Kristen behind him. They started down the sidewalk in single file. Suddenly a trio of massive floodlights snapped on at the east end of the block.

"Holy shit," gasped Belamo.

"Get out the other way," Kristen heard Wareagle mutter back to them. "I will hold them at this end."

Before they could even swing all the way round, though, more floodlights burned toward them from the west end of the block. The distinctive clacking of rifles being slammed against shoulders into the ready position echoed in the night. Then a pair of helicopters sliced through the dark over the rise of buildings, converging from the north and south.

"Drop your weapons and put your hands in the air!" a voice ordered through a bullhorn from one of the choppers.

McCracken, caught in the spill of one of the floods, let his pistol fall to the ground. Belamo and Wareagle followed suit with their rifles. All of them raised their arms above their heads.

"Do not move! Stay where you are!"

"We make a run for it, boss?" Belamo whispered Blaine's way.

"One of us has to get out with a little present Carlisle gave me."

"Six snipers with Starlight scopes atop the buildings, Blainey," Wareagle reported. "Under strong cover."

"Kristen," Blaine whispered.

"I'm ready. Tell me what to do."

She was their only chance. With the focus of the rifles unquestionably on the three of them, she might make it if they provided a significant enough distraction.

"Johnny," McCracken muttered. "Sal."

Wareagle nodded, shoulders tensing slightly.

"Fuck," rasped Sal.

McCracken started to lower his hand toward the pocket containing the 3.5-inch floppy disk Carlisle had given him. Kristen was trembling, fingers held even with her shoulders.

"Wait, Blainey," Wareagle said suddenly.

McCracken turned to follow the big Indian's eyes. While the choppers hovered overhead, a phalanx of armed troops were approaching from the east end of Good Hope Street, boots clacking against the street. The man leading the way carried no gun. The soldiers behind him had theirs unmenacingly shouldered. The man in front came to within six feet of the tensed McCracken and saluted.

"Sorry for the inconvenience, Captain. But this seemed the safest way to avoid a misunderstanding. I'm Colonel Ben Power."

Blaine returned his salute. "It's been a long time since I've been addressed as captain, Colonel."

"Then let me be the first to welcome you back to the ranks. But enough small talk, Captain. You're already late for an appointment I'm supposed to deliver you to."

"Appointment?"

"With the President. Let's move."

CHAPTER 29

"I thought it best we speak alone initially," the President said to Blaine McCracken.

The news that McCracken had been spotted by one of the teams assigned to watch for him had reached the President as he tried unsuccessfully to sleep. He dressed quickly, kept abreast of what was transpiring down on Good Hope Street in Anacostia, and was waiting in his office when Colonel Ben Power personally ushered McCracken in.

"Please, make yourself comfortable," the President said, offering him one of the matching wing chairs in his private office.

"That's a bit difficult for me."

"Under the circumstances, I quite understand."

"Not just these circumstances, sir." Blaine groped for the correct explanation. "It's been a long time since I've been on the inside." His eyes swept through the room. "Especially this far in."

"Your file forewarned me of that."

"How did your people find me, Mr. President?"

"It begins with a tape...."

The President went on to explain how a former KGB chief's bugging of the CIA director's office had provided them with a recording of the final conversation between Tom Daniels and Clifton Jardine. The conversation had ended with the director giving tacit approval to Blaine's utilization. Accordingly, the assumption was that Daniels had come to Rock Creek Park for a meeting with him.

"At that point," elaborated the President, "our thinking

was that you could provide us with the specifics the recording left out."

"At that point, I didn't know any more than you did. Less, even."

"We learned of your 'appearance' in the Coconut Grove the previous night and that it was Daniels who had expedited your release from police custody. Later we became aware of your near-disastrous plane ride back to Miami. Someone wanted you dead, very likely the same party behind the murders of Daniels and Jardine."

"They got two out of three."

"And you dropped out of sight. Not surprisingly, we were unable to find you. But we assumed the quest you were on could only lead you back to the capital, and we blanketed the city with men armed with your picture."

"You'll need an army of men armed with more than that to stop this government from falling, sir."

The President stood up and grasped the back of his chair. "Who's behind it? Just tell me that."

"Mr. President, how much do you know about the Trilateral Commission?"

By the time Blaine had finished his tale, leaving out mention of the Delphi's nuclear stockpile for the time being, the President had sunk into the chair. His shoulders all but disappeared into its high back. His features paled. His lower lip was trembling.

"You say that Carlisle furnished you with the names of those who were part of this Delphi when he disappeared," he raised when McCracken had at last finished.

Blaine's response was to pull a 3.5-inch floppy disk from his pocket. "Some of which would have later left on the same terms he did. Since his information stops at 1980, others listed will be dead, and undoubtedly there'll be a number of names missing."

"Like Samuel Jackson Dodd's, no doubt. What about the when and how? Did Carlisle have any notion about that?"

"No, but Tom Daniels did," Blaine told him, recalling

Daniels's final plea to him in Rock Creek Park. "Six or seven days from now."

The President's face paled. "Of course."

"Sir?"

"One week from tonight I'm scheduled to address a joint session of Congress on my new strategy for economic revitalization."

"The entire leadership of the nation together at the same time . . . Lambs to the slaughter, sir."

The President gripped the arms of his chair. "And instead of those actually responsible, the Midnight Riders will be blamed."

"In an apparent revolution," Blaine picked up, "that will leave the military no choice but to assume control."

"Only until they can circumvent the Constitution to call for a special presidential election."

"Which Dodd has positioned himself to win. But he's not going to be elected president, sir, he's going to be elected savior. And the people will accept anything he and the Delphi force upon them."

The President's face regained its color. He shook his head deliberately. "No, in spite of everything, I still don't buy all of this. I don't care how deep the Delphi's reach into government extends, they've misjudged the country's reaction. They'll never get away with this."

McCracken was suddenly struck by something he'd forgotten, one of the last words spoken by Tom Daniels.

"Mr. President, what is Prometheus?"

What little color remained in the President's face drained out instantly. His eyes grew frightened. He rose and walked stiffly to the room's bar. He started to pour himself a glass of water from a pitcher and then changed his mind. He spoke without looking directly back at McCracken.

"Prometheus is a national version of the emergency broadcast system. A communications network built to endure even the severest electromagnetic pulse in space and provide reliable communication in the event of the unthinkable."

"Sounds like an unnecessary extravagance in this era."

"But we have no idea what the future might bring, do we? The system was on the verge of completion when I took office. But I made sure the public and Congress thought it had been abandoned, another multi-billion-dollar albatross that didn't work." The President stopped and looked back at Blaine. "In actuality it couldn't have worked better. I renamed it Prometheus. Besides you, there aren't five other people in this country who know of it by that name."

"Tom Daniels knew."

"And by connection the Delphi. Only—"

"How does Prometheus work?" Blaine interrupted.

"Satellite relays with dozens of redundant systems along with the most advanced software and hardware ever put into orbit," the President answered, watching McCracken nod his head. "What I've just said doesn't seem to surprise you. Why?"

"Dodd Industries, sir. Check the contractors. That's where they'll all lead back to."

"Even so," the President followed, "Prometheus' existence would only facilitate strategic communications. How could that possibly aid the Delphi's plan?"

"Look, sir," Blaine answered, moving toward him, "I don't know a down-link from an up-link. But I do know that everything with communications today comes down to satellite relays. Big machines talking to each other. Without an electromagnetic pulse to spoil the mix, Dodd links Prometheus up with standard orbiting broadcast satellites and replaces their signal. Like magic, the Delphi take over the airwaves to facilitate the taking of control by the military. And thus Dodd."

"The country left with no choice but to listen." The President regarded McCracken quizzically. "Wait, there's something you're not telling me, something you're holding back."

"I wasn't a hundred percent sure until this moment. But now the rest of their plan makes perfect sense."

"*Rest* of their plan? Good Lord, what more could there be?"

"In a nutshell, sir, the Delphi is presently one of the major nuclear powers on the face of the planet."

The President's face sagged and he headed slowly back to his chair.

"Miravo Air Force Base," Blaine continued.

"Retasked to dismantle short-range nuclear artillery shells."

"No, retasked to allow a number of the warheads to be smuggled off the base and stockpiled."

The President sat down. "Five other bases have been retasked as well. Can we assume the same holds true for them?"

"I think the enemy we're facing got all of what they needed from Miravo. But their salvaged stockpile isn't going to be used inside our borders."

"Where, then?"

Blaine took a deep breath. "I started down this trail in the wrong direction, sir. It wasn't the lunatic fringe doing the plotting, it was another fringe. . . ."

"An international cadre of madmen from the radical right," the President summed up succinctly after Blaine had finished the explanation passed on to him by Carlisle.

"Whom the Delphi will help bring to power and then utilize to help control and manage the entire world. The Trilateral Commission itself was founded on a doctrine that wasn't much different."

"I don't think the Trilat's charter said anything about a council of lunatics running civilization."

"A means to an end and nothing more. Even if they fail, the resulting disruption makes the Delphi winners because other nations will be ill equipped to respond to the disaster that has taken place in the United States while the transition takes place."

"The question becomes, Can all this still be stopped?"

"Bill Carlisle gave me the name of the only international Delphi representative he was sure of: Travis Dreyer."

"Also known as the South African Hitler."

"Dreyer will be able to fill in the missing details, maybe even the identities of the remainder of the Delphi's chosen lot overseas."

"You plan on going to South Africa and making him talk?"

"Ideally, I can come up with the information without him ever knowing I was there."

The President thought for a moment. "There's one week left before my address to Congress. That's all the cushion I can give you."

"And you can make good use of that same cushion at home, sir, while I'm in South Africa," said Blaine as he held up the floppy disk Bill Carlisle had given him.

"The members of the Delphi."

"Preempt them, sir. Arrest them on any charges you can come up with. They couldn't know about my meeting with Carlisle. The advantage is ours. Surprise them and maybe we avoid the day of the Delphi altogether."

The President looked anything but optimistic. "If we fail, I'm afraid I'll only have one option left: moving the entire government to the proper emergency locations. The Delphi can't kill who they can't get to."

"No, but you'll end up with a national panic on your hands, and those you're trying to save from the Delphi will be questioning your sanity."

"I'll take that over sitting by while Washington gets overrun by illegitimate troops who have orders to assassinate the country's elected and appointed leaders. Let Congress impeach me. At least the country is saved."

"But for how long? Dodd will still be out there, and he'll

find a way to get his special election. The point is that for every strategy we undertake, short of total preemption, they have a contingency."

"We're not giving up, Mr. McCracken."

"Not at all, sir. We're just getting started."

Blaine met with Johnny Wareagle inside an empty White House office twenty minutes later, as soon as his meeting with the President had concluded.

"Didn't want you and Sal to feel left out, Indian," McCracken started, "and there happens to be a task that's right up your alley. The way I see it, the Delphi would never have shipped their entire store of nuclear weapons to their international representatives. They'd want to keep plenty in reserve as a future bargaining chip, as well as backup."

"I understand."

"The bulk of the weapons must still be in the United States and we've got to find where they've been stored. Otherwise the Delphi lives to fight another day."

"Leave it to Sal Belamo and me, Blainey."

"With the President's blessing, by the way." McCracken paused. "It's strange, Indian," he continued uneasily, "here we are working on the inside, as far inside as you can get, with the resources of the entire nation behind us, and we're still alone."

"There is a point in that, Blainey."

"Love to hear it."

"The inside is a state of mind, not one of being. From our beginnings in the hellfire we have always worked outside the system, but only to better accomplish what the system needs. I came to Sandcastle One last night after Traggeo. But when I saw he was part of something much bigger, I realized he had only been a lure the spirits had cast before me to draw me there." Wareagle stopped and took a long look at McCracken. "To you and what we face now. What we must save."

"Save *them*, right? Those who've denounced us, red-flagged us, denied we even exist. We've prevailed in spite of them."

"Then who are the true outsiders? We see ourselves as part of a country, and a world, that sometimes must be saved from itself and its own excesses. Those in power created these excesses, or at least allowed them to be. They steer and manage an entity they stand beyond, *without*, to watch evolve. But they don't see what that evolution has wrought within."

"We do."

"Then you understand."

"I think so. Next thing you know the spirits will be trying to speak in my ear, too."

Wareagle flashed a rare smile. "Perhaps they have already started and you need only to listen."

No sooner had Johnny left the office than Kristen Kurcell barged in, much to the dismay of the FBI agents assigned to watch her. She closed the door in the lead one's face.

"I guess you're planning what they call the fast exit, eh, McCracken?"

"Let me do what I do best, Kris."

"And what happens to me?"

"You stay alive."

"Not good enough," she said resolvedly.

"Look, Kris—"

"Don't bullshit me, McCracken. I'm a part of this, in case you've forgotten. I threw everything away to find out why my brother died." She hesitated, but her eyes lost none of their fire. "Samantha Jordan was in love with me, you know—"

"I got that impression."

"—and I killed her."

"I'm sorry."

"I'm not. She was part of what killed my brother, full of lies and deceptions. Even all those times she tried to seduce me, the lies were there. I could have quit my job, but I didn't because above everything else I thought she was my friend. Another lie."

"Maybe not. You admitted yourself she could have had you killed right away, but didn't."

"Again, to serve her own interests."

"Isn't that what everyone does?"

Her gaze grew suddenly uncertain. "You don't."

"I'm different."

"I know," Kristen said.

Taking a quick step forward, she pulled Blaine's head down and kissed him with all the passion pent up within her. Blaine could feel every bit of her emotion and her fear. He wrapped his arms around her and instinctively responded. The moment lingered as she jammed her hands against his chest and drove him back against the wall.

"Take me to South Africa with you," she said after at last pulling away, eyes demanding the response she wanted.

He raised his hands and grasped her shoulders. "Just be here when I get back, when all this is over."

"It's never going to be over, not for me anyway. My life's in the sewer."

"Try swimming, even treading water. I've been there. It works until the time comes to climb out."

"What if I don't want to climb out?"

"Then you drown."

"You're a son of a bitch, McCracken. You're—"

Before the next word had left Kristen's lips, Blaine had covered them with his own. She tried to push him off briefly and then relented, returning his kiss with a passion equal to her earlier one.

This time it was McCracken who pulled away first.

"Now we're even," he told her.

The contents of the floppy disk given to McCracken by Wild Bill Carlisle had been transferred to hard copy and distributed to Ben Samuelson, Charlie Byrne, General Trevor Cantrell, and Angela Taft in the Situation Room first thing

Wednesday morning. Their reactions ranged from shock to disbelief to disavowment as they scanned the eighteen-page document that contained files on the twenty-one men and women who had served with Carlisle on what had become the Delphi. Four of the twenty-one had died and two more had been incapacitated by illness, leaving fifteen in all. The President stressed the fact that some of those fifteen would have been forced out of the Delphi or left by their own choice, as had been the case with Bill Carlisle. The rest had stayed to form the nucleus behind the threat the government was currently facing.

Before the meeting had even begun, crack troops dispatched by General Cantrell had taken control of Miravo and all other bases retasked to handle the dismantling or destruction of nuclear warheads. At the very least, then, the group could rest assured that the Delphi's nuclear stockpile would not be expanded further.

Under the circumstances, that didn't really reassure any of the members of the inner circle. After reading through Carlisle's list of Delphi members, Charlie Byrne leaned back and tapped his knuckles together. Cantrell ruffled through the spent pages. Samuelson shoved the document away from him and stared it down as if afraid it might lunge back his way. Taft was shaking her head.

"How certain can we be of the accuracy of this information?" opened General Cantrell.

"*Absolutely* certain," responded the President. "To waste our time arguing otherwise is playing the old ostrich game of sticking our heads in the sand."

"There are three senators on this list," Byrne pointed out.

"Also three military men," Cantrell added. "An admiral and two generals. All three major branches of the armed forces covered."

"It's the representatives from the private sector I'm more concerned about," said Angela Taft. "Three of these men became political legends without ever running for office or even granting an interview. Consultants who've troubleshot in the background for the last three administrations, including this one. Men who understand power and know how to wield it."

"How familiar are you with the representatives from business, Charlie?" asked the President.

"You don't have to go beyond the front page of *The Wall Street Journal* to recognize their names, that's for sure, sir. But it goes way beyond that. Three of these men control companies that are among the largest multinational corporations based in this country. And the other two are billionaires several times over."

"Not hard to figure out where the resources came from to finance their right-wing allies across the globe, is it?" the President commented as he turned to Samuelson. "Now, Ben, how do we go about bringing them in?"

Samuelson was still flipping through the pages deliberately. "A coordinated, simultaneous effort to prevent the possibility of any of the representatives being forewarned," the head of the FBI said without any hesitation, barely looking up from the report. "Of course, since we don't know which of the fifteen we can safely rule out, the round-up will have to include all of them."

"Lots of states to cover," the President cautioned. "I counted ten for the fifteen names on the list."

"We're prepared, sir."

"How long before you can bring it off?"

"Lots of men have got to be moved into place, and there's the added complication of setting up a workable communications link. Say, between midnight and dawn tomorrow, Thursday. Catching the representatives at home should facilitate matters considerably. Of course, there are some factors we'd better get squared away right now."

"Go ahead."

"Do we inform the locals and take them along?"

The President shook his head. "The people on Carlisle's list probably damn near own the locals. Absolutely not. Next?"

"What exactly, sir, are we going to charge them with?"

"To paraphrase Rhett Butler, 'Frankly, my dear Ben, I don't give a damn.' But how does treason grab you?"

Samuelson nodded, satisfied with the response.

"Can we make that stick?" asked Angela Taft.

"So long as we exercise all proper procedures," answered Samuelson, "yes, I think we can."

"What about Dodd?"

"He's taken up temporary residence in *Olympus*, sir," Samuelson replied, referring to the space station Dodd had backed in a coventure with NASA.

"Good timing."

"He's got to come down sometime," said Charlie Byrne.

"And when he docs, Ben," the President told the director of the FBI, "I want the son of a bitch brought to me with his balls in a sling."

CHAPTER 30

Clive Barnstable, a member of South Africa's Interior Ministry, met McCracken just inside the international terminal of Jan Smuts Airport and escorted him away from Immigration toward the diplomatic entry point.

"I wish my instructions had permitted me to employ some backup," he complained.

"Those were *my* instructions," Blaine told him. "I don't want to draw any more attention to my presence than is absolutely necessary."

Barnstable, a rail-thin man wearing a linen cream-colored suit flecked with sweat, ran his handkerchief across his forehead. "Whatever you say."

The commercial flight out of Dulles had landed on time just before dawn on Thursday. The flight was seventeen hours long, and that fact, coupled with the five-hour advance in time, meant McCracken had essentially lost an en-

tire day he could ill afford to. His request to be met and
assisted by an expert on Travis Dreyer and the AWB had
been made through standard channels, nothing done that
would raise any eyebrows.

"I've got a car waiting outside," Barnstable told him.

"We'll take a taxi."

"The car's *illegally* parked."

"Must have diplomatic plates, then."

Barnstable's shoulders slumped further as he caught on to
McCracken's thinking. "You're right, of course," was all he
said.

"What about the information I requested?" Blaine asked
Barnstable as they moved toward the single check-in desk
within the confines of the diplomatic entry point.

Barnstable's thin frame bobbed a bit. "It's waiting for you
at a secure location." His tone became harsh. "This better
be more important. The entire schema of Whiteland is not
something to be pulled out on a whim."

"Whiteland?"

"That's the name Dreyer's given to the private state in the
Eastern Transvaal the AWB has formed."

"Tell you what. Let's jump in that cab and you can give
me the full briefing on the way."

The President accepted the news from Samuelson at six
A.M. Thursday with more frustration than rage. He had again
slept not a wink, waiting for word that the coordinated capture of the known members of the Delphi had been successfully completed. When the duty officer informed him that
Samuelson had arrived downstairs, he knew otherwise.

The President had tied his robe haphazardly over his pa-
jama bottoms so that a large expanse of bare chest was revealed. He paced the length of the bay window in his office
as the FBI director issued his report.

"So how many did we get, Ben?" he asked before
Samuelson was finished, his voice strangely calm.

"Four of the fifteen, sir. That leaves eleven."

The President stopped pacing. "I can subtract myself, Ben. I'm also pretty good at adding things up, and right now I'd say the four we did get left the Delphi around the same time as Bill Carlisle."

"Their initial statements do reflect that, sir."

"And what about the others?"

"None of my people can say for sure how any of them managed to avoid our nets. No two cases appear to have been the same. They just disappeared."

"A coordinated effort, then."

"As much as our capture of them would have been."

"So they must have known we were coming."

The head of the FBI stood there rigidly. "Sir, I know the responsibility for this lies with me, as does the apparent leak, since my people were the only ones involved. I can say only that I planned the operation with this very possibility in mind. Not a single one of my field commanders knew exactly what their assignment was until thirty minutes before zero hour. In some cases even the location was withheld or obscured until that time. Yes, it's conceivable a few of the eleven caught wind of what was going on or were warned by sources. But *all* of them? No, it couldn't have come from my people."

"Are you suggesting that one of those in our inner circle is the informer?"

"Not necessarily, sir. We know the clock's ticking on this. It's conceivable the Delphi member withdrawal was already planned and our missing them was a combination of bad timing and bad luck."

"And if it's not, Ben?"

Samuelson hesitated before responding, not able to fully hold the President's stare. "Then we must assume the Delphi knew we were onto them *prior* to the dispatch of my people."

"And if that's the case, they would also be aware that their timetable is no longer a mystery to us, either."

"Yes, sir, in all probability."

"Then we might be giving them no choice but to move things up and not wait for next Tuesday night at all."

The head of the FBI said nothing.

"All right, Ben, under the circumstances I think we can dispense with the subterfuge. I want these men found. And if they can't be found, I want them cut off." The President stopped just long enough to collect his thoughts. "That means freezing all their personal and business assets. And I want the lines of those involved in the government tapped."

"Should I get a court order?"

"I think an *executive* order should do quite nicely."

"Of course," Samuelson said, and hesitated. "Sir?"

"Yes, Ben."

"Have you considered going public with this? Expose these bastards for what they are in front of the nation before they can put their plan into effect."

"I've considered that and a hundred other possibilities. But even in the best-case scenario, that the people actually believed me, I can't see anything but panic resulting. It also could lead to the Delphi becoming desperate enough to utilize their nuclear stockpile. That's their trump card, Ben, the major unknown in all this."

The President did not add that the two men McCracken had vouched for were at present searching for that stockpile. Similarly, on McCracken's advice he had not informed the members of his inner circle of where Blaine himself had gone off to, or mentioned anything about the Delphi's international interests. It was conceivable, McCracken had insisted, that the enemy's reach extended even inside that circle, and now it appeared his fears were not without substance.

In any case, whatever advantage McCracken had briefly provided had been lost and, with it, trust. Under the circumstances, the only people the President had to rely on were a single operative presently in South Africa who had been considered an outcast until yesterday and two of his cohorts. Only one option remained.

The President would order General Cantrell to put the Evac plan into action tomorrow morning. At that point, unless something changed over the next twenty-four hours, the government would be taken out of harm's way.

Out of Washington.

Barnstable brought McCracken to Johannesburg's lavish Carlton Hotel in the Carlton Center, where Blaine would spend the rest of the morning familiarizing himself with the layout of Whiteland. A laptop computer and a collection of rolled-up blueprint-type plans awaited them when they entered the room.

"What's the computer for?" Blaine asked Barnstable.

"Much of what we know about Dreyer, the AWB, and Whiteland is contained on the Interior Ministry mainframe. There's too much to copy so I brought this laptop along so you can tie into the system."

McCracken spread the blueprints out across the bed while Barnstable activated the modem and tied into the Interior Ministry's data banks. Whiteland was so vast that it required eight of the blueprints to encompass the entire area. According to Barnstable, the AWB had staked their claim to the roughly 20,000 acres of land three years ago to establish what amounted to a separate nation. The South African government had ignored the gesture partly to avoid the confrontation Dreyer was looking for and partly in the hope that the problem would just go away. It didn't, of course, and in fact was compounded as the de Klerk administration inched ever closer toward ending white rule. Soon some executive powers would be handed over to a multiracial transition team, the first universal elections tentatively scheduled for later this year. Accordingly, emotions were running high with the extremes further polarizing themselves from the center. This had resulted in a dramatic rise in the AWB's ranks. New recruits, Barnstable reported, arrived almost daily, and construction to meet the resulting demand at Whiteland was proceeding at a frantic pace.

This trend was illustrated by the one-month-old blueprints Barnstable had provided. With few exceptions, Whiteland was not unlike any other town or settlement. Some areas were a bit more provincial, even primitive, because they were not yet supplied with running water and indoor plumbing. By all indications, Dreyer was having trouble keeping up with the need for housing.

Whiteland's town center was just that, a quartet of criss-crossing streets set in the middle of the territory the AWB had simply laid claim to. Only a small portion of it was property of the Dreyer family. The rest had been owned and protected by the state until Travis Dreyer had dared the government to stop him from settling it. Apparently, the five-acre parcel of land owned legitimately by the Dreyers in the southeast portion of Whiteland had become home to the AWB's command center. Blaine turned his attention to the blueprint featuring this complex.

The command center was situated with its rear close to the woods that enclosed the entire property. It was three stories in height built atop four underground levels of concrete bunkers that could be totally sealed from the outside world. A ten-foot-high electrified fence eliminated virtually any hope of accessing it stealthily from the rear. There was no additional fence, and no other elaborate security precautions to contend with, nor had Blaine expected any. After all, what kind of impression would the residents of Whiteland have if their capital was more like a fortress or a prison? Still, Blaine assumed a regular patrol of guards would be in place about its perimeter.

"What about these open lines here?" Blaine raised, pointing to a small corner of the blueprint.

"Air-conditioning ducts," Barnstable explained from just over his shoulder. "The equipment had yet to be installed when we obtained this information."

"From sources inside Whiteland, I would assume."

"Yes."

"Still present?"

Barnstable frowned. "The one who supplied this intelligence never came out. The one before that got his hand blown off in an accident. Still got a few inside, but we don't ask much of them these days. No sense placing them in jeopardy if we aren't planning to move on what they tell us."

"Would they be available to me?"

"*You?* Some of 'em got families and want the piss out of there as it is. I don't think they'd be agreeable to helping a man with your intentions." Barnstable stopped and leaned over the table. "Those kinds of intentions leave widows and orphans."

"So once I get in, I'm on my own."

"*If* you get in, you mean."

"Shouldn't be too hard, Barnstable. I just become one of those new recruits you said signs up every day."

McCracken continued to study the blueprints and pertinent intelligence data after Barnstable departed to manufacture the identity Blaine would require to gain entrance to Whiteland. He returned from the Interior Ministry shortly after noon.

"I've arranged for your background to fit what Dreyer is most comfortable with," he explained and pulled a manila-colored envelope from his pocket. "A frustrated out-of-work husband and father." He gave Blaine the envelope and drew his sleeve up to check his watch. "That contains the identity papers you'll need to be accepted. There's a bus leaving for Whiteland from the city in forty minutes time."

"And all I do is climb on board?"

"Whiteland maintains an open-door policy. Only trouble is that there's no contact with the outside once you're inside it. It's not just a question of not being allowed; there are no phones and no mail service. All delivery trucks are unloaded at a central area on the town's outskirts, and their contents transferred to the appropriate areas by Whiteland personnel."

"He's not making things easy for me, is he?"

Barnstable shrugged grimly. "Even if you find what you're looking for in there, getting out with it promises to be bloody hard. And I'm not authorized to help you in that regard."

"I'll worry about that when the time comes."

The meeting place for the AWB's newest recruits was Johannesburg's outdoor flea market located near an old factory warehouse converted into the Market Theater. The bus was already there when Barnstable dropped Blaine off a block away, fifteen seats taken by men who had gathered here from various points throughout the country. Men who wore their hate and hopelessness plain on their faces. They needed someone to blame for their ills, someone to strike back at.

The bus left at one o'clock sharp and McCracken spent the nearly four-hour ride to South Africa's newest township in the fourth seat from the rear. Whiteland lay halfway between Johannesburg and Kruger National Park, and for part of the last stretch he caught glimpses of the Olifants River. The bus turned off the highway ten miles past the signs for Marble Hall onto a bumpy, hard-packed gravel road. It passed a number of sentries and signs explicitly warning unwelcome visitors to turn back. Two miles later the bus pulled through a fortified gate and up to a trio of austere white buildings.

Blaine was instantly reminded of the induction center he had been bused to after enlisting in the army in 1968. Men in the trademark khaki uniforms and dirt-scuffed brown boots of the AWB waited with handshakes as the passengers stepped down off the bus. Three more stood proud vigil on horseback. The men on the ground were smiling. Those on horseback simply stared straight ahead. But their eyes were all the same, harsh and unforgiving. Blaine knew them all too well. They were the eyes of men who lived off hate and intolerance. And he knew equally well that the defeat in the eyes of those who had accompanied him here on the bus would soon change to hate as well.

A balding, mustachioed man who introduced himself as Colonel Smeed made brief introductory remarks, after which standard interviews were conducted. Blaine drew the colonel himself. When his turn came across a table inside one of the three buildings, he repeated the well-rehearsed background of the identity Barnstable and the Interior Ministry had created for him. The colonel accepted it matter-of-factly, jotting notes in the prescribed areas on a number of forms.

When all the interviews were over, the new recruits were assembled back outside. Smeed and the other AWB troops snapped to attention with a click of their heels as a jeep approached. Blaine could see a man he recognized as Travis Dreyer standing on the floorboard, holding the frame of the windshield for support. The jeep slowed to a halt and Dryer jumped down, his shiny black boots crunching gravel on impact. He approached stiffly, arms swaying in mechanical fashion by his side and chest protruding absurdly out. He was clean-shaven and had close-cropped corn-colored hair. His eyes were a light crystalline shade of blue.

An ivory-handled nine-millimeter Browning pistol was showcased in a standard AWB Sam Browne gun belt. It hung too low and flapped against his leg as he crossed in front of his rigid troops.

"At ease," he said and kept going.

He continued up the line of new recruits, regarding each with a hard stare. Blaine was afraid he was going to linger too long before him, but he paid him the same heed he had paid the others. Dreyer nodded one last time at the group as a whole before climbing back into his jeep and retaking his hold on the windshield.

The jeep drove off and Colonel Smeed ordered the sixteen new recruits to join him back on board the bus, which proceeded on a slow cruise through Whiteland while the colonel provided his standard narration. Blaine memorized the sights and locations, placing them for scale and context against details recalled from his careful study earlier in the day. The blueprints and information obtained over the computer had not done Whiteland justice. There was ample evidence of fresh plantings, and a number of men toiled tirelessly about the grounds surrounding the simple modular homes. Lawns were being planted, gardens dug. Flowers were in bloom.

As the bus continued to crawl through Whiteland, Blaine noted there had already been one extension to the school building and that another was currently in progress. There were kids playing soccer in khaki shorts and shirts. Women toted canvas bags full of groceries. A few people peddled about the freshly paved roads on bicycles.

McCracken could see in the commercial district that Barnstable's intelligence was already outdated; he counted at least three shops not mentioned in either the intelligence reports or the blueprints. If he had been set down here without knowing where he was, he would have guessed this was a farming community. The only sounds that disturbed the illusion were those of the heavy construction equipment racing to keep up with the demand for housing and other facilities.

Some of the people on the streets waved, smiling. The gestures were inviting, but the expressions on their faces were closed.

Blaine was so busy with his efforts to memorize the community's layout that he simply tuned out the colonel's narration. Almost before he realized it, the bus stopped before a chain link fence that surrounded Whiteland's training compound. There was nothing elaborate or overly impressive about what was going on within. Men were being taught hand-to-hand and close-in fighting in small groups. Another group was parading about. One was working with rifles equipped with bayonettes.

The dummies they were spearing were painted black.

McCracken listened distantly to the colonel expounding

on the high regard in which security was held here in Whiteland. He emphasized the fact that every man and woman who was accepted for residence had to be willing to defend his or her principles at any cost. They were in the midst of a war, the colonel told them, and they formed the nation's, and the white people's, last stand and hope.

Blaine heard the nonstop clacking of rifle reports and followed the recoil of the barrels. The targets coughed white specs and straw into the air, hardly in ratio to the number of bullets being fired. He pictured similar scenes occurring all over the world. Hatred was being sanctioned, provided with guns under a veil of legitimacy. Left unchecked, the Delphi's plan would spread violence and intolerance everywhere, making it easier for their representatives to achieve control.

But their day could still be stopped, starting here.

Tonight.

CHAPTER 31

Night deepened over Whiteland. McCracken's long day of indoctrination to his new home was complete for now, his reward a stiff cot in a thirty-six-bed dormitory. He lay beneath a window open to the harsh spill of the evening security lights. Blaine had recorded their presence earlier, along with a number of other measures he would have to overcome.

Though the AWB was always pictured on horseback at their rallies, they used jeeps to patrol the grounds at night, two men in each. There were also a number of security cameras that the residents had undoubtedly been told were for their own protection.

Slipping out of the dormitory would not be a problem. Thereafter, however, he would have well over a mile to cover to reach the command center. The security cameras were fixed on the doors, so Blaine climbed quietly out a window, taking care not to disturb his sleeping dorm-mates. The thick haze that hung before the security lights would help obscure him from the passing jeeps. His progress came in quick dashes intermixed with slithering headlong crawls through well-lit areas When a security patrol loomed near, he was able to take cover behind the freshly planted shrubbery.

He reached the outskirts of the command center without incident and lay prone on the grass in the darkness. No fence enclosed the command center other than at its rear, but the floods mounted on the building spilled light out at a radius wide enough to force him to take a roundabout route. Blaine clung to the shadows and used a prone approach over ground to avoid detection by the dozen or so guards who were trained to counter a commando-style assault, not a one-man reconnaissance.

McCracken reached the rear of the command center without incident. He passed several horses tied to a post near the building's back right-hand side and had reached up to still one's sudden stirring when he noticed the long rope clipped to its saddle. He removed the rope and carried it with him as he continued on.

Twelve feet separated him from the security fence that rimmed the compound's rear. There were no windows in the back of the command center building, and only a single door, which was sealed from the inside. He had grabbed the rope with these very limitations in mind. Careful scrutiny of the plans that morning had furnished him with accurate detail of the roof's layout. The chimney was just where he had expected it to be, its shape indistinct in the darkness. Blaine tied the front section of the rope into a lasso and backed up as far as the fence would let him. Then he hurled the rope outward with looped end leading.

It smacked against the top of the command center and bounced back down.

He cleared the roof on the second try and grazed the

chimney on the third. The fourth saw the lasso drop over the shape of the chimney and settle. Blaine took up the slack and felt the rope lock on. As soon as he felt the rope was secure, he grabbed hold tightly and began to scale the command center.

Samuel Jackson Dodd stood uneasily before the single small viewing portal located directly behind the slate black desk in his private quarters upon the space station *Olympus*. A slightly larger portal was contained in the station's severely limited observation deck, and a third, the smallest of all, could be found in main control. Originally he had envisioned an entire viewing wall to be constructed in these quarters reserved solely for him or his personal guests. But the engineers had found his request technologically laughable and stricken it from the plans. What did they know? Did they somehow think that by restricting his view from this vantage point they could also restrict his grand vision?

Dodd turned from it back toward his desk, atop which rested the computerized signal switcher and voice regulator that made secure communications between the Delphi's international representatives possible. The LED readouts for all were flashing, except that of Johannesburg's. Dodd felt himself growing increasingly impatient. He had thought long and hard over how best to explain the need for a drastic change in strategy. Though crucial to the ultimate plans of the Delphi, these men were difficult, often impossible, to deal with.

Atop his desk in the space station's observation room, Johannesburg still had not come on-line.

Committing himself to construction of the space station *Olympus* had seemed the most risky venture of Dodd's entire career. Even with underwriting by NASA, the total costs promised to stretch beyond the $40 billion mark. Add to this an estimated $100 billion cost to maintain the station over its thirty-year lifetime, and the downside if things went wrong, as everyone was predicting they would, was unlimited.

Sam Jack Dodd had learned long ago not to listen to others.

Olympus exemplified his commitment to the marriage of business and government, and even more his ability to get things done. With budgetary constraints as they were, NASA never could have undertaken the project alone. By the same token, no one in the private sector possessed the financial or technological resources to get it off the ground. The answer to this, as with everything, was a joint effort. In return for underwriting the project, NASA scientists and astronauts would have exclusive use of *Olympus* for its first three years. After that time a new subdivision of Dodd Industries would begin selling trips into space for civilians at, of course, exorbitantly expensive prices. Sam Jack Dodd wasn't worried; his market research had assured him that there would be a five-year waiting list and this project would be well in the black within a decade of operation.

A pair of new shuttles NASA was building would serve as space taxis. His marketing people projected that hitherto earthbound scientists alone could fill every seat for seven years. Insurance costs, the original deal breaker, were negligible because NASA had absorbed them into its budget.

Dodd turned back to the small portal and gazed out over what little of space he could see. From this angle only a small portion of the station itself was visible. Even when seen in total, though, *Olympus* was hardly a breath-stealing sight. When it came to construction pertaining to space, form ran a poor second to function. As a result, the station had a squat, tubular look to it, almost like an overweight spider. The bulk of *Olympus* was little more than a massive truss made of steel supports sandwiching the five spherical nodules that formed the station's heart. The central and largest nodule housed the main labs, combination cafeteria/meeting hall, and Dodd's private quarters. Three of the smaller nodules contained living quarters for crew and guests, while the fourth housed the command center.

The symmetrical girders and neatly arrayed scaffolding-like supports were marred by what looked like stubborn space debris in the form of the primary heat exchangers, solar panels, and main engine components. Indeed, *Olympus* was little more than an elaborate and cumbersome spaceship that doubled as a massive orbiting laboratory. Thicker, tubular assemblies ran toward the central nodule from three separate docking bays, only one of which was currently functional. Eventually all three would allow shuttles to conveniently off-load their passengers, whose first exposure to *Olympus* would be a zero gravity dash through the tubes leading into the central nodule where gravity was equalized.

The station itself maintained a constant rotation through its geosynchronistic orbit 22,400 miles above the center of the United States. The air was filtered by solar-powered engines, pumped out at a comfortable seventy-six degrees. Dodd kept having to remind himself in this his first visit that he was actually in space and not walking the hall of a high-tech office or luxury hotel. It had taken a full week of intensive training to prepare him for this. Future visitors would be required to spend two weeks in training, further justifying their fee and raising the station's profit margin. The first paying space travelers could purchase the entire package at a start-up price of $25,000, growing to near $50,000 within the first year. It had not yet been determined if the space-walk portion of the five-day sojourn would be extra or not.

Dodd squeezed his eyes closer to the small acrylic portal. Twenty-two thousand four hundred miles below him the small speck of the United States had slipped from his gaze.

How could things have gone so wrong? How could a single man have placed all his work in jeopardy?

Thanks to Blaine McCracken, the original members of the Delphi were on the run. Because sufficient warning had been provided, all had managed to get out safely, but their

usefulness had been placed in severe doubt. Some members
had panicked. They had lived their true lives in the shadows, and having the light suddenly thrust upon them was
more than most could bear. A few were advocating that the
operation be canceled, at the very least postponed. Dodd
knew that agreeing to either would only provide the fearful
with more time to betray the Delphi's cause. They might decide to turn themselves in and trade their stories for freedom. Loyalty was fleeting.

Sam Jack Dodd realized he needed a way to make that
work for him, to placate the Delphi while at the same time
appeasing the group's foreign representatives. It was a matter of utilizing what the circumstances had provided, which
in this case happened to be considerable. The remolding of
the strategy actually had a number of distinct advantages.
The problems it posed were ones of logistics and timing.
But the Delphi member inside the President's inner circle
had assured him all could be pulled off with nary a hitch.
Dodd had no choice other than to listen and hope the rest of
the international representatives so crucial to his plan would
listen as well.

On the communications system resting atop his desk, Johannesburg at last came on-line.

McCracken had spent considerable time that morning in
his room at the Carlton studying the air-conditioning system of Whiteland's command center for a reason. Since it
would be required to furnish air to the four underground
bunker levels as well as the three above ground, huge con-
densers and fans would be required, along with wide
enough duct work to push sufficient quantities through.
The plans had indicated the massive condenser units were
located on the roof, meaning the start of the labyrinthine
network of ducts would be found there as well. Blaine
knew also from the plans where Trevor Dreyer's office
was located. The contents of that top-floor office were
what had drawn him here. His plan now was to gain access

to that office by following the duct work to the crawl space directly above it.

Time was on his side except for the fact that those within the command center would soon notice that the air conditioning had malfunctioned. Even after they did, his hope was that it would take some time before a work crew could be dispatched and his handiwork on the roof uncovered.

Atop the roof now, McCracken quickly located the massive condenser unit. Finding no simple on-and-off switch, he began yanking out every exposed cord and wire until the thing shook and shut down. He followed the line that led from the condenser across to what he had first thought was a huge skylight but quickly realized was the intake duct for the chilled air. The plans had actually underestimated its size. Its rectangular cover was three by four feet, even easier for a man to negotiate than he had imagined. He had the top pried off within thirty seconds and breathed easier when he saw that the start of the duct work was elbow-shaped, eliminating the anxiety-generating necessity of negotiating a straight drop.

He slid immediately feet first into the galvanized steel and started to make his way toward the office of Travis Dreyer.

"Gentlemen," Samuel Jackson Dodd opened after the communications check had been satisfactorily completed, "this meeting has been called to inform you that circumstances have forced a rather drastic change in our final plans. The timetable is being moved up from next Tuesday to forty-eight hours from now. Seven P.M. Saturday, Washington time."

"*What?*" a number of the voices seemed to blare at once.

"That's absurd!" roared Germany.

"Our people are already in place," Japan returned. "Recalling them with such short notice would be impossible."

"And we," started Johannesburg, "cannot be ready to go until we have received our warheads."

"Calm yourselves, gentlemen. You will not be asked to do so until it is safe for us to make the shipment. It is only the American end of things I have elected to move up."

FRANCE. "But a simultaneous move by all parties was agreed upon for a reason. Without that simultaneity, the success of our own strikes is instantly placed in jeopardy."

"Gentlemen," began the Washington representative calmly, "we are all in jeopardy already. Our only chance for success is to advance the timetable here in the United States as has been laid out with my approval."

"You will lag behind us by only a week, ten days at the most," Dodd picked up immediately. "And when your day comes, the results may well exceed your original expectations, thanks to the new contingency we have adopted for the United States."

The observation deck of *Olympus* fell into silence. None of the LED lights flashed across their respective slots.

"Then when can I expect my warheads?" raised Johannesburg finally.

"They remain secure and will be transferred to you as soon as we have been able to stabilize the situation in the United States."

"And to what do we owe this change in plans?" demanded Germany.

"During the course of our last meeting, I briefed you on the involvement of Blaine McCracken. That involvement has now revealed to the U.S. government that they are backed into a corner." Dodd paused. "There is also the possibility that McCracken has uncovered the international nature of the Delphi."

"And our identities?" raised England.

"He could conceivably be aware of them. Accordingly, at the close of this meeting I will fax you the most recent picture we have on file of him. Just be on your guard."

"On our guard? The entire operation is in jeopardy and that is all you can say?"

"Our operation, Japan, is not in jeopardy at all. It has

only required the adopting of a contingent strategy we've
had ready for some time. In short, McCracken's involvement has given Washington only one way to turn, and when
they do so, we will be waiting."

"What do you mean?" asked France.

In response Samuel Jackson Dodd laid out the revised
plan for them step by step.

*"It has only required the adopting of a contingent strat-
egy we've had ready for some time. In short, McCracken's
involvement has given Washington only one way to turn,
and when they do so, we will be waiting. . . ."*

Blaine McCracken listened to what must have been a me-
chanically synthesized voice, Sam Jack Dodd's probably,
begin to detail the revised operation that would overthrow
the U.S. government. He had managed to pick up bits and
pieces of earlier parts of the discussion while crawling forward through the duct that ran along the complex's third-
floor ceiling. But it wasn't until he reached the spot over
Dreyer's office that he could hear all the words clearly.

He lay prone inside the steel duct to enable himself to
press his ear against it more easily. A cold sweat rose to the
surface of his flesh as he listened, terror increasing with
each successive sentence.

The President was playing right into the Delphi's hands.
The government of the United States was going to fall.

Saturday at seven P.M. . . .

Not even two days from now.

And unless Blaine could get word back to Washington in
a matter of hours, no one would be able to do a thing to prevent it.

Dreyer rose from his chair, exhilarated. His greatest
dreams were on the verge of coming true. In forty-eight
hours the United States would be thrown into total chaos.
Thereafter, the rest of the process that would bring the AWB

to power in South Africa would be carried out without impediment.

The leader of the AWB heard the whirr of the elaborate communication system's internal fax machine and placed his hand in front of the slot. The single page emerged only slightly rolled and possessing virtually all of the original's clarity. Dreyer gazed at the picture of Blaine McCracken.

His eyes bulged.

He knew this man, had seen him recently, had seen him . . .

Today!

McCracken was among the new recruits who had arrived that afternoon! McCracken was *on the premises now*!

Nervous sweat dripping off him, Dreyer started from his desk toward the door to his office. He needed to find Colonel Smeed. They had to be both cautious and thorough in dealing with a man of McCracken's prowess. Handle it right and Dreyer could become a hero among the Delphi, the man who rid the group of Blaine McCracken. His heart began to beat faster.

Near the door, Dreyer realized the air in the room was heavy and moist, far warmer than it should be. Dismayed, he reached up and placed his palm against one of the air-conditioning registers; it wasn't working.

"Jesus," Dreyer gasped, realizing. "Jesus. . . ."

McCracken retraced his path through the duct, no longer bothering to mask the sounds. He reached the roof and replaced the cover over the central duct. There was no time to reconnect the hoses he had yanked free or repair the damage he had done to the condenser. He simply retrieved the rope he had piled near the chimney and twisted the other end into a loop as well. His plan was to secure this end round a tree branch on the other side of the electrified fence and then pull himself over it to freedom.

Blaine heard the sounds of footsteps charging up the stairs that led onto the roof just as he was ready to toss the rope. Capture clearly was unavoidable. If Dreyer believed he had overheard the meeting of the Delphi that had just concluded, he would be killed almost instantly. His best chance to survive and maintain some hope, then, was to create the illusion that he had yet to gain entry to the command center.

McCracken rushed back to the primary duct he had dropped through initially and was pretending to work the cover off when the roof door crashed open. He made sure the troops saw him toss the duct cover away before they were upon him, led by Colonel Smeed.

"I think we should have another talk, Mr. McDowell," Smeed said, a pistol tight in his hand.

CHAPTER 32

"Thank you for seeing me, Mr. Matabu," Kristen Kurcell greeted the man staring intently at her from behind the desk.

Bota Matabu leaned his tall, thin frame forward, his chair creaking slightly. "After the great assistance you provided my delegation during our visit to your country, it is the least I can do for you, Miss Kurcell."

"I hope so, sir, because I'm about to ask you for a great deal more."

Matabu's huge, deep-set eyes did not waver. He folded his fingers together and rested his chin on his thumbs. His silk suit looked to be a top designer label, Italian probably, Kristen surmised. The patterned tie picked up the slight cream windowpane in the gray to create a look befitting the powerful and controversial leader Matabu had become. As the African National Congress's third-ranking member, he was Nelson Mandela's chief troubleshooter who supervised the strikes, work stoppages, and armed resistance to white reactionaries and police brutality in the townships.

"I'm listening, Miss Kurcell," he followed, but Kristen paused before resuming.

Since the FBI had assigned men to her for protection and not restraint, she'd had little trouble slipping out of the hotel in Washington without their knowing. She had timed her escape to coincide with catching a flight to Johannesburg, where she was determined to find Blaine McCracken. He had confided the rough sketch of his plan to her before they had parted, and in the succeeding hours she'd had time to see the folly of it. There were too many things that could go wrong, and if any of them did, McCracken would be left utterly alone.

Instead of sitting passively by, Kristen decided to do whatever she could to aid Blaine. The helpless feeling that still remained inside over her brother's death was torture enough. She couldn't sit idly by and wait for someone else she cared for to die.

Kristen had contacted Matabu before leaving Washington, and one of his private cars was waiting to pick her up when she reached Johannesburg in the dark early hours of Friday.

"Your phone call from the States was very disturbing," Matabu continued when Kristen did not speak. "Also vague. You said our movement was in great danger. May I assume this has something to do with a policy of some sort your government is considering?"

"No," Kristen told him. "Not at all. The danger to the ANC comes from my country, but it has nothing to do with the government."

Matabu's large eyes narrowed. "I am confused, Miss Kurcell."

"Mr. Matabu, there is strong reason to believe that American nuclear weapons have fallen into the hands of the AWB."

Matabu's eyebrows flickered. Beyond that, he showed no reaction. "I would have thought such a powerful and dangerous revelation would have been delivered through considerably different channels."

"As it would surely have been, if the force responsible was not also mounting a concerted effort to overthrow my country's government."

Matabu's head rose slowly from his hands. "Am I to assume that there is a connection between these two pursuits?"

"The force I speak of is determined to seek international domination by the radical right, to forge a worldwide cabal of men like Dreyer."

Matabu's stonelike composure wavered ever so slightly. "And how have you come by this information, Miss Kurcell?"

"Through a man who saved my life after I was taken prisoner by the group behind this threat to both our nations." Kristen paused. "The only man who might be able to stop it from happening."

"Yet you have come to me."

"Because that man came over here to infiltrate Whiteland, Mr. Matabu. And I think he's in trouble."

With the stage set, Kristen proceeded to tell her tale from the beginning. By the time she had finished, Bota Matabu's gaunt face glistened with a shiny layer of sweat. His deep-set eyes had lost their harshness and their certainty. When he finally spoke his tone was softer, almost muted.

"Then this man, this . . ."

"Blaine McCracken."

" . . . sought to gain access to Whiteland to uncover the substance of the . . . What did you call them?"

"The Delphi."

" . . . the Delphi's plan in order to stop it."

"Here and in the United States, Mr. Matabu. And if he fails, both of our nations will pay the price."

"What exactly would you like me to do, Miss Kurcell?"

"Find out if he's in there. Help him if he's in trouble."

"You believe me capable of a great deal."

Kristen tried to look as determined as she felt. "I know,

Mr. Matabu, that you have held a number of meetings with
members of the ECC," she said, referring to the End Con-
scription Campaign that had been founded by young whites
fed up with forced service to uphold the policy of apartheid
they did not support. Often called the "alternative Afrikaners," these whites were part of a grass-roots movement to
bring the races together in peace.

"I believe," she continued, "that several of these meetings
had as their basis the planting of ECC members in Whiteland
to provide accurate intelligence of the AWB's plans."

Matabu nodded, obviously impressed. "Just suppose that
I have been able to place a small number of white sympathizers inside Whiteland. Suppose these sympathizers have
cellular communicators with them that they use to forewarn
us of planned AWB strikes against the townships."

Kristen's spirits lifted. "Then you must be able to make
contact with them."

"I'm afraid only they can contact me. Their next report
from inside Whiteland is due at dawn. We will have to wait
until then."

Matabu called Kristen back into his office Friday morning after the report from one of his Whiteland infiltrators
had come in.

"Please describe this McCracken," he told her, standing
rigid before his desk.

"Tall and broad, with black, wavy hair," Kristen said, picturing Blaine McCracken in her head. "He has a closely
trimmed beard and a scar running through his—"

"That is the man," Matabu confirmed. "Apparently last
night he was caught trying to sneak into the AWB command
center."

"Is he alive?"

"Only for now, I'm afraid."

The first rays of the morning sun turned the hole Blaine
was stuffed in into an oven. Touching the iron walls with

his bare skin singed his flesh, and it took every bit of self-control to keep his breathing steady. They had stripped him down to his shorts the previous night before sealing him in this cramped cubicle, where the heat seemed to suck the oxygen right out of the air. The humidity was stifling, and with each passing minute the sun fed it further.

The sun was a major problem, but the boxlike hole itself posed an even greater one. When he was in a seated position, Blaine's head was close to the grated top, which focused the light into even harsher beams. The hole was too small for him to stretch his legs out fully in any direction without his bare shoulders rubbing up against the sizzling walls. So Blaine had no choice but to keep his legs tucked in close to his chest, the cramping in his already weary muscles starting almost instantly.

He stretched them as best he could, knowing he had to stay strong and ready. Once the opportunity for escape arose, he must be prepared to seize it. If not, the President and the entire United States were going to fall into a deadly trap.

The shadow of one of his guards passed over the grate above him. Blaine stilled his thoughts as if they were words. The logistics of the setting ruled out a desperate dash for freedom, even if there had been a way to pry the grate off. Guns would be trained on him at this very moment. Dreyer had been waiting the night before when McCracken was brought down from the roof. Secure in the notion that Blaine had not managed to learn anything of value, the leader of the AWB had chosen the most dramatic of demises for him:

Blaine was to be shot by a firing squad at noon, right about the time the President would be embarking on a path certain to ensure the fall of his administration.

In the Situation Room of the White House, General Trevor Cantrell had the floor. He stood before a color-coded map of Washington, indicating various pickup points keyed to one of the three destinations the government was going to be moved to.

"How long to manage total evacuation?" the President asked.

"Eight to ten hours for those·currently in the capital, and that's a liberal figure, sir."

"I'd like to hear the procedure again," requested National Security Advisor Angela Taft.

"A simple message will be played over every Washington radio station every fifteen minutes. CNN and all other news broadcasts will carry a certain commercial every ten minutes. A number of selected group leaders will be personally telephoned and asked to begin a chain system to reach all those readily accessible. Beyond that, Emergency Communications, or EMER-COM, has on file all the numbers of those on the Evac list who carry beepers: roughly seventy percent. That will insure we don't miss anyone."

"Have you determined exactly how many are in town?" asked Charlie Byrne.

Cantrell looked to Ben Samuelson of the FBI before responding. "With Mr. Samuelson's help, I've determined that number to be between ninety and ninety-two percent. Best strategic estimates in the past have run somewhere around three-quarters, so we're well ahead of the game."

"No effort, I assume, has been made to contact those who are not readily accessible," said the President.

"No, sir, and for obvious reasons. A possible leak has to be avoided at all costs. I'm afraid those not included in the Evac will have to accept being left out of the government for as long as it takes to restore order."

"Assuming we end up losing that order," said Charlie Byrne.

"And just how do we keep the city from realizing the people governing the nation have taken their collective leave?" followed the President.

"None of the pickup points are in public areas. All helicopter drops will be made by army choppers, hardly an un-familiar site in the city."

"What about those charged with the transportation end of things?" raised Angela Taft.

"All pilots and drivers are currently on alert, ma'am. We run drills constantly, so they're none the wiser about what's going on. We won't lose time on their account."

"But if we try to pull all this off in eight to ten hours," started the President, "plenty of people are going to take notice, the media included. I think we should spread it out further, through all of tomorrow if necessary."

"Tomorrow's Saturday," reminded Ben Samuelson, echoing his sentiments. "The people we've got to get out won't be working anyway. Makes perfect sense."

"Agreed, but I strongly suggest that those slated for Mount Weather leave as soon as we go to alert status," Cantrell stated, referring to the justices of the Supreme Court, Cabinet members, and selected other government officials. "That would include you, sir."

"And I'm willing to accept that so long as you're confident we can control things from inside Mount Weather. I had only a cursory tour and there wasn't much I understood about the technical aspects."

"You can run the country as confidently from Mount Weather as you can from the White House, sir. In fact, replicas have been constructed of the Oval Office and White House press room to make the country think you're still *in* Washington, if you so choose."

"I'd still be more comfortable overseeing things from where I am now," the President said, hedging.

"Speaking of which," began Ben Samuelson, "someone's got to coordinate security for the city if the siege comes. That's the job of the FBI." He looked toward Cantrell. "The general and I have already discussed this."

"Troops from the Seventh Light Infantry are in position to move in now, sir," Cantrell explained. "Once in place they could be placed under the direct command of Mr. Samuelson."

"Let's back up a minute, General," said the President. "How do we move the Seventh LID in without attracting the very kind of fuss we seem so determined to avoid?"

"My suggestion," Angela Taft threw in, "would be to say nothing until the siege begins, if it begins. Then, sir, you inform the media—and the nation—from inside Mount Weather."

The President nodded, as satisfied as he was going to be. "Okay, people. According to my watch it's four A.M. I want to be ready to move by dawn."

"It's the best I can do, I'm afraid," Matabu said with grim detachment after explaining the final elements of his plan to Kristen. In the wake of learning about McCracken's impending death by firing squad, he had put the plan together quickly with the reluctant support of his plants from the ECC inside Whiteland.

"It'll be enough," she told him.

"I'm afraid I do not share your confidence."

"That's because you don't know Blaine McCracken."

Matabu checked his watch. "But I do know we'd better get moving if we want to be in position on the chance he makes it out."

The sun had continued to sap the strength from McCracken, taking his hope along with it. Brief lapses into unconsciousness threatened his sense of time. He came awake from each one fully determined to remain alert, yet unable to control his drifts. He could barely swallow. His breath came in short, fitful heaves. The sweat had stopped running off him as his bodily fluids dried up.

McCracken slipped out of consciousness again, welcomed the cool comfort his mind was able to conjure up in that state. A noise drew him back, something familiar yet out of place.

The *wop-wop* sound of one helicopter overhead was instantly joined by another. As Blaine tried to angle his body to peer out through the grate, he heard metallic bursts of heavy automatic fire ringing through the air.

Whiteland was coming under attack!

He let himself hope this was the work of Barnstable and the Interior Ministry, that a rescue was being attempted. But his hope sank as quickly as it had risen. A hundred helicopter gunships were nothing compared to the single well-placed bullet that would swiftly end his life. Even Johnny Wareagle would be hard-pressed to get him off the grounds under current conditions.

Still, the fire from above continued, returned by AWB soldiers with their automatic rifles. The ground enclosing his hole trembled as men dashed in all directions. Blaine could hear multiple orders being shouted and easily imagined the pandemonium transpiring above his head.

Suddenly a pair of shadows crossed over his grate. Blaine heard a key jangling in the lock beyond. Noon, it seemed, was coming early.

The grate was raised. "Hurry, mate," a voice called. "We've come to get you out!"

"No," Blaine said hoarsely.

"What?" The voice sounding exasperated now, the face attached to it lowering.

"We'd never make it. Not like this."

"But— "

"Just listen to me."

The man did, then sped off, leaving a pair of cohorts over Blaine's cell. The minutes dragged on as the battle above continued. Then the grate was raised again long enough for a small pack to be dropped through.

"Hope you know what you're doing, mate."

"You and me both."

"Fucking kaffirs!" Dreyer screeched, ivory-handled nine-millimeter Browning pistol held cocked by his side.

He could see the pair of helicopters fleeing to the north, one bleeding smoke and oil, the ten-minute battle apparently over. Colonel Smeed's jeep pulled up alongside him.

"Casualties?" Dreyer demanded.

"A dozen or so wounded. None killed. Just a nuisance run."

"This is the first time Matabu's hit Whiteland, Colonel. I don't like that. I like it even less since he's adding choppers to the kaffir arsenal." Dreyer's mind veered in midthought. "What about our prisoner?"

"Safely under guard."

"I want to see for myself," Travis Dreyer said and climbed into the jeep's back. "It's almost noon."

Smeed jammed the key home and unlocked the grate while Dreyer waited behind him. A guard hoisted the grate, allowing Smeed to peer down inside.

Dreyer watched Smeed's back go rigid.

"Bloody hell," the colonel muttered.

"What?" Dreyer demanded. *"What?"*

He shoved Smeed aside and followed the path of his stare. "Fucking shit!" Dreyer bellowed.

The balled-up shape in the khaki uniform inside the hole belonged to an AWB guard.

"Find McCracken!" he yelled at Smeed. "I want him in irons and I mean immediately!"

The chaos that had followed the chopper attack was nothing compared to that which came next. The entire complement of AWB soldiers fanned out through the complex and surrounding brush to search for the escaped prisoner. Dreyer cursed himself for opting for the dramatic, rather than for a simple execution last night when the opportunity availed itself. He longed now for another chance to center McCracken in his gun sights. The man couldn't have gone far in his weakened condition. Dreyer's men would find him.

On McCracken's instructions, the three ECC plants posing as guards had supplied him with an AWB khaki uniform and Sam Browne belt, and then returned when the rush of troops dispersed in all directions to begin a frantic search. To anyone who bothered to notice, it seemed they were simply removing the unconscious frame of the comrade who had fallen prey to the escaped prisoner. One of them laid out a stretcher. Another feigned lifting McCracken out of the hole.

"Make yourself comfortable," he said, starting to ease Blaine toward the stretcher.

"Not me—you."

"Me?"

"We're trading places. I'll take things from here."

The contents of a full canteen included in the pack had had a miraculous effect on McCracken. He felt alert and strong, lost bodily fluids at least partially replenished.

"A car will be waiting for you at the entrance of the road leading in to Whiteland," the familiar voice of the leader advised him. "A black Mercedes."

"Who are you?"

"Friends."

Blaine tightened his gun belt. "They'll figure this out."

Two of the men lifted the stretcher bearing the third upward.

"We won't be far behind."

They moved away and McCracken started off in the opposite direction. In the light of day, even with the chaos, it was only a matter of time before someone recognized him, an easy task since the guards were virtually all clean-shaven, whereas he wore a beard. The sooner he got out of Whiteland, the better. The cover of troops already spreading outward to search for him would have to be enough.

Blaine followed a phalanx through an open gate into the nearby brush and trees. Around him men hacked at the brush and bushes to ease their search for the escaped prisoner. McCracken kept his distance, already angling to circle back for the road. His best chance lay in keeping to the woods for as long as possible. He picked up his pace, straining to maintain his sense of direction.

His route took him into the path of a team slicing through the brush in the direction he had come from. He tried to escape recognition by mimicking their hacking motions, thereby keeping his face and beard covered. But he couldn't avoid a familiar figure that appeared suddenly before him.

"You!" bellowed Colonel Smeed.

His pistol came up as McCracken lunged forward. He managed to knock the hand aside, but a shot rang out and echoed in the air. Blaine lashed out with a palm-heel strike that mashed Smeed's nose and pitched him over. The damage, though, had been done, the gunshot certain to draw much of the AWB to this area. Blaine jumped over the colonel's body and began to run.

Footsteps converged upon him from the sides and rear. Blaine could not afford any tricks or feints. His only chance was to reach the road and the black Mercedes, not knowing who waited inside it nor what exactly his fate would be upon reaching it.

McCracken's mouth had gone desert dry again. He pushed his weary, battered body through the brush. Adrenaline swept through him. He grew stronger with each step.

The road appeared and Blaine lunged through the last of the trees onto it. If his bearings were correct, he had covered a good half mile in the woods outside Whiteland, that much more to traverse in the open before he reached the Mercedes. McCracken pushed himself into a sprint that had brought him almost all the rest of the way when he heard truck engines coming fast in his wake. Refusing to slow up, he clung to the road's side in case he had to take refuge in the woods once more and ran with pistol in hand.

He could see the head of the road now, a black Mercedes backed into the woods for cover, its nose alone visible. He chanced a quick glance over his shoulder and found the trucks were still a hundred yards behind him. Turning back to the Mercedes, he saw a pair of black men holding automatic rifles emerge from the front seat of the car, while a familiar figure slid out of the back.

"Hurry!" screamed Kristen Kurcell.

McCracken was twenty-five yards away when the black gunmen opened fire on the lead truck that had just spotted McCracken. Its windshield shattered and it spun across the road. A second truck rammed into it. The gunmen kept firing, starting to move back for the car as Blaine reached Kristen. She hugged him and dragged him into the backseat of the car while the two gunmen jumped into the front.

"Thank God," she moaned. "Thank God."

Waiting inside the back was another man who grinned tightly at Blaine.

"We seem to share the same enemies, Mr. McCracken," said Bota Matabu.

CHAPTER 33

The Mercedes screeched away, one of the gunmen keeping a vigil on the rear while the other drove.

"They are not behind us," he reported, the relief clear in his voice.

Kristen watched Blaine's eyes sweeping about the car's interior. "A phone! Does this car have a phone?" he demanded of Matabu.

"No."

"Then get me somewhere that does!"

"I have a small substation thirty minutes from here," Matabu offered. "That is as close a place as any where there will be a phone."

McCracken shifted nervously about, aware that this was the man who had obviously arranged to save his life. Thanks would have to come later. Blaine looked back at Kristen.

"How much does he know?" he asked Kristen.

"Everything I do," she replied. "Which apparently needs some filling in."

"I'll say," McCracken acknowledged.

"Sir, the helicopter is prepped to leave," General Cantrell announced at six A.M. sharp Friday morning. "An identical chopper will take off five minutes before yours and a second identical chopper will follow five minutes after. All three will receive identical air support in the form of gunships."

"What about the rest of those bound for Mount Weather?"

"They will all have received the order before we take off. Pickup vehicles, other choppers mostly, will be waiting at the assigned rendezvous points."

"You move fast, General," the President complimented.

"We've been prepared for a much worse scenario for generations," Cantrell reminded.

"Everything's relative, I suppose," the President said as he rose. "I'd better get a move on."

The presidential chopper, flanked by a pair of protective gunships, hovered over the Mount Weather helipad that was visible only from directly overhead. Although it had been cleared to land, wind conditions were not favorable and the pilot had to continue hovering until a window opened up.

The President sat along with Cantrell, Charlie Byrne, Angela Taft, and a team of personally selected Secret Service agents in the passenger hold. At last they felt the chopper's landing pods touch down and watched a phalanx of guards from within Mount Weather sprint into positions around the helipad to join those already posted upon the surrounding Blue Ridge Mountains. Cantrell stepped out first and made sure all were in place before signaling the President to join him.

"Faster!" Matabu ordered as they came to the final stretch leading to his substation.

His driver swung onto the hardpacked dirt road, pushing

the big car even more and jostling its passengers. The road led to an isolated farm, and Blaine was out through the rear door before the Mercedes had come to a complete stop. A pair of black men with shotguns sprinted out of the house at the sight of his AWB uniform.

"No!" ordered Matabu, as he emerged in McCracken's wake. "Let him in!"

Matabu helped Kristen from the backseat and followed Blaine toward the house.

McCracken charged through the door and quickly reached the living room. Scanning the room he spotted a phone resting on an end table. Within seconds of picking it up, he reached an international operator. In just a few moments more, the direct line the President had provided him with was ringing.

"Emergency Communications," a voice greeted.

"What?"

"You have reached Emergency Communications or EMER-COM," the voice continued. "State your name and designation."

McCracken had never heard of EMER-COM. "My name is McCracken and I don't have a designation."

"Please vacate this line. Failure to do so—"

"Look, the President gave me this number. I've got to reach him."

"You are in violation of national security."

"Bullshit! Check the exchange this call was routed from. You'll find it's the President's private number. He gave it to me so I could relay certain information directly to him. I've got that information now and I need to pass it on, which means you've got to patch me the fuck through to him wherever he is!"

The man hesitated, Blaine certain he was checking the original routing, but keeping his fingers crossed nonetheless. "Patch-through being effected now."

McCracken heard the soft clacking of what sounded like computer keys on the other end and settled himself to wait.

* * *

The call came in over the chopper pilot's headset when the security detail leading the President through the stiff wind was halfway to the elevator built into the mountain.

"EMER-COM for the President."

"We've just landed at Mount Weather. He's on his way into the installation."

"Catch him, please."

The pilot leaped down from the bridge and cupped his hands in front of his mouth before calling out. The strong winds swallowed his shout. He yelled again to no avail. The presidential entourage boarded the elevator, and the black steel door closed behind them.

"Sorry," he said into his mike after climbing back into the chopper. "I missed him."

"The President is no longer accessible," EMER-COM informed McCracken.

"Christ . . . He's entered Mount Weather then, hasn't he? No, don't bother answering. Just patch me through to him inside the mountain. Patch me through to *anyone* inside the mountain."

The elevator descended a hundred feet into the Blue Ridge Mountains. Its doors opened to reveal a long corridor with guards stationed at attention on both sides.

"Very impressive, General," the President complimented Cantrell.

"These are special operations troops who were moved in to supplement standard security only yesterday. They're here just in case our opposition elects to try taking Mount Weather itself as a last desperate act."

"I feel safer already."

"Mount Weather Communications Control."

"Go ahead," EMER-COM instructed McCracken.

"Please put the President on the line."

"He has just arrived on station."

"Get him. Tell him the balls are cracked again."

"What?"

"You heard me. That's the message. Do it!"

The President advanced down the corridor toward the nerve center of Mount Weather flanked by Charlie Byrne and General Cantrell. Angela Taft brought up the rear just ahead of the quartet of Secret Service agents. Suddenly a man in uniform appeared before them and saluted.

"Sir," he addressed the President, "a call for you has been relayed through Emergency Communications. It's on the line now."

"From who?"

"The caller said to tell you . . . the balls are cracked again."

"McCracken!" the President realized, looking at General Cantrell. "Where can I take it?"

"Down here, sir."

The President had started after him when Cantrell nodded almost imperceptibly to the troops closest to the group. In the next instant, their guns were leveled directly at the President, Charlie Byrne, Angela Taft. The Secret Service agents who had accompanied the group instinctively formed a protective shield around the President, flirting with the notion of drawing their weapons.

"Don't do it, gentlemen," Cantrell ordered and drew his own pistol. "My men have orders to shoot as soon as they see steel."

The agents' hands froze, then slowly dropped.

"Now back off," Cantrell told them, "hands in the air." After they had obeyed, he addressed the special troops lining the corridor. "Detain all base personnel and secure the communications station!"

A portion of his troops dashed off to complete their pre-arranged assignments.

"You're a son of a bitch, General," the President said, face-to-face with the Delphi traitor who had penetrated his inner circle.

The general held his pistol on him while a team of his remaining troops slammed the Secret Service agents up against the wall and checked them for additional weapons. "And you're under arrest, sir."

Several minutes had passed before a different voice came on the line from inside Mount Weather. "The President is not available."

"Did you give him the message?" Blaine demanded.

"Wait a minute, who is this?"

"We can reach you from this end when he is settled if you give us your number."

McCracken hung up the phone.

"What's wrong?" Kristen asked from the doorway, Bota Matabu alongside her.

"They've got him," Blaine said flatly. "We were too late."

Kristen exchanged a glance with Matabu, both aware of what that meant.

"It's called the hole theory," Blaine had explained back in the car after relating the substance of what he had heard above Dreyer's office the night before.

"The what?" asked Kristen.

"Has to do with using a perceived threat to make someone withdraw to where he thinks he'll be safe, into a hole, so to speak. But the hole is really a prison, and the subject falls into a trap."

The Delphi had contrived to use the White House's discovery of their original plan to their best advantage. The Evac would closet the entire government in secure locations, presumably to wait out the coming battle in safety. But those secure locations would now be turned into detention centers little different from Sandcastle One, where those charged with running the country would be trapped, to be either incarcerated or killed.

Kristen stood watching as McCracken hovered over the phone. "What happens next?"

"The Delphi presides over the destruction of Washington

with the blame cast elsewhere, prepared to emerge from the rubble as the only effective governing body. The country will be forced to accept them—even be *glad* to accept them. And Dodd too, of course, because there's no alternative. They've got nowhere else to go."

"Like us . . ."

Blaine's eyes bulged, thoughts triggered. "Maybe not."

He picked up the receiver again and dialed another long-distance number, pressing out the digits as quickly as he could recall them.

"Who are you calling?" Kristen asked, perplexed.

"An army of our own."

"You killed Clifton Jardine," the President snapped at Trevor Cantrell, inside the office that would serve as his, Charlie Byrne's, and Angela Taft's cell.

"He didn't realize how close his man Daniels had come to us. He called me for my input prior to the meeting he had scheduled with you."

"And now . . ."

"You know the drill as well as I do, Mr. President. And now we ravage the city of Washington. By this time tomorrow, the occupants of both Greenbrier and Site R, as well as the others slated to arrive here, will be under detention. The government will have been effectively unseated."

"So Sam Jack Dodd can move in after your fireworks show is finished." The President's rage began to boil over. "How many innocent people do you plan to kill? How many will it take to scare the country into supporting what you have to offer?"

"Enough, sir, so that they won't be sorry when order is restored at last."

"Don't 'sir' me. I think we can dispense with your facade of respect."

Cantrell looked honestly hurt. "It's no facade, Mr. President. My respect for you carries over into the office you hold and the nation itself. What I've done, what *we've* done, is for the long-term good of that nation."

"Right," the President agreed wryly, "because the Delphi see themselves as the only ones capable of running the entire world."

"That's the point, sir: only by running the world can we successfully run the country. Unification, centralization—enemies controlled by dependence."

"Meaning those fascists the Delphi's sleeping with."

Cantrell's eyes narrowed in suspicion and then widened in understanding. "Obviously McCracken uncovered more than you let on to us."

"Held back on his advice."

"All academic at this point, in any case. Call them whatever you want, but we'll accept any bedfellows who can help us make our country strong again. As for you, sir, I'm afraid it was just bad timing. It could have been anyone."

"Well, it wasn't anyone; it was *me*. And I'm betting you're all going to fall on your asses. Do you honestly think you can just ride in and *take* Washington?"

"Not exactly, sir," Cantrell said confidently, backing up toward the door, "because we're already there and no one's left to stop us."

"You're forgetting someone, aren't you?"

The general stiffened. His hand stopped short of the knob. "McCracken? We'll deal with him when he comes to effect your rescue."

"I don't think he'll come for me, General. I think he'll be coming to stop you. In Washington."

Cantrell tried to look confident. "Then he'll die with any others who try to provide resistance."

"We'll see, General."

"Yes, sir, we will, because Mr. Dodd has arranged a satellite feed to allow us to view tomorrow's proceedings. I've saved you a front-row seat."

PART FIVE

THE BATTLE OF WASHINGTON

WASHINGTON:
SATURDAY, APRIL 23, 1994; NOON

CHAPTER 34

"You mean these are the only people you can call on?" Kristen Kurcell shook her head. "With all your contacts, this is the *best* you can do?"

McCracken leaned back against his seat in the Washington-bound Metroliner's first-class compartment. With Union Station just minutes away, he had finally explained to Kristen who he hoped would be awaiting them in the capital. Her reaction had not been terribly surprising.

"Let's wait and see if I've done anything at all," he said flatly.

More shock crossed Kristen's features. "You mean you aren't even sure they're coming?"

"Afraid not."

Blaine's mind flashed back to the second phone call he had made the day before from Bota Matabu's ANC substation thirty minutes from Whiteland.

"You're fuckin' nuts, man!" the voice on the other end of the line had responded to Blaine's request.

"That doesn't change the fact that you might be the country's last hope."

A hearty laugh broke a brief silence. "Country's last hope? Ain't that a trip. . . . Shit, maybe I'll just sit on the sidelines and enjoy the show."

"You won't like what's left when it's over. Nightmare city for everything you've always stood for and believed in. And need I remind you that you owe me?"

"You had to bring that up, didn't you?"

"You missed your chance twenty-five years ago. Today's

your lucky day: you get another one—by helping to stop a
group aiming to accomplish the exact opposite."

"Anybody ever tell you the age of Aquarius was over,
Mac?"

"More than that's gonna be over unless I get some help."

Immediately after that phone call ended, McCracken had
begun plotting how he and Kristen could return to the
United States. Aware the Delphi would be watching for him,
he had turned down Matabu's offer to spirit them into the
country covertly on board a diplomatic flight. Instead Blaine
opted for an arduous journey linking Kristen and him up
with a tour group in London bound for New York and then,
finally, onto this Metroliner that would take them to the capital. In all, the trek had taken a nerve-racking twenty-seven
hours, partially accounting for Kristen's short temper.

"What about the damn army?" she persisted. "All your
old friends. Isn't this their kind of work?"

"It would be if I knew who among them I could trust,"
Blaine told her. "You're forgetting that high levels of the
military are involved in this. And you can bet that anyone
close enough to Washington to do us any good who isn't
part of the Delphi has been sent off on drills and maneuvers
as far away as possible."

Kristen leaned back herself and sighed. "They've thought
of everything."

"Not quite," McCracken reminded.

McCracken had the driver leave them off on Constitution
Avenue near the Lincoln Memorial. The beautiful spring
Saturday had brought the tourists out in force, none of them
realizing what the city would be facing in a scant few hours.
The Mall itself was littered with strollers. A few young men
were playing Frisbee. At the Washington Monument, the
line to make the climb to the top circled the building three
times.

As Kristen moved past it at Blaine's side, her gaze drifted
all the way down the Mall to the U.S. Capitol. At first she

thought the group McCracken had contacted had failed to show up. Then she noticed the large cluster of casually dressed men and women who were setting up some sort of exhibition past 14th Street in front of the Smithsonian complex. She looked back at McCracken and saw a smile inching across his features.

"It's them, isn't it?" she said.

His response was to pick up his pace as he walked toward the group. A thinnish man sporting a ponytail and a tie-dyed tank top over his cutoff jeans saw them coming and moved away from the group to meet them, a slight limp slowing his gait.

"Not bad," Blaine greeted.

"Hey, man, ask and you shall receive," Arlo Cleese returned.

Blaine turned to Kristen. "I don't suppose I have to introduce you."

She took a long look at Cleese and then gazed back at McCracken. "But you could explain to me why a man who declared war on America a generation ago is now going to try and save it."

"Thing is, lady," the leader of the Midnight Riders responded, "the enemy I was fighting then's about the same one I came here to fight today. Not much really changes."

Behind Cleese the Midnight Riders who had accompanied him to Washington continued unloading paintings and other wares from a collection of colorfully painted Volkswagen vans onto tables that had been set up to display them. Old-fashioned peace signs dangled round a number of necks. Leather moccasins and Jerry Garcia glasses were among the most popular accessories.

Most of those helping to unload the vans, though, were dressed nondescriptly and wore no accessories at all. They moved cautiously, deliberately, not bothering to acknowledge the arrival of these two strangers in the group while never allowing their eyes to stray too far away from them.

Kristen managed to meet those eyes a few times and the sight chilled her. These were the true remnants of the lunatic fringe, dwellers on society's outskirts for the better part of their lives. The eclectic verse of the Weathermen, Black Panthers, and Students for a Democratic Society still strummed in their minds. It was as though they had stepped out of a time capsule to at last stand ready for the battle so long delayed, the battle they had joined the Midnight Riders to wage. The difference was that they had come to save the government they had once seemed determined to overthrow.

"How many?" Blaine asked Cleese.

"Couple hundred was the best I could do."

"I was hoping for more," he said.

"Lucky to get this many, man."

"Firepower?"

"None of the big stuff. Lots of explosives, grenades, a few rockets. A goddamn insurgency grab bag. See, all our vans come equipped with secret compartments. Plenty of room to store goodies."

"The stuff you bought from the Alvarezes?"

"What we could carry, anyway. You didn't exactly give me a lot of notice."

"I don't believe this," Kristen muttered.

"Tough bitch," Cleese said to McCracken.

"I don't think she approves of my choice in friends."

Cleese again glanced at Kristen. "Maybe because she figures we'd rather see the country go up in flames."

."The thought had crossed my mind," Kristen shot back.

"Depends on who's about to throw the match, sister. If we're the lunatic fringe, what do you call the dudes who are about to burn the city? Everything's relative, and we're not the real crazies anymore. Hell, we never were, not to this extent, anyway. We never wanted to take the country over. We just wanted to make sure the people who already had it took note of our positions. We mighta been wrong and we mighta been assholes, but we believed in what we were doing. We were just sick of watching the country fuck itself up, and today makes it seem like we were right all along."

Cleese peeled away a section of hair on the right side of his head to reveal a nasty scar. "Got this outside the '68 convention in Chicago. Cop with a billy club. I was on my knees at the time. He was smiling. That's the kind of mentality that's gonna be running things come morning 'less something gets done. I won't lie and say we haven't talked about doing it ourselves more times than once. Saving the country from that cop with the billy club's probably gonna be the closest we ever come. What the hell? That's close enough."

"What's it mean, big fella?" Sal Belamo asked after the contact exchange he and Johnny Wareagle had been issued to report their progress rang unanswered.

They had been at it for nearly two days now, scouring an ever-expanding perimeter around Miravo Air Force Base in search of the Delphi's stockpile of nuclear weapons. The helicopter they had been provided with had allowed them to cover lots of ground, all for naught so far. A refueling stop at this small airfield bright and early Saturday morning gave Johnny a perfect opportunity to call in a fresh update to the special number provided. The lack of response on the other end in Washington indicated the worst had happened, or was about to.

"You thinking the two of us should call it quits and head home, big fella?"

"No, Sal Belamo. Finding the nuclear weapons remains our task. The rest is Blainey's."

They hurried across the tarmac and climbed back on board the chopper.

"Bad news," the pilot, Tom Wainwright, reported, looking up from his gauges. "Got one mother of a storm whipping up through the Rockies. Blizzard conditions sure to take effect within an hour right where we're headed."

"The next airfield is forty minutes away," said Wareagle. "Just get us that far."

The storm had thrown a thin blanket of snow over the airfield by the time they got there. In another few minutes, Wainwright told them, the winds would have made landing impossible.

"You boys don't mind, I'd like to be on my way."

"Your job's not finished yet," Johnny said to the pilot as Sal climbed out of the chopper to see about the vehicle that should be waiting for them. "I have a message you must deliver."

Tom Wainwright looked back at Johnny. "To Washington?"

"No," said Wareagle and gave him a sheet of paper. "Arizona."

Wainwright studied the coordinates printed on the top. "Take me forever to get to these in a chopper."

Johnny pointed to a trio of Learjets parked just off the tarmac. "One of those has been held for our use in case we need it. When you reach the coordinates, give the man in charge this." And he handed Wainwright an envelope containing two pages of the clearest writing he could manage during the choppy flight to this field.

"Are you sure they'll let me land?"

"Use the designation underneath the coordinates."

Wainwright's eyes widened as he scanned down the page. "What the . . ." He looked up at Wareagle. "I was over there, too. This designation is *twenty-five* years old."

"That's why they'll let you land."

By the time Sal Belamo drove onto the tarmac in a four-wheel drive GMC Jimmy, Wainwright was already heading for the Lears.

"What now?" Sal asked through the window.

The coating of powdery snow on Johnny's shoulders and hair enhanced the copper color of his skin. "We move southwest toward the mountains we haven't checked yet."

Belamo sighed, eyes turning to find the blizzard had already chewed into the sky as far as he could see in that direction. "I was afraid you were going to say that."

Colorado Boy Scout Troop 116 was in the midst of a wilderness retreat in the Rockies when the storm began its sweep. The sudden twenty-degree drop in temperature had stirred a number of them in their sleeping bags, so many were awake by the time the first flakes started falling.

At first the surprise spring storm was fun. Snowball fights in the half-light that starts an hour before dawn were the stuff that great stories were made of. It was not long, though, before the boys' laughs gave way to chills and whimpers. The bitter wind froze the thin layers of sweat that had formed over their faces and hands. Only a few had brought gloves, and the rest were steadfastly jamming their fingers deep into their jacket pockets to no avail.

The scout leader, Frank Richter, an ex-marine, assessed the situation as calmly as he could. He knew the storm was going to be a big one from the first snap of the wind. He also knew that unless he was able to do something fast, some of his young charges would not be making it back alive. Richter tried the radio he never failed to carry on a retreat. As he had expected, though, the storm had stolen whatever small hope he held of making contact this far out of range. That made his immediate goal getting back into radio range at the same time he looked for shelter for the scouts.

The storm's fury had swept over them like a blanket by the time Richter packed the radio safely away. He ordered the boys to wrap their sleeping bags about their shoulders for added warmth and leave everything else that wasn't vital to their immediate survival behind. Busying themselves with carrying out orders, the boys managed to hold fast to their sense of calm, but Richter could spot the fear starting to show in their eyes as he moved up the line.

The scouts of Troop 116 were between the ages of twelve

and fifteen. Once they set out, Richter knew his place was
at the head of the pack, leaving the rear precariously unsu-
pervised, which meant that one or more of his eighteen
charges could simply slip away to be taken by the storm.
Accordingly, the last orders he shouted through the howling
winds were for the boys to pull the tie cords out of their
sleeping bags. Richter collected and strung them together,
then pushed the resulting single strand through a belt loop
on each of his scouts' pants before setting out.

The quickest route to shelter was to the southwest. But
walking into the thick of the storm was unthinkable under
the circumstances. Richter knew Troop 116's best hope was
to move northeast to keep the wind at their backs.

The storm seemed not to care which direction they set out
in. Its swirling winds battered the scouts without letup. A
quarter mile into the trek, Richter felt like an ox pulling a
plow, nothing but dead weight behind him. He pressed on
down a trail that had become nothing more than an extension of the vast white veil coating the Rockies. He couldn't
see more than a few yards ahead of him. His own hands and
feet were starting to numb.

Richter gritted his teeth and pushed himself on, forcing
the blood into his weary, stiffening muscles. Minutes later
he looked up and realized he could no longer see the mountain peaks surrounding them. Beneath him, though, the trail
had widened and flattened out, vaguely familiar again.

Familiar enough to make Richter stop suddenly.

The sheer edge of a cliff loomed not more than a yard
ahead of him. A straight drop to a white death for all the
boys if he had taken another two steps. The precipice was
almost invisible from this vantage point.

*They were on a road! A swirling, wide path that curled
its way down the mountain!*

If they followed it they would eventually find shelter. He
shouted encouragement to the boys and told those in front
to pass the word along.

Only a short time later he spotted what looked like a vast

black hole in the side of the mountain just to the right of the road. From Richter's knowledge of the terrain he believed it might be the entrance to an abandoned silver mine, one of the big ones that was more like a man-made cave.

Frank Richter led Troop 116 into the cavern and ordered the boys to assemble camp as best they could with what they had managed to bring with them. Two of the older boys were sent with flashlights to explore the mine's reaches. Richter set up his radio.

"This is two-niner-bingo," he said into the mike. "Does anyone read me? . . . This is two-niner-bingo. Does anyone copy? . . . I am reporting a mayday. Is anyone out there? Over."

Richter eased off on the microphone and prayed for a voice to filter through the static.

Nothing.

"This is two-niner-bingo," he repeated. "I have a scout troop marooned in the storm. If anyone can hear me, please acknowledge. If there's anyone out there, please acknowledge. Over."

Again only static.

"Frank," called one of the older boys he'd sent exploring.

Richter halfheartedly turned away from the radio.

"There's something you'd better take a look at."

"Think we can drive them out?" one of the boys asked as Richter stood before the pair of heavy transport trucks.

The scouts who'd checked the back reaches of the mine had found them covered by dark tarpaulins they had yanked off to expose the trucks' cabs. Richter's final years with the marines had been spent in the shipping and receiving department at a base in Germany. He'd seen trucks like this before, which was all the more reason why their presence here boggled his mind.

What in the hell were they?

"Frank," another boy called, but Richter had already

moved between the trucks and squeezed behind the rear of the one on the left.

"Stay back," Richter told him and pulled off the tarp covering the cargo door. The door was unlocked and Richter had little trouble sliding it upward. He shined his flashlight inside the hold.

"Oh my God," he muttered, eyes bulging. His beam had illuminated more than a dozen olive green fiberglass containers, all five by four feet in size. Richter didn't have to read the bold printing on their sides and top to know what they contained.

"Frank, what is it? Frank?" one of the boys called to him after he charged past them.

They trailed him back to the front of the mine where Richter returned to the radio. His hand trembling, he retrieved the microphone.

"This is two-niner-bingo," he said, rushed and desperate now. "Someone please answer. Someone please come in. Mayday . . . Mayday . . . Mayday . . . Over."

Again Richter pulled his hand from the button. The static returned. His eyes gazed back toward the rear of the mine.

"Two-niner-bingo," a splintered voice said through the static.

"I read you! Who is this? Over."

The reply couldn't break through the garble this time.

"Say again. I did not copy that. Over."

More garble answered his call. He waited until the static was all that was left before returning to his microphone.

"All right. I'm assuming you can hear me better than I can hear you. I'm trapped in an abandoned silver mine with a scout troop somewhere in the mountains between Weaver and Kendall Gap. We need a rescue party." Richter stole a gaze back at the hopeful young charges hovering over him, then spoke again with his voice lowered. "And there's something else. We found something in the mine."

Still not believing it himself, Richter managed to report that the two concealed trucks were loaded with nuclear warheads before a sudden screaming amongst the kids made him turn. He caught a brief glimpse of something dark and shiny whistling his way and felt the smack against his skull before oblivion took him.

The voice started to fade shortly after giving its location, and Duncan Farlowe pressed his ear right against his short-wave radio's speaker to better hear it. A sudden scream followed by a thud signaled the end of the transmission and jolted Farlowe enough to make him yank his head away. As he soothed his twisted neck with one hand, the sheriff of Grand Mesa wasn't thinking of the scream at all; he was thinking of what he heard the speaker claim he had seen in a pair of trucks.

Had he heard right?

If it wasn't for Kristen Kurcell and Miravo Air Force Base, Duncan Farlowe never would have believed it. Farlowe figured he had a damn good notion now of what Kristen's brother had seen that had gotten him killed. And, judging by the way their leader's message had abruptly ended, this scout troop might well be about to share David Kurcell's fate.

Farlowe moved to the window and opened it to see clearly out into the storm. Much of the snow gathered on the windowsill blew into the room, and he brushed the rest away. This cabin near the grounds of an old ski resort had provided him safe refuge since Tuesday, when Grand Mesa's municipal offices had been blown up. He figured something would be coming to chase him back to the world, but he never imagined it would be *this*. The irony drew a smile from him.

The sight outside the window changed it to a frown. By now there wouldn't be a road open from anywhere a rescue party for these Boy Scouts was likely to originate. Could even be he was the only one to have heard the message anyway. Not many folks had call to leave their shortwaves powered up these days.

That made Farlowe the sole hope this Boy Scout troop had to survive. It took ten minutes for him to get the right clothes on and another ten for him to trudge over to the ski resort's garage. The Sno-Cat in the front of the line of vehicles, a tank with a cab instead of a turret, would do just fine. Pack it up with as many provisions as he could salvage and off he'd go.

"And there's something else. We found something in the mine."

"My lucky day," Duncan Farlowe mumbled to himself.

The voice came over the chopper's radio fifteen miles before Tom Wainwright's Learjet reached the coordinates in central Arizona Johnny Wareagle had given him.

"Identified aircraft, you have entered restricted airspace and are advised to turn back immediately."

"Tower, I have a message to deliver to your commanding officer. Request permission to land."

"State designation."

Wainwright gave the designation Johnny Wareagle had instructed him to, hoping it made more sense to whomever he was talking to than it did to him. The pause was very slight, the voice much softer when it came back on.

"Permission granted. Come right to heading two-five-zero. We're dead ahead."

Wainwright eased into his descent and passed over a thick grove of tall evergreen trees. The sight revealed a quarter mile beyond it made his eyes bulge in disbelief.

"Holy shit," he muttered.

What he was looking at, descending toward, was . . . impossible.

"Our commanding officer will be waiting on the tarmac," the voice in his headset droned. "You are cleared to land."

CHAPTER 35

They sat in a circle, positioned on the grass of the Mall so each had a clear view of either the Capitol or the Washington Monument. In addition to Cleese, Kristen, and McCracken there were four Midnight Riders, two men and two women.

"Like you folks to meet my recon team," Cleese started. "This is Luke, Sally, Freedom, and Bird Man."

Each of the Riders gave a brief acknowledgment as they were introduced. The bulk of the others had already begun to position themselves discreetly in small groups throughout the city, in touch with Cleese by walkie-talkie.

"These four been with me from the beginning," he continued. "Lord, how many nights we spent figuring ourselves on the other side of this. . . . Anyway, I gave each a section of the city so we can put together a notion of what we're up against. Bird Man, why don't you lead off."

Bird Man had light curly hair and a beak-shaped nose that curved downward and in, accounting for his nickname. "Lots of trucks made out to look like sanitation and DPW. Plenty of people milling about them, not doing much of anything."

"Dress?" Blaine raised.

"Run-of-the-mill, everyday normal civilian. They're trying awful hard not to be noticed. That's why I noticed them."

"How many?"

"Don't matter, because they're just the advance team," interrupted Luke. He removed his wraparound sunglasses to reveal a pair of dark steely eyes and a face Blaine recognized from wanted posters picturing the members of the Black Panthers' most radical cell. "Sort of keeping an eye on the surroundings. Larger complement figured on getting out of the sun to wait things out."

"Where?"

"The Old Post Office Tower," Luke said. "Stores are all packed, but nobody's buying much. Restaurants are jammed, but lots of people are just lingering. Shit, I probably woulda done it this way myself."

"The Clock Tower," Blaine realized.

"Huh?" from Cleese.

"The two tallest points in the city center are the observation deck in the Old Post Office Tower and the top of the Washington Monument. You want to take the city, you got to own those."

"Sniper fire?"

"Put a squad in each and it would be like target practice."

"Not to mention they'd be able to pin down exactly where any resistance was coming from," said the woman named Freedom. She had blond hair tied into braids and was busy rolling a baby stroller back and forth alongside her. "They spot us and pick us off all the way down Pennsylvania Avenue."

Cleese looked toward McCracken. "Rockets? Take 'em out sure and fast?"

Blaine shook his head. "You're still thinking like a revolutionary."

"Long-time habit."

"Form a new one: start thinking like a soldier."

"Give me a for instance."

"What's important to them is also important to us. For the same reasons."

"Don't get you, Mac."

"You will." McCracken paused. "How good are your shooters, Arlo?"

"Good enough. But that kind of gun wasn't on my shopping list with Alvarez."

"Leave that to me. I want to hear more about these trucks."

Freedom leaned forward. She stopped moving the stroller briefly and the baby inside whimpered.

"Me and Raindance took in some of the best sites Washington had to offer," she said, working the stroller again. "Saw trucks in the area of the White House, Capitol, Supreme Court, you get the idea."

"The Delphi's weapons will be inside," explained McCracken. "The men Bird Man saw posted around the trucks are guards in case anybody perceived to be a threat wanders too close. But there are plenty more in the area he didn't see. Come show time they'll move to the trucks and pick up their weapons."

"Don't have to walk around obvious that way," Luke picked up. "Just join the chaos and head to where their hardware is waiting."

"That means they left us the opportunity to cut them off from it," the woman named Raindance concluded, her skin pale enough to make McCracken wonder if she had ever seen the sun before.

"Don't underestimate their security," he cautioned. "They might have a minimum posted on the streets, but you can rest assured there's plenty under cover in the vicinity of each of those trucks. To take them on, we'll need some cover of our own." He looked toward Cleese. "How's your supply of explosives?"

"Enough to do the job." His face had gone almost as white as Raindance's, but it was hardened with resolve. "And they were gonna pin this whole damn revolution on us."

"All the evidence would have pointed in your direction," Blaine confirmed. "With the government fractured, Dodd probably would have taken charge of the investigation himself."

" 'Cept if it wasn't for you, I'd be dead now."

"But the trail tying you to Alvarez and the weapons that end up pulverizing Washington would have still remained very much alive. You're just a symbol, a fabricated enemy the Delphi needs to seize their day."

" 'Long with the nation."

"That's the point."

Cleese nodded. "We hit 'em early and hard, we fuck up their day big time. Thing is, how do we do it?"

McCracken held Kristen Kurcell's eyes briefly before beginning his explanation. "We start with the Old Post Office Building. . . ."

Frank Richter regained consciousness slowly, the world a blur before him that sharpened more slowly than the picture on a cheap television. His head throbbed and he felt something soft pressed against his skull.

"What happened?" he asked in a raspy voice.

Above him a boy pulled a blood-soaked jacket from his head and rebundled it in search of an unsoiled patch.

"They put us in here," one of the older boys said. "After they hit you."

"They?"

"The men," another chimed in. "They had guns."

"How many men?"

"I think five. Yeah, five."

"One was really big," added another. "And ugly."

Richter gazed around him in the darkness broken only by the collective spill of the boys' flashlights. "Where are we?"

"Another part of the mine," from a fourth.

Wherever they were, Richter realized it was at least a little more temperate than the front chamber of the mine had been. But it was still damn cold, and whoever their captors were, they hadn't let the boys bring in their sleeping bags. He gazed about and saw them shivering in their thin, spring-weight jackets.

Clearly the contents of the trucks back in the old mine's

front chamber accounted for their captivity. And the fact that there was no way their captors could let them out of the mine alive with that information was just as clear.

Richter pulled the bloodied jacket from his head and struggled to his feet. There was no sense bothering with the front of the mine; even if the passage back was unguarded, the men would hear them coming in plenty of time to respond.

"Has anyone checked this chamber for another way out?" he asked.

"A couple of us did," said one of the older boys. "We couldn't find one."

"We've got to keep looking," Richter told them all. "I know these mines, and I'm telling you there's *always* a way out. All we have to do is find it."

Johnny Wareagle and Sal Belamo both knew their journey was about to come to a premature end. Grim-faced and resolute, they sat in the Jimmy's front seat staring into the teeth of a storm that just kept biting. Johnny had taken over the wheel three miles back, and for that long he'd been able to coax the Jimmy through the mounting piles of white collecting on the road before them. Now, though, those piles had at last climbed higher than the wheel axles in enough places to turn their progress into a maddening progression of stops, starts, and skids. Both knew all progress would cease in the next few minutes. The Jimmy would simply grind to a halt, its wheels churning fruitlessly.

"We gonna walk the rest of the way into this part of the Rockies, big fella?" Belamo asked just to break the silence in the cab.

He turned Johnny's way and noticed the big Indian's eye catch something off to the right where the road gave way to a gulley. Wareagle slid the truck onto the road's indistinguishable shoulder and brought it to a stop against a drift that came up level with the hood.

"What gives, big fella?"

"Look, Sal Belamo."

Sal followed the line of Johnny's gaze and saw an orange sheen rising out of the vast blanket of white.

"Looks like a—"

Wareagle had climbed down through his open door before Sal could finish the thought. Belamo met him knee-deep in snow on the shoulder. Directly below them in the gulley lay what looked like a bulldozer without a shovel.

"A Sno-Cat," Wareagle said through the snow slapping at his face.

"Declawed, you ask me."

The front of the Sno-Cat's treads had been hidden completely, the rear of them covered halfway. Sal and Johnny worked their way down the fairly steep drop into the gulley toward it. Johnny reached the cab first and jerked open its door. An old, bearded man was slumped against the driver's seat. A trail of clotted blood lined the right side of his pale face starting on his forehead.

"He's alive," Wareagle reported after checking his neck for a pulse.

"I'll get the coffee and first-aid kit," Belamo said and he started to claw his way back up the hill.

The old man stirred, the chill wind seeming to revive him. He shifted slightly and Johnny noticed an old Colt Peacemaker revolver holstered at his hip. He had a tarnished silver badge pinned to the lapel of the heavy jacket that covered his thin frame. The old man's eyes opened slowly and fixed themselves on Wareagle.

"If I'm dead, just let me know which place I ended up."

"Still earth," Johnny told him. "The toughest place of all."

"That's the god's honest truth."

The old man sized him up again. "Storm make you miss the turn-off for the reservation, Injun?"

"Not exactly."

"Then what exactly brings you out in a storm that'll kill whoever it can?"

"Finding at least one it hasn't been able to yet."

"Good point." The old man touched the swollen lump on his forehead where the trail of dried blood originated. "Guess I'm not as good at driving these babies as I used to be. Couldn't see a damn thing. One minute the road was there and the next . . ."

Wareagle's eyes had strayed to the cramped space behind the Sno-Cat's two-man cab. Atop a clutter of supplies lay a twelve-gauge shotgun.

"Bunch of Boy Scouts got themselves holed up in an old silver mine fifteen miles from here up Mountain Pass," the old man said, noting Johnny's interest. "That stuff in the back's to keep them going if I get there in time for it to matter."

"And the shotgun?"

The old man glanced at it himself before responding. "They're not alone."

"We can't move the trucks in this," the man standing on Traggeo's right insisted. His name was Boggs and he too was a survivor of Salvage Company, one of four Traggeo had recruited personally.

"We don't have a choice," the big man told him.

The numbing cold had done little to ease the pain in his right forearm where Johnny Wareagle's knife had ripped through five days before. Traggeo could block it out only until a quick motion or slight graze against the damaged flesh brought it back. Each burst of pain filled him with a vengeful yet envious hate. He had missed his chance to kill the legendary true-blood back at Sandcastle One and could only hope fate would give him another opportunity to prove himself to the spirits.

"There was a voice on the other end of the radio," Traggeo continued. "Someone heard the distress call. They'll be coming."

"The storm will stop them, too," said Boggs.

"Not when there are kids to rescue. They'll find a way up here. We've got to move the trucks."

Boggs shrank back into the cover provided beyond the entrance to the mine. The five former members of Tyson Gash's ignoble Salvage Company had been safe and warm back in their camp set in another section of the mine when they heard the commotion. Traggeo hadn't decided what to do until a few of the kids discovered the trucks and the lone adult began broadcasting over a shortwave radio. That had forced his hand.

"We get the trucks out," Boggs said, "those kids still know what was inside."

"Then," Traggeo told him, "before we leave we have to make sure the rescue party gets here too late to help them."

They didn't try budging the Sno-Cat until Sheriff Duncan Farlowe had completed his tale.

"Looks like we found what we been looking for, big fella," Sal Belamo said at the end.

"Looking for?" questioned Farlowe before Wareagle could respond. "What the hell you boys up to? Wait a minute, this is about Kristen. You boys are here thanks to Kristen!"

"Yes," Johnny affirmed without going into further detail.

"She okay? Just tell me if she's okay."

"For now. Like the rest of us."

Farlowe grasped his unspoken meaning. "That bad?"

"Worse," said Belamo.

"We must reach that mine," Wareagle added.

He took the wheel when they set out, Sal Belamo seated next to him. Sheriff Duncan Farlowe had squeezed himself amidst the provisions in the cab's back, cradling the twelve-gauge shotgun in his lap. The Sno-Cat wouldn't budge at first, the storm's fist holding fast. But then Johnny stopped fighting the grade and steered the 'Cat downhill just to get started. The strategy worked. Its tank-like treads began to turn. Huge plumes of snow jetted backwards as the Sno-Cat pulled free of the drift with a jolt. Not wanting to suddenly challenge the grade, he leveled the 'Cat out before beginning a gradual climb that ended when its treads carried it over the ridge and back onto the road.

Their sense of triumph, though, lasted only as long as it took for the road to scale sharply upward. The mountains rose up before them as shadowy giants looming through the swirling fall of white from the sky. Each yard the 'Cat managed became precious. Its churning treads fought the storm every inch of the way.

"Is this the only route they can take out of the mine?" Johnny asked Sheriff Farlowe.

"They ain't goin' anywhere till we—" Farlowe stopped himself. "You're not talking 'bout the kids, are you?"

"No, I'm not."

"But they matter to you; I know they do. And I know you wanna help get them safely out of this."

"Go on," Johnny said.

"You didn't think I intended on driving right up to that mine and knocking on the front door, did you?"

Johnny looked back at him.

"See, the thing is, I think I can get us inside without whoever's guarding those trucks being the wiser."

"It's a rescue party," Traggeo announced, the Sno-Cat plainly visible advancing up Mountain Pass through the storm.

Traggeo stepped back into the cover of the mine entrance. He had set a four o'clock departure time for his team and their cargo. Keeping to that plan meant leaving at the height of the storm, and he knew how very precarious that would be. Yet the risk posed by the storm was less than that of discovery of the cave's contents by a significant rescue party. With four o'clock looming, he had been about to move to the rear chamber of the mine to deal with the members of Troop 116 when the sound of the 'Cat's engine had instantly changed his priorities.

"The two of you," he said, pointing to Boggs and another Salvage Company alumnus named Kreller, "will come with me."

Before stepping outside, Boggs and Kreller securely fastened their jackets against the storm and pulled ski masks over their faces. Traggeo left his face uncovered, willing to accept the frigid snap against his exposed flesh in exchange for optimum vision. With no opportunity for shaving his head, his own hair had grown into a layer of black stubble that became speckled with thick white snowflakes the moment he left the shelter of the mine. He longed not only to be rid of the stubble but also to have the fresh scalp of a victim to replace it with.

Eliminating the threat posed by the approaching Sno-Cat, he knew, was only part of his problem. More rescue parties would be coming in the wake of this one as soon as the weather cleared, and Traggeo couldn't risk waiting for them to arrive. He had to get his trucks and precious cargo away from here before anyone else followed in the Sno-Cat's path.

He found the perfect setting for an ambush an eighth of a mile from the mine at a point where the road bent out of a slight curve into a straightaway. He placed Boggs and Kreller into position to await the 'Cat's passing. Then Traggeo withdrew his pistol and patted the scalping knife sheathed on his other hip.

"Hear that?" Farlowe asked Wareagle as the tunnel inside the old silver mine at last began to swerve upward.

"Voices," Johnny replied.

"Straight ahead. Usually gets a bit steep the last stretch leading from one chamber to another. . . ."

The two of them had left the Sno-Cat twenty minutes earlier. Farlowe estimated it would take at least that long to find a rear entrance to the silver mine and work their way to the main chamber. Accordingly, Sal Belamo wouldn't start the 'Cat moving again until fifteen minutes after their

departure, hoping to lure a portion of the Delphi guards outside the mine as he drew closer to it.

The shaft they entered had turned dark after the first corner. Their flashlights had taken over from there, Farlowe
following the path as if he had been down it a hundred
times before. In point of fact, he had never once been in this
particular mine but had been inside a hundred others, all
having a similar construction.

The grade of the last stretch, though, was significantly
steeper than he had led Johnny to believe. The big Indian
ended up behind the sheriff, helping him pull himself toward the main body of the mine and the sound of the
voices.

Wareagle was wary as he moved toward their source until
he clearly discerned the voices belonged to children. The
ground leveled for a few yards before rising steeply once
more toward a wooden hatchway. Johnny yanked it open
and a shower of rubble dropped on him and Farlowe. He
climbed up and lent the sheriff a hand. He let Farlowe ease
ahead of him to lead the way toward a dozen fading flashlights huddled closely together fifty feet from them.

"You boys oughta know these mines are off-limits,"
Farlowe announced softly, and the beams turned toward
their approach. "Looks like I'm gonna have to arrest ya."

The grateful eyes of Troop 116 found him in the spill of
the beams. A lone adult pulled himself uneasily to his feet
and clung to the shoulder of an older boy.

"Thank God," moaned Frank Richter. "Thank God you
found us."

"You can thank God if you want, but you better thank my
friend here, too," said Farlowe as Johnny Wareagle drew up
alongside.

Mount Weather's communications center was laid out in
the form of a mini-amphitheater. The floor had a steep
enough rise to ensure a clear view for anyone seated in the

fifty or so seats, only three of which would be needed tonight.

As the minutes ticked ever closer to seven o'clock, the President, Charlie Byrne, and Angela Taft were ushered to chairs in the first row under the watchful eyes of a half dozen armed guards. General Trevor Cantrell was already inside, standing directly in front of a massive screen that took up the better part of the front wall. The high-resolution monitor was significantly longer than it was tall, its proportions closer to those of a motion picture screen than to those of a normal television.

"You'll be happy to know, sir, that the Evac operation went even better than planned," Cantrell said to the President. "Ninety-four percent of those on the list are presently sealed in at either Greenbrier, Site R, or here."

Cantrell stepped aside to reveal the screen in its full expanse.

"Impressive use of the taxpayers' money," the President noted.

"And appropriately, sir, we have Dodd Industries to thank for what you are about to see," he explained, and used a sophisticated remote control device to turn the monitor on.

The screen instantly lit up with a crystal-clear overview shot of Washington, D.C., south from L'Enfant Plaza and D Street to K Street in the north. The west and east borders were 23rd Street at the rear of the Department of State and 2nd Street behind the Supreme Court and congressional offices.

"This is a picture broadcast from a satellite in geosynchronistic orbit over Washington," Cantrell continued. "You're looking at a full overview shot, but with the touch of a few buttons we can zoom in on virtually anything."

To demonstrate his point, Cantrell worked his hand-held remote to direct one of five different-sized squares across the screen. He clicked down when the square was centered over the Washington Monument. Instantly the screen changed to a shot of the lines of people still waiting outside for their turn to reach the top. It was incredibly crisp, the President noted, almost like a television camera scanning the stands at a baseball game.

"I could bring this in close enough to read the face of a watch on one of the tourists," Cantrell explained. "I can also split the screen into a maximum of sixteen segments to ensure we don't miss anything." He smiled as he adroitly displayed the capabilities outlined. "I thought you would appreciate viewing the day of the Delphi for yourself," the general said when the demonstration was complete.

The digital clock over the door read 6:47:35 in bright red numbers. Across the remainder of the large front wall different sections of the country were represented on grid maps that instantly displayed the routing of information and data over lines. Each of the grids was lit, or "hot," according to the current jargon. A few sporadic flashes indicated a power failure or system trouble that was quickly bypassed. Men and women in swivel chairs were pressing information into keypads attached to sophisticated monitor screens set back between the front wall and the gallery where the President was seated. This was standard procedure at Mount Weather, where the nation's communications and data transmissions systems were monitored at all times. Only in the event of an emergency declared by the President could these systems be overridden and the emergency network known as Prometheus be switched on in their place. Otherwise, Mount Weather simply kept abreast of what was going on and instantly compensated when any system failure became evident.

Cantrell moved behind the team of specially trained Delphi monitors who had replaced the real workers, eyes fixed anxiously on the clock. As 6:50 approached, he moved beyond the wall to a black box mounted near the sliding steel access door. As Chairman of the Joint Chiefs, he carried on his person at all times a master key fit to the specifications of slots capable of triggering a number of emergency procedures. He removed it from his pocket and held its flat, thick end up for the President to see. Then he slid it easily into the slot tailored for it. A red light over the box turned to green. Cantrell turned the key.

A red switch emerged with a quick *pop!* as the security plate before it slid away. The clock read 6:49:45.

"I am about to bring your term in office officially to an end, sir," Cantrell announced to the President.

At 6:50 precisely he flipped the switch into the off position. An alarm chimed three times. The colors over all of the grids on the front wall changed from green to red and held there. The alarm chimed three more times.

The President watched in horror as the grid lights that looked like a road map for the entire country went out, spreading from east to west. As of that moment, the satellite feeds responsible for putting television and radio on the air were shut down. People in the midst of phone conversations had them ended in the middle of a word or a sentence. All forms of data being transferred were lost en route. Technology was unforgiving; it made no exceptions. Prometheus had taken over.

The battle of Washington had officially begun.

CHAPTER 36

McCracken and his team of five Midnight Riders approached the Old Post Office Tower from different directions. Originally the headquarters for the U.S. Postal Service and later a clearinghouse for government office overflow, the building had become home to a lavish indoor shopping mall called the Pavilion. Taking full advantage of the inner courtyard's enormous uninterrupted area, the Pavilion was to Washington what Faneuil Hall was to Boston and Ghirardelli Square was to San Francisco. There was ample space to shop and stroll, and there were plenty of tables in the Pavilion's food court to enjoy a snack or a meal, while natural light filtered through the restored glass roof nine stories above.

At the same time, a sense of history had been preserved with the complete restoration of both the twelfth-floor observation deck and the famed Congress Bells. The melodic chimes could be heard throughout the city whenever occasion dictated. McCracken couldn't help but wonder if activating them might not be the signal for the Delphi to begin their attack at seven o'clock.

He had a surprise in store for his adversaries just prior to that.

The wide open area of the Pavilion made it an ideal gathering place for a hefty complement of the Delphi's troops. Similarly, McCracken was certain they had already secured the observation deck, where all strategic points in the capital's center could be reached by sniper fire. A few good marksmen could take out every Washington police officer or stray marine from the 8th and Eye Company who attempted to offer resistance. Accordingly, the importance of this building could not be overestimated.

It was six-fifty when Blaine and the five members of the Midnight Riders handpicked by Arlo Cleese entered the Pavilion. For McCracken, picking out the Delphi troops was as easy as moving his eyes. Their civilian dress could not camouflage the hard resolve in their stares, as well as the lack of shopping bags by most of their sides or their empty plates at the tables where they lingered. Especially now, with the operation just minutes away, they couldn't have been more obvious if Blaine had asked them to identify themselves by raising their hands.

His problem was that their number made up only half of the Pavilion's current occupants.

McCracken and the five Midnight Riders made their separate ways into an alcove that housed the start of the tours of the observation decks and Congress Bells. All six squeezed onto the elevator, which climbed toward the ninth-floor chamber where the musical bells were controlled. One of the Midnight Riders stepped out there. McCracken and the rest stayed in the compartment and continued on to the twelfth-floor observation deck, where five men wearing green U.S. ranger uniforms turned toward them in surprise when the compartment doors slid open.

"I'm afraid the tower's been closed," one of them announced apologetically.

"Oh, that ruins my day."

Following McCracken's lead, the four Riders drew their silenced semiautomatic pistols and opened fire. The five Delphi crumpled. The Riders had begun to drag their corpses aside when the fire alarm began to wail, set off three floors down by the final member of their party.

6:54, Blaine's watch read.

That meant the civilians in the Pavilion had six minutes to clear the building. He had to hope that was enough.

Blaine hurried to the observation deck's western perch, which looked down three stories on the sloping glass roof of the Post Office Tower itself. He drew his harmless-looking shoulder bag forward and pulled the four mounds of detonator-rigged C-4 plastic explosives from inside it.

In the command center of Mount Weather, the computer operators working behind screens located between the front wall and the gallery had been charged with monitoring various sectors of Washington. One of them swiveled his chair toward General Cantrell, a hand pressed against his headpiece to hold it in place.

"Sir, a fire alarm is going off at the Old Post Office Tower. Civilians are evacuating."

Cantrell stole a glance at the wall clock, which read 6:55:30, and then worked his remote control. The viewing screen filled with an overhead shot of the building currently holding by far his largest single concentration of troops.

"Sir," continued the man in charge of the grid containing

the building, "contact has been lost with the observation deck."

"What the hell . . ."

Cantrell moved closer to the screen.

"Civilian evacuation from building proceeding, sir. Troops have been dispatched to the deck."

"Get me someone down there on the line, son," Cantrell ordered.

The Post Office Tower's glass roof was of the sloped variety that came to a pinnacle in the center. The fragmented shards of two tons of three-inch-thick glass would make for deadly weapons indeed, but only if they were blown downward. To cause that kind of explosion, Blaine had to be sure the *plastique* ended up close to the structural stress points found in each of the four corners. His tosses just after the 6:59 mark were as measured and precise as he could manage: two right on the mark, the others close enough.

"Down!" he screamed back to the Riders.

As instructed, all dove to the floor on the eastern side of the deck, using the raised platform that held the ranger's booth for cover.

The explosion came seconds before seven o'clock.

Blaine had his head and ears covered, which didn't stop the piercing screech made by two tons of glass shattering from all but deafening him. The deck's safety wire, in place to keep birds from straying in, could not stop the storm of deadly shards from surging inward. McCracken and his men remained tightly bunched on the floor until they were certain the potentially fatal shower was over.

Blaine heard the screams and wails of horrible agony from the Pavilion. He brushed the thick blanket of debris from him and lunged to his feet. The sight below off the tower's western side was mind-boggling. So much of the glass roof had been blown away that he had a clear view of the Pavilion and the effects of his handiwork. The shards had done their job even better, and bloodier, than expected.

Bodies lay everywhere, cluttered in heaps. Some writhed and reached for help. Most were still. The coppery scent of volumes of blood drifted up into the air and mixed with the lingering stench of C-4 *plastique*. McCracken tried not to consider how many of the downed might have been civilians who hadn't been able to flee the building in time. He hoped there hadn't been many, but in any case he knew he had to turn his attention elsewhere.

He located ten M21 sniper systems, which consisted of modified M14 rifles equipped with Zeupold scopes. The Delphi had chosen the best around. Ironic that it was about to be turned against them.

"You know what the bad guys look like," Blaine said to the Riders. Three of them had joined up with Cleese after disillusioning returns from Vietnam, and two of these were snipers. The remaining two knew guns and scopes strictly from their work with the Weather Underground. "When the time comes, kill them all and let God sort 'em out."

With that, McCracken disappeared into the stairwell.

The occupants of Mount Weather's command center watched the explosion in total shock. The satellite feed lacked sound, but their imaginations more than compensated for that, as the glass roof of the Old Post Office Tower exploded in a single bright flash and disappeared downward. Cantrell involuntarily arched away from the screen. The President rose to his feet, horrified and revitalized at the same time.

"McCracken," he muttered. "McCracken . . ."

Cantrell was moving down the row of monitors, furiously barking orders. Not surprisingly, contact had been lost with the building and several personnel were trying to establish contact with someone else in the sector. Desperate voices converged in his transistorized headset, forcing him to strip it off.

In all the excitement, the general lost track of the digital

wall clock and did not turn its way until seven o'clock was
almost two minutes passed.

"Order operations to begin in all sectors!" he roared to
the monitors in touch with the Delphi troops in Washington.
"Now!"

"Something unexpected, General?" the President teased.

Cantrell had swung to face the commander in chief when
the voice of Samuel Jackson Dodd filled the room.

"What's happening, General?" Dodd asked in a strangely
flat tone, even though an identical picture was being broadcast to his space station.

Cantrell gazed up at the camera that allowed Dodd to
monitor the command center from *Olympus* as well.

"I . . . don't know, sir."

"I do: McCracken. It's McCracken." Dodd's voice was
still flat. Since hearing of McCracken's untimely escape
from Whiteland, he had been expecting something like this
to come to pass.

"Sir, we have no way of—"

"General, I don't want to hear any excuses or denials.
Alert all Delphi units to be on the watch for anyone meeting
his description." Dodd paused, his breathing audible through
the unseen speaker. "We haven't won yet."

The next several moments gave the President reason to
grimly question Dodd's final pronouncement. Cantrell had
divided the screen into eight shots of Delphi troops scam-
pering toward trucks parked in the vicinity of their primary
targets.

Of course, since the trucks were placed in a manner to
make them blend into the scene, the assigned guards had
paid little heed to bystanders walking past them. Neither the
guards nor the men scanning the satellite's cameras had noticed a woman wheeling a baby carriage who wedged a wad
of plastic explosives against the side of one truck. Or a pair
of couples walking hand in hand who barely had to break
stride to jam their bombs against two additional trucks. In

all, seven of the enemy vehicles, each loaded with weapons, had been found and sabotaged by the Midnight Riders.

The logistics of the operation dictated the necessity of remote instead of timer detonation. So as not to attract potential scrutiny, in each case a Rider different from the one who had set the explosive was holding the detonator. The original seven were well versed in such matters, having practiced their deadly trade for the Weathermen, SDS, or the Black Panthers back in the sixties. Unfortunately, the seven responsible for setting the explosives off were not. In turn, six of the seven prematurely pressed the red buttons on their detonators at the first sign of approach by the Delphi troops. The dizzying explosions utterly destroyed the trucks and the weapons within them. But in only one case, as the satellite broadcast back to Mount Weather, did the explosion also consume the converging Delphi troops at the same time.

Nonetheless, the President exchanged hopeful gazes with Charlie Byrne and Angela Taft.

"Right on, brother," the National Security Advisor muttered, referring to Blaine McCracken.

Cantrell pulled back to a wide overhead view of Washington's center to better assess the damage. Seven plumes of black fiery smoke were clearly visible, each denoting a lost truck. The headset he had just replaced over his ears burst alive with activity again, as his command liaisons in the capital ordered replacements hurried out.

"You're losing, General," the President said confidently, still on his feet.

"Let's take a look at something else then, sir," Cantrell shot back.

He worked the remote control again and focused on a grid dominated by Georgetown's trendy M Street. The President felt his stomach sink at the sight. A parade of civilian-clad gunmen wielding automatic rifles ran in all directions, strafing anything that moved. Car windshields and tires blew out on screen. Plate-glass store windows were reduced to splinters. People, *innocent* people, were cut down as they tried to flee. The carnage was sickening. Bodies toppled everywhere. Those surviving the initial barrage lunged through the fractured windows of upscale boutiques and eateries in search of cover. The automatic fire was unrelenting, the President's sensibilities devastated despite the lack of sound.

Cantrell was working his control box again. "And that's not all. . . ."

He had split the huge screen in two. On the left-hand side, a commando-style assault was in progress on police headquarters near the U.S. Courthouse. The inside of the building wasn't visible, but it didn't have to be. Not a window had been left whole. A quartet of squad cars lay tipped on their sides in ruins, signifying hits by either small rockets or grenades. All that remained of the main entrance was a huge jagged chasm. Smoke spilled out through the remnants of windows. Uniformed bodies lay on the front lawn and across the steps. The wheels of a toppled motorcycle, its rider pinned beneath it, continued to spin. Although only headquarters was portrayed, it was clear this same scene was being played out at strategic precincts throughout the city.

The President struggled for breath. The right half of the screen was just as bad. The 8th and Eye marine company used as White House, Capitol, embassy, and functionary guards also put on regular full-dress marching exhibitions at their barracks. Though seeming to be concerned solely with protocol, the members of the 8th and Eye were no less competent as fighters and thus a threat the Delphi had to respect. Accordingly, the President watched in horror as a squad of Delphi troops fifty strong rushed through the brick archway into the barracks courtyard where an exhibition was underway. Random gunfire strafed the participants, their ceremonial rifles useless for defense. The gunmen turned their attention on the panicked members of the audience as well, cutting droves down as they attempted to flee the bleachers. A series of mind-numbing explosions then rattled the barracks structures that enclosed the courtyard. Buildings and vehicles were engulfed in flames. A few 8th and Eye marines who had responded fast enough to arm themselves were massacred effortlessly.

General Cantrell worked his remote control to change the screen to a quartet of overhead views of Delphi trucks the Midnight Riders' recon had missed cruising the streets from Georgetown to L'Enfant Plaza, from Union Station to the State Department building. At predetermined spots, Delphi troops were dropped off and dispersed on planned sweeping routes.

"It would seem, sir," Cantrell said to the President, "that the tide of the battle has already turned."

From his darkened office, FBI director Ben Samuelson had been trying every means of communication at his disposal to reach the outside world since the battle had begun. Spotters he had placed on the roof relayed enough about what was going on for him to realize the Seventh Light Infantry Division he had supposedly been in contact with all afternoon was nothing more than a voice at the other end of the line. He had been duped; the *country* had been duped. The Seventh LID wasn't in Washington and wasn't coming. The enemy had the city to itself.

For the first time since the J. Edgar Hoover Building had been opened, Samuelson had ordered a Con-Red. Hoover's own personal paranoia had led to some rather extreme inclusions in the building's plans. These included steel blast shutters capable of resisting rocket fire that could be lowered over all entryways as well as windows on all executive office levels. In addition, there were concealed firing ports built into parapets on all four sides of the building, four on each side making sixteen in all. Samuelson's first order when the truth of the treachery became known was to order members of the FBI's Hostage and Rescue Team he had stationed in the building into position in those ports. Samuelson had chosen these troops over the Bureau's SWAT and anti-terrorist commandos for their expertise in marksmanship. After all, if the building came under attack, what he would need more than anything would be men who could shoot the tip of a pen off at a hundred yards.

Once in position, the Hostage and Rescue Team's members provided the Delphi trucks cruising the surrounding streets with their first direct resistance. Emptying clip after clip through the well-fortified ports, they succeeded first in slowing the random strafing, and then in drawing a heavy concentration of attention and fire on themselves. Two minutes after retaliation had commenced from within it, the Hoover Building's exorbitant security was being given its first test. Grenade and small-arms fire tore chips from its heavy concrete construction. Personnel within cringed and sought cover as the steel security shutters buckled under fire from M40 grenades. Clearly the steel second skins would not be able to repel heavy rocket fire—say, of the Stinger variety. The minimal staff Samuelson had kept with him inside were grimly aware of this, as well as the fact that the stand they were making in the city's center, while ultimately doomed to fail, might be crucial to buying enough time for reinforcements to arrive.

Of course, not all of them at this point knew that all cellular, land-line, and direct link communication had been rendered inoperative.

A special agent hustled into Samuelson's office in a crouch, something wrapped in a blanket cradled in his arms. "Got it here in one piece," he said, almost out of breath, and lay the contents of his arms on the carpeted floor.

Samuelson yanked the blanket off to reveal an old-fashioned MARS, or Military Amateur Radio System, beneath him. The director knelt and switched it on. Then he brought the clumsy pedestal microphone to his lips.

"This is the FBI calling all on-line military bases," he started, not waiting for the tubes to warm up. "This is the FBI calling all on-line military bases. Over."

Samuelson knew that with a communications black-out in place, all bases would have automatically transferred to this mode of communication. What he could not have known was that those bases within a hundred miles of the capital, including that of the SEALS in Virginia, had been nearly emptied by a sudden joint exercise scheduled by General Cantrell. The nearest one that received Samuelson's message came on-line from North Carolina within seconds.

"Attention, caller, this is Fort Bragg command central," a stern voice announced. "You are operating on a military restricted channel. Please vacate this channel instantly. You are violating federal access laws and trespassing on private communication channels as specified by the Federal Communications Commission. Over."

"Bragg," Samuelson picked up, "this is Director Ben Samuelson of the Federal Bureau of Investigation. Designation four-zero-box-niner. The city of Washington is under attack. We are requesting immediate support. Over."

"Did you say attack, sir? Please say again. Over."

"You're damn right I did." Samuelson simply removed his finger from the activator button, consciously omitting the standard transmission closing.

"FBI, please state one more time for confirmation. We have 'The city of Washington is under attack.' Over."

"Goddamnit, people are *dying*!" Samuelson roared while outside fire continued to pound the J. Edgar Hoover Building. "Move your ass, son, and get us some help!"

Less than a minute later, Commanding General Lester Kerwin of Fort Bragg had established an open channel with Ben Samuelson over the MARS. Samuelson filled him in rapidly on what form the attack was taking, and on the fact that the President and all top members of government had been evacuated from the city. Samuelson could not say whether or not they were safe.

For now Kerwin elected to concentrate his initial resources on Washington itself. He could either deploy Delta Force commandos or risk a more extravagant response in the form of the 82nd Airborne. The disadvantage to the latter selection was that the 82nd was strictly an attack unit. "If it moves, kill it" was the 82nd's credo, and the Washington theater of operations promised to have plenty of friendly civilians running around. Delta Force, on the other hand, operated with far more discretion, but in far fewer numbers than the 82nd. Worse, Delta Force was trained to rely on lots of advance reconnaissance and intelligence to determine their footing, neither of which was going to be available today. And since they were a fast-attack team, armored backup was not something they were familiar with, and the siege the capital was facing indicated the heavy stuff might be required.

In the end Kerwin opted for the only real choice he had. He would send the 82nd into Washington and have Delta Force prep for the potential retaking of Greenbrier, Site R, and Mount Weather.

"Director Samuelson, the 82nd Airborne is prepping now. Over."

"How long? Over."

"ETA four hours to your beacon. Over."

"*Four hours?* There might not be anyone here alive in four hours. Over."

"Sir, that's shaving two off *optimum* time. Over."

"This is the capital of the country we're talking about, General. Over."

"It's my country too, Director. We'll be there as soon as we can. Over and out."

As Samuelson lowered the microphone, a hail of rocket fire shook the Hoover Building. The lighting died and the emergency generators kicked in instantly, casting a murky gray light over his office.

"I'm going upstairs to the ports," he told the crisis team, collectively hugging the floor of his office as far from the shuttered windows as they could manage. "I want to see for myself what's going on out there."

* * *

The ferocity of the opposition's attack surprised even McCracken. He emerged amid the wounded from the Pavilion in the Old Post Office Building, and, to set up a cover for himself, helped carry a few bleeding bodies out through the foot-deep pile of shattered glass.

The sounds of several smaller explosions from the city beyond reassured him that Arlo Cleese's Midnight Riders had followed his instructions to the letter. Gathered in their small groups, the Riders would now await Cleese's signal to move in. These groups were dominated by the hard-edged men and women for whom violence had come easy in the sixties and would again tonight. Vastly outnumbered by the Delphi troops, they would utilize a hit-and-run strategy aimed at slowing the enemy down long enough for help to arrive from somewhere. Even with all the precautions the Delphi had taken, Blaine knew five or so hours was the best window they could hope for, and the plan he had laid out was aimed at holding the city for that long.

McCracken managed to reach the Mall via 12th Street to find that it had become a sea of chaos all the way to the Lincoln Memorial. Delphi gunmen rushed to the area by truck descended upon the thousands of bystanders who were scattering from the Lincoln Memorial and the Washington Monument. Several ended up in the algae-rich waters of the Reflecting Pool when their path was cut off in all other directions. Blaine carried only his SIG-Sauer and had to fight against using it. Revealing himself would serve only to bring a hail of gunfire upon him. Hanging back, he raised his walkie-talkie to his mouth.

"McCracken to Tower. Come in."

"Tower," replied one of the Midnight Riders he had left in the Old Post Office Tower's observation deck.

"Got lots of unfriendlies down here on the Mall. Take 'em down."

Seconds later, the charging troops began to fall to his snipers. Their discretion of fire was excellent, impressive under any circumstances. Bodies continued to topple before

Blaine's eyes, the remaining Delphi troops searching frantically for the source of the unseen resistance.

"Yo, Mac," Arlo Cleese's voice squawked over Blaine's
walkie-talkie from the back of a Volkswagen van parked on
Pennsylvania Avenue, Kristen Kurcell by his side.

"Right here."

"The bros and sises are all in position."

"Order them in."

CHAPTER 37

"You sure you don't need me along?" Duncan Farlowe
asked again.

Johnny Wareagle gazed back to the center of the abandoned silver mine's rear chamber where Troop 116 remained gathered. "It's best for you to guard the boys."

Farlowe frowned. "Easy job for me, tough one for you.
Gun mighta helped ya out."

"Sal Belamo needed them more."

"Take mine," Farlowe said and handed over his Colt
Peacemaker, leaving him with the twelve-gauge shotgun he
had stubbornly worn slung from his shoulder all the way
from the 'Cat.

Johnny accepted the pistol with a simple nod and headed
on toward the passage leading to the front of the mine. The
darkness slowed him only slightly, and as he had expected,
there was no guard at the other end. Two men remained in
the front chamber, fifteen feet apart and positioned so they
could stare out into the storm to watch for the others in their
party who had ventured out to await the Sno-Cat.

The one standing to the rear never knew anyone was behind him until Wareagle clamped a huge hand over his
mouth and another atop his head. A quick wrenching motion snapped the man's neck and he went limp in Johnny's
arms. The other man heard the muted crack and swung

round fast. Wareagle used the corpse's rifle to snap two shots into the second man's head.

He then turned his attention to the two trucks parked in a darkened corner of the mine's front chamber. Dark tarpaulins still partially covered their long shapes. Johnny tugged one all the way off to find that the trucks were of the heavy cargo variety, long trailers attached by hitch to the cabs. He didn't have to peer inside to know they contained a dozen or so nuclear artillery shells each. He also knew that he and Sal would face a daunting task in driving one of the trucks down the mountain road, never mind two. The solution could have been as close as the mountain's edge, except for the untold damage that could result upon the trailers' impact a mile below if the radioactive material inside the warheads somehow leaked out. No, both trucks had to be *driven* out of here.

Even to Wareagle, that task seemed daunting. He needed a plan that would minimize the vast risks confronting him. One came to mind instantly, though the means to implement it were severely lacking.

Then again, maybe they weren't.

Johnny surveyed the exposed truck before him again and realized there was a way Duncan Farlowe and Troop 116 could help him out after all.

Traggeo was holding position between Boggs and Kreller when the Sno-Cat slowed to a halt before reaching the curve beyond which they were perched.

"Check it out," he ordered them. "Don't be subtle."

Without goggles, it was impossible for Boggs and Kreller to see much more than two yards ahead. The storm winds had shifted and blew the blinding white sheet directly at them as they advanced toward the curve. They had no choice but to ward the assault off with one arm raised before their faces, leaving only the other one for their M16s.

The stalled Sno-Cat came into view when they reached the slight curve in the mountainside. Boggs and Kreller slid back against the ice-encrusted face and eyed each other before launching their attack. They rounded the curve with guns spitting fire. The glass of the Sno-Cat's windshield fractured and the storm swept into its cab.

The men stopped firing. Boggs approached the Sno-Cat warily while Kreller hung back. The treads on the 'Cat's right side rested precariously close to the edge and Boggs was careful not to jar it when he climbed up to peer inside what was left of the cab. He threw the door open with one hand, rifle ready in the other.

The cab was empty. Splintered glass and already thickening snow lay on the driver's seat in place of the driver who had taken the 'Cat this far. Boggs leaped down and had swung round to shout toward Kreller when a barrage of gunfire stitched across his midsection and slammed him against the Sno-Cat's frame. As Boggs's corpse dropped to the snow, another barrage chased Kreller back against the mountain's icy rock face, where a hand closed on his shoulder.

"He's got us pinned down," Traggeo told him, his eyes sweeping the crevices and ledges above for the gunman's position.

A peculiarly even coating of snow hung over his stubble-lined head. His blazing eyes swept the mountain again.

"I'm going after him," Traggeo said. "You try to make it back to the mine."

"The mine?" Kreller raised.

"We've walked into a trap meant to keep us away from it. Whoever's doing the shooting isn't alone."

"The warheads . . ."

Traggeo nodded and slid sideways enough to ensure the angle of his climb would allow the mountain to serve as cover. Kreller followed Traggeo's impossible progress through the snow and ice briefly before starting to inch his way back in the mine's direction.

Kreller had just rounded the length of the curve, shoulders pressed against ice-layered rock, when a rumbling

found his ears. He came cautiously away from the sheer
rock wall in order to catch sight of the sound's source.

His eyes bulged.

One of the trucks carrying the nuclear stockpile was bar-
reling through the snow, lights on and engine grinding in
low gear. The truck took the curve leading onto the straightaway just ahead, and Kreller saw that incredibly it was pulling *both* of the cargo trailers. It swerved as its tires fought
to maintain their desperate purchase on the road through the
snow's hold. The second of the trailers fishtailed madly,
drawing sparks when it scraped against the mountainside.

Kreller held his ground and leveled his rifle on the cab as
the truck bore down on him.

Johnny Wareagle ducked an instant before the windshield
fractured. Glass blew into the truck's cab, the storm fast to
follow. He clung to the wheel and felt the thump of the big
truck slamming into the gunman and hurtling him aside.

Troop 116 had been all too happy to assist Johnny in im-
plementing his plan. Even with their help, though, the process took dangerously long, forcing Sal Belamo to hold off
the enemy by himself for a much greater than anticipated
duration.

The trailers Wareagle was hauling whiplashed madly
from side to side, and a dangerous curve was coming fast.
Johnny knew applying the brakes now would send him off
the mountain and shifted the truck into its lowest gear to regain control. He let the heavily armored trailers kiss the
mountain's side and ride against it through the curve. Sparks
flew out and dissipated harmlessly in the snow.

As Johnny steered the big truck on, the back trailer
grazed up against the stalled Sno-Cat and pushed it even
closer to the edge. The road dipped into another straightaway and Johnny eased off on the gas to let the big truck
coast. He was experimenting with the brakes when he saw
Sal Belamo waving his arms on the side of the road. Johnny
couldn't risk trying to bring the truck to a complete stop, so

Belamo had to run to catch up, the last stretch covered in a long leap to the passenger side sill. He managed to grab the mirror and kick his legs up after him.

Wareagle leaned over and threw the door open. The door nearly brushed against the mountain as Sal Belamo pulled himself all the way inside and closed it behind him.

"Thanks for stopping," Sal huffed. "You ask me, they should take your license away."

Johnny wiped the melting snow off his forehead and aimed the big truck through the storm.

Traggeo had stopped his climb up the mountain when he heard the sound of the truck's engine. A brief crackle of gunfire followed and then the two-trailer rig slid toward him, its windshield shattered. He had fully expected an unknown enemy to make a concerted effort to seize the mine's contents. But driving a double-hitched rig out through *this* storm? The thought was too incredible for him to even have considered it. What kind of man would attempt such a thing?

Even if Traggeo had been able to angle himself for a clear shot at the crazed driver, a direct hit would almost surely result in the precious cargo being lost over the mountain's side. No, he had to catch up to the rig and somehow take control of it.

Toward that end, he began a rapid descent of the ice-encrusted mountain. He was halfway down when the rig slid by, allowing him to catch a glimpse of the driver. In that instant everything became chillingly clear.

Johnny Wareagle!

To the victor of this battle would go the spoils of the trailers' contents. But more important to Traggeo was being granted a second chance to slay the legend. Win this battle and the scalp of Johnny Wareagle would be his. With it would come the legend's vast power, Traggeo certain the spirits would have no choice but to accept him.

The rig had passed out of sight down the mountain by the time Traggeo reached the road and rushed for the Sno-Cat.

The satellite feed hooked up to Mount Weather and Samuel Jackson Dodd's space station served a far larger purpose than simple entertainment. It was also an eye that could see the whole of the battle as it unfolded. Cantrell had always expected some pockets of limited resistance. It was the satellite, though, that was making it possible for him to deal with this unexpected, and organized, opponent his Delphi troops had to contend with. The explosion at the Old Post Office Tower had dealt him a devastating blow that instantly cut his manpower by a third. The ever-so-crucial timing of the operation would be considerably off as a result. Cantrell scrambled to compensate and redirect his forces accordingly.

He had divided the screen into eight sections, one of which featured an overview shot of the Mall, where sniper fire had begun cutting down his men there at will.

"The observation deck," the general realized, and worked his controls until a shot of the remnants of the Old Post Office Tower replaced one of the eight images pictured. Barrel flashes coming from within its tower confirmed his suspicions. "Ground control, we have sniper fire originating in the Old Post Office Tower. Neutralize it."

Seconds after the command was issued, Delphi marksmen stationed atop the Washington Monument turned their attention away from fleeing bystanders and onto the observation deck of the Old Post Office Tower. They opened up with a nonstop barrage of automatic fire at shapes they had no reason to expect were not friendlies until now. Instantly the shapes vanished. But the firing from the observation deck continued to the east toward the Capitol, the one perch the Monument snipers could not home in on.

"Destroy the tower," Cantrell ordered. "Repeat, destroy the tower."

* * *

"We got trouble at the Capitol Building, Mac," Arlo Cleese told Blaine over the walkie-talkie.

"On my way," McCracken returned and spun round to begin a dash down the Mall.

The sound of explosions made him turn back toward the observation deck of the Old Post Office Tower. Rockets from hand-held launchers had obliterated the top floor and a good portion of those immediately beneath it. Flames peeked out from gaping fissures in the tower's white-stone structure. Melodic, almost ghost-like strains of the Congress Bells filtered into the air as debris slammed into them. Five good men and a prime advantage had been lost.

Blaine gritted his teeth and rushed on. Night was descending, and he held to the hope that this would favor the hit-and-run tactics of the Midnight Riders. They had split into a dozen teams focused entirely about Constitution, Independence, and Pennsylvania avenues. McCracken ran into the first team huddled amidst the masses behind the cover of the Vietnam Veterans' Memorial.

"Feels pretty strange for this to be keeping me alive," said a balding man who must have spent the years that had claimed the listed names protesting the war.

McCracken placed his hand against part of one of the year's rolls, struck by a different sort of irony. "It does at that."

Delphi troops were spilling their way up from the area of the Lincoln Memorial. The Riders swung toward them and opened fire with their automatic weapons, taking the Delphi troops totally by surprise. A covered truck passing on Constitution Avenue screeched to a halt and jolted into reverse, Delphi reinforcements hanging from its rear ready to lunge out to join the battle. McCracken charged toward the truck and pulled the pin from one of Cleese's stock of grenades as he ran. It was airborne in the next instant, followed immediately by a second. The first hit the ground and rolled under the chassis when the truck came to a stop. The second wobbled toward the truck's open-flapped rear.

The explosions came within an instant of each other. The truck spun sideways when the first erupted, swallowed in heavy flames. The second explosion caught those men who had already managed to drop down.

McCracken turned round to see another horde of enemy troops storming his way from the southwest. The Delphi's intelligence was incredibly precise. Their ability to know the source of every explosion, ambush, and attack was severely restricting the effectiveness of what should have been a brilliant guerrilla-type strategy.

How were the Delphi able to mount reactive strikes so accurately?

Blaine stole a glance at the darkening sky. Much of the day of the Delphi was about Prometheus, about satellites orbiting thousands of miles overhead. Could one of Dodd's be—

Of course! That was it!

McCracken left this team of Riders to the battle and started across Constitution Avenue. He kept his pace as fast as he dared without revealing himself, staying low on the sidewalk to use the parked and abandoned cars as cover. Minutes later he reached the trio of buildings known as the Federal Triangle without incident and rushed toward a familiar monolith with an M stenciled near the top. What better place to make his way through the city than beneath it, where the eyes of Sam Jack Dodd could never find him?

Blaine sprinted the last stretch to the Federal Triangle Metro station and plunged down the stalled steps of the escalator.

The sixteen-member Hostage and Rescue Team on the Hoover Building's top level had already suffered six casualties by the time director Ben Samuelson got there. The enemy was using rockets and grenades to pummel the structure. The steel blast shutters had buckled and even caved in at several points, allowing dusk and enemy fire to filter in.

Samuelson helped tie tourniquets round a pair of leg wounds, then armed himself with a scope-equipped M16 and took the place of one of the downed men in an empty port. The remaining team members fanned out across the once-fortified floor.

"You better have a look at this," one of them called from his port overlooking Pennsylvania Avenue.

Samuelson crawled over and peered down to see a dozen or so figures had entered the battle on *their* side, taking the Delphi troops laying waste to the Hoover Building by surprise. They weren't police and they certainly weren't soldiers. Their ambush worked spectacularly at first, but the tide changed as the enemy became aware of the new combatants' presence. Since they had failed to leave themselves a clear escape route, the figures found themselves trapped and forced onto the defensive. Samuelson seized the opportunity to order his marksmen to concentrate their efforts on trying to catch the opposition in a cross fire. The friendlies, though, whoever they were, had already been overwhelmed by the hail of Delphi bullets concentrated in their direction. Those who tried to flee were cut down even faster than the ones who held as fast as they could to their cover.

"Who are they?" Samuelson asked out loud. "Who the hell are they?"

"Bad news," Arlo Cleese told Kristen, lowering the walkie-talkie from his ear.

"What?"

"Team that managed to take the White House right out from under these bastards is under siege. Not enough firepower. Fucked big time."

"What are you gonna do?"

"Just one thing avails itself, sister."

And Cleese pulled himself through the curtain and into the driver's seat of the van. Incredibly, a number of civilian vehicles were still braving the battle in search of flight or at least safety. Cleese chased the ponytail from his face, gunned the van's engine, and steered it into a sharp U-turn toward the other end of Pennsylvania Avenue.

It didn't take long before the White House came into view. Initially, in a surprise charge, a pair of Midnight Rider teams had overcome the attacking Delphi troops from the rear. They managed to secure a hold on the building's front, only to face dozens of reinforcements rushed into the area. They had expended virtually all their ammo and grenades in repelling the opposition's advances and could continue to do so only if Cleese found a way to get them restocked.

Surging down Pennsylvania Avenue toward the ravaged White House, there was only one option he could see.

"Hold on," he told Kristen.

She watched him smile and then chuckle. He was laughing hysterically by the time the van lunged toward a chasm blown out of the iron fence enclosing the grounds and past the corpses of a number of marines who had died trying to fend off the Delphi's initial assault.

A hail of bullets trailed the van as it surged onto the White House lawn. The sound of several shells testing the van's armored steel skin reminded Kristen of popcorn popping as she slid back into the rear to get the equipment ready for immediate dispersal. She felt a thump to her leg, like a hard kick, and looked down to see blood spreading through her jeans. Her hands went for the wound instinctively and felt the mangled flesh.

"Heeeeeeeeee-yahhhhhhhhhhhhh!" Arlo Cleese's bellow rose above the sounds of the gunshots, and he pushed the van up the White House steps on three blown tires. He jerked the wheel sideways at the last to bring the passenger side door even with the entrance. The fresh supply of armaments could now be distributed from some semblance of cover. Pushing down the shock from her wound, Kristen began passing the heavy machine guns and rocket launchers up to Cleese in the cab of the van. She could see blood flowing down his right arm as he handed the weapons to those beyond.

She had just crawled up to join him when the hands that had lifted the fresh weapons out reached in for the two of them. Kristen watched the scene dazedly as she was carried into the front of the White House. Between eight and ten surviving Riders hurried to get the tripods set up and the pair of .50-caliber machine guns in place atop them. There were six portable rocket launchers as well, and a half box of grenades to be distributed down the short line offering resistance.

By the time they set her down, Kristen couldn't feel her leg anymore. It was all she could do to crawl to the window to watch the battle raging outside. She smelled acrid smoke and realized part of the White House was burning. Dimly, she registered a stubborn fire alarm continuing to wail from one of the floors above.

Kristen caught glimpses of the remaining Riders struggling to repel another determined assault by the Delphi. Their new machine guns clacked off with little pause and the already distinctive thumping *poof!* of grenade blasts were sounding with regularity. A trio of off-target Delphi rockets smashed into the White House's second level and showered remnants of the ceiling down upon her.

A Rider wearing a bandage around his head dragged a resistant Arlo Cleese into the foyer and deposited him next to Kristen.

"Can you fucking believe this?" he moaned, trying to rub the life back into his right shoulder, which was even more mangled than her leg. "I can't even hold any of the fucking guns I delivered."

"We're going to die," she said flatly.

Cleese pulled a half-gone marijuana cigarette from his jacket with his good hand and then flicked a lighter against it.

"Not if our friend Mac has anything to say about it." He inhaled deeply and then held the joint out to her. "Care for a toke, sis?"

* * *

The switch thrown at Mount Weather had crippled the city's famed Metro in its tracks, the vast tunnels reduced to nothing more than safe havens for those who had managed to flee the battle aboveground. McCracken charged past hundreds of terrified faces in the dim emergency lighting. The air conditioning had died along with the power, and already the heat was stifling. The lack of circulation made the rank stench of fear all the worse.

Blaine had been careful to choose the proper feed line to take him in the direction of the Capitol Building and followed the cement walk as far as he could before leaping down onto the dead tracks. He then picked up his pace again, conscious of the echoing clip-clop of his shoes against the rail ties. The best chance the Midnight Riders had now was to hold firm to the prime landmarks on the Delphi's target list, like the Capitol Building, long enough for help to arrive.

The route from the Federal Triangle complex to the Capitol was elbow-shaped, L'Enfant Plaza station lying at the bend. McCracken sped on again after pausing there long enough to catch his breath, and reached the Capitol South station to find it empty except for a few dozen refugees from the battle. Bounding up the steps of another stalled escalator, he reached the top and the outdoors out of breath. In the failing daylight Blaine could hear the sounds of rocket and light arms fire, and could see constant flashes of light reaching him from nearby the Capitol.

A block later his knees nearly buckled at the sight of it. The Capitol's marble dome had been splintered by rockets and its topmost portion had caved in. The rest of the dome looked like the bottom chunk of a shattered glass. Additional chasms had been dug out of the stately fronts of House and Senate, as well as the Rotunda centered between them. The long steps leading up to all three were littered with bodies, both Riders and Delphi by all appearances. The Riders, though, were holding firm in their defense of the building. Vastly outnumbered and unquestionably running

low on ammo, they held their ground determined to repel
any direct assault that would lead to the building's total destruction.

But the massive concentration of Delphi troops lining 1st
Street and Union Square would not be denied much longer
unless Blaine could find a way to stop their mounting force.
He had the night's first darkness now to conceal his approach. But what was he going to approach *with*? What
could he possibly use to . . .

McCracken's eyes fell on a gasoline tanker abandoned in
the center of Canal Street. He charged toward it and jumped
into the driver's seat. The keys were missing, but he had the
engine hot-wired and revving less than a minute later. Then
he lunged back out and opened the main spigot, which operated off a gravity feed. By the time he started the tanker
forward, gas was already flooding out through the open
spigot.

Blaine crept the truck down Canal Street, weaving
through stalled traffic. Fortunately 1st Street was wide open,
and he upshifted to gather speed. He relied on the sounds of
heavy fire from the Capitol to conceal those of the surging
tanker. If the night could hold sight of it back just until he
crossed over Constitution Avenue, he knew his plan stood
an excellent chance of success.

He eased onto 1st Street and gave the tanker gas. When
it hit twenty miles per hour, he opened the door and angled
his body so he could keep pressure on the gas pedal until
the last possible moment.

McCracken jumped just as the tanker crossed between the
double-line formation the Delphi troops had erected in their
siege of the Capitol. Their machine-gun fire sliced through
its engine and stitched a line of punctures in the massive
tank. The remainder of the gas flooded outward.

The explosion came when the tanker slid past the
Garfield Monument and crashed into a truck parked perpen-
dicular to the street. The flames jetted out in all directions,

lighting up the night. Fire dashed along the trail of gas that had followed the tanker all the way here.

The initial explosion had consumed over half the Delphi troops stationed before the Capitol. Others had been scorched by flames or just the heat of the blast. And the fire wasn't finished yet. It continued to spread along the line of the freed gas in what amounted to a wall of flames, cutting off all but a circuitous route to the Capitol. The Delphi retreated, their vehicles and much of their equipment left behind for Blaine to make use of.

McCracken tempted the flames with a quick dash up to a truck that was just beginning to catch. He peered into its rear and grasped a machine gun known as a SAW, or Squad Automatic Weapon. The SAW fired belt-fed 5.56 rounds. Since the rounds were light, Blaine would have no trouble toting the thousand-round belt that made the SAW the perfect weapon for what remained ahead of him. Making sure the belt was properly fixed and chambered, he slid away from the flames into the night.

At Mount Weather, General Trevor Cantrell enlarged the scene of the huge explosion and fire outside the Capitol to half of the entire screen. As he watched it, his face squeezed even more tautly into a grimace. To an observer, he looked as though he was holding his breath.

Behind him the President was resting his hands confidently on the railing in front of the first row of chairs in the gallery. The awful damage that had been done to the White House and the Capitol, not to mention the Supreme Court, State Department, Hoover Building, and numerous others, didn't seem to matter so long as the resistance continued that was keeping the structures from being utterly overrun and devastated. He knew as well as Cantrell did that real help was still hours away. But he realized too that the day of the Delphi relied on the concept of quick shock for its expected success, in and out before anyone knew what hit them. That was forfeit now. And the longer the troops of the

Delphi had to contend with the resistance fighters, the greater the chances that their true purpose and identities would ultimately be revealed.

"General Cantrell," the President spoke forcefully to compel attention. When the general glanced toward him, he continued, "I am willing to accept your unconditional surrender."

Cantrell's lower lip trembled and his eyes flashed. "I've had quite enough of this," he said, though it wasn't clear to whom.

He steadied his headset before uttering his next words. "Ground command, this is Mountain Leader." Cantrell held the President's stare emotionlessly. "Send in the heavies."

"Come in, Arlo," Blaine said into his walkie-talkie.

"Right here, Mac," came the wheezy reply.

"You've sounded better."

"West Wing never agreed with me."

"You're in the *White House*?"

"Till they blow it out from under me."

McCracken could hear the dizzying explosions clearly in his ears now. "Ours or theirs?"

"Both."

"Kristen?"

"Right here. Wouldn't sound any better than me."

"How bad?"

"She been better."

"What about the rest of the Riders around the city?"

"Good to the last drop, Mac, and that's what we're down to. Maybe fifty left who can still fight. That's it."

Blaine felt the momentary euphoria over his success at the Capitol ebbing fast.

"Hold on," Blaine said, picking up his pace toward the Mall. "I'm on my way."

"Might be gone by the time you arrive. Might be—"

Another blast drowned out Cleese's words and then replaced them with static.

"Arlo?" Blaine called, knowing there would be no reply. "Kristen."

He began to sprint, willing to risk a dash through the heavily patrolled streets to reach the White House faster. He had just turned onto Pennsylvania Avenue, thinking about grabbing a vehicle, when he heard an all-too-familiar high-pitched grinding sound.

A pair of M-1 tanks were coming his way side by side right down the center of the street. The cars in their way were shoved effortlessly aside. Beyond them Blaine could see another pair of tanks creaking in the opposite direction toward the White House. He hid in the shadow of the Federal Trade Commission building and was briefly caught in the spill of lights shining out from a Bradley personnel carrier passing along Constitution Avenue, its deadly 14mm cannon poised for action.

The Delphi had broken out the heavy equipment they must have been stockpiling in the city for some time, in closed sections of parking garages probably. Short of a miracle, the battle was over. McCracken figured if he was going out, he might as well do so in style. Take down one, maybe even two of the tanks with what he had left on him.

He waited for the pair of M-1s to pass by him down Pennsylvania Avenue and had started to make his move when the sound of distant humming brought his eyes skyward.

And the miracle he needed greeted his gaze.

"What?" General Cantrell bellowed, working the remote control to place a single view on the entire screen. "This can't be. . . . *It can't be!"*

The President's eyes glistened with tears of uncomprehending thanks. Charlie Byrne had sunk back into his chair, near fainting. Angela Taft's smile stretched across the entire width of her face.

The huge television screen showed paratroopers dropping from the belly of a transport that streamed through the night, the numbers 9-1-1 stenciled in red across its side. Their parachutes opened in one beautiful, swift motion and floated toward the open ground of West Potomac Park beyond the Lincoln Memorial.

CHAPTER 38

The mannequins that made up the first drop drew fire only from the top of the Washington Monument. Colonel Tyson Gash of the 911 Brigade pulled the unlit cigar from his mouth and spoke to the trailing C-130.

"Savior Two, enemy fire originating in Monument top. Take it out."

"Take the *Monument* out, sir?"

"That's an order, son. We gotta get our boys down safe."

"Roger, sir."

As Savior Two banked under the 911 Brigade's flagship, the plane's gunner locked the top of the Washington Monument into the firing grid of the C-130's wing-mounted dual 20mm Vulcan miniguns. He pressed the red triggers under each of his thumbs. Three hundred rounds sped metallically out of two sets of six churning barrels and the gunner closed his eyes to the results. He didn't open them again until the C-130 had passed over its target.

In essence, the Vulcans had sheered the top of the Monument clean off. The sharply angled tip of the obelisk was gone, leaving only a jagged edge in the stone. The three stories beneath it had been peppered black with 20mm fire and seemed a wind's gust away from toppling as well.

"This is Savior Two, Rescue Leader," the pilot said into his headset. "The field is clear."

Gash gave the drop signal and the four transports filling out the line behind him began to spill the eager soldiers from their bays. He had initially considered directing the battle from within the flagship circling the city. But one sight of the inferno that was spreading through the ravaged capital of the United States set his stomach churning. This was the moment for which he'd been training men for five years now. This was the battle he knew his 911 Brigade would have to fight sooner or later. He had greeted the message delivered by Johnny Wareagle's pilot seven hours before with excitement and vindication. The country needed him after all. But the excitement vanished at the sight of Washington burning, nothing but hate and revulsion left in its place.

Gash discarded his cigar and moved backwards to join the men who would be dropping from Rescue Leader in the next pass.

"We're gonna fry these sons of whores," he growled to one of his sergeants. "And we're going to enjoy every goddamn second of it."

McCracken's eyes continued to peer skyward as a sea of black parachutes opened in direct line over West Potomac Park. Another transport with a red 9-1-1 on its side zoomed over his head.

It was Tyson Gash, alerted to what was going on, no doubt, by Johnny Wareagle!

The spread of Gash's paratroopers was even and precise, the only light catching them that from the flames flickering out of what remained of the Washington Monument's top. The drop concentrated entirely in West Potomac Park south of the Lincoln Memorial across Independence Avenue. Blaine figured what Gash and the 911 would need most now was a quick intelligence appraisal of what was going on. So he started down the center of the Mall toward the troops that would already be gathering into recon units.

His step had never felt so light. The Midnight Riders had done it! They had held the Delphi off long enough for help to arrive, though not from the expected source.

McCracken broke into a sprint down the Mall toward the ruins of the Washington Monument.

* * *

In the Mount Weather command center, half of the giant screen showed the paratroopers deploying quickly as another fleet of C-130s with red 911s across their sides circled the Potomac for an equipment drop. The other half closed on a solitary figure sprinting down the far end of the Mall in the paratroopers' direction.

Blaine McCracken.

"Kill him, General," the voice of Samuel Jackson Dodd ordered, filling the room. "Whatever it takes, I want him dead."

"Sir, the men we would have to commit to—"

"I want McCracken *dead*!"

"You ask me," Sal Belamo muttered, "we should pull over and call a cab."

Johnny Wareagle kept his eyes fixed on the road and his attention riveted to the task of getting the double rig down Mountain Pass. They were coming to the steepest and most precarious portion of the road, and the weather was at its least forgiving. The snow collected in the gaps of the fractured windshield and crystallized, further limiting Johnny's view. He hammered at the remnants of the glass with a naked fist to try to loosen the icy particles and succeeded only in putting more cracks in the windshield. The best he could do now was push as much of the glass out as he dared, lest the snow and ice block his vision altogether.

Johnny had done his best to memorize Mountain Pass during the trek up it in the Sno-Cat. But the dips and darts all looked the same and each slight misjudgment sent the two trailers he was hauling into a dangerous sweep. He could see their tires flirting with the edge in his mind. The storm conspired with the length of the rig to make it impossible for him to watch for any possible pursuit. Before him, meanwhile, the wildness of the storm frequently obscured what little view remained. Sal Belamo had tried to serve as spotter, but that hadn't worked, leaving Johnny with only his eyes.

And the spirits.

He could feel their hands over his. He could hear their words in his ears, leading him to make sudden adjustments in his route that kept the rig from pitching over the side. Johnny could see at most only ten feet ahead of him at a time, and he broke down the journey into segments that long.

"Wake me when we get off the mountain," said Sal Belamo, feigning a yawn.

Traggeo shoved the Sno-Cat on through the storm. Its dangerous perch near the mountain's edge had made him fear initially that righting it would be not only impossible but also deadly. He'd been able to manage the task, though at a severe handicap in time that gave the rig hauling two trailer-loads of nuclear weapons an even more considerable head start. But the nukes were only part of this for Traggeo now, and a small part at that, since he had glimpsed the face of the driver.

Fate had placed the two of them on this mountain together, because by killing Wareagle and taking his scalp, all he sought could be gained. Traggeo would swallow the great Indian's power and at last be accepted by those who had disdained him. He would wear the hair of Wareagle forever; there would never be call to change it. Future victims he claimed would merely recharge his spirit. He would no longer need to absorb their power by wearing their scalps.

The snow pummeled Traggeo through the shot-out cab. The environment inside the Sno-Cat seemed no different than the environment beyond. But at least he was moving, and finally, after an agonizing ten minutes, he caught a brief glimpse of the massive rig two hundred yards ahead of him.

Traggeo pushed the 'Cat for still more speed and its treads responded. The gap closed to a hundred yards, then to fifty, sight of the rear trailer now grabbed in longer stretches through the storm.

At twenty yards, the second trailer was a snake slithering S-like across the muddied grounds. Traggeo kept the Sno-Cat charging on. Its front kissed the trailer's rear bumper. The trailer jolted a bit and then steadied. Traggeo stomped forcefully on the accelerator pedal.

The Sno-Cat lurched forward and mounted the hitch assembly protruding from the trailer's rear, catching hold briefly. Traggeo checked both his .45-caliber pistol and killing knife, then pulled himself out through the Sno-Cat's shattered cab. He scaled its hood and leaped to grab hold of the trailer's roof. His gloves just managed to close on the sill and he pulled himself atop it. Johnny Wareagle was a mere hundred feet away now, and Traggeo began his advance across the top of the snow-covered rig.

McCracken had reached the halfway point of the Mall between the remnants of the Capitol and the Washington Monument when the first of the Delphi troops converged on his position from Constitution Avenue. He checked the area quickly for cover. The rear of the Smithsonian's Air and Space Museum was thirty yards away and he charged toward it, using a burst from the SAW to shatter the wall-length windows and clear a path for him inside.

The logistics of the museum gave him the semblance of hope. Its many areas for concealment would allow him to use a hit-and-run strategy comparable to the one the Midnight Riders had employed for the entire city. He began to search for a spot amongst the various displays of aerial history to lay his initial ambush.

A large poster drew his attention to an alcove of the museum reserved for Vertical Flight. It advertised a special demonstration that was being given on a daily basis all week. Intrigued by the accompanying photo, Blaine edged closer and realized his best chance for survival might lie in putting on an unscheduled demo of his own.

* * *

Colonel Tyson Gash touched down in West Potomac Park and shed his parachute amidst the last of his black-clad commandos. In all, the logistical limitations had allowed him to get a 500-man contingent in, roughly one-third of the 911 Brigade's total ranks. These same limitations had prevented the luxury of heavy air support. The 911 Brigade had its own fleet of Apache attack helicopters that were tailor-made for this kind of encounter. But Apaches required assembly that couldn't possibly be completed without more time and a sufficient platform.

Despite this drawback, the 911 had other heavy arms to rely on, thanks to LAPES. LAPES stood for Low Altitude Parachute Equipment Setup, and it was the most important element in effecting the kind of counterstrike the 911 Brigade was trained for. In years dating back to Gash's boyhood in World War II the casualty rate in paratrooper drops often approached a staggering 80 percent. The reason for this was not that they were cut down out of the air; it was that the enemy armaments awaiting them on the ground were simply too much to overcome. Accordingly, military planners had come up with a number of schemes to neutralize this advantage, ultimately evolving into LAPES.

Gash watched now as a fresh set of C-130s sliced in over the Potomac. The first in the procession nearly scraped the top of the Lincoln Memorial and dropped to within six feet of West Potomac Park's grassy plain. At that point, an onboard officer with the title of loadmaster began to work his magic. The loadmaster had already opened the C-130's rear flap in the midst of its descent. Now, when the plane was six feet off the ground, he activated a cargo chute that shot outward and opened twenty-five yards behind the C-130. Instantly a much larger chute automatically deployed behind the first and opened as well. The second chute was attached to a single M-551 Sheridan tank, and the force of its opening dragged the Sheridan out from the cargo bay. The fast-attack, aluminum Sheridan bounced once and came to a halt, fully ready to go, armed with a hypervelocity 110mm cannon and Shillelagh missiles. The team assigned to man it was inside and firing up the Sheridan inside of a minute later.

Three more C-130s dropped another trio of Sheridans, followed by additional LAPES passes that spilled a half-dozen Humvees equipped with tank-killing TOW missiles into the park. The trick for each of the pilots after deployment became pulling their planes' noses up to climb back over the Potomac fast enough to avoid the trees that rimmed the park. Each managed the daunting task and headed for a midair rendezvous to await further orders.

Colonel Tyson Gash checked his watch. The 911 Brigade had pulled the entire drop off in under nine minutes, an incredible three entire minutes better than their best-ever practice run. Without hesitation, following the specifications laid out en route from base, the vehicles rolled out toward their assigned grids. The remaining ground troops began their spread as well. Gash himself took command of the force that would take control of the Mall.

He grimaced as he led his men up toward the ruined structure of the Washington Monument. Maybe they shouldn't fix it at all when this was over. Maybe they should leave the Monument just the way it was as a memorial to the battle of Washington.

And the troops that were about to win it.

Traggeo continued to creep along the slippery top of the second trailer. The storm battered him relentlessly, and more than once he feared the winds would spill him to the road below or even off the mountain's steep side. By brute strength and force of will he managed to keep his center of gravity low and find the best footholds present on the ice-encrusted trailer top.

The most precarious move was having to leap five feet from the second trailer onto the first. After managing it effortlessly, Traggeo picked up his pace across the top of the lead trailer with new confidence. The sound of his steps was swallowed by the cushion of snow. The cab came into clear view quickly and he readied his final attack.

Mountain Pass had taken the slippery shape of an endless S. Wareagle kept the rig's pace steady, riding the storm as best as he could. He seemed to have formed a truce with the wind and snow, allowing him to concentrate on negotiating the multiple curves of the road. Each motion of the wheel had become an exercise in madness, as he waited to see if the tires could keep their hold.

The remaining portions of the windshield had begun to fog up from the warm breath misting from his and Sal's mouths. Johnny had taken to leaning forward at regular intervals to wipe the clouds away before the storm turned them into opaque shields frozen over the glass.

He was dragging his sleeve across a remnant of the windshield when a gloved hand shattered the glass next to it and grabbed hold of his forearm. A swift yank brought his upper body through what little remained of the windshield onto the tractor's hood.

"Shit!" Sal Belamo bellowed, freeing his gun and starting it forward.

"The wheel!" Johnny screamed back at Sal as the rig began to waver. "Take the wheel!"

Johnny twisted his body to find Traggeo grinning fiercely down at him. The killer kept him pinned with his left arm while his right slashed a huge knife downward. Wareagle remembered the wound his own knife had made in that arm five days before and deflected the blow on the same spot. Traggeo howled in pain and jerked the knife upward.

Johnny reached up and grabbed the killer by the jacket to yank him from the roof. He had begun to pull when the rig whiplashed madly across the road and slammed into the mountainside, separating the two men and catapulting both of them forward.

Sal Belamo's fingers had found the wheel seconds before,

but he couldn't see well enough over the big Indian's body to enable him to regain control. As a result the only choice he had was to jerk the rig into a veer away from Mountain Pass's edge. Without being able to work the brakes, Sal knew what was coming before he felt the tires lock up.

The truck skidded sideways across the white blanketed road. The passenger side took the brunt of the crash, jostling Sal all around the cab. Belamo was trying to go for his gun when the truck bounced off the mountain and tipped over. The two trailers teetered briefly before dropping onto their sides, coughing up a fountain of snow. Sal tried to rise to see what had become of Johnny. But his leg was caught under the seat, his frame pinned in place and his gun rendered useless as a result.

"Fuck!" he bellowed.

Johnny Wareagle, meanwhile, lunged up from the snow-bank he had landed in. His eyes found Traggeo struggling to his feet not far from the edge and he moved a hand to draw Duncan Farlowe's Peacemaker from his belt. But his grasp came away empty, the pistol lost in the fall and stolen now by the storm.

Fifteen feet away Traggeo was drawing a .45 pistol the fall had spared from inside his jacket, and Johnny threw himself forward. A tunnel seemed to open up and propel him, the gap closing quicker than should have been possible. Johnny never reached Traggeo, but he reached the pistol and kicked it out of the killer's hand. His right wrist stung again, Traggeo managed to whip his eighteen-inch blade forward in his left.

If Johnny had tried to follow up his kick with a second blow, the knife would have found him. But the spirits speaking through the storm had been there to lend advice, and Johnny had already backed off to draw his own knife, which was a virtual twin of Traggeo's.

The mad killer was grinning, teeth whiter than the storm. The snow covered both of them up to the knees and the two giants began to circle each other in equally deliberate motions. The spilled truck blocked the road forward. The toppled trailers cut off all passage to the rear. The result was a small patch of snowy ground no more than five hundred feet square to serve as their arena.

Johnny should have known his journey here would have confronted him again with the killer he sought to cleanse the name of his people. The circle always completed itself. Following Traggeo had brought him to the Delphi. Pursuing the Delphi had brought him back to Traggeo.

Traggeo held his knife high. His steps were crouched and wide. Wareagle kept his blade low at the midsection, his feet crisscrossing through the snow in narrow gliding motions. Measuring his chances for success, Traggeo was the first to lunge, his knife coming down on an overhead sweep.

Johnny stepped back from the blow that was supposed to serve as distraction for Traggeo's primary attack. He anticipated the coming kick perfectly and blocked it hard right on the knee. The mad killer groaned in pain.

Traggeo put his injured leg down gingerly and grimaced as he backpedaled. He was having trouble putting weight on it and he angled his crouch to protect that side. Johnny knew he had the advantage now, but would have to make use of it before Traggeo fought back the pain.

He charged in and blocked Traggeo's defensive poke easily with his left hand and drove his knife forward with his right. Traggeo managed to shift at the last and the blade merely grazed his shoulder. He accepted the pain and rammed Johnny's face with the back of his hand. The blow staggered Wareagle and blinded him long enough for Traggeo to launch an upward cut dead on line with his throat. Johnny was able to avoid the blow with a lurch backward that left his heels teetering on the very edge of the precipice.

Traggeo instantly realized the precarious position Wareagle had left himself in, but he did not strike right away as most would have. Instead he angled forward deliberately, his intent being to keep Wareagle unbalanced on the edge. Unable to move backward, in response the legend would have to sidestep through the treacherous snow that could betray his footing at any moment. Traggeo could see Wareagle's feet probing uncertainly, and he committed himself to holding off his next attack until the inevitable slip came.

The slight buckle he detected in one of Wareagle's knees was his signal to pounce.

Wareagle saw Traggeo's knife coming and twisted from its path. The edge, though, denied him the full range of motion he needed and as a result the blade dug into his right side. Traggeo tore it free and blood spattered into the white snow.

The mad killer's grin widened. He was going for the kill.

Johnny spun away from the edge, a counterattack readied, and this time the knife whizzed by without a touch. Traggeo tried to pull it back, but Johnny clamped down on his wrist. His hope was that the killer would try at all costs to tear free of his hold by yanking with even more resolve backward. Johnny would need only to hang on to be drawn back to firm, secure footing once again. Instead, though, Traggeo rerouted his momentum *forward*. Johnny lost his grip on the mad killer's wrist. His already dubious balance wavered and his left foot slid off the precipice.

Sensing the advantage, Traggeo tried a vicious swipe across the scalp he so desperately wanted to own. The momentum of ducking beneath it stripped Wareagle's right foot from the ledge as well, and he slipped off the mountain's edge into the white oblivion below.

In the end the opposition had determined Samuel Jackson Dodd's final move for him. Watching the paratroopers spread through the capital along with their tanks and Humvees had been too much for Dodd to bear, even before the initial encounters proved devastating for his Delphi troops. Whoever these new arrivals were, they were ferocious and skilled soldiers who could scarely contain their enthusiasm at being released to their deadly task.

The satellite pictures showed one of his tanks being killed by a TOW missile fired from a Humvee, even as the other M-1s continued to blast away successfully at prime locations in the city. It didn't matter. All his tanks would soon encounter the fate of the first. And the largest concentrations of the remaining Delphi troops were faring no better, as the fast-moving Sheridan tanks easily homed in on them, forcing retreat after retreat.

Strangely, this ghost team of deadly rescuers seemed to care no more for the physical state of the city than his troops did. Their Sheridans blasted holes in any building the Delphi sought to use as cover. And the fast tanks' Shillelagh missiles were as relentless as their 110mm cannon.

The rout, clearly, was on. The further the ghost team spread out through the city, the more this would become merely a mop-up operation for them. The Delphi troops had been too weakened and depleted by their earlier encounters with the guerrilla force led by McCracken to mount any credible resistance.

So Dodd had no choice but to trigger the electronic satellite signal that activated the only option he had left, his last chance to secure the day of the Delphi's anticipated results. Red digits poised over the monitor began counting down from the twenty-minute mark.

Sam Jack Dodd watched the seconds shrink away and settled back to wait.

The 911 Brigade had been outfitted and trained to encounter a much different enemy than the one it was facing tonight. An elaborate terrorist strike had always been the prime expectation, or even a covert enemy insurgence. In these and other scenarios, the presence of nuclear weapons was both planned for and expected. As a result, three of the 911's Humvees were equipped with the latest nuclear-tracking devices designed to sniff out bombs wherever they were hidden within a city.

The systems automatically triggered upon activation of the rest of the three Humvees' communications and weapons systems. Having no reason to expect it, the driver of the lead Humvee didn't even notice the red blip on the grid screen to the right of his console until a full minute after it had begun to blink.

"What the fuck . . ."

He tapped the screen with one finger and then two, hoping the message would change. When it didn't, he reached for his walkie-talkie.

"Tracker One to Rescue Leader," he called. "Come in, Rescue Leader."

Over a hundred Delphi troops surged into the Air and Space Museum in pursuit of McCracken, after briefly reforming outside. Nothing was left to chance this time. Expecting McCracken to be waiting to catch the largest group possible in the spray of his weapon, they had entered in small groups through varied points. The troops proceeded to move about the first floor of the museum in a wide spread. A few might be shot, but in the process their quarry would have to give away his position. In seconds the rest would have converged upon him.

A third of the Delphi troops climbed to the second floor in case McCracken had chosen this strategic position from which to fire upon them. But the quick and deadly firefight they had been expecting didn't come. They were nervous and edgy as a result. They knew McCracken was in the building; they just had to find him.

Some of the troops widened their spread to include cubicles, alcoves, rest rooms, souvenir shops, anywhere their quarry might have been hiding. A team even swept the movie theater, half expecting McCracken to burst out at them through the massive screen.

He didn't.

The troops on the second floor were the first to hear the buzzing. By the time they had pinpointed the source of the noise, though, a figure whirling over them had opened fire with a belt-fed machine gun, mowing down dozens of their number and drawing an orange streak across the upper reaches of the Air and Space Museum.

McCracken had been hiding atop an old Douglas DC-3 while the troops had fanned out through the museum. When he rose at last into the darkness, his head nearly touched the ceiling of the Air and Space. He made sure the thousand-shot belt for his SAW was weighted evenly over his left arm and then squeezed the Hoppi-copter's control handle with the hand on that side. The single rotor on the one-man helicopter began to turn, and Blaine braced his body over to begin his attack run.

The Pentecost Hoppi-copter was developed in 1945 with the aim of moving foot soldiers over otherwise impassable terrain. Only twenty were produced, and the military quickly gave up on the Hoppi for its cumbersome bulk and expected high maintenance. A prototype had ended up here in the Air and Space Museum, where the poster Blaine had seen minutes earlier advertised its full restoration and daily demonstrations.

Without pausing even to check the contraption out fully, McCracken had rushed into the Vertical Flight exhibit and strapped himself in.

The Hoppi-copter was indeed cumbersome. Basically it was nothing more than a steel cage attached to a single blade above it which boasted a fifty-two-inch spread. The relatively small engine was perched on the cage's rear and dug into Blaine's back after he had strapped himself in and tightened the harness. The Hoppi was bulky and poorly weighted, helping to account for its quick dismissal from service. McCracken couldn't imagine trusting it to difficult terrain in the outdoors, but within the open confines of the Air and Space it would serve him nicely.

The Hoppi had a single control button built into the handle grasped in Blaine's left hand. Squeezing it regulated the speed of the rotor blade, and thus the height the Hoppi could be taken to. The way the rider angled his body, especially his legs, determined direction.

It was as simple as any machine Blaine had ever operated and he had learned everything he needed to about it in the quick climb atop the Douglas DC-3. He left the engine on, hoping the low hum wouldn't attract attention. Then when the enemy had worked itself into the wide spread he had been expecting, he squeezed the handle and lifted off, beginning to fire as soon as he soared over the first of the Delphi troops.

The various exhibits of the Air and Space flew by in a darkened blur as he continued to rotate the SAW to catch all the astonished troops beneath him in its 5.56mm spray. He nearly collided with the tip of a ballistic missile and had to angle his body in sudden severe motions to avoid smashing into a model of the space shuttle and then with the prototype for NASA's X-15 fast flier.

He fired with virtually no pause whatsoever, not daring to give the men below time to regroup or even aim their weapons toward him. The belt slid nonstop across his left forearm, scraping his flesh through the shirt-sleeve. The SAW was light enough to handle the effort nicely, and after his early near collisions, he settled into a rhythm of using his left to control the Hoppi while his right worked the SAW.

The remaining enemy forces were in total disarray when he drifted upward, grazing the steel supports mounted beneath the museum's glass roof. His last attack was made in a classic dive pattern that took him beneath the second-floor balcony. The final complement of Delphi troops were rushing to flee, firing wildly in their wake. McCracken answered their fire with a burst that shattered the glass on the Independence Avenue side of the museum and spilled another dozen bodies to the floor.

The few troops still on the second level tried for him

again at that point. McCracken pulled immediately into a rise up and over them and managed to fire one last burst from the SAW when the Hoppi's engine began to sputter from ebbing fuel. He reached the floor just before it ran out and unbuckled the harness quickly to shed the Hoppi's weight.

McCracken swung toward the sound of more glass shattering on the back side of the Air and Space just as the Hoppi clanged to the floor. A fresh charge of troops surged forward, dressed totally in black and armed to the teeth. McCracken lowered the SAW and smiled.

"Hold your fire!" a familiar voice from long ago ordered and these troops that must have belonged to the 911 went rigid. "We got us a friendly."

Out of the glare of focused beams attached to several of the M16s stepped a barrel-chested shape chomping on an unlit cigar.

"Nobody the fuck else but you could have done this, McCrackenballs," grinned Colonel Tyson Gash, working the cigar from the left side of his mouth to the right.

"Looks like we finally get a chance to work together, after all, Colonel."

"Way I see it," Gash said, still advancing, " 'bout time the both of you decided to sign up with the 9-1-1."

"I figured Johnny had been to see you," Blaine returned and let himself smile.

"Don't start the celebration yet, Captain," Gash cautioned. "We still got a shit load of a problem left to contend with."

CHAPTER 39

McCracken and Gash jogged at the head of the procession, skirting the clutter of bodies Blaine had left behind inside the Air and Space Museum. A Humvee was revved up and waiting directly outside the museum's entrance on Independence Avenue.

"We've got a positive fix, sir," a soldier who had come to meet them halfway told Gash.

"Where, son?" the colonel asked, the unlit cigar working still in his mouth now.

"Lincoln Memorial, sir."

"Shit on a pistol."

"Fix on *what*?" Blaine wondered.

"A nuke, Captain. We'd better get moving."

Ben Samuelson had begun firing wildly, desperation taking hold. Only three members of his Hostage and Rescue Team were still in position, the rest either seriously wounded or dead. The battle had claimed a number of special agents as well who had taken their places. And below, the Hoover Building itself was burning. The sprinkler system fought to contain a blaze that continued to be fed by fire from the M-1 tank that had positioned itself near FDR Memorial Drive. Each shell shook the building and sent showers of concrete into the air. The security doors and shutters had been breeched and any moment now the troops in the street below would come surging in.

Samuelson had decided the only course left to him was to continue firing until the end. The city was falling and FBI headquarters was falling with it.

More tank fire slammed into the building. One shell pounded the top level where he crouched, and then a second. Samuelson watched more of his people blown over, blood flowing from tears and gashes, some of the wounds destined to be mortal.

"Goddamnit," he moaned. "God*damnit*!"

He popped a fresh clip into his M16, leveled it on the tank across the road, and opened fire.

The M-1's turret exploded in a fiery blast that shoved the tank sideways.

Samuelson stopped firing and looked down at his M16.

A second explosion pounded the M-1 on its opposite side and lifted the flaming tank into the air before toppling it over.

What the he—

A flood of black-clad troops rushed into the square and opened fire on the positions held by the Delphi, overwhelming them with sheer force as well as skill. For an instant Samuelson recalled the other group of friendlies that had perished earlier in the battle for a similar effort. But this force was different. Samuelson could see it in the confident, precisioned way they moved. Around him what had been grim stares on the faces of his remaining defenders an instant before turned to stunned disbelief and then glee. Hoots and hollers replaced the eerie clacking of gunfire as the enemy was slaughtered in a wholesale, unforgiving fashion on the street below.

Instead of joining in the celebration, Samuelson found himself plagued by a nagging question.

Who the hell *were* these guys?

In the White House, not a single Midnight Rider had been left unscathed by the battle. Other than a few bullets left in pistols, their ammo had run out a few minutes before. Those still able to move had joined Kristen Kurcell and Arlo Cleese in the back foyer. Cleese had lit up a fresh joint and was offering it around.

There were plenty of takers.

The troops beyond would be rushing the White House any moment. Sitting here, nice and relaxed, maybe they'd be able to take a few more by surprise.

Suddenly gunfire began to erupt anew outside. The Riders gazed at each other through eyes dulled by the pungent marijuana smoke, wondering if anyone was missing. Even if there had been, though, the intensity of the gunfire could never have come from a single person, or even a small group of their companions. This was something else entirely, a whole new battle picking up where theirs had left off. Not one of the Riders had the strength or resolve to even check out what was happening.

"What the fuck?" one muttered.

And seconds later they heard and felt the barricaded front doors blown open. Orders were shouted, precise and professional. Heavy footsteps filled the hall. One set reached the doorway leading into the back foyer at the same time the barrel of an M16 poked its way through.

"What the hell is this?" asked a man who was dressed completely in black-out gear, from his feet to the dark stain on his face.

"It's a party, soldier," Cleese said, his mind starting to clear to the reality of what must be happening. "And you're the guest of honor."

Traggeo lingered near the edge for several moments after Johnny Wareagle had slipped off, peering over the mountain in search of him. When what little he could make out through the storm gave up no sign of the legend, he knew he had won. The victory felt somewhat hollow without the trophy of Wareagle's scalp, but another trophy awaited his inspection.

Traggeo slid along the edge of Mountain Pass to the second of the two toppled trailers to check the condition of its deadly cargo. The angle of its tumble had left it only a yard from the precipice, so he worked carefully. Using his knife he was able to jimmy the locking mechanism on the rear hatch door. The guide rails must have bent slightly when it tipped over, because progress in getting the door to slide upward came agonizingly slow. Finally Traggeo was able to force the door into the rails and open it. He peered into the trailer through the storm.

It was empty. The green containers were gone.

Traggeo blinked his eyes, not believing the sight. A feeling made him step away from the trailer's rear and gaze back into the storm. He shivered.

An apparition stood there, the ghost of Johnny Wareagle,

as white as the storm itself. But this apparition held in his hand a century-old pistol that was caked with snow. His face was scraped and bloodied. The arm not holding the gun hung lower than the other. A frosty patch of red glistened on his side where Traggeo's knife had wedged home.

Traggeo stiffened and sneaked a hand to that same knife now sheathed on his hip, out of the ghost's view.

"You!"

As Wareagle had dropped over the side he had spotted a narrow ledge ten feet down. He landed on it with both feet, slipped off, but managed to grab hold of a protruding rim with his left hand. He badly wrenched his shoulder in the process, which made first climbing upon the ledge and then back onto the road extremely difficult tasks. His plight was complicated all the more by the necessity of clinging to the rim until he was sure Traggeo was no longer peering down from above.

Traggeo was behind the second trailer by the time Johnny retook the ground. Not wanting to risk a close-in kill, he searched hurriedly through the snow for Duncan Farlowe's pistol and found it not far from the cab's toppled frame. He had just gotten the Peacemaker raised when the man he had hunted stepped away from the trailer and faced him.

Traggeo feigned a quick glance back up Mountain Pass so he could work his knife from its sheath.

"Those Boy Scouts," he muttered, stalling.

"They helped me unload both trailers before I set out."

"Then the warheads . . ." The knife was in hand now, almost ready to throw.

"Yes," Wareagle said, completing the thought for him.

They were still in the cave, watched over by Duncan Farlowe and the boys of Troop 116.

"Then I will have to go back for them," Traggeo said.

He wheeled and threw the knife in the next instant. Johnny Wareagle didn't even move. Duncan Farlowe's Peacemaker coughed twice from his hip, both bullets catching Traggeo square in the chest. The killer couldn't believe his eyes. But he wasn't gazing at his wounds. No. He was staring straight ahead, wondering how his knife had missed its target. It had been dead on line; he was sure of it. Then it was gone, almost like the storm had somehow swallowed it before it reached Wareagle.

Traggeo started to stagger, dying eyes locked on the apparition of Wareagle.

"Ghost," he said and fell backward over the mountain's edge.

"Not yet," Johnny told his corpse.

The 911's bomb disposal unit was waiting on the steps of the Lincoln Memorial when Colonel Tyson Gash's Humvee pulled up, its doors already open. Gash rushed toward them, McCracken right by his side.

"It's here all right, sir," reported the chief of the unit, a corporal named Revens.

"Where?"

"We've already searched the building, sir, and found nothing," Revens continued, "which means it has to be underneath."

"Underneath, soldier?"

"The catacombs," said Blaine.

Gash and the members of the 911's bomb disposal unit, trained in all manner of explosives including nukes, turned to look at him.

"This used to be swampland, Colonel," Blaine explained. "Layers of tunnels and caverns had to be dug to support the memorial's weight when it was built."

"Do you know how to access them, sir?" Revens asked him.

"I will as soon as we're inside."

In the command center of Mount Weather, General Cantrell had done what he would have considered laughable only hours before: he had surrendered unconditionally to the President. The facility's regular security personnel were already in the process of disarming and detaining Cantrell's crack troops. The President's team of Secret Service agents had been brought to the command center where they took direct responsibility for the general.

"I want to get back to Washington," the President said anxiously to Charlie Byrne. "Now that this is over we've got plenty of—"

"Wait a minute," interrupted Angela Taft, her eyes still on the big screen. "If it's over, what's going on down there?"

Before her, a full quarter of the screen was taken up by a horde of men and vehicles converging on the Lincoln Memorial.

Samuel Jackson Dodd watched the clock tick down to the eight-minute mark and then returned his attention to his screen. The troops that had forced him to resort to this stratagem were storming inside the Lincoln Memorial. A slight tremor of fear slid through Dodd. If they knew about the catacombs, there was plenty of time for them to reach the bomb. Disarming it, though, would be something else entirely. He had left a subtle surprise to make that effort almost surely go for naught.

The bomb would detonate at the 2:00 mark instead of at the traditional 0:00. The center of Washington would be reduced to rubble, the disappearance of the nation's leaders even easier to account for in the process. Greenbrier and Site R remained under his control. Regaining control in Mount Weather would be accomplished in the wake of the blast.

Once Dodd took office, of course, he would have to rebuild the capital from scratch. The challenge intrigued him. His first act as the nation's commander in chief would leave an indelible mark on all of history, at the same time that it helped to solidify and consolidate the Delphi's hold on power.

Dodd resisted the temptation to announce to the surprised occupants of Mount Weather's command center what was about to happen. It would be far more effective to surprise them and watch the shock on their faces when the explosion vaporized the center of Washington less than six minutes from now.

He filled his viewing screen on *Olympus* with a single overview shot of central Washington and settled calmly back to watch.

The Lincoln Memorial's supporting understructure of catacombs was filled with walkways accompanied by wooden safety rails. Tours had been given of them on a regular basis until tests revealed dangerously high levels of asbestos. Since removing it was not practical, the catacombs had simply been shut down.

McCracken had located the entrance to them on the lower floor of the Memorial. Gash's men shot their way through a locked steel door and surged inside.

The darkness of the catacombs was broken by a series of single bulbs strung overhead. Blaine had found the switch to activate them on the wall next to the ruined steel door. In spite of the spring warmth, the walls were icy cold to the touch. The deeper inside the troops ventured, the more in evidence were the soda straws and stalactites fashioned by the dripping and freezing water. There were puddles of water sloshing beneath their feet, and the clammy chill made Blaine wonder why they hadn't frozen. He could see the breath misting before his face. Revens's hand-held nuke locater was beeping now as well as flashing, and McCracken knew they were getting close.

"It's right up here," Revens announced. "No, wait. Stop."

"Well?" Colonel Gash raised.

"Just to the right," Revens gestured. "In that ditch, I think."

Gash moved slightly ahead of them toward the ditch in question. The unlit cigar was still in his mouth.

The nuclear warhead rested comfortably in a yard-deep depression in the ground. No effort had been made to con-

ceal it, since a century's camouflage already in place would
have seemed to make that superfluous. A timer rigged atop
the black casing was ticking down to the seven-minute
mark.

"Converted low-yield artillery shell," Revens identified
and looked back at Blaine. "One of those you told us was
stolen, no doubt."

"Low yield or not, it's enough to put the government out
of business for a long time if it goes off," Blaine told him.

"It won't be going off, sir," Revens assured as his team
went about their individual tasks in quick, coordinated motion. Tools were brought out, cases containing varying sizes
of magnifying glasses and lenses unloaded. There was also
a machine that was designed to the specifications of a
stethoscope, only rigged to a sound board with dials and
gauges. He recognized a second device as an instant X-ray
machine.

To McCracken, it all seemed too simple, too pat. For
Dodd to have come this far, gone through all this, and leave
no extra surprises at the end was not something he could accept. So what was it? What were they missing?

Another bomb perhaps, a second one, to be ignored after
this one had been found?

No. The portable locater would have picked up two blips
if that were the case.

"I know this baby well," Revens continued. He was
crouching in the ditch now, eyeing the shell confidently.
"Won't even have to use all this stuff to shut her down."

Revens turned the waist-high warhead on its side and affixed a pair of suction cups to the locking mechanism on its
underside. The suction cups were connected to an elaborate
sensor mechanism that looked like a laptop computer but
was actually a master unlocking system allocated to battalion field commanders so they could manually deactivate
their warheads in any eventuality. The final fail-safe procedure in the loop.

As Blaine watched, numbers began flying across the device's small screen. Four locked home and began flashing.

"Halfway there," Revens said to McCracken and Colonel Gash.

The clock, facing upward with the warhead tipped onto its side, ticked to 3:59.

A fifth number joined the others on the screen and began flashing. The next two followed at intervals of fifteen seconds. When the machine correctly identified the eighth and final one the screen emptied except for the eight numbers. Revens hit the keyboard's execute key.

The clock had reached 3:20.

The two men on either side of Revens brought the instant X-ray machine, along with what looked like an electronic stethoscope.

"Now we check for booby traps before I remove the lock."

"No!" Blaine said, dropping down into the ditch. "This warhead would have an internal clock, wouldn't it?"

"Yes, but—"

"Then why bother with one we can see?" He looked back at Gash. "It's here to fool us. It might read two minutes and forty-five seconds, but we don't have that much time left."

"What do you suggest, Captain?" Gash asked him.

Blaine swung toward Revens. "Remove the lock now."

"Sir, if I do that and it's booby-trapped . . ."

"They wouldn't bother with a booby trap. They would have figured the clock was enough."

Revens looked at Gash. The colonel nodded.

The clock read 2:30.

Reluctantly, Revens cupped the sophisticated housing that fastened the lock required for detonation into the warhead. With the proper unlocking code entered, he turned it to the right. It clicked into place at the 2:19 mark and he started to twist it back to the left.

Click.

2:13 . . .

Revens moved his left hand up to join his right and used both to grasp the locking mechanism's ridged edges. If the warhead was booby-trapped, they'd all know soon enough.

2:08 . . .

Revens held his breath and started to slide the locking mechanism toward him. He had it in hand and cradled like a baby as the countdown clock facing the ceiling ticked to the two-minute mark.

EPILOGUE

"This country owes you a lot, Blaine," the President said yet again, "one hell of a lot."

Three days had passed since the battle of Washington had ended, and this was the first time in that period that McCracken had met with the President alone. The commander-in-chief had insisted on returning to the White House after spending only a single night at Camp David. Tyson Gash's 911 Brigade had left the task of mopping up the city to the 82nd Airborne, who arrived just over four hours after the battle of Washington had begun. Had the 911 stayed long enough for the media to descend once Prometheus was deactivated, they would have been hailed as heroes. Gash would have been able to name his terms for return to the service that had spurned him. Instead, just before dawn the men of the 911 were trucked to Andrews Air Force Base, where their transport planes were waiting to ferry all troops and equipment back to their Arizona base. The only ones not making the trip were the few casualties, and their hospital stays promised to be as quiet as they were short.

The 82nd served as backup for Delta Force in the retaking of Greenbrier and Site R as well. None of the temporary inhabitants of either locale fully understood what had happened. There were numerous rumors, but hard facts were difficult to come by and the truth remained elusive. Only the President, Charlie Byrne, Angela Taft, and Ben Samuelson knew the whole story, and they had no intention of sharing it.

By Monday, incredibly, the government was up and running again. Since very little damage had been done to the Capitol's interior, Congress held a virtually normal session even as construction crews began the massive repair job outside. The nation's representatives attacked their roles with renewed vigor and pride. In that sense the very basis for the day of the Delphi had been proven wrong. The government emerged from the crisis stronger than ever.

"It's not finished yet, sir. It's not over," Blaine told the President as they strolled through the Rose Garden.

"You're talking about Dodd, of course."

"What happens when he comes down off his space station, Mr. President?"

"What would you like to see happen, Mr. McCracken?"

"I'd like to be standing there to personally slap the handcuffs on him and place him under arrest for treason."

"Which, I'm told, still carries the death penalty with it."

"Under the right circumstances it does, sir."

The President stopped. "And could the country handle the trial, Blaine?"

"I'm not sure the country could handle *not* having the trial."

"In this case I don't agree with you, Blaine. In fact I question which McCracken I'm speaking to. The one who spent the last dozen years on the outside, or the one who spent the last week on the in? The former would be advocating Dodd's arrest, incarceration, and the biggest trial this nation has ever seen. The latter would realize allowing everything he tried to do to come out might tear this country apart."

"You're making the same mistake Dodd did, sir: you're not giving the country enough credit."

"Maybe. But a trial would give Dodd a forum for his ideas, and if his lawyers found a way to get him off, he could conceivably emerge from this in an even stronger position. Right or wrong?"

"Right," Blaine conceded.

"And we could be facing all this again some other time, if not from Dodd, then from someone else. Right or wrong?"

McCracken's eyes gave his answer.

The President looked at him thoughtfully. "After all this is over and done with, I want to keep you on the inside, and the only way you can stay here is to think in those terms. There's got to be some other means to deal with Samuel Jackson Dodd."

The space shuttle *Atlantis* squeezed against the docking bay of the space station *Olympus*. Its occupants felt a hefty thump as the seal took hold.

"Docking achieved," the pilot announced.

"Enter when ready," the station commander greeted.

Sam Jack Dodd had followed the shuttle's approach carefully, wondering what or who might be waiting on board for him.

"Mr. Dodd?" a voice called from within *Atlantis* over Dodd's private channel.

"I believe that must be the voice of Blaine McCracken," he responded. "I'm gratified you made the trip personally."

"Sorry to disappoint you, but I'm speaking to you from earth. I've had my fill of traveling on space shuttles."

"Of course, that nasty Omega business."

"I see my reputation precedes me."

"You'll be meeting me on the ground, I suspect."

"Nope."

"Your surrogates, then."

"No again. Your limousine will be there, as expected."

Dodd smirked. "In that case, I assume that you're calling to make some sort of deal on behalf of—"

"Wrong for the third time. You must be having a bad day, Mr. Dodd."

"Whose side exactly are you on, Mr. McCracken?"

"The side of anyone who is willing to stand up against men like you."

"Like *me*? I should point out that might well include yourself. After all, what more do the two of us want than what's best for the country?"

"I guess I want plenty more. Like making sure we maintain self-determination. The country's got to chart its own course, Mr. Dodd. It's not up to individual men or groups to force the future down anyone's throat. I saw the results of that Saturday night, and I've seen them before. Lots of people died down here for no reason at all. Lots more were injured. And just about everyone else is scared."

"That's the point! You're missing it!"

"And you missed it a long time ago. A country's not a business, not a simple commodity. It's a living, breathing entity. We grow, we change. If the day of the Delphi had worked, there would be no growth, no change. There would be only a prescription based on your diagnosis to be filled and swallowed. Sorry, Mr. Dodd. The country might be sick right now, but it doesn't need the kind of medicine you advocate."

Dodd wandered to the small viewing portal before responding over the speaker. "For a simple killer, you know how to turn a phrase. I look forward to meeting you on the ground."

"Like I said, I won't be there."

"You're letting me off?"

"I didn't say that either."

"But the country must be spared embarrassment, mustn't it?" Dodd smiled to himself. Hope rose anew. "Of course I should have known." Once again, the government's weakness had worked to his favor. "Don't expect me to promise I won't try it again," he added defiantly. "Don't expect me to promise anything."

"I don't."

"We'll meet someday, Mr. McCracken."

"No, Mr. Dodd, I don't think we will."

* * *

McCracken was visiting Kristen Kurcell in the hospital when the space shuttle *Atlantis* touched down with Samuel Jackson Dodd on board, met only by his standard private security detail. Baffled but no less wary, Dodd climbed into his limousine and was driven off. He knew McCracken would be coming for him before too long and intended to be ready.

The bullet she had taken inside Arlo Cleese's van had done a lot of damage to Kristen's leg. Surgery had been performed early Sunday morning and she'd finished her first therapy session an hour before Blaine's arrival on Wednesday afternoon. The pain had been excruciating, the simplest motion suddenly difficult.

"I always wanted a personal trainer," she said to Blaine. The furrows pain had dug in her face during therapy were still evident. "You wouldn't be available, would you?"

He sat down close to her on the bed and took her hand. "For the right price."

"I mean, I've got to figure you're an expert. Saturday night was just routine to you."

"It's never routine. Some are just worse than others."

"This one?"

"Definitely in the top three." Blaine slid closer to Kristen and stroked her hair with his free hand. "But maybe the next one will hold off for a while, long enough for me to help you mend that leg anyway."

"Money will be a problem. I'm currently unemployed, in case you forgot."

"I've got friends in Washington now. Let me see what I can do."

"Must feel strange."

"Having friends?"

"In Washington, anyway. Plan on staying?"

"Depends on how I'm treated," Blaine told her. "I was a resident before. I didn't like the company. No pun intended."

"Times change."

"Not really. But people do, and maybe the cycle's come round again. It's not who you bring to the dance, Kris, it's who you leave with."

She looked down at her heavily bandaged leg. "No dancing for me for a while."

"Then we'll have to find something else to do in the meantime."

He pulled her head close to him and kissed her warmly.

"Looking for something, Indian?"

McCracken stopped a yard short of Johnny Wareagle, who was staring intently at one of the black slab sections of the Vietnam Veterans Memorial.

"The missing names of those who served with us," Johnny said without turning. A sling he had already stopped using hung down from his damaged left shoulder. "I have stood here imagining them incised on the black amid the others, Blainey." He swung slowly at last. "I liked the sight."

"You've got some favors coming to you too, Indian."

Wareagle gazed back at the memorial. "Enough to make them add the names, Blainey?"

"Maybe. Folks here in the capital are in a real appeasing mood right now. Saturday night gave them another way of looking at things."

The nuclear warheads Wareagle had kept from Traggeo's possession were still under heavy guard in the abandoned Colorado mine. There was no way to salvage the green containers Boy Scout Troop 116 had helped him unload until the renewed spring warmth melted all of the snow and made it safe for trucks to negotiate Mountain Pass. Tomorrow, maybe, or the day after.

Wareagle regarded McCracken skeptically. "Are these folks looking through your eyes, Blainey, or are you looking through theirs?" He paused and took a step away from the memorial. "Years ago we shared our separate partings from them because we had convinced ourselves we were outsiders. But we were wrong, too close to the center to realize where we stood in relation to those who scorned us. *They* are the true outsiders. Yet they don't realize it, because from their perspective everything revolves around them."

"The battle of Washington may have broadened that perspective."

"Only for a time, Blainey. Take advantage of it while it is there."

"I plan to, Indian."

It began with a nineteen-point single-day drop on Wall Street, fueled by rumors of an investigation into fraud over government contracts. The IRS issued its own statement. The Justice Department had convened a grand jury. In a mere forty-eight-hour period, Dodd Industries and its many subdivisions had plunged to the verge of bankruptcy as panicked selling shook markets all across the world.

On the nation's docks, the longshoremen's union refused to load or unload any Dodd freighter. Dodd Industries' international shipping business was brought to a halt when its jets were denied clearance to file flight plans to airports from Los Angeles to Sydney, to Tokyo, to London. A strike shut down the conglomerate's industrial and manufacturing plants. And all this shared a front-page item on every major national daily detailing a long litany of bribes Sam Jack Dodd had passed to help build his empire. Indictments were pending.

It was just the beginning. And also the end.

Samuel Jackson Dodd would never stand trial for treason. The carefully placed rumors of his part in the near destruction of Washington were enough to do the job, even if the collective truths of his past hadn't suddenly been exposed.

With the authority and backing of the White House, Blaine McCracken had put his strategy into effect by making quiet visits to a number of individuals in the proper unions, brokerage houses, and government agencies. None were told all, but all were told enough to want Samuel Jackson Dodd put out of business for good. Dodd might escape jail, but not the scandal certain to strip him of his vast power and prevent the day of the Delphi from ever dawning again.

Coming soon from Tor Books . . .

THE KINGDOM OF THE SEVEN

A Blaine McCracken Novel

by Jon Land

Enjoy the following preview!

PROLOGUE

"What d'ya make of that?"

Officer Joe Langhorn turned slowly into the sun, inching the Arizona Highway Patrol car toward the shape on the side of the road. On first glance he had passed it off as a Hefty bag discarded by some lunkhead in a Winnebago too impatient to wait for the next rest stop. But now he was thinking it could be a coyote or even a mountain lion. Road kill of a bumper-bending sort.

"Jesus Christ, Wayne, is that a . . ."

His partner, Wayne Denbo, held a hand up to shield his eyes, then pulled it away along with his sunglasses.

"Shit," Denbo muttered. "Pull over."

"I'll call it in," from Langhorn, reaching for the mike stand.

"Wait till we're sure."

Denbo climbed out his door first once the cruiser had ground to a halt on the sand-washed pavement. He had redonned his sunglasses, gun flap unsnapped out of habit. Langhorn drew up even in time for the next wave of sand to slap him in the face.

"I'm sure enough now," he said after it had passed.

The shape suspended halfway over the shoulder embankment belonged to a man. The flapping of a black shirt spilling out of his pants accounted for the illusion of a discarded Hefty bag. His outstretched, sand-caked arms were tawny enough to look like the limbs of some unfortunate mountain predator. Not a coyote, but road kill quite possibly after all.

Langhorn waited with his gaze half on the cruiser while

Denbo leaned over the body and felt about its neck for a pulse.

"He's still alive," Denbo said, looking up.

"I'm calling this in now."

" 'The fuck, Joe. Bring my thermos over."

It was a Dunkin' Donuts jumbo, the kind that came free with enough coffee to fill it. Except Wayne Denbo always filled it with iced tea. Every day that Joe Langhorn could remember since they'd been paired up on this route.

The ice had long melted and what contents had survived the morning sloshed about inside. Joe Langhorn delivered it to his partner, who had just turned the man-shape onto his back.

"He hasn't been here long," Denbo reported. "Couple hours maybe."

"Hit by a car maybe?"

"Don't think so. He's got no bruises or abrasions I can find."

Langhorn gazed around into the emptiness that stretched in all directions. "Where's his car? How the fuck he get out here?"

The shape moaned. Denbo lifted his head and tapped his cheek lightly.

"Mister? Come on, mister, wake up. Come on. . . ."

"You check for ID?"

Denbo flipped his partner a wallet he had pulled from the shape's pants pocket. Langhorn bobbled it briefly, then grabbed hold.

"Name's Frank McBride," he reported, after locating the man's driver's license. "From Beaver Falls. Twenty miles west down the highway."

"Twelve walking 'cross the sand."

"You figure that's how he got himself here?"

"Look at him."

Langhorn didn't really want to. Whatever it was would make a man walk a dozen miles straight into the heat of the day was beyond anything he could conceive. "Thinking about calling this in, Wayne."

But Denbo still had the shape's head cradled, a half cup of brown-black iced tea pressed against his lips. He saw something tucked into the inside pocket of his jacket and reached for it.

"What's that?" Langhorn asked.

"Airline ticket envelope." Denbo opened it. "Empty."

"Maybe they canceled his flight, so he decided to walk."

The senior man's eyes scorned his partner for the failed attempt at humor.

"Sorry."

Denbo lifted the iced tea away from the unconscious man's lips. "Come on, Mr. McBride. It's okay now. You're all right. Wake up. Wake up."

The shape stirred slightly. His eyes opened: uncertain, wavering, frightened. His lips began to take in the tea.

"That's it. There we go. Not too fast now."

Denbo pulled the cup away and McBride was left with dark brown droplets washing the sand off his chin. His lips trembled, then opened, moving.

"I think he's trying to talk, Wayne," Langhorn pronounced. "I think he's trying to say something."

Denbo moved his right ear closer.

"Did you walk here from home, Mr. McBride? Did you walk here from Beaver Falls?"

The shape tried to force out a word and spit sand forth in its place. His hand latched desperately onto Denbo's sleeve and drew the patrolman closer.

Joe Langhorn heard a muttered rasp, something like air bleeding from a tire. The rasp came again and then Wayne Denbo pulled away.

"What'd he say, Wayne?"

"I don't know."

"Come on, what'd you hear?"

Frank McBride was just lying there, not trying to talk anymore.

Denbo gulped down the rest of the tea himself. "One word."

"*What* word, for the love of Christ?"

Denbo looked up from the empty cup. "Gone, Joe. I think he said *gone.*"

By the time the officers got him into the back of their patrol car, McBride was out again, eyelids jittering like a dreaming dog's.

"What do you think he meant, Wayne?" raised Joe Langhorn. "What do you think he meant when he said *gone?*"

"Beaver Falls."

"Huh?"

Denbo settled himself in the passenger seat. "I said Beaver Falls. Know anything about it?"

"Population of maybe a thousand. Nothing 'round it for miles. Folks live there like their privacy. Residents call it the Falls. Beaver got lost a long time ago." Langhorn met Denbo's stare and got the message. "Not on our patrol, that's what you're thinking."

The senior man's eyes tilted toward the backseat. "We should run him home."

"Call it in's what we should do. Stay with him while we wait for the ambulance to get here."

"Forty minutes if we're lucky," Denbo told his partner. "Long wait for a guy who maybe just needs to sleep one off."

"He walked out of the desert."

"Fight with his wife, maybe."

"Way he's dressed, that empty airline folder in his pocket, I'm thinking maybe he got home and saw something he didn't like. Made him leave in a hurry."

"Start the car, Joe," Denbo ordered. "Beaver Falls is barely out of our way."

* * *

Joe Langhorn never would have admitted it, but he breathed a silent sigh of relief when the town of Beaver Falls came into view. A part of him deep within had feared it was going to be . . . gone. Melted into the ground or reduced to rubble, like in some thriller novel they sold in the discount paperback section of Wal-mart. But it was there, rustic colors baking in the midday sun.

A squat collection of buildings no more than three stories high formed the town center along a half-mile drag. There was a church on one side of town. A K–12 school rested on the other. Couple restaurants, a bar, post office and bank. The single parking lot was half full.

Joe Langhorn snailed the squad car through the outskirts past some of the residents' homes and headed into the center of town. He pulled into a parking space in front of the sheriff's station marked RESERVED.

In the backseat Frank McBride shifted uneasily, threatening to come awake.

"Wait here," Wayne Denbo instructed.

"The hell I will," followed Langhorn, joining him on the hot pavement. They entered the sheriff's office one behind the other.

It was empty. A cup of coffee that had long lost its steam sat on a big desk with a SHERIFF JOHN TOULAN nameplate. A half-eaten donut rested next to it on a napkin. There were three other desks and a counter for the receptionist/ dispatcher, all unoccupied.

"Musta left in a hurry," said Langhorn.

Wayne Denbo moved behind the counter and reached for the microphone attached to the communications base unit. "Sheriff Toulan, this is the Arizona Highway Patrol. Come in, please. Over."

Silence.

"Sheriff Toulan, come in, please. Over."

More silence.

Langhorn and Denbo looked at each other. They started for the door.

"Maybe they're out looking for McBride," Langhorn offered.

Back in the street Denbo stiffened. "Look over there. 'Cross the street."

Langhorn followed his eyes to an old-fashioned diner called Ruby's dominated by a long counter.

"What do you see?"

"Nothing."

"Right. Even though it's lunchtime."

Denbo started moving and Langhorn quickly followed him. Bells jangled when the senior cop entered the diner, presently lined by empty counter stools and unoccupied booths. Half of the stools had plates of breakfast food resting before them, most partially eaten. A blackboard advertised a western omelet special, and three orders with varying amounts left looked lonely in one of the booths.

Langhorn stuck his hand in a half-gone cup of coffee and swept his tongue across his fingers. "Hours old. Looks like they never got past breakfast, never mind lunch."

"Enough time maybe for Mr. McBride to walk himself across the desert?"

"What the fuck, Wayne? What the *fuck*?"

They backed out through the door. The bells jingling startled Langhorn and he unsnapped his gun retainer.

"Let's take a walk," Denbo suggested.

In the post office, the lone counter had been abandoned with four letters resting atop it. Four stamps waited nearby to be licked.

The bank, too, was empty, the floor dotted with stray bills, a few checks, and deposit slips.

At Beaver Falls' single filling station, a Chevy Cavalier waited at the pump with the nozzle from the regular slot jammed into its tank. The gas had come to an automatic stop. The Cavalier's driver's door was open, key still in the ignition and no driver to be found.

Each window Langhorn and Denbo passed, each closed

door they stopped to knock on brought the same results: nothing.

Langhorn was palming his gun butt now, flirting with whether or not to draw it. "Let's get out of here, okay?"

"Whatever it was musta happened fast."

"Wayne, let's get out of—"

"If they were all together, where would they be?" Denbo followed, his eyes drifting up the street toward the school.

"We got to call this in, Wayne."

"One more thing to check."

The school door closed behind them with a rattling clang. The main office was just on the right and Wayne Denbo led the way in.

Beyond the front counter, a trio of secretary's desks were empty.

The two highway patrolmen advanced down the narrow hall separating the offices of the principals and guidance counselors. The first three were empty as well.

They moved on to a room packed with copying and mimeograph machines, attracted by a dull hum emanating from a space-age Xerox with multiple paper slots protruding from one side. The top slot had overflowed and spit neatly printed paper everywhere. The machine's small LED readout flashed a continuous message:

PAPER OUT

The Mr. Coffee against the far wall brimmed with a steaming full pot. Three styrofoam cups had been set out as if to await its contents.

"Nothing," Joe Langhorn said from the doorway. "Fucking nothing."

"You take the back end of the building," Wayne Denbo told him. "I'll take the front." He pulled the walkie-talkie from his belt. "Stay in touch."

Judging by the maps dangling from the front wall in the

first classroom he entered, Denbo figured this must be the school's social studies section. Textbooks and notebooks lay open on unoccupied desks, some with pens dropped haphazardly upon them. What little of the blackboard the maps left exposed showed a sentence uncompleted, abandoned in the middle.

Denbo moved on to the next classroom.

Identical sheets rested atop each desk. Denbo stopped near one in the rear and hovered over the chair, as if the kid was still seated there. Social studies quiz. Twenty questions, all multiple choice. Junior high school stuff. Kid from this desk had gotten through the first nine.

"Wayne?" Langhorn's voice called over the walkie-talkie.

"Here, Joe."

"I'm in one of the science labs. It stinks down here. Got all kinds of stuff in vials and tubes left out. Instructions on the board saying what to do."

"Don't do anything. Don't touch anything," warned Denbo, worried about chemicals being left out that weren't supposed to. He tried thinking about what it was like for Frank McBride. Back from a business trip to find his whole town missing. That had been hours ago. Maybe McBride had seen something then that might help decipher what had happened here in the Falls.

"Wayne, you there?"

"Yeah, Joe."

"I'm heading your way. We're calling this in. I've had e—"

The walkie-talkie went cold in Wayne Denbo's hand. He brought it back to his lips.

"Joe? Come in, Joe, come in. . . ."

No response.

"Joe!"

Denbo was already sprinting down the hall. The stink Joe Langhorn had referred to, like rotten eggs, drew him toward the science labs.

"Joe," he kept calling into his walkie-talkie. "Joe."

"Joe."

His own voice bounced back at him, and Denbo looked through the door of the second lab on the right. Joe Langhorn's walkie-talkie lay on the floor, speaker facing up. Denbo backed into the corridor and drew his gun. His mouth felt like someone had papered it with Kleenex. He started running, heels clacking against the linoleum tile and contents of his gun belt bouncing up and down.

He burst through the front doors and reached the patrol car breathless, one hand on his knee as he reached for the door.

In the backseat the slumped form of Frank McBride was gone.

"Jesus," he muttered, only halfway in when he grabbed the mike. "Base, this is Seventeen. Base, come in!"

"Go ahead, Seventeen," returned dispatcher Harvey Milkweed.

Denbo muttered a silent thanks, glad there was still a voice out there to greet him.

"We got a situation here, a major situation."

"What is your location, Seventeen?" asked Milkweed. "Are you requesting backup?" He'd rooted himself to a desk after a brief visit to the Gulf War left him with part of a land mine stuck in his leg. Milkweed hated the desk, missed situations.

"Backup? We need the whole goddamn national guard down here in a hurry. We need— Wait a minute . . . What the . . . Oh my God . . . Oh *my*—"

The hairs on Harvey Milkweed's neck stood on end. He leaned forward in his chair.

"Seventeen, what's going on? Seventeen, come in. . . . Denbo, what's wrong?"

Milkweed waited.

"Denbo? Denbo, come in!"

There was no response, and Milkweed realized there wasn't going to be.

Wayne Denbo was gone.

Jon Land is thirty-six years old and lives in Providence, Rhode Island where he is at work on his next bestseller for Tor, THE KINGDOM OF THE SEVEN.

HIGH-TENSION
THRILLERS FROM TOR

☐ 52222-2   BLOOD OF THE LAMB $5.99
          Thomas Monteleone   Canada $6.99

☐ 52169-2   THE COUNT OF ELEVEN $4.99
          Ramsey Cambell   Canada $5.99

☐ 52497-7   CRITICAL MASS $5.99
          David Hagberg   Canada $6.99

☐ 51786-5   FIENDS $4.95
          John Farris   Canada $5.95

☐ 51957-4   HUNGER $4.99
          William R. Dantz   Canada $5.99

☐ 51173-5   NEMESIS MISSION $5.95
          Dean Ing   Canada $6.95

☐ 58254-3   O'FARRELL'S LAW $3.99
          Brian Freemantle   Canada $4.99

☐ 50939-0   PIKA DON $4.99
          Al Dempsey   Canada $5.99

☐ 52016-5   THE SWISS ACCOUNT $5.99
          Paul Erdman   Canada $6.99

Buy them at your local bookstore or use this handy coupon:
Clip and mail this page with your order.

Publishers Book and Audio Mailing Service
P.O. Box 120159, Staten Island, NY 10312-0004

Please send me the book(s) I have checked above. I am enclosing $ _____ .
(Please add $1.25 for the first book, and $.25 for each additional book to cover postage and handling.
Send check or money order only—no CODs.)

Name _____

Address _____

City _____ State/Zip _____

Please allow six weeks for delivery. Prices subject to change without notice.